Dream Scout

HIS MAJESTY'S ELITE

By
Missy Sheldrake

Dream Scout
INDEPENDENTLY PUBLISHED
By Missy Sheldrake

First Published in the United States 2021
ISBN: 978-1-7345896-3-4

Illustrations, typesetting, layout, cover design, and writing by Missy Sheldrake.

www.missysheldrake.com

ISBN: 9798517459640

Fonts:
Great Victorian Swashed
Garamond
FairydustB
CINZEL DECORATIVE

For the Dreamers, the Wanderers, and the Forgotten

Believe in your Dreams!

Missy Shuldhal

The Haigh

Long Arm Pass

*Belvitch City

Cerion

Hywilkin

ion

*Cresten

Elespen

THE KNOWN LANDS

*Zhaghen

Third Sunteri

Book One
THE GROVE

1

The Way of the Grove

To Elliot, My Sheshi (Dear One),

There are some places in our world so hidden, most don't even believe they exist. Places no one can happen into because they are so well protected. Imagine instead a world where we could move freely across borders, where a sister, a daughter would not be shunned forever for leaving home.

I understand allowing it draws fear. Even here, the high elves of Ceras'lain are always on defense. Their magic is well-known and sought-after, so their ramparts must always be fortified. Their warriors are forever anticipating a siege.

Where you are, in the Grove, the Ancients wish to go the way of the fairies, to have the Grove fall into obscurity and legend.

But once the Sorcerers set their sights on a place, once they find a Source they can drain, they will dominate it or die trying. Everyone everywhere fears them. Even the humans.

I have learned so much in the libraries of the elves,

1

little brother. There is so much more I wish to write, but I know I must not go too long, for your sake.

How I wish we could be as close as we always have been. I have searched for some way, but there is none. I fear our days together are gone from us forever, all because of fear.

Though I am loved here in my new home with the elves, I deeply regret having left you behind. I miss you desperately. Keep me in your mind. I beg you, do not make me Forgotten.

Be safe, Sheshi. Celian vore estier'analla (I am with you, always).

Mari

A brisk wind howls across the mouth of the den, and I brush the auburn fringe from my tear-stung eyes to gaze at the darkening sky in the direction of Ceras'lain. It's getting late, and I've already been away too long. The Ancients will notice. They always notice.

Reluctantly, I fold the note into a tight square, drop it, and crouch low. I step forward, feeling the change shiver over me as fur and whiskers sprout from my skin. My hands and feet shrink to velvety paws, and I flex my claws into the dry gravel as I pick up the note between my pointed teeth.

Nearby in the safety of the den's shadows, Sare fox opens one eye to watch me. If I were any other creature interrupting her newborn pups' supper, she'd likely tear me apart. She knows me, though, the wood elf boy who can choose to be just as much a fox as she is. She trusts me as much as she trusted her own mate, who was lost to the goblins before he could see his pups born.

I slink deeper into the small cave, past Sare and her four suckling kits. In a dark, hidden space I tuck Mari's note beside dozens of others and nudge my stash of sticks, cleaned bones, and leaves over it to cover its scent.

At the cave mouth the howling wind screams louder, and I slink toward it just in time to see the trawling glow of red warning light catch across the gravel.

"*Wanderer's son*." The wisp's voice, a spirit of the Grove sent by the Elders, is the whisper of wind through the leaves. Its presence is peaceful despite its jarring color and scolding words.

"*You shall be late*."

I try hard to suppress the anger that wells in me being addressed as *Wanderer's son*. Couldn't they call me Warrior's son, for Father? Or dream scout, as I am? Even just my name, Elliot, would be better than *Wanderer's son*. Why should I have to carry my mother's shame on my shoulders? She's the one who has strayed from the paths set before her. Her mistakes aren't mine.

Whatever they call me, I'm bound by the Grove's will to obey. We are all ruled by the Ancients, the sacred sentient trees who are our providers and our purpose.

I curl up, tucking my nose into the fluff of my red tail. As soon as I close my eyes I feel the pull of the Dreaming, but I don't let it take me fully. I let my wood elf side slip away just a little until I settle into two parts of a whole: the fox, asleep, and my second self hovering outside of him.

As a dream scout, I have three choices while I'm asleep: I can slip all the way into the realm called Dreaming and visit the dreams of anyone else who is sleeping, or I can scout through the realm of the In-between; the strange, fuzzy space between sleeping and awake that allows me to go anywhere the Ancients choose undetected and spy on the Waking, or, finally, I can simply rest.

I can even use my abilities as a means of travel. Once asleep, I'm able to steal outside of my body, navigate through the In-between, and call myself through to the Waking anyplace I like, as long as I never cross outside the borders of the Grove.

"*They are starting…*"

I leap from the mouth of the cave into the current of the wind and let its essence carry me forward. In this state there is no wind, nor ground, nor sky. They're there, but they aren't. My feet churn in a running motion but don't actually propel me.

The Grove unfurls beneath me, its lush green treetops sprawling toward the mountains and rivers beyond our borders. For a moment I'm distracted by the lure of Cerion, the land of men.

"*Wanderer's son,*" the wisp teases, and I whip my attention toward it.

"Take me, then," I call, bracing myself.

Its energy catches me and pulls me fast, like a fish caught on a line. It streaks me away from mountains, rivers, and men, and I barely have time for a single breath before I'm deposited on the path just outside the Great Grove known as the Sanctum.

"*Late, late,*" chides the wisp before it disappears through a delicate curtain of willow fronds.

Here, because of the protective spells cast by generations of Elders, the roaring wind has died down to the caress of a gentle breeze. I close my eyes as the power of the Ancients washes over me, and in my mind, I imagine myself solid and whole.

Concentrating, I draw my fox self across the miles until our two halves meet, and I snap fully into myself in my true, wood elf form. The sensation of the change rustles my hair as I take a step out of the In-between and return fully to the Waking.

"*Late,*" the wisp whispers from the other side of the willows.

I hesitate, staring at the feathery leaves, knowing what's waiting for me beyond.

Will tonight be different? Will I finally be given some duty? Some purpose? Or will I continue to spend my days the same way I've spent my years, feeling useless and unimportant while all my friends and family actually have things to do?

Sometimes I feel like Mari isn't the only one who's been Forgotten.

"*Late,*" the wisp pulses brighter this time.

Stepping into the Great Grove feels like a rite of passage every time. My people are the chosen children of the Ancient Ones, protected by their might, nurtured by their wisdom, provided for by their generosity. Entering this sacred place steals my breath and fills me with a sense of euphoria that clears away my worries, my thoughts.

The majesty of the Ancients is a wonder to behold. Within the Sanctum, we lovingly call these trees the *Rianave*.

To say they are remarkable wouldn't do them justice. To compare them to any other tree would be a severe insult. There is no creature, force, or plant in the Known Lands that compares to our mighty *Rianaves*. Their trunks are so broad it would take twenty grown humans with their arms stretched wide to circle the base of them, and their branches so tall they disappear into the sky above, which is now dyed deep orange by the setting sun.

Wondering how dozens of them managed to grow in such perfect rows, how their trunks could be so impossibly straight and immaculate, how they could hold such incredible power, overwhelms me with awe.

Dozens of my kin are already grouped with their families, gazing toward the sky. I creep through the flowering glade at the center of the Grove to find my place between my older brother, Sulien, and my younger brother, Kaini. Kaini raises his brow at me with a look that promises he'll be telling Father how late I was tonight.

Silently, I kneel in the space they left for me. Father doesn't notice. He and Sulien are already enraptured by the wisps floating far above in the *Rianaves'* branches. The glowing creatures are the embodiment of the *Rianaves'* spirits and the spirits of all the Elders whose bodies have returned to the earth. I shift on my knees slightly, trying not to think about how many of our fallen ancestors lie buried in the soil beneath me, twined in the roots of our Ancient Ones.

Kaini jabs a finger into my side to antagonize me, but when I shake my head fiercely and point up at the twinkling glow, his eyes slide upward reverently.

"*No secrets from us,*" the *Rianaves'* deep voices resonate across the Sanctum. The wisps' lights pulse with each word, twinkling like thousands of fireflies.

"No secrets," I join my voice with the others. I feel a pang thinking about Mari's secret letters, but I keep my gaze to the wisps and let their rapture clear my heart of guilt and my mind of troubling thoughts.

"As t*he Grove wills it,*" thunder the *Rianaves*.

"As the Grove wills it."

"*Protection for all,*" the *Rianaves* promise.

"Protection for all," we reply.

"*Duty above all.*"

"Duty above all."

"*Keep hidden, always.*"

"Keep hidden, always."

"Roots in soil, limbs in sky."

"Roots in soil, limbs in sky.

"We are one with the Grove."

"We are one with the Grove."

As the mantra ends, the wisps sweep down from the trees. I cup my hands in front of me as is the custom, and the wisps glide from one person to the next, first touching their forehead and then dipping into their waiting hands.

Mine isn't the same one who fetched me from the cave. This one has a pinkish tint to it, the color of healing. I'm not injured or sick, so I'm not sure why it comes to me. Cast in its pinkish glow, I wait while it hovers at my heart, beaming warmth and light across my face and chest.

"In time, you will come to see," the wisp assures me.

Something had been troubling me, but the wisp's words clear all remnants of it away, leaving me feeling loved and fulfilled. All around us, the wisps deliver similar messages of encouragement, advice, and healing, resulting in an ethereal sort of murmuring that sends a shiver of a thrill through us all.

"Thank you," I whisper, feeling a renewed sense of purpose.

The wisp sinks through my cupped hands, leaving behind a hearty bowl of my favorite meal: stewed pheasant with fresh, hot wheat nut bread. I wait for the wisp to descend into the ground beneath me like the others do, where it will join with the roots of the *Rianave* and the spirits of those who came before us, then I take just one bite of my bread before covertly tucking it into my gathering bag.

"Is that what you wanted?" Kaini wrinkles his nose at my pheasant, and I turn slightly and drape my arm over the bowl to keep him away. "Pheasants are remarkable birds," he cranes his neck to peer over his meal of mostly vegetables, "shame that one ended up in your stew."

He reaches a hand toward me, his fingertips glowing bright pink with healing magic like the wisp.

"Kaini, stop!" I growl, curling myself around my bowl protectively.

On my other side Sulien nudges Father, who leans over his own meal to look at the two of us. He gives us both a warning look, and Kaini shoves his glowing hand into the thick moss to hide it.

"Elliot was late again," he tattles, diverting Father's attention. He spears a chunk of roasted spring parsnip and stuffs it into his mouth innocently.

"Doing what?" Father asks. His tone is calm and disinterested, but I know it will change drastically depending on my answer. Suddenly it occurs to me I received no direction from the wisps. For me, tomorrow will be another day with no duties or accomplishments.

I stall, taking a bite of my stew as I stare at the honor beads dangling from Father's broad, muscled shoulders. My eyes trail to the burnished skin of his upper arm and across the various designs burned there to mark his status and prestige as one of the Grove's proudest warriors. I wonder if he's ever spent a day of his life feeling useless.

His long, braided hair and feathers swing forward across his arm as he sternly meets my eye, demanding an answer.

"Sare fox had her litter," I tell him after finally swallowing the chunk of pheasant. "Four kits. I brought her some mice."

"Always with the foxes," Sulien grunts, smirking. "It's too bad there isn't another of you, some female fox scout. That would be a match."

"We're not all searching for a mate like you, Suli," I answer around another mouthful of stew.

"He does stink a lot more like a fox than usual," Kaini declares, pressing his nose to my arm to sniff it.

"Stop," I growl and swing my elbow hard into his nose. It cracks.

As Kaini squeals and claps a hand over his bloody nose, the chatter around us goes silent. A healer sitting nearby rushes to tend to him, but Kaini waves them off with one hand while the one clamped over his bleeding nose glows pink.

Furious, Father snatches my bowl and clamps his other hand around my arm to pull me to his other side, separating us. While Sulien tries to comfort Kaini, Father tightens his grip on my arm painfully and glowers.

"He—" I start, but Father shakes his head sternly, once, and shoves my bowl into my hands.

"You are the older one," he says firmly. "You should have more restraint."

"But—"

"And you should not have left your mother alone."

"But—"

"Not another word, Elliot," Father warns. "Eat."

I hunch over my meal, shoveling it into my mouth and barely tasting it as I glare at the moss in front of me. Father always takes Kaini's side. Always. He says it's because I'm older, but that isn't why, and we both know it. The fact that he mentioned Amma is just further proof. He brought her up just to needle me.

I'm sick of being the only one to stay with her day and night. He should be there, too, at least sometimes, but he refuses.

She damaged his good standing in the Grove by letting Mari slip away and become Forgotten, and then she went and got herself declared a Wanderer. He resents her, and he resents me because I'm just like her. And just like my sister.

He acts like it's just a matter of time before it happens to me, too. Before I become a Wanderer like Amma or a Forgotten, like Mari. Maybe he's right. Maybe someday I'll leave this place and find my own path. Maybe someday I'll become both Wanderer *and* Forgotten. Then he'll be sorry.

2

The Hamlet

The Hamlet is an intricate web of rope bridges, wooden houses, and platforms built high in the forest canopies. Sulien and Kaini walk together toward the lower houses, the stone-and-thatch cottages tucked into the bases of sturdy oaks, elms, and walnut trees. As a high-ranking warrior, Father's house is at the front of this grouping since it's his duty to protect the Hamlet against any threat that might come to it. Being down low would give him the easiest, quickest access to defense.

That's what they tell us, but the arrangement is just symbolic. So many layers of ancient, heavy magic protect the Grove that it would be impossible for any intruder to make it this far into its depths.

Beside me, Father slows and looks up into the branches, where dozens of houses glow in the waning light of dusk. Where Amma is sure to be sleeping. Wandering.

"Will you come say goodnight?" *At least*, I want to add, but even asking what I did could be considered insolent.

His jaw tightens. He swallows and shakes his head.

"I'll tell her for you," I say, trying hard to keep the anger from my voice. Up ahead, Sulien ducks into Father's cottage, and Kaini makes a face at me before he goes inside, too.

"Do not Wander tonight," Father orders, ignoring my offer. I hate that he barely acknowledges her anymore. It's like if he doesn't admit she exists, her mistakes can't affect him.

I start to walk away without replying, but he grabs my arm again to stop me.

"Elliot."

I want to look at him straight in the eye, to glare, to be defiant. I want to argue, just this once. Instead, I stare at the bronze studs of his vest just above the fringe, woven into the thick leather, intended to protect his heart. I don't know why he needs those studs. Even if he were bare-chested, I can't imagine any weapon that could penetrate the stone within.

"Yes, Father." I raise my arm a little, hoping he'll let go, but he only does when Oakson approaches with Hana, his dryad niece, who watches Father with wide eyes as the two men greet each other.

"Patrolling Blackbird's Spine tomorrow," Oakson says, clapping Father on the shoulder. "Hana as well."

"And Sulien and I," Father rumbles proudly as he raises his spear to the man in salute.

Hana smiles at them, a glint of excitement flashing in her eyes until she catches my gaze and mouths a sincere, "Sorry."

I shrug. I'm not sure why she's sorry. It's not like she had any choice in being assigned to go while I was left behind. It's not like any of us do.

"Go on, Son," Father says to me dismissively. Then, to make matters worse, he gives me a hearty nudge toward the nearby ramp. I rush off quickly, before Hana can pity me any more.

I walk round and round up the ramp, and the higher I go, the better I feel. Up here, with a view of the night sky and the peaceful whisper of the wind through tender spring leaves, nothing ever seems as bad as it had been far below.

Amma's house is on the third highest platform from the top of our tree, who we call Grandymum. A sturdy oak of four-hundred sixty-three years, Grandymum has been home to our family for generations. Amma's mother was a dream scout, and her grandfather before her, and his father, and his mother, for as far back as the stars can be counted.

It's large for a treetop home and so old that the bark of the tree has grown around it, enveloping its walls in sweet-smelling wood that has always made me feel like we're getting a constant hug from Grandymum.

When I reach our platform, it seems like Amma isn't at home. Where the two other, smaller treetop homes are warmly lit and bustling with shadows across the shutters and laughter and music inside, Amma's house is dark and silent. I jog quietly across the platform hoping not to draw the attention of our neighbors, and I press my hand to the door. The magic guarding the house knows me. The door swings open under my touch, welcoming me home.

Inside, it's just as dark and silent as it seemed from the outside. I pause in the entry and hold my breath, listening closely. When Amma's long, deep breaths fill the empty space, I exhale with relief and open the glow lamps for their gentle light.

This house will be mine one day. It's a thought I've been having more and more often lately, and I hate myself for it. It used to be such a faraway idea, but as I find her in the gathering room, that time seems so much nearer now.

In her oversized chair, sunk deep into the cushions, buried in furs and worn sisal blankets, she looks feather-frail. Here, I don't open the glow lamps. I don't want to see anything more clearly. I know her eyes, gazing blankly into the night, are white as milkweed fluff. I know her hands are knobby as the twisting branches of oaks, and cold, so cold, despite all those blankets. Despite the warming air of Midspring.

I know I can touch her shoulder, her face, her hair, and never rouse her. There's only one way to try to wake her up. I have to be careful, though. I'm not sure how far she has gone, and even though I didn't exactly promise Father I wouldn't Wander, there are places Amma goes where I'm too afraid to venture.

When I was first coming into my skills, we used to sleep in the same bed so she could guide me through Dreaming. It's easier to find each other there when you're touching in the Waking. But I fell out of that habit as I got older and more comfortable in my dream scouting, so I haven't done that for a while.

Tonight, though, I feel the need to be close to her. She's so wasted by her neglect for the Waking that I can easily fit beside her on the chair even though I take up more space than I used to.

I nudge myself beside her carefully and tuck her icy hand under the blankets, close to my chest. With a long, deep breath to center myself, I try to relax. I fall asleep and drift easily through the In-between and on into the Dreaming.

In Amma's dreams, moonlight casts stark shadows over barren

lands. Crickets, bullfrogs, and owls sing their night choruses, but the sound is distorted and eerie. I close my eyes in the realm of Dreaming and remember things she taught me long ago. Things she has long since forgotten:

Remember, as there are two parts of us, there are always at least two sides to everything. A side that dwells in light, and one that dwells in shadow. If you stand in the sunshine, you will always cast a shadow. If you turn your back to the light, you risk becoming one with the shadow.

I look down at the long shadow stretching from my feet across the dirt, and I turn to face the shining moon. Full and powerful, its blue light charges me with hope. The sounds around me rise in pitch, settling back to normal and familiar.

In the distance, standing in a patch of grass at the edge of the barren earth, a red doe watches me. With a step, I transform myself from wood elf to fox, but I don't move closer. I won't approach her. She's skittish, and I don't want her to run.

The red doe takes a step and her form shimmers oddly, writhing and twisting until suddenly, harshly, my mother stands in her place. Anxious she'll bolt, I step, too, transforming back to my true form.

"Amma," I call softly across the space, which has expanded from fifty paces to at least a hundred in the span of two breaths. "Turn to the moon."

She cowers slightly, hunching in on herself, and points past me. I know what's there. I have seen the shadows, and I refuse to give them power by facing them. She needs to wake up. Now.

"Amma!" I shout, fueled by my fear and impatience. "It's been six days!"

At first, she's too frightened to grasp the meaning of my words, but after a moment she stands a little taller, and understanding flashes across her face. She takes a single step backward and her figure shimmers and disappears.

As soon as she's gone, the moon sinks lower in the sky and the sun rises with the most vibrant display of pinks, reds, golds, and lavender. I slip out of Dreaming, back to my sleeping self on the chaise, and feel Amma's cold finger stroking my cheek.

"Sleep, little fox," she whispers, raspy and tired. "The hour is late. Do not fret over me. I'm awake."

Her words give me the permission I need to sink into rest, into my own Dreaming, where the colorful sunshine is such a welcome, joyful contrast to her darkness. I lift my face to the light and bask in it, and my thoughts roam back through the day, all the way to Mari's letter.

Sister.

Here in Dreaming, I can cross borders. I can go anywhere in the world I want to go. I can take whatever form I want. With Amma safely awake, I let go of my worry for her just for a short stretch of time. I let myself soar.

In fox form, I run over the crests of mountains and dip into valleys filled with quaint villages. I follow along the banks of a great, rushing river and leap over forests of pine, marveling at every sight I pass. I know exactly where to go. My nose twitches and I sniff the air and catch a familiar scent: earth, lavender, straw, and reeds. Mari. Mari.

In my memory I see her sitting in a beam of sunlight beside our sleeping amma, her fingers deftly weaving strands of grass into a gathering basket, her eyes smiling as she tells me story after story, never tiring of my company. Mari, who always found a purpose for me, who never made me feel useless or unworthy, who loves me more than anyone ever has. Even more than Amma.

Mari. Sister.

My paws blur beneath me as I streak past the impressive white wall of stone that marks the border between Ceras'lain, the land of high elves, and Cerion, the land of men. The journey across leagues is a breathtaking adventure. After standing in the darkness of Amma's dreams, I need this exhilaration, this escape.

I dive low, spying the guards of the White Line: elegant high elves taller even than father, dressed in gleaming white armor and cloaks. I slow slightly as I pass a nest of cygnets, the giant, lizard-like bird mounts the elves ride on patrols and into battle. One of the great birds lifts its head to sniff in my direction, and I dart away and catch Mari's scent again. She's close. So close.

I race along the rows of archways toward a rushing waterfall and slow to search the balconies as my sister's scent grows stronger. When I finally catch sight of her, I nearly stumble with surprise. She looks so different against the backdrop of intricately carved ivory elven stone. Standing at the railing of her veranda, her long hair and silky dressing gown billowing behind her, she smiles serenely into the breeze. Her hands caress her belly as she gazes up into the sky like she's making a wish, her eyes glinting with starlight.

I crawl closer to perch on the wide railing beside her. So close, but so very far away. I started in Dreaming, and even though I honestly wasn't going to Wander tonight, I can't help myself. I need to know she's safe, she's real. I need to feel just a little closer to her.

I shouldn't Wander, and coming here without having followed a path, that's exactly what I'm doing. I don't care, though. This close to my sister, Father's warnings seem to carry much less weight.

Concentrating, I make the slight shift from Dreaming to the In-between and feel the strands between my second self and my true form asleep in the sitting room stretched thin.

It took me a long time to get used to that feeling when I was first given my gift. It used to send me into throes of panic knowing that my true self was left so exposed, so oblivious to everything around me in the Waking. Now it doesn't bother me so much. With practice, it has become second nature.

In the In-between, I know what I see is real. Nothing here is conjured by my imagination. This Mari is the Mari who exists in the Waking. I see her clearly, but she can't see me. Not unless she knows to expect me and makes a true effort to look. Still, I can't resist trying. I step closer, balancing on the railing, and shift into my true form.

"Mari," I whisper, leaning nearer, "I'm here." She doesn't answer, of course, so I just sit on the railing beside her, staring up into the stars with her. She starts to hum the same melody she used to sing to Kaini and me to get us to sleep, and when the song is done, she sighs.

"I will teach you of the Grove, my little one, and of your grandmother and grandfather, and your uncles Suli, and Kaini, and Elliot, who is my favorite brother," she giggles, "but you mustn't tell anyone I said so, my sweeting. It isn't right for a sister to have favorites."

Her smile fades slightly as she looks away from the stars toward the waterfall with a distant, sorrowful expression. "Amma, I hope the boys are caring for you. I hope you're looking after my dearest brother."

"Darling," a deep, melodic voice calls from inside the sheer curtains that billow out over the balcony like silvery clouds.

Mari deftly wipes a tear away as her high elf husband crosses the balcony and takes her in his arms. I can't help but stare as he bends to kiss her. As a wood elf, Mari is two-thirds her husband's height and much less willowy. His ears are sleeker and more pointed, and his skin seems to glow in the moonlight, while Mari's is more tan and solid-looking.

Elves have always fascinated me, which isn't surprising. High elves tend to fascinate everyone they meet. Everything about them is entrancing: how tall and lithe, how strong but elegant. Even his white silk sleeping robes intricately embroidered with silvery thread seem magical.

"Come and rest, my love," he murmurs at the end of their kiss. The way he looks at Mari makes it seem like she's his whole world.

"Oh, Elowyn, I miss them so," my sister cries softly, burrowing her face into his chest.

"I know, my only," Elowyn gathers her into his arms, draping her small frame with his long, sweeping sleeves.

"*Celian vore estier'analla,*" he whispers. I remember the phrase from her letter: "I am with you."

"I have such an awful notion…" Mari shivers.

"Then come, and we shall Ruminate and put your mind at ease," he whispers, drawing her hands to his lips and kissing them tenderly. "These feelings always seem so much worse during the dark hours."

Mari nods, and Elowyn draws her through the silver cloud curtains. I start to follow, but when I get halfway across the balcony, I feel myself abruptly pushed back. I raise my hand and try to press it nearer to the curtains, and there's a resistance in the air like I'm pressing on an invisible pillow. With that sensation comes a feeling of warning, and a strong message in my mind: "*Go no further.*"

"Wards," I murmur, immediately recognizing the protective spells cast by Mages. I step into fox form and sniff the air, committing the scent of melted wax, flowers, and salt to memory. Elf magic has a different, softer feel to it than the magic of the Grove, which is earthy and root-like.

In the In-between and even in the Dreaming, we dream scouts have limits. I can't cross through a ward cast by a Mage. For now, I leave Mari and Elowyn behind and leap into the sky, letting myself float on the breeze until I wake slowly, naturally, curled into the furs and blankets of Amma's over-sized chair.

3

Keep Hidden, Always

"Calm your breath, young one, and drink. Eat. There, now. Food in the belly always helps us feel more grounded."

I open my eyes slowly, squinting into the beams of morning sunlight that splash through the open window. Motes of dust swirl between me and the rest of the world like lingering bits of dreams, sparkling against the dim background of the sitting room. I yawn and reach my arms overhead and stretch my legs long, flexing my toes and feet.

Chimes jingle from the direction of our kitchen, and with them waft the enticing aromas of spices, eggs, and butter. My stomach growls.

"You don't understand," Amma's reply is hushed and frantic.

"Shh, not just yet. Here, what a lovely plate. Eat first, hm? We'll have plenty of time for talking later."

"If you believed me, you would not say that," Amma answers coldly.

"Eat, Lorelai," answers our guest, more sternly this time.

It sounds like Avela, Elder of the Seers, but that's impossible. Elders never make visits. They're far too important to venture out of the Sanctum, away from their *Rianaves*, to come calling in the Hamlet. If a Druid seeks an audience with an Elder, a request is made, and the Ancients decide whether or not the Druid is worthy to meet with the Elder. But it's always in the Great Grove. Never at home.

I push the furs off and creep toward the voices, rubbing my growling stomach to try and quiet it. When I peek into the sun-splashed room, I'm dazzled by what I see. I was right. It's Avela. I take a step back and try to focus.

Elders carry with them an immense amount of magic, mostly from regularly drinking the Lifesap of the *Rianave* trees. Avela is one of the most revered of all the Elders. Our humble kitchen seems too small to contain her. She beams with such glamour I have to blink my eyes rapidly and rub them to get used to the sight of her.

Her leather tunic twinkles and flashes in the sunbeams as she meanders through the small space. Her long, glittering gray hair grazes her heels, swaying behind her like a moonlit waterfall. Feathers and crystals adorn her intricate braids and dangle from piercings in her ears.

With each step she takes, tiny chimes jingle softly, and when she turns away from Amma to take the clay kettle from the fire, the elegant gossamer wings sprouting from her back catch a spray of sunlight and cast it shimmering gold and green across the walls.

In her shadow, Amma is a gray, withering ghost. Her stringy hair hangs into her plate, her white eyes stare blankly ahead. She makes no effort to eat, despite Avela's urging. The sight of her is so pitiful, I forget all manners and graces in an Elder's presence and rush to her side.

"Amma," I say, touching her shoulder so she knows I'm beside her.

At the hearth Avela fusses with the kettle, turning her head only slightly when she realizes I'm here.

"Elliot," Amma whispers. She clings to my arm urgently, like she's afraid at any moment the two of us will be torn apart. "Elliot, you saw them, didn't you? Elliot was there, Elder Avela. My son saw the shadows!"

At that, Avela turns to look at me. Her eyes search mine for a long, intense moment, and she shakes her head at me and nods to the dish of food in front of Amma.

"There are always shadows," I reply, spooning up a bit of egg from her dish. I hold it to her lips, and she sniffs it and opens her mouth to take the bite. "Turn yourself to the light and you can't see the shadows, Amma."

She chews and swallows, and I feed her another bite. The memory of Mari sitting on this same stool, feeding Amma this same way, drifts back to me. Avela brings two steaming mugs to the table, one for me and one for herself, and none of us speaks again until Amma's plate is empty.

"Ah," Avela says, sipping her tea as her gaze dances over us both. "She is returning. Your turn to eat, child," she says to me, "Eat. It will ground you."

She sweeps a hand across the table, conjuring a similar hot meal which I dig into gratefully. An Elder's meal is second only to the gifts of the wisps and the *Rianaves* themselves.

Halfway through my meal, Amma speaks up.

"Blackbird's Spine will see Sorcerers today."

Mid-bite, I drop my spoon to my plate and stare between them, wide-eyed. "What, Amma?"

"Blackbird's Spine. Sorcerers. They are planning and plotting."

Avela chuckles softly through her nose and gives me a pitying look. I grab my tea and gulp it down, cringing and coughing as it burns my throat, then tell them, "Father is going there today, with Uncle Oakson and Hana and Sulien. They said so last night after supper gathering."

"Elliot, be calm," Avela says, sipping her tea. "I have not seen this, Lorelai. None of us have."

"Because you close your eyes to outsiders," Amma says defiantly. I set down my tea and cover her hand with mine, trying to quiet her.

"You overstep," Avela warns, her wings stretching upward behind her, "just as you did when you entered the Sanctum this morning."

"You what?" I ask, staring in disbelief at my mother, who has refused to answer the call of the wisps for so long now that she's lost her privilege to join us in meals or enter the Sanctum at all anymore. She's too much a Wanderer, now.

"Elder, please forgive us both," I say urgently. "I was supposed to be watching her, but she left while I was sleeping. She didn't know what she was doing, she—"

"Child, child," Avela interrupts me with a reassuring smile, "we know what it is to be lost in Dreaming. To be a Wanderer. We have seen it many times before. At this point, your mother has no real understanding of what she sees, or where she is, or even what actions she takes."

Under the cover of my hand, I feel Amma tighten her fist. Her white eyes narrow angrily, and I grip her hand to try and calm her.

"They will come with dark magic," Amma warns, this time through clenched teeth.

"Dear ones, I assure you we have not foreseen it," Avela says again, emptying a pouch of shining stones into her hand. "Here. I shall cast the stones right now so you can be at ease. Elliot, watch closely and tell your mother what is shown."

"I don't CARE about your sticks and your stones," Amma shouts, sweeping her arm across the table in a frenzy.

Avela calmly raises a hand and the flying dishes and mugs hover in mid-air.

"People will die!" Amma rants. "There will be floods, there will be fires! It is already happening!"

She jumps to her feet and starts pacing wildly, like a cornered beast.

"I have looked into shadow! I have seen the eyes of Marked men! I have followed the black path and gone deeper than any of you have the courage to go, searching for the truth!" She points toward Avela, grimacing with fury.

Avela stares at her, horrified. "You have looked into the faces of Sorcerers, Wanderer? Have they looked into yours? Have they seen you?"

I grip the edge of the table to keep myself on my stool as Amma paces, cupping her hands over her ears and shaking her head maniacally.

"Keep hidden, always, Amma," I whisper, just as shocked as Avela. "You taught me that."

Amma screams in anguish and starts to drop to her knees, but Avela sweeps her hand again and Amma freezes just like the dishes and the mugs, her arms dangling slightly in front of her, her face twisted with regret.

"Child," Avela calls me, and when I can't manage to tear my gaze from the eerie, floating scene, she puts her arm around me and turns me away. I feel the power of the Grove flowing off her like water over the falls, spilling into me, filling me with comfort. I feel myself relax and I lean into her welcoming hold.

"Long have you suffered from all of this," she soothes. "All of you, and your mother as well."

I nod tearfully, thinking of how Mari was driven away by Amma's rantings and the unending pressure of having to care for her.

"I wish I could have shielded you from this. I know how

frightening it must be," she whispers kindly, "but perhaps it was best for you to see it, to learn the importance of keeping within the laws. Not only for the Grove, but for your own well-being."

I nod again, speechlessly, and work to keep my gaze from Amma, who still dangles motionless, held by Avela's spell.

"You are too young for this burden," Avela sighs and rubs my shoulder comfortingly. "I shall take her with me and place her in the care of the fold until she can recover."

"I promised Father I would watch over her," I whisper, feeling my throat close with emotion.

"We will send him word she is safe. Do not fret, dear one. Every child of the Grove is precious. The fold will help her heal."

I nod again and watch the glint of her vest dance through the tears that blur my eyes.

Growing up in the Grove, we're told of mysteries everyone accepts without question. The fold lies somewhere beyond the Sanctum. It's the place where Druids go who need more attention than wood elf healers can provide. If they are worthy of the Ancients' favor, they'll survive what ails them. Even though the fold can heal like no one else in the Grove, it doesn't always succeed. Life here has its cycle just like everywhere else, and some are beyond help.

Not everyone who enters the fold returns alive.

Those who don't make it are taken into the ground to serve the Ancients even after their lives are finished. Those who have been to the fold and return keep it secret except to whisper gratitude for its generous healing. They never tell what it looks like, or who met them there, or what was said or done.

At the very least, Amma will be changed if she returns. *When* she returns. When, I tell myself again firmly.

I blink rapidly, trying to clear the tears before they spill, but one traitor slips down my cheek and rolls to my chin.

"Take some time for respite," Avela urges warmly, patting my cheek with the soft pads of her fingertips. Jingling. "You have suffered so much in so little time. In a few days, the Ancients will show us their will in this matter. Until then, enrich yourself for the good of the Grove."

"For the good of the Grove," I repeat numbly.

Avela gestures to the hovering dishes and mugs, and they float back to the table and stack themselves neat and clean. She then beckons to Amma, who floats into her waiting arms and curls up like a child. As old and small as Avela looks, carrying Amma doesn't seem at all difficult for her.

"Say farewell for now," Avela whispers to me, tipping Amma's face toward mine. She looks so peaceful, her eyes closed, her face slack. I kiss her on one sunken cheek, then the other.

"Come back to us all better, Amma," I whisper, shaking. I wish Father were here.

"As the Grove wills it," Avela murmurs, and with a flutter of her beautiful wings, the Elder pushes off from the floor and soars straight through the wall like it isn't even there.

4

Blackbird's Spine

As soon as Avela leaves, the calm goes with her. I stare at the neatly stacked dishes and mugs, and my thoughts race. I was there in the Dreaming with Amma. I felt the shadows at my back, but I didn't look. If I had, what would I have seen? Sorcerers? If I turned, would they have seen me, too?

The thought terrifies me so much, my teeth start to chatter. I run to the sitting room and drop into the chair, but I can't relax enough to slip into the In-between, so I pull my boots on, grab my bow, and run outside down the empty platform that winds around Grandymum's trunk.

Every time I come to the side overlooking Father's cabin, I crane my neck to see if it looks like anyone is at home. The glow lamps are off, the chimney clear of smoke. That doesn't mean anything, though. Especially not on such a bright spring day.

I slide on two feet down the last few steps of the ramp and dash down the stone path through the center of the hamlet. People stare as I hop over a pair of geese and dodge around a group of old ladies busy sewing gathering sacks.

"Where are you going in such a rush, little fox?" one of them calls after me. "Come listen to a tale."

"Sorry, Grandmother!" I shout over my shoulder as I reach Father's house.

"Father?" I call, pushing the door open slowly. "Suli? Kaini?"

No one answers.

"Kaini?" I call again. Father's cabin is smaller than Amma's. Warriors' homes aren't meant for larger families. It's the custom for children to live with their mothers unless they're boys. Our family is unusually larger than most, with more boys than most. I push open the door to the only other room in the cabin: a bunk room with two large beds, one for Sulien and Kaini, and one for Father. Both beds are piled with rumpled furs and blankets, and the floor is littered not just with Sulien and Kaini's sleeping clothes, but Father's too.

The sight and smell of it makes my heart ache for Mari. She never would have let it get this way. I wish they had all seen how much they took her for granted while she was here.

I consider lying down and trying again to scout, but it's too stuffy, and the smell is too strong, so I close the door and head back to Amma's.

Partway up the ramp, I stop and lean close to the tree trunk. I press my ear and hand to the bark and whisper, "Grandymum, did you see Kaini today? Do you know where he went?"

A light breeze rustles Grandymum's leaves, shimmering across the canopy to the north, and north of that, and north still, like a drop in the lake rippling out from the center.

"Lit-tle Kay-niii," Grandymum's voice enters my understanding ancient and rough, like the creak of dry branches rubbing together. "Ek-ko pool." She speaks slowly, stopping at every consonant, drawing out the words like they're strange to her.

"Echo pool?" I whisper thoughtfully. Good. He didn't go with Father.

"Ek-ko pool," creaks Grandymum. "Climb-bing trees with lit-tle ones."

"And Father and the others? Are they at Blackbird's Spine already? Is something happening there?" I press both hands to her trunk, waiting for an answer as the breeze ripples outward again. She waits for an answer for an awfully long time, so I slide my hand along her bark as I climb up the ramp again.

"Bat-tle," she creaks, and I stop mid-step and press myself against her trunk again.

"Battle? At Blackbird's Spine? What sort of battle? What's happening?"

"Bah. Slow down, lit-tle one."

"Sorry, Grandymum. But please, what's happening there?"

"Black sky wat-ter," she replies with a long, weary sigh.

"Thank you!" I shout and take off up the ramp again. I don't know what it means, but it doesn't sound safe. What if Avela was wrong and Amma was right? The door swings open at my touch, and I close it behind me and make sure it's guarded before I fling myself onto the chair and squeeze my eyes shut.

"Calm," I whisper, breathing in several long, deep breaths. "Calm down. Calm down."

I think the words over and over until I feel relaxed enough to pull away into my second self. I take fox form for speed and agility and dive out of the open window to race on the wind, soaring through tree limbs and leaping over the canopy.

Blackbird's Spine is to the north, beneath an ominous black storm cloud that looms heavy over the treetops. As I near, an angry funnel spears down from the churning sky into the stony ridge below, flinging rocks and dirt and broken tree limbs out of the obsidian ravine that marks the northern border of the Grove from Cerion, the land of men.

Secure in the In-between, I dive low and run along the edge of the enormous black, spine-like stones all the way to the last one, which is long and pointed like the beak of a bird. On one side of the great ridge stands a group of eight Druids, including Father and Sulien.

Facing them on the other side are four humans dressed in billowing black robes and deep crimson cloaks. Between the two groups, rivulets of black rain pour into the ravine. Black sky water, just like Grandymum said.

I stop on the edge of the ravine right beside Father and his companions. He grips his spear in one hand and his sling in the other, watching the incredible force of the driving storm and the violent cyclone, completely untouched. No wind flutters the feathers adorning his braids, no rain spatters his leather vest. As strong as the wind is within the storm, and as torrential as the black rain falls, none of it crosses the magical barriers that shield us from the outside.

The inky rain pools on the sharp edge of stone between our wards and the drop into the ravine, and sticks and leaves litter the ground on the Sorcerers' side, but there is a crisp, clean line that nothing can cross.

"I thought we were here for a fight!" Father shouts angrily over the roar of the storm. He drives the butt of his spear into the ground, and the others beside him howl in agreement.

"*They* aren't," Hana speaks up from behind the line, pointing at the dry ground at the edge of the wards. "That's what the black rain is for. They're trying to find a break in our defenses."

"By the Grove, Hana, you're right," Oakson says. "Look at the way it's pooling against our border."

"Do not fire against them," Father commands, his voice booming over the rumble of the storm. "Sulien, go and tell the others. Hana, Oakson, stand back. Do not get too close."

I follow my brother as he jogs along the edge of the spine to pass Father's message to two more groups of eight waiting along the ridge. When he's done, I leap into the air and run high above them, careful to stay on our side of the border. I don't know what might happen if I cross while we're under assault, and I don't want to risk exposing the rest of them.

Across the ravine, the four figures join hands. Their cloaks and robes whip around them wildly, revealing the skin of their faces, necks, and arms, stained by the dark, swirling lines of Mage Mark.

Sorcerers. Just like Amma said. Just like in Mari's letter: *once the Sorcerers set their sights on a place, once they find a Source they can drain, they will dominate it or die trying.*

It doesn't matter whether or not there's a battle right now. My blood runs cold. They're after the Ancients. They want the *Rianaves.* The Lifesap. Panting with fear, I pull myself from Amma's house, reeling myself in until I snap together again in one piece. Beside Father, I take a step and tug his arm urgently.

"Elliot!" he yells, enraged by my sudden appearance.

"Amma said there would be Sorcerers here today!" I shout, "You have to leave, all of you!"

"What do you think you're doing?" Father bellows, not even listening. He pushes me away from the others, toward the tree line. "It isn't safe, Elliot—"

His voice is cut off by a gut-wrenching thunderous rumble coming from down the line, followed by screaming. We start to run toward the sound, but it's too late. The ground beneath the blackbird's beak crumbles, and before we can reach any of them, three of our men plummet into the blackened ravine.

"Go home NOW," Father seethes, shoving me backwards again. I stumble into the brush at the edge of the forest and watch in disbelief as the rest of them rush to aid the three who were lost.

Shaken, I lean back against the trunk of an oak, close my eyes, and fling my fox-self out toward the hamlet. As I reach the path to the Great Grove, I gather myself to whole again and run as fast as I can to the guardians at the entrance.

Twice my height, wearing cloaks of silky leaves that pool on the ground around them, the pair of guardians thump the ends of their spears into the ground and announce in perfect unison, "Supper is at sunset, child of the Grove."

Their eyes, as wide as my fists, flash gold and green. Within the flutter of their cloaks, I catch flashes of burnished scale armor. Their presence is meant to be intimidating, and I take a few hesitant steps back to gather my courage.

"I need to see Elder Avela, please," I say. "It's urgent. Something happened at Blackbird's Spine."

"They know this already," the Guardians answer. "There is no need to fear."

"No need to fear? There are Sorcerers!" I shout, and several Druids passing by stop to look at me curiously.

"Isn't that the Wanderer's son?" I hear one of them ask, and the Guardians each raise a judgmental brow.

"Go home, young one. There is no danger. The Grove protects us."

"Yes, there is! I need to see Avela! Please!"

"She is unavailable, but you are welcome to return at supper gathering."

"Then I need to see Amma!" I shout louder, up into the tops of the towering *Rianaves* beyond. To my surprise, a single golden wisp emerges from the shimmering canopy above and hovers gently in front of me.

"*Home*," it says brightly, and without a second thought, I turn and walk back to the Hamlet.

I climb the winding ramp, cross the platform, close the door behind me, and drop into the overstuffed chair. My wisp escort pulses silently nearby, exuding a calming energy. Suddenly feeling very sleepy, my head drops to the side, my eyelids grow heavy, and I sink into a pleasant, restful sleep.

5

In Dreaming

In Dreaming, there are paths to follow. Amma has always told me these are trails into the choices of our lives. They appear as mossy walkways, or smooth steppingstones across a brook, or long, winding footpaths edged by sheer cliffs.

Or, in Amma's case, sometimes they're black, shadowed passages that twist and turn through places we should always avoid.

My dream begins with a song. In the Great Grove, we have gifted chanters who tell stories of our past and lift their voices to soar into the sacred canopy of the Ancients. I have always appreciated these songs and felt connected and grounded by them and awed by their beauty, but the voice that greets me in this dream outshines any I have ever heard in the Waking.

Journey
How I long for a journey
across the sea
across the leagues
ocean flashing
Sea salt splashing
golden sunrise
far away from me
far, far away from me…

The song sounds familiar, like home, even though I'm sure I've never heard it before. A forest as dense and magical as our Grove unfurls around me, with silver and gold butterflies darting around willowy tree trunks and golden beams of sunlight dancing across brilliant green grass.

The path leading me to the voice is fresh mulch, soft and fragrant. I consider it carefully before I take a step. I have always been taught that in Dreaming, the paths we choose can shift the course of our lives in ways we might never have imagined. When I finally decide to take a step, my foot sinks pleasantly into the spongy surface, and I'm overwhelmed by a profound feeling I can't explain.

My feet barely touch the ground as I'm drawn to the longing in her song and the beauty of her voice. My fingertips graze the mossy tree trunks, and each tree I pass whispers to me of so much love and encouragement that my heart feels like it will burst with warmth.

In all my life in the Grove, I have never felt so deliberate, so absolutely sure I'm on the path I'm meant for.

The trail guides me to a tall hedge of wisteria where I can stay hidden but still glimpse what's beyond. Through the screen of branches and purple flowers is a glen bathed in the glow of afternoon sun. The singer, the most beautiful human girl I have ever seen, kneels alone against the mossy trunk of a tree.

Her bright red hair is like flames, not only in its color but also in its strange style; short and spiked up from the crown of her head. Her skin is tanned golden and dappled with freckles that remind me of the patterns of stars in the night sky. Her eyes are so intensely green they rival the moss and the grass. They look like the way the light shines into a clear pool of water, illuminating it from deep within.

I yearn to move closer and show myself to her. It doesn't feel right to lurk behind branches. Not when I'm so sure we're meant to meet. Why else would the path lead me here? Is this a trick? Some test sent by the wisp, by the Ancients, to see if I'm capable of following the rules?

Keep hidden, always.

We do not show ourselves to others. Even when I know I'm fully in Dreaming, it's dangerous.

Something else Amma always taught me comes to mind: "We are all as we see our ownselves in this place." It gives me an idea. This human is just a dreamer. There are hundreds of thousands of them in the Dreaming at any given time. I could change myself to something nothing like myself.

I'll make myself a dream for this human, so I can meet her, and she'll never know me as I really am. When she wakes up, she'll remember something wonderful. Not me.

The Dreaming is such an accommodating place that as soon as I imagine the high elf I want to be, I begin to shift. I stretch taller as my arms and legs grow elegantly. My brown doeskin leggings, boots and tunic transform to elegant elvish styles, embroidered with intricate

designs like Elowyn's robes. My shaggy red hair tames itself to drape my shoulders like silk. When I move, the jewels in my braids jingle softly like Avela's charms.

I tighten my grip on the elegant recurve bow that appears in my hand. Nervous she'll see through my disguise somehow, I move slowly to the edge of the glen. She's so engrossed in her song she doesn't notice me at first, but then she looks up and our eyes meet, and she draws a sharp, startled breath.

I realize too late I'm still gripping my bow, and I quickly stow it across my shoulders to assure her I mean no harm. She watches me with wonder as I step closer, my heart racing so fast I can barely think.

Suli's joke about finding a mate pops into my mind, and I shove it away quickly. I've never been as interested in finding a match as he is. But this human…finding her feels like a moment I have hoped for all my life but didn't know it. It's almost the same as when I'm split apart in the In-between, and my two selves snap back together again.

"Please," I call, holding my hands out to show her I'm here in peace. Even disguised as an elf, my voice sounds wrong after hearing hers. Inferior.

"I didn't mean to interrupt," I say, trying hard to sound more elf-like. "Your voice drew me to this place. May I?" I gesture to the grass beside her, unable to tear my gaze from hers.

Her nod of agreement feels like the moment the sun breaks the clouds after a week-long rainstorm. We stare at each other for a long time, until I can't bear her silence any longer. I start to sing the song that drew me to her, surprised I remember the words and melody so easily. When she joins in, I feel it again, a sense that this moment is a waypoint in my life that has always been here, waiting for me to arrive. By the time the song is finished, I feel as light and joyful as leaves dancing in the wind.

She stares up at me as the light through the trees pulses softly around us like a heartbeat. The trees whisper encouragement and I search her eyes, wondering how I have come this far in my life without ever knowing I could feel this way.

"I heard your song from across the leagues of Dreaming," I murmur, trying hard to keep sounding like the high elf I'm pretending to be. "It hastened my feet to run to you, to see if your beauty matched that of your voice."

"Oh," she whispers, and even that one soft word thrills me. Her cheeks bloom pink, and her eyes dart to my lips and back to my eyes. When I realize she means to kiss me, I feel a quick pang of regret. This is only a dream to her, but to me, Dreaming and Waking are woven too tightly together. What started out as a curious exploration feels wrong, now. Deceptive.

I brush her chin with my fingertips, and she tilts her head back to gaze into my face, her green eyes dancing with emotion. I want to show her the truth, but I can't. I shouldn't.

"We are all as we see our ownselves in this place," I whisper.

"What does that mean?" she asks breathlessly.

"It means you are not as you seem, and neither am I." It's the closest I can come to revealing the truth without breaking the laws of the Ancients.

She leans in closer and closes her eyes, and I gather her into my arms and kiss her in a way I never would have had the courage to in the waking. I have never kissed anyone before. I have never really wanted to. Not like this, anyway. Not so deeply, not with someone I feel this connected to even though we never met before.

This is a dream, I remind myself. Only a dream. But I know after this, I'll never be the same. Somehow, this dream has sealed a destiny that's just beginning to reveal itself to me.

I don't know how long we spend together kissing, never speaking, until she fades back to the Waking and leaves me alone in the meadow. I sit for a while, watching the birds and clouds drift overhead, thinking about her. I never even asked her name, and she didn't ask mine. That's probably best, I think, though my heart sinks at the thought that I might never find her again.

With a sigh, I stand up and step forward into my familiar, more comfortable fox form. The shift helps clear my head and heart a little. As the mulch path fades, two new paths emerge at the edge of the meadow.

One path is wood, polished so smooth it looks like the flat, gleaming edge of a crystal. The other is black and dull like mold devouring the bark of an infested tree. I take a step back, shocked. I have never seen a black path in my own dreams before. Only in Amma's. When a hulking shadow emerges at the edge of the dark, gaping opening in the tree line and stands watching from the beginning of the path, I spin to face the light, my heart thudding hard in my chest.

My claws grip the grass and loam and propel me toward the shiny wooden trail. I run as fast as I can, never looking behind me. Green leaves and gray limbs blur past, giving way to polished, deep brown wood on either side of me. Ahead I see a door, a room, a bed draped with curtains and canopies. I'm running too fast. I slide, careening forward until I skid to a stop underneath the bed, hidden by drapes and plush velvet ruffles.

Panting, I creep forward and poke my nose through the ruffles to sniff the air. More humans. And salt. Ocean air. Smoke, wood, stone, and iron. Lavender, velvet, lemon balm. So many complex scents, all blended.

"Prince Tirnon, forgive me, but precisely what will gazing out of your window into the dawning hours accomplish? At least *try* to sleep."

Prince? Where has the path brought me this time?

"I can't sleep," answers a younger voice from a short distance away. "Not now. Is Finn on guard?"

"He is sensibly asleep, Highness," the first voice scolds gently.

Through the stretch of silence, I peer above me at the cut wood and the fine, soft mattress poking through the slats, filled with several birds' worth of feathers. I think of beds and blankets and stuffed chairs and suddenly I'm overcome with a feeling that somehow without meaning to, I've split myself into the In-between.

One part of me is here, wherever this is, and the other part is back home in the Grove. But how? This has never happened to me before. I'm Wandering, and deep.

A heavy sigh breaks the silence, and the prince says, "They have a right to know, Erol. If I were down there, I would want to know."

My curiosity overrules my bewilderment, and I creep further from my cover to peer out at the two men. They're a strange pair, standing outside on a balcony like Mari's. Except this is not Ceras'lain. These are humans. I try to focus, looking between the two intently. There must be a reason the path brought me here, so I must pay attention.

The prince, just a few years older than me, wears a strange outfit of heavy-looking embroidered fabric that catches the firelight and the moonlight with a dull shine. A circlet of polished metal rests on his head, and his hair is cropped short like a warrior, but there are no braids, feathers, tattoos, or beads bearing his station. He leans on the railing, peering out over something I can't see from here, but I don't dare move closer to find out what.

Erol is older and much more simply dressed, but his clothing is just as strange and heavy-looking, and his shoes are stranger still. They're like indoor moccasins, but with odd wooden blocks stuck to the bottom that make him stand more on his toes, and that click on the stone when he walks.

"Sometimes peace is best kept with secrets," Erol says. "A long road lies ahead, Highness. A long and trying road. But you will not be alone. We are all here to guide you."

He pats the prince on the back to comfort him, and when Tirnon rubs his face and shakes his head, I realize he's crying.

"Get to bed, now," Erol says much more gently. "Things always seem worse when we're exhausted. A prince needs rest to rule, hm? Come."

Even though I know they can't see me, I duck back through the ruffles before they turn toward the bed. Erol's block shoes click on the stone as they near, and Highness's softer shoes shuffle alongside. Above me, the bed creaks and the mattress puffs out feathers that drift past my nose to the floor. The shoe clicks are muffled as Erol walks around on the carpet, and I scoot to the other side of the bed and peek through the ruffles to watch him hang the prince's heavy coat on a rack.

His footsteps cross the room again to the balcony, but the prince stops him.

"Leave it open, please," he calls.

"There's a chill in the air," Erol argues, and the prince sighs.

"I feel closer to my subjects with it open. Good night, Erol. Thank you."

"Highness." Erol replies and clicks across the room. I watch him go, closing the enormous, wall-sized wooden door behind him with a bang that echoes through the room.

My gaze roams to the symbol embroidered on the back of the prince's coat. The emblem of Cerion.

I sniff the air again, inhaling the saltiness and all the intricate scents woven into this strange land. My ears twitch as I become aware of all the unusual sounds mingling beyond the balcony: the distant crash of waves into the cliffs, the occasional shout from far away, the squeak of a wheel, the clang of metal and ropes against stone, the call of sea birds in the night.

"Watch over Father, please," the prince murmurs above me. "Keep him safe, keep him here with me. I'm not ready. Not yet. Please, make him well again. Give our healers all the strength they need to ease his ailments."

He whispers the prayer again and again until he finally falls asleep, and I pull myself quickly away, off the balcony, beyond the sprawling palace lawns and walls, over hundreds of crowded rooftops.

I'm dazzled by how many there are. So many roofs of all shapes and sizes, houses and towers and buildings. So many people. Past them, the sea reflects the moon and stars like a mirror all the way to the horizon. To me, it looks like the edge of the world.

The moon shines straight above me, and I cast no shadow as I turn to the north and the east and push myself back toward home, racing until the ground beneath me turns lush and green, and the Ancients tower in the distance. I streak through the Hamlet, through the window to where my true self dozes in Amma's chair, and I snap back into myself with a gasp of relief and wonder.

6

What Happened?

When I wake up, the glow lamps are turned off, and someone has shuttered the window beside the chair to the cool spring breeze and the moonlight. Moonlight? How long was I asleep?

I scoot back in my chair and rub my eyes as I blink sleepily into the darkened room, trying to remember when I dozed off. My stomach growls, and I'm sure it was at least a few meals' worth of time.

"The wisp," I mutter and shove the furs aside. "Where did it go?"

A shadow moves in the corner of the room past the shuttered window, in the chair that used to be Father's.

"What happened?" it demands, and I scramble backwards to duck behind the cover of the chair. Chills prickle my arms and neck. My panicked heart thrums, rushing blood to my ears. When the shadow chuckles, I realize it isn't any of the ones in my dreams, or Amma's.

"Father," I exhale with relief. "I thought you were something—someone else."

"I told you not to Wander." He gets up from his chair and moves closer, clamping his hand on my shoulder. Even in the dim light I can see the heaviness in his expression. His proud shoulders are slumped forward, his tunic torn and stained with blood just above his belt.

"What happened?" he asks, taking the words out of my mouth.

I work hard to suppress a yawn, feeling emptied out and exhausted despite my long sleep. I need to ground myself. I need to eat something. Father seems to notice and shakes my shoulder like he's trying to wake me up more.

With my time in the Dreaming still fresh in my mind, I race through all of it trying hard to pick out what I want to tell him and what I don't. If he knew about the human girl, he'd be furious. If I told him of the gleaming wood path that led me to the prince of Cerion, he'd probably think I'm mad enough to belong with Amma in the fold. I shift uncomfortably, wanting more than anything to pull free from his grip. I don't dare do that, either.

"Elliot," he jostles me again and bends to meet my eyes, and this time I see a hint of something I don't see often in him. Fear. "What happened with your mother?"

There it is in his voice, too.

"I…" I swallow nervously, thinking past the dreams to try to remember. "The wisp…" I scowl and rub my brow, remembering being sent home, being lulled to sleep, then having those paths set before me. Was I Wandering on my own, or were the Ancients directing my dreams?

"Go and wash your face and do what you must to wake up," he says, and pulls his hand away to run it over his face. "I forgot how hard it is for you dream scouts to readjust. When you come back, you will tell me everything that happened with your mother before they took her."

I do as he says and trudge to the small washroom tucked at the back of Amma's house, where I splash my face from the basin of spring water and stare sleepily at my reflection. It's strange how I can feel so changed after those dreams, but still look exactly as I did yesterday. Same shaggy orange hair falling into my eyes, same hazel eyes, same long chin and pointed nose.

I scratch at the black, whisker-like lines tattooed across my cheeks, the marks of a four-footed shifter, and I close my eyes to shut away my reflection and work to gather my thoughts. Father isn't here to talk about my Wandering. He wants to know what happened to Amma.

I go out, and I'm surprised to find him in the kitchen. The glow lamps are turned all the way up, and he's poking at the dying embers of the fire in the hearth.

"I went into Dreaming to tell her to wake up," I say, slumping onto the stool. I can still feel her in this room as though if I just turned to look, she'd be sitting on the stool beside me, her white eyes staring, her limp hair hanging into her plate. "She was surrounded by darkness in there. Shadows everywhere. I had to look at the moon to be safe."

He stays hunched beneath the mantel and nudges dead kindling onto the coals, causing a spray of sparks and smoke to puff into the chimney.

"When we woke up, she told me to rest. I…" I trail off cautiously. If I told him I saw Mari, he'd be finished with the conversation. He'd be finished with me. She's Forgotten, after all. "I was tired, so I did as she said. I slept. Then I woke up and Elder Avela was here, and—"

The fire catches, and he stands up and turns to me, eyebrows raised skeptically.

"She was, I swear," I whisper. "And…" I slide from the stool and go to the shelves to find something to eat. "She made Amma and me eat—"

"She cooked for you?" Father's eyebrows hitch even more. He reaches past me and grabs a clay jar of grain from the shelf, and another of dried hickory nuts, and a bowl of Amma's favorite mulberries that I found an early harvest of a few days ago.

I nod, stepping back so he can gather what he wants, and I don't say anything else. I don't want to tell him the things Amma said or how she behaved. I don't want him to know she looked into the face of shadow. It would only make him hate her more than he already does. He wouldn't understand.

"And?"

He pours water into the hanging pot, then dumps in the grain and the nuts without measuring any of it. And the fire isn't even hot enough yet. When he reaches for the bowl of mulberries, I jump to take them from him. I picked them for Amma. I won't let him ruin them.

"Let me," I insist. "You're injured. Kaini would scold."

"I'm healed," Father grumbles, but hands me the bowl and drops onto his old stool at the table anyway.

"Where are they?" I ask, trying hard to steer the conversation away from Amma. "Kaini and Sulien?"

"Sleeping," Father grunts, his hand sliding over the hole in his tunic. "It's the middle of the night."

I glance at him and look away quickly, stirring the raw grain and water together, watching how some of it stays dry, floating at the top of the water and the rest sinks to the bottom, settling beneath.

Amma once told me it made her think of the Grove, where everyone remains safe and covered under the canopy, and yet some of us float above, seeing things differently than the rest of them. But eventually, we all sink down, drenched in the magic that protects us.

"I asked you a question." Father's voice startles me back to the present.

I jump and look at him again. It's the middle of the night after a long day of battle. Everyone else is asleep, and yet he came straight here without even changing out of his bloodied tunic to wait for me to wake up. Maybe he hasn't abandoned Amma after all. Maybe, deep down, he does care.

"Amma had a rage fit," I tell him, skipping over most of what happened. "She threw some dishes and Elder Avela stopped them with magic, but Amma was too deep in it, so Elder stopped her too. She said

I'm too young to have to watch over Amma when she's like that."

"You're fifteen, and the only one of us—" he starts defensively but stops himself abruptly when he realizes he's not actually arguing against me, but against the words of an Elder.

"She said they'd take her into the fold." I stir the pot and watch the last flake of grain sink down to join the others.

"If she had any control at all," Father gets up and starts to pace, shaking his head angrily. "She thinks of only herself. And now I'm left to fix it."

I stare at him, trying hard not to show my own anger. He always makes everything about him. Ever since Mari pointed it out to me, I've noticed it so much more. He's obsessed over how our actions make him look as a father or a husband, and nothing is ever his fault.

"She told us what was going to happen today at Blackbird's Spine, but Elder Avela said none of the Seers saw it. That's why I was there. To bring her warning to you," I say with a tone that nearly crosses into insolence.

"So, you ignored the word of an Elder in favor of your mother?" He shakes his head with a half-snort. "You were a distraction that nearly cost the lives of three of my men. Do you have any idea what kind of danger you put us all in? You were not meant to be there, or to see any of that! You're becoming just as bad as she is!"

This time, I can't hide the anger that boils under my skin. I glare at him, furious.

"If you cannot look at me with respect, you will not look at me, Elliot," Father rages, pointing at me to punctuate each word.

My pulse thuds in my ears, drowning out all sound as I stand up, toss the spoon onto the table, and storm out of the kitchen. I duck into the room Mari and I used to share and yank the door behind me. The moment it slams shut, I regret my decision to come in here. I haven't set foot in this room since the night she left. I had forgotten it was even here. Forgotten.

It's been months, but nothing has changed. It still carries her scent. The walls are still covered with her weavings, paintings, and writings. The vellum pages, tacked to the wood with sticky sap, rustle gently when I brush past. I turn to the bed we used to share, still rumpled and untouched, and I remember lying there watching her slip out of the window, her pack strapped to her back, her birds fluttering around her. I remember.

The door clatters open and Father storms in. I brace myself for his fury, but he stops and looks around at the writings and drawings, and all the things Mari left behind, and he goes quiet.

We stand together in silence, me staring at the window, him gazing distantly at her writings.

"Your mother did this," he shakes his head. "She did it to all of us. If she had just controlled herself, if she——"

"Lorelai," I bark defiantly. "You can't even say her name anymore, can you? It's Lorelai."

Enraged, his nostrils flare, his face goes red, his jaw tightens like chiseled stone until veins bulge at his temples. I back up behind the end of the bed, ready to duck if he swings.

"You will not go the way of your mother," he growls, but doesn't chase me. "I hear your lies already. The way you leave things out, just like she did! It's unacceptable. It's time you learned to honor your father and respect the Grove."

The courage I gathered being surrounded by Mari's essence dies a little, and I tuck myself further into the safety of the little corner made by the bed and the curved wall. I stay silent, knowing anything I say will just infuriate him more.

"The Elders agree that she failed to teach you well," he says, and I bristle. He still refuses to call her by name, and now he's insulting her schooling of a skill he knows nothing about.

"They're considering my request to carry the Dream Stone."

"The Dream Stone?" I whisper in disbelief.

It would allow him to navigate the Dreaming just like we do. He could follow me anywhere; go wherever I go. But he has no skill in it. No training, no real understanding. It isn't something just anyone can do. Dream scouts have to show a talent for it early and be nurtured through the learning of how things work. It takes years before initiation, years of practice and discipline before it can be understood enough to be useful. To be safe.

"They're considering it." He watches me, searching for a reaction. I do my best not to give him one.

"You wouldn't do that for Amma even when they offered it to you," I say, staring at the fine inked lines of Mari's detailed drawing of kestrel feathers. "Why do you ask for it now?"

"Because she was a grown woman, capable of making her own choices. She chose to go down dark paths, she chose others over——" he stops himself, squaring his shoulders and twisting his neck to crack it. "She knew the consequences, and she chose. You are a fledgling. And you're my son." His last words are gentler, but I'm too stuck on what he said about Amma to notice.

What he thinks is that Amma sunk deeper and deeper into Dreaming because there was someone she loved there more than him.

He's been wounded by that assumption for as long as I can remember. He's still wounded. But he never tried to understand it from her side.

The Dreaming is a different world. Everything is so much more intense there. It's so much more real, even when it isn't. What no one knows but me is something I'll never tell him. Not without Amma's permission. What she does there is noble and brave, and nobody sees it. When they finally do, maybe they'll understand. Or maybe by then it'll be too late. I don't know.

"When will they decide?" I utter, barely able to eke out any sound with the words. I can't think of anything worse than Father following me around the In-between and the Dreaming. I'd never be able to read Mari's letters again, or travel the new paths I've found, or explore anything, ever. Not with him there.

"Elder Avela gave you a respite of a few days."

I nod, even though I don't want a respite. I've been waiting too long for a purpose. I want to do something meaningful. I want to be useful.

"The Elders will consult the Ancients and make a decision. We'll join them for Vigil when we are called," Father shakes his head. "Until then, Elliot, no Wandering."

"Who do I go to with questions?" I ask, knowing a fledgling like me wouldn't be left without some kind of guidance, even for a few days.

"Waterfowl," said Father nodding toward the outside wall in the direction of Waterfowl's house, who shares the platform with us. "He and Amma Julane have agreed to keep an eye on you. Not all of us are on respite. I have patrols. But I expect to see you at morning meal and supper."

"Yes, Father." It could be worse. At least he isn't forbidding me from going into Dreaming.

"What about Amma?" I ask. "Can I visit her?"

"Not in Waking or in Dreaming," Father forbids. He looks around the room like he's seeing Mari's things for the first time, then shakes his head and walks out.

"Be at breakfast," he calls before the outside door closes behind him.

Through the open door of Mari's and my room, the faint scent of smoke wafts toward me.

"Breakfast!" I yelp and run to the smoking pot at the hearth. Inside, all the water has boiled away, leaving the smoldering nuts and grains blackened and burned. A shiver goes through me. Somehow, it feels like a portent.

The Sylvan Next Door

While scraping the charcoal out of the pot, I hear an unmistakable tapping just outside of the shuttered kitchen window. It comes in patterns of three: *tap, tap, tap*, like the branch of a tree rapping at the shutter.

"Who's there?" I ask, brushing the wall with my fingertips.

"Lit-tle Ha-na," Grandymum creaks.

My heartbeat quickens, and I leave the half-scraped pot to go lift the latch for her.

Outside the window there's only a very narrow section of platform to stand on, too small for even a walkway. Hana sits perched on the branch-like railing, the tendrils that sprout from her back twining around it to keep her safely tethered. When she stands up and leans against the window frame, the vines arrange themselves gently around her legs like a long, flowing skirt.

"He's gone, right?" she whispers, and when I nod, she ducks inside and hops lightly from the windowsill. The springlike tendrils sprouting from her long black hair twist and curl toward me like saplings searching for sunlight.

"*He* was in a rage," she says, tucking her thumbs into her belt.

"What else is new?" I grumble, returning to the pot. "He hates me."

"You were raging, too," she presses, coming to squat beside me.

While she talks, her vines explore the area around her, crawling up the hearthstone, curling around the leg of a nearby stool, even poking into the pot I'm scrubbing.

"I saw him when he arrived," she said. "I was about to come, myself, and see if you were awake. But then he showed up, so I asked Grandymum to let me know when you were alone again. Grandmother Avela said your amma had a portent. She saw what was going to happen today, and then it did happen, and none of the other seers saw it."

I stop scrubbing and look into her curious gray eyes. She blinks, waiting for me to say something. I hold my tongue. It's not right to speak out against an Elder. Especially not in anger. Especially not to accuse them of being wrong. But I can't ignore the thought that if Avela had believed her to begin with, maybe Amma wouldn't have raged. Maybe she'd still be here instead of at the fold, where I'm forbidden to visit her.

When I don't speak up fast enough, Hana just keeps going like she always does.

"I saw you there today, too. You were scouting, weren't you? It's strange to see you just appear that way. No wonder your father was so shocked. Did you see Blackbird's head crumble? Loran, Jevren, and Kyli all fell into the ravine after that, but Uncle and I used our vines to snag them and pull them out. I got Jevren, since he's smallest. It was the first time I ever got to use my darlings that way, to save someone."

She holds her hands out lovingly, and the vines that had made up her skirt snake into her palms and grow thicker and sturdier. I imagine her standing at the edge of the ravine, plunging them down into the depths to fish out a grown man.

"How did you do that?" I ask, setting aside the mostly scraped pot. "I mean, how did you manage to pull him up without falling in, too?"

"Roots in soil, limbs in sky," she says, grinning, and the vines in her open hands start to sprout long, sturdy roots to help her make her point. "I'd show you, but I don't want to damage Grandymum with my roots."

She tosses her long black hair over her shoulders, rustling the leaves that sprout from the bark-like skin of her arms. When she drops her hands to her sides, the vines settle back into skirts again. She sighs wistfully and strokes them like she's smoothing them down.

"Someday, my darlings, you'll be just as strong as Uncle's, won't you? He pulled two men out at once!"

"I wish I had stayed to see it," I say, honestly awed by her abilities.

"It was fiercely frightening, plunging my sweet helpers down toward all that black water." Hana exclaims. She stands up and spies the bowl of mulberries resting on the mantel, and she takes a few to nibble on after I nod reluctantly.

"But the strange thing is, it never did cross the protections. It just pooled against our magic and puddled down at the bottom, lapping like

it was trying to get in. Uncle Oakson said he was proud of me for figuring it out, that they were testing our borders. But think of it," she leans forward, clutching the bowl to her chest, her eyes wide. "Sorcerers."

She says it with such a thrill, but all I can think of are the shadows in Amma's dreams, and the black paths, and the warnings to turn to the light. Gently, I take the bowl from her hand and tuck it back on the shelf. I know Hana. If I let her, she'll finish the whole thing and leave none for Amma.

"You're awfully quiet," she complains, licking the red juice from her fingers. "Aren't you going to say anything?"

"It's just a lot to think about," I say, shrugging. "What you went through, and that Amma knew it would happen."

"She saw things the Elders didn't," Hana agrees. "I wish I could go into the Dreaming like that, like you two do."

"Believe me," I say, staring at the neatly stacked plates and cups on the table, right where Avela left them after Amma's rage, "you don't."

"Mm," Hana gives a non-committal shrug and wanders past me out into the gathering room. I follow her and open the glow lamps, and her vines creep toward the light when she drops into a chair.

"So, what happened here?" she asks, absently sticking a finger into a neglected potted violet on the windowsill. Its withered petals stretch toward her. Its stems and leaves grow plump and green, completely restored by her simple gesture.

"Whispers say you came back from Blackbird's Spine shouting, and the Ancients had to send a wisp to calm you," she says, tickling the leaves with a smile.

"Whispers?" I ask defensively. "Whose whispers? I can't do anything around here without people noticing and making something out of it, can I?"

"Why are you acting so angry?" Hana asks. When she leans against the back of the chair, her vines fan out around her, caressing Grandymum lovingly.

"Oh, I don't know," I growl. "Maybe because they took Amma away, and nobody will let me see her. Or maybe it's because no one would listen to her about the warning. Or maybe it's because when I tried to do what I'm supposed to do and report the things I saw while I was scouting, I was sent a wisp to keep me quiet. Or maybe it's because Father asked the Elders for access to the Dream Stone, and now he's going to be following me around in the one place I can actually get away from him and his—"

"No!" Hana claps a hand over her mouth, and one of her vines sweeps across her fingers curiously. "He didn't!"

"He did," I grumble, kicking at the edge of the sisal mat.

"Elliot," Hana whispers, trailing off. For once, she's speechless. I shrug. I am, too.

"They won't let him," she says after a long stretch of silence, but even she doesn't sound convinced. "It's too complex. Especially with how your amma is. They would have you guided by someone experienced."

"What do you mean, how Amma is?" I ask her defensively.

"I didn't mean it that way! I meant…" she moves closer and rests a hand on my arm, and her vines gently graze the sides of my tunic, "I meant, she has such power behind her skills. Generations' worth of power. And you have that, too. If you can't be taught by her, then you deserve to have a teacher just as strong as she is." She drops her voice to a whisper so quiet I'm sure Grandymum can't even hear. "Not him carrying some rock, bumbling around."

She gazes sincerely up at me, and my eyes sting with the threat of tears. She has been there for me for as long as I can remember. She understands how left out I've felt lately. She's been there for me—we've been there for each other.

I want to tell her how grateful I am to have at least one person left in the Grove who understands me, but I can't manage to form the words. She leans in, her vines absently pulling at me until we're close enough that I can feel her breath on my face. She leans closer, closing her eyes.

The human girl's face flits into my mind and I stand awkwardly, savoring the memory of the dream, ignoring the real girl right in front of me.

"Maps!" Hana yelps randomly, causing me to jump. She turns around quickly, and her vines go limp, obviously disappointed.

"Maps?" I ask dimly, feeling foolish and regretful.

"That's why I came. I wanted to see if the recorded border at the ravine matched where the black water pooled," she explains.

"That's why you came?" I mutter lamely as she brushes past to the long shelves where our generous collection of old rolled-up maps are carefully stored.

With her back turned, one of her vines snakes to my eye level and makes what can only be explained as a head-shaking motion of disappointment. I shrug apologetically, and it slithers over Hana's shoulder to poke curiously at the shelf.

Most Druids in our grove have no use for maps. They've lived here all their lives and they know our woods instinctively. The maps on our shelves were mostly created by my great-grandfather who had a dangerous interest in the lands outside our territory and would often go exploring in the In-between to create detailed drawings and records. From his archives Amma's family saved nine maps, but we really only ever look at map five, which is the center of them all: Sorlen Grove, our home.

I carefully take the map from the shelf and unroll it across the sisal carpet, and Hana and I kneel to find Blackbird's Spine.

"There," she says, and one of her vines taps a spot on the map marked with the name and border of the ravine. "It really does look like a blackbird, doesn't it? And the border goes right along the bottom of the ravine, right where the black water pooled." She sits back, letting her vines prop her up. "It's amazing that your grandfather got it so accurate. So, you were right. They were trying to figure out the borders."

"You said it first," I remind her, engrossed in the details of the map. "That they were testing our defenses. Look at this…" I brush my finger across a perfectly straight, silvery line I've never noticed before which runs through the Great Grove to the west-southwest all the way off edge of the map.

"What's there?" Hana asks, pointing at the bare mat where the line would have continued.

"Cerion," I whisper and jump up to get map four, which would match up to the edge of it. Her vines help me smooth the second map across the floor and line it up. "Look, Hana." I trace my finger over the line, across two rivers, a mountain range, the ocean, and the cliffs of Cerion. "Look, this line of silver goes straight through Cerion's palace."

I stare, remembering the prince and his attendant, and the view of the kingdom and the smell of the ocean. I try to tell her I've been there, but the words don't come. Something warns me that even though it was the first time, it won't be the last. I need to keep it secret for now. Druid magic works this way, sometimes. Makes us keep things to ourselves for reasons we don't really know until later.

"Humans," Hana scoffs, wrinkling her nose with distaste. "Awful creatures. They have enough land of their own. Look at all that!" She sweeps her hand across the map. "And that's only to the west! Why do they need to bother us?"

"It's not all humans," I argue. "Just the Sorcerers. The wicked ones."

"Are you actually defending them?" Hana asks. Her eyebrows go up, and her vines duck backwards slightly like they're shocked.

"I'm just saying they can't all be bad." I shrug, thinking about the human girl and the prince. "Can they?"

"I don't know," she rolls her eyes. "But I do know that Uncle Oakson was pretty rattled about what happened. We went to Grandmother Avela after it was all over yesterday, and he asked her to talk to the Ancients about sending a message to their king. He thinks the humans should be informed there are Sorcerers running around Cerion, causing trouble. Grandmother didn't seem convinced, but she said she'd put it to the Grove to decide."

"How would they even do that?" I ask, wide-eyed.

"Well, you know anyone who leaves the Grove is Forgotten forever, never to return. So they couldn't send a messenger," Hana chews her lip thoughtfully.

"Maybe they'll send a bird," I suggest, thinking of Mari's letters delivered by her sparrow, Kyu.

"If they even decide to do anything." Hana shrugs and starts rolling up the scroll. "The Ancients know that we Druids can hold our own. They prefer us to stay out of human affairs, and I don't see that changing for a few Sorcerers."

I nod, pondering the polished wood path that just happened to lead me straight to palace of Cerion, straight to the prince. Again, I try to tell Hana about it, but the words fail me.

"Come on," she says, handing the rolled-up scroll to her tendrils. "Let's put these away. The sun's up, and I'm starving."

"Yeah, better not be late for breakfast," I grumble, rolling up the second map. "Kaini'd love that."

8

Mages and Wards

Breakfast in the Great Grove is similar to supper, except instead of sitting with our families, we gather with others who share our gifts. That gives me a choice between the dream scouts, the shapeshifters, or the tree whisperers. Most days Hana and I meet up together since we share the gift of talking and listening to trees. Being the born granddaughter of Elder Avela, she almost always has something interesting to talk about, but today while we walk down the ramp toward the Grove among the other Druids of the Hamlet, Hana leans close to me and whispers, "You should try to get a spot near Waterfowl at breakfast. There are whispers he might have something to tell you."

She won't give up any more than that, so we part ways after we duck through the fronds of the willows at the entry to the Grove. As tradition dictates, I look for Father first to offer him a morning greeting. I find him gathered not with the warriors as usual, but with the star speakers, the keepers of the Grove's ancient history. It has been so long since he gathered with them, I nearly forgot he had the gift of looking to the stars to see the past of our people.

I bow my head when I reach him, and I wait politely for him to pause his conversation with the group of a dozen or so others of his talent. Eventually he turns to me.

"Good morning, Father," I say dutifully, like we weren't just fighting before sunrise.

When he places his closed fist on the crown of my head as a blessing, it's like nothing happened between us hours ago. That's how it's meant to be. In the Great Grove, every morning is a fresh start.

We're expected to let go of things that happened before this moment and move forward with peace in our hearts.

"Go with the Grace of the Ancients," he tells me.

When he drops his hand and our eyes meet for a quick glance, I'm surprised by how calm he seems. Nothing like the anger that still broils deep in my belly. He truly embraces the Way of the Grove. I'm not sure I ever want to.

I weave through the groups of gathered Druids: healers, seers, animal kin, shapeshifters, historians, storytellers, plant-kin, and so many others until I reach my own, the dream scouts, at the very heart of the Grove.

I gaze far up into the *Rianave* leaves and fragrant spring blooms fluttering against the deep blue morning sky, and let myself get swept into the deep, peaceful energy of morning pulsing from the wisps above, the trunks between, and the moss below. Waterfowl's hand on my shoulder startles me, and I blink and shake my head, tearing my gaze away to him.

The markings on his face are different from mine. Instead of two lines like whiskers on each side of his nose, he bears a single slash of black across his eyes in the mark of a bird. The effect makes his bright blue eyes seem to glow brightly in the shadow of his brow, and gives him a stern, frowning gaze despite his calmer nature.

The style he wears his dark hair, with blue and green mallard feathers tucked into the sides and the top spiked high like a crest, suits him well as a man who is sometimes a mallard, just like I'm sometimes a fox.

"Elliot is on respite," he calls out to the other dream scouts with a knowing twinkle in his eye and shakes my shoulder excitedly. "Ahh, what a word, what freedom!"

All around us, the other scouts laugh and nod. I don't let on that I disagree.

"What will you do with your respite, Elliot?" asks Glorine, a rare dream scout who has no ability to shift. She tucks her hand into the crook of Waterfowl's elbow and leans against him while she waits for my answer.

"What won't he do is a better question," Waterfowl quips merrily, and everyone laughs. The wisps start to descend from the treetops, and as we all take our seats on the mossy ground to accept the gift of breakfast, Waterfowl leans toward me and winks.

"Eat well, little fox," he says, opening his palms to receive his meal. "I imagine you have some great adventures in your near future."

The wisp that comes to me is pure white, the color of renewal. The gift of its energy washes over me with a feeling of purity, hope, and cleansing. I feel a buzz of excitement for the new day and all it promises to bring me.

It descends into my waiting palms, leaving me the most generous breakfast I've ever received from the Grove: a heaping bowl of sun-warmed summer blueberries—even though it's only Spring yet—with a jug of creamy, tingling *Rianave* nut milk to pour over them, two fluffy sweet cakes baked up with maple butter, and a giant roasted goose egg.

I glance wide-eyed at Waterfowl beside me, who offers me a wink that lets me know he must have had something to do with this, and I dive in to devour the best breakfast I've ever had.

Murmurs of conversation flood through the Grove as everyone settles into their morning meal. In our small circle, talk turns to the tasks of the day.

"We have been offered an invitation," announces Waterfowl after a gulp of hot brew from his mug. "Those of you who have been called to scout the borders may remain here within the embrace of the Ancients today."

My own surprise is echoed in the expressions of those around me, who whisper to each other with excitement. I remember a few times when Amma had been allowed to remain in the Grove all day when I was much younger, but that was many years before my initiation. Since then, I've seen other groups invited to remain all day, but never the dream scouts. I used to hope for it long ago, but I eventually forgot about it.

"You may remain as well, if you wish," Waterfowl tells me. "I think you've never scouted from within the Great Grove before. It's an experience you won't soon forget."

"No, sir, I haven't," I answer excitedly. Maybe today will be different, now that Amma is cared for. Maybe this time, finally, I'll find some purpose.

But then my thoughts flicker to the last time I was in Dreaming, when the first black path I ever encountered outside of Amma's dreams appeared to me. Waterfowl must notice, because he turns to offer me his full attention.

"What troubles you, young one?" he asks. "The shadows cross your face."

"Exactly that," I answer without a moment to think of my reply. Being here among the Ancients has taken away my doubts and restraint. "The last time I went in, for the first time ever, I was shown a black path just like Amma's."

"That must have been frightening for you," he says with understanding.

I nod silently.

"Before then, what did you see?" Waterfowl asks. This time, I catch myself and form my answer carefully.

"Something beautiful. More beautiful than anything I've ever seen before."

"And so you have experienced balance," Waterfowl says. "The Ancients know, Elliot. They know what you are ready for and what you are not. They will never show you a path that isn't meant for you in one way or another."

"But how could so much darkness be meant for Amma?" I ask, lowering my voice and leaning closer so the others can't hear.

"She has been titled a Wanderer for straying from the paths set before her, not for following them. What you know of her dreams are what you're meant to know for your own journey. You must not forget what you've seen, but you must learn to separate your experience from hers. Yes, she is your mother, but you are on two distinct, personal paths. You are called Wanderer's Son not to punish you, but to remind not to follow her. Be mindful. Do not stray from the paths set before you."

"Father said I mustn't visit Amma while she's in the care of the fold. Is the dark path that appeared to me a path to see her?"

"It could be, or it could be something else entirely," Waterfowl gazes across the Grove in Father's direction. "I would not speak against your father's wishes, Elliot, but barring the Ancients themselves, no one has the right to tell you where you cannot go in Dreaming. If a path opens to you, that path is yours to explore."

I look at him, wishing I could ask a question I know must be forbidden. Druids are meant to remain in the Grove. Crossing borders is forbidden. But I went to Cerion last night. Cerion, the kingdom surrounding our Grove, which has no authority over us. Cerion, where the Sorcerers stood when they attacked our borders with black rain.

Sharply observant, Waterfowl seems to recognize my need for a private question. He guides me to a quiet space on the outskirts of the Grove, nestled between *Rianave* roots taller than my head. This close, the thrum of the Lifesap pumping beneath its bark is distracting enough to steal my breath. Again, Waterfowl notices and he takes me by my shoulders to looks into my eyes.

"What if a path leads me outside of the Grove?" I whisper, nervous the *Rianave* will hear me.

He looks at me for a long time. If he has any reaction, he hides it well. Finally, after a long stretch of thoughtful silence, he says, "It is the Grove's will that you would be shown such a path. As long as you follow it only in Dreaming or in the In-between, and as long as you keep yourself grounded here within our borders, there is no harm in exploring where you are led. It is only considered Wandering when you willfully stray from the trails."

Like when I went to see Mari. The *Rianaves* would never send me a path to her.

A brisk wind brushes past us, ruffling my hair and the fringe on my vest, and blowing a feather loose from Waterfowl's crest. His words are exactly the reassurance I need. A heavy burden lifted from my shoulders.

"I will warn you, though," he says with his arm around me as he guides me back to the others, "if you are to leave the Grove, even in Dreaming, it would do you well not to speak to others about it. Spreading knowledge about the outside lands can sow temptation and curiosity. The Ancients might agree you're strong enough to resist such things, but there are many others, even grown men, who are not. That which you experience on the outside, keep to yourself, Elliot. For the good of the Grove."

The Sanctum is empty now, save for the dream scouts who have propped themselves comfortably around the meadow to begin their journeys. Waterfowl and I settle into the moss beside them, and as soon as I close my eyes, I feel my second self float away.

In Dreaming, I stand amid the *Rianaves,* feeling their warmth and encouragement wash over me like the waves of Echo Pool at the peak of summertime. It's an unbelievable feeling, soaring high into the branches of the Ancients where the wisps live, looking down at myself and the rest of the dream scouts below, asleep. Protected. Loved.

I feel myself pulled gently away from them, turned, placed into the sky, where a path made from puffs of clouds stretches out beneath my feet. In wood elf form, secure in the In-between, I take step after step to the south.

Far beneath me, the world spreads out like great-grandfather's map. I see the perfect sunburst of the Rianave grove, and the obsidian slash of Blackbird's Spine, and the vast stretch of blue water that makes up Echo Pool and the greater lake called Mistsheen beside it. Up this high, the southern range of mountains looks like tiny, snow-capped anthills.

I run along the cloud path, hopping from one puff to another over the ocean, caught up in the game of crossing the expanse like steppingstones across a brook. The path curves slowly downward as ocean becomes land, and I descend deep into broad, wet leaves.

The air in this place is thick and hot, worse than a bad summer in the Grove. I feel myself strangely pulled through space, unable to choose my own direction, until I speed so fast, I have to squeeze my eyes shut to keep from feeling sick.

When I open them again, I'm standing in a hallway outside an unfamiliar room in a large wooden house. The shutters of the room have been pushed open, allowing the morning sunlight to beam inside and splash along the wooden floorboards and colorful carpet. Six beds line the walls, each with its own personality. Some are neatly made; others are messy and piled with trinkets and dolls.

I can't figure out why I'm here until I step through the door and turn to my right to see the human singing girl, sound asleep. I creep closer to the bed and look at her curiously, feeling strange to be given this chance to see her asleep in her own world instead of in Dreaming. She looks as if she has just dozed off, with her book open in her hand and her quill still tucked into it.

Sunlight spills across the page of the open book and paints a golden line across her lips, freckled cheek, and apple-red hair. Here in the In-between, she's just as breathtaking as she had been in Dreaming.

I stand looking at her for what feels like half the morning. Deep within me, I feel a charge of affection and belonging. A thought edges in. She's dreaming right now. I could see here there, instead of standing here watching her sleep.

I walk away from her bed and feel the shimmer of the Dreaming brush over me like cobwebs, rustling my hair, prickling my skin. Once there, I make a second change. It's a necessary one, but one I feel guilty about anyway. I think of my high elf disguise, and when I become him on the outside, the spongy mulch path appears before me. I follow it and her song to a bright, cheerful glade where she dances freely among the flowers and birds. Entranced by the beauty of her spirit, I weave through the tall fronds of grass and meadow flowers toward her.

"Is that you, my darling elf?" she calls. I open my arms to greet her, and she runs to my embrace and presses her lips to mine.

Through this dream, in between kisses, we sit in the grass among the spring blossoms, and I hold her close and listen as she tells me so many things. Her name is Mya, and there is a sorrow in her voice, a longing I'm in some ways familiar with.

She tells me her father has left her with strangers, and though they're kind to her, she wishes every day for his return. She fears he hates her. She aches to find her own place in the world.

Her words stir the same feelings in me about Father and the Grove, and about exploring new places and venturing down exciting paths, but I don't dare speak about them and reveal more of myself than I should. I only draw her closer and listen, letting the pleasant tones of her voice wash emotions over me.

After some time, I begin to forget about the Grove and the Ancient Ones. She becomes my world, stirring feelings and wishes I never knew I had before I met her.

"My voice gets me into trouble," Mya breaks through my musing, nuzzling deeper into my arms. "I try to control it, but sometimes I forget. What if Pa finally had enough of it? What if, this time, he isn't coming back for me? What if I'm left on my own?"

"Sometimes our parents' actions might make them seem selfish or cruel," I tell her, marveling at how velvety smooth my elf voice sounds. "When we begin to understand them for who they are, it gets easier."

"Do you think he's coming back?" she asks tearfully.

"If he does not," I say honestly, "then he has chosen to cast away one of the greatest treasures of our world."

"Oh," Mya's awed whisper sends a thrill of tingles through me. We kiss until her dream ends and she fades from my arms, leaving me alone in the glade.

Before I have time to miss her, the tall grass shifts oddly at my knees, rustling apart to reveal another path. This one is made of smooth stones, neatly arranged side by side. Scowling, I push to my hands and knees and when my hand touches the stone, the path bursts forward into the distance, disappearing beyond a thick, sunny hedgerow.

Intrigued by this new path, I jump to my feet and jog, letting the high elf disguise shimmer away to my fox-self for speed and scent tracking. When I cross through the hedgerow I'm met with a brightly lit fog and the tickling sensation that I've once again shifted out of Dreaming into the In-between.

I take a cautious step expecting to meet with the same path, but instead I'm dropped so abruptly onto a much wider stone lane that my breath is knocked out of me.

The shift is so strange and swift that for a moment I can't even remember what happened, or how I got here. Am I in Dreaming? Is this the In-between? I realize soon enough the source of my confusion. I had been a fox, but now, somehow, I'm my true self. My wood elf self.

I stumble slightly, trying to orient myself. This place is crowded. I can't remember ever visiting a place so crowded. Humans rush past on a cobblestone road framed with buildings of stone and brick and lined with tables full of strange objects.

A constant barrage of shouting, clomping, and wood and metal wheels clattering against uneven stone jars me. The colors, the crowd, the flashes of jewels and coins and shiny pots are too much. Overwhelmed, I rush across the cobblestone road seeking shelter in the quiet shade of a glinting white building.

How did I get here? The feeling that at any moment I could be whisked away again like a leaf on the wind is unfamiliar and terrifying. I try hard to feel the peace of the Grove while I stand here, but the chaos of this bustling human place is too distracting, too unfamiliar, too harsh.

I press myself back against the wall of sparkling white stone, hug my torso tightly to try to keep myself together, and squeeze my eyes shut in an effort to find some grounding.

"YOU DO NOT BELONG HERE!" a forbidding voice screeches into my mind, and I scramble away from the building in terror.

I turn to look for the source of it, expecting to see something terrifying, furious, and immensely powerful, but there is nothing. Not only is there no one there, the building itself is suddenly obscured by a shift of the light.

"Oh," I whisper, fascinated, as one robe-wearing human after another vanish into the space where I once stood.

I back away further, and the more distance I put between myself and the building, the more it comes into focus. When I'm nearly a block away, I marvel at its remarkable golden domed roof, and the gleam of the massive, smooth white stone walls that look like they were carved from a single piece of stone.

Once I'm used to my surroundings, I find myself dazzled by the splendors of the city surrounding me. I stare at the hundreds of baubles on tables, and wonder at men walking past, carrying tall poles stacked with twisted breads, or colorful hats, or swaying scarves.

"Sister, *why* do you vex me so?" a voice drifts from my left, and I turn toward a young man walking beside an annoyed-looking girl slightly younger than he.

It must be like the Grove where we call everyone Uncle or Auntie, and Grandmother or Grandfather, because the two of them are complete opposites. He has such dark hair, while the girl's hair is light and golden. He is tall and frail-looking, and she is shorter, sturdier, and muscled. She's unmistakably a warrior, dressed in leather armor with a sword strapped to her hip, while he wears long, billowing robes like the Sorcerers at the ravine.

Sorcerers. Suspiciously, I step back into fox form and creep closer to them, sniffing the air. The one in robes does carry the scent of human magic with him: Parchment, candle wax, incense, and a sense of intensity.

"I'm not vexing you, Gaethon," the girl scoffs. "I'm just telling you not to lose track of time again."

"A Mage has better things to do than—"

"Than eat?" she interrupts, exasperated.

The way they argue, they're probably sister and brother after all. They smell like they came from the same place.

I sniff again. Yes, and that's definitely the scent of human magic. Anger wells inside me until I realize the scent is somehow clean and pure. Mages and Sorcerers are as different as light and shadow. He isn't one of those. There's a sense of diligence about him. Of clarity and brightness.

"Please, Lisabella," Gaethon mutters as his fellow Mages rush past, gesturing strange greetings to him.

"I swear if it weren't for the wards, I'd storm in there and drag you out myself," she says jokingly, "just so I wouldn't have to listen to Mouli!"

"Yes, well, they're there for a reason..." his bored, dismissive tone strays in and out of the In-between strangely, like he's already part here and part there.

Wards. That makes sense. Just like the Grove, Mage places carry thick and forbidding magical protections. That's what scared me off so quickly. I wonder if our wards and warnings back home are as terrifying to outsiders as that building's warnings were to me.

I slip to the girl and sniff the air around her, just to see. She carries no magic with her except a very faint scent of it, which most likely just lingers from her being so close to her brother.

"Just..." Lisabella sighs and shake her head, and Gaethon offers her a smirk. "I'm going to be late," she says.

He nods in response, then a strange look comes over him and he turns his head in my direction. The blur around the Mage shifts slightly, and for a quick moment he comes into clear focus. To my shock, his eyes meet mine directly.

We both draw a startled breath, and he stumbles backward into his sister's grip as I skitter away in disbelief. Had he really seen me? It isn't possible. *Keep hidden, always.*

"Brother?" Lisabella asks with concern, propping him up.

Panicked, I duck under the cover of a booth a few paces away while Gaethon blinks rapidly, massaging his furrowed brow with his fingertips.

"I thought I saw something," he mutters, then collects himself and brushes her away. "Give His Highness my regards."

My heart races as I watch the Mage disappear beyond the magic of the warded walls. That has never happened before. It should not *ever* happen. Lisabella shakes her head and starts to walk away, and I follow her in a daze through the crowded market, trying to make sense of it all.

"*It is the Grove's will that you have been shown such a path,*" Waterfowl's words echo through my mind, convincing me I didn't stumble on this brother and sister for no reason. But why am I suddenly being shown so many humans?

As Lisabella reaches the gates of the palace of Cerion, I gape at its noble towers and parapets in awe. I've been in there, just last night.

Gently, the cobblestone street beneath my feet falls away, and I glide backwards. The castle shrinks in the distance until it disappears beyond the crests of mountains, then the puffy white clouds, and finally the wispy fronds of the *Rianave* canopy until I float back into myself again, cradled tenderly by the soft moss of the Sanctum.

9

The Rianave

I wake slowly, staring along the perfect, straight trunks of the *Rianaves* to the point where they converge into the canopy far above me. All around me, the other dream scouts lie sleeping, their breathing slow and even. It's an eerie feeling, like waking up in the middle of the night in a dark, silent house. I don't move for a while. I just lie in the moss, thinking.

Still dazed by my journeys, I imagine myself walking along the trunk of the nearest *Rianave* as though it's a path, and I count the paces in my mind. When I reach one-hundred fifty paces all the way up in the leafy fronds of the tree's crown, I catch sight of something out of the corner of my eye moving across the ground beside a different *Rianave*. I prop myself on my elbows to look closer, just in time to see the hint of a shadow disappear behind the *Rianave's* massive roots.

Scowling, I gaze back into the canopy for some sign that the *Rianaves* saw it too, but they remain stoic and silent. Not even a wisp peeks out from the sunbeams that scatter across the moss and ferns of the glade.

I slink toward the roots where the shadow disappeared and notice something very strange. What I think at first is a huge black snake slithering along is actually a broad path made of shadows or smoke. It creeps slowly in my direction, and I freeze and hold my breath, terrified.

"Turn away from shadow," I whisper to myself and turn abruptly to face the other direction.

A breeze shivers across the leaves in the canopy far above, and its chill prickles my arms and the back of my neck. I squint toward the sun and take a step into a beam of light that dances across the moss, closing my eyes to bask in its warmth.

Abruptly, the beam is snuffed out, leaving me chilled again. When I open my eyes, I'm standing in shadows again, the dark path just one step from the toes of my boots. As soon as I notice it, it edges closer.

I've never seen a path behave this way before. Not in Waking or in Dreaming. Mystified, I glance across to where the dream scouts sleep, expecting to maybe see myself lying there and realize I'm in the In-between, but I'm not. I'm awake.

The path creeps closer, and I turn from it to walk briskly across the glade until I'm only a few paces from the massive trunk of a different *Rianave*. The thrum of the Lifesap pulses in my ears. Just a step or two more and I won't be able to avoid touching its bark.

I look over my shoulder and see the path has chased me all the way to this point, making a straight, direct line across the Grove. Frantically, I shuffle backwards, desperate to avoid it, but it edges ever closer until my hands graze the smooth bark of the Rianave and I fall against it.

"*Elliot Eldinae*," the *Rianave's* voice thunders so deafeningly inside my mind I feel like my head will split open from its sheer power. The ground beneath my feet rumbles with warning. When I look down at my boots, the black path is gone. My knees buckle underneath me, and I try to pull my hands away, but they stay stuck. A golden glow surges up my arms as I slide down to kneel at the base of the root.

I try to muster the words to apologize for touching this sacred, mighty being uninvited, but my voice fails me. Golden light swirls further up my arms, caressing my shoulders, dancing into my eyes, cradling me from head to toe.

"*Elliot Eldinae*," my name echoes through my mind again, but this time it comes as a chorus of all the *Rianaves* in the Sanctum. The effect is so euphoric I lose all ability to think, to wonder, to speak. Images emerge between us so fast I have no time to see what they are or what they mean before they fall away to be replaced with something else.

Fleetingly, I glimpse Mari's face, and Mya's, and the prince in Cerion, and the Mage Gaethon, and the Sorcerers at the ravine. I see my house nestled in Grandymum's branches, and Hana's vines reaching, and Sare Fox and her kits, and Father, and Kaini with his hand clapped over his bloodied nose, and Amma in her chair.

"*Long have your ancestors served us faithfully,*" the *Rianaves* declare, and with their words come an overwhelming sense of gratitude.

"*Why do you turn away from dark paths?*" they ask after a long time watching pieces of my past shuffle between us.

"Amma told me to," I whisper, fighting through my mind to find the words.

"*What did she say?*" they ask me.

I try to think of a reply, but it's difficult to focus through the euphoria. Eventually they find the answer themselves, tucked into a memory. Amma's voice: *"Remember, as there are two parts of us, there are always at least two sides to everything. A side that dwells in light, and one that dwells in shadow. If you stand in the sunshine, you will always cast a shadow. If you turn your back to the light, you risk becoming one with the shadow."*

I shiver again, and the *Rianave's* gentle hold glows brighter, warming me and filling me with comfort.

"Wise words from Amma," the *Rianave* holding me offers kindly. *"But what if, in our service, you were to face the shadow? Look into Shadow for us, young one. Courageous one. As your mother has before you. See what we must know. Know we are with you, always."*

The golden light pulses around me, cradling me with such comfort I can't help the tears that spill down my face. When I feel like it's too much to bear and I can't take any more of its warmth and affection, the *Rianave* sets me gently on my feet and the golden light fades to leave me standing alone facing the trunk, my hands by my sides.

I stare in wonder at the smooth bark in front of me, my whole body buzzing with energy from the experience. I feel unreal, like if I took a step, I'd soar straight up to the clouds again. After a long time, I wriggle my toes and my fingers and begin to feel myself grounded in my body again. *Roots in soil, limbs in sky.*

My stomach growls.

"I'm here," Waterfowl whispers beside me, and I yelp and nearly jump out of my skin. He rests a hand on my back and quiets me, warning me not to wake the others before he guides me away from the *Rianave* and closer to the gathering.

Once we're a few paces away, I start to feel more like myself but still charged with the energy I just experienced. Waterfowl leans closer to me as if trying to absorb some of it himself, though I know as well as he does that's not possible.

"Whatever they showed you, Elliot," he says, meeting my gaze with admiration, "know it is their will."

"But they said—" I start, but he stops me quickly, raising his hand.

"It isn't for me to know," he whispers, smiling. "You have been given a great gift this day. One that only comes once in a lifetime to most of us. The wisdom of the Ancients, face-to-face. I'm proud of you."

I blink and turn to look at the *Rianave* I touched. In the moment, what it told me made perfect sense. Now that it's over, I find myself doubting.

"It goes against what Amma told me," I tell Waterfowl. "It goes against..." I shiver, imagining Amma's dreams filled with dark paths and threatening, shadowed figures. "I don't want to go there, ever."

"Trust in what you've seen, young one," Waterfowl says. "If the Ancients have shown it to you, then they are with you."

"Know we are with you, always," I whisper.

"As the Grove wills it," Waterfowl says, and bows his head to the *Rianaves*.

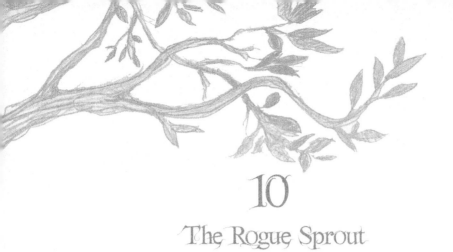

10

The Rogue Sprout

F eeling bold with my true self safe in the Great Grove, I dash through the In-between in fox form, relishing the feel of the wind in my fur and the damp forest ground beneath my feet.

The outer Grove that buffers the Great Grove from the rest of the world is thick with mist. It holds few paths and even fewer landmarks, making it feel untamed and dangerous.

I know well which parts to avoid, even here in the In-between. Dark creatures reside in this part of the forest. Goblins. Pookas. Sylphs. Wildwood. Wraiths and scaly slydragons. Aberrants. For our safety, the wards woven into the great cedars and elms here seep with warning and redirection.

Through the afternoon, I skirt along the edge of the mist through the darkest parts of the forest. When no shadowed paths appear, I break off along one of many streams flowing from the mountains toward Echo Pool.

After my hours spent exploring mist and shadow, the massive bowl of crystal turquoise water is breathtaking. Bordered by sheer stone cliffs as tall as the *Rianaves,* it sparkles brightly in the sunlight, reflecting a perfect blue sky. I leap from the cliff and skim across the smooth surface of the water to the opposite side, and land lightly on the narrow, rocky footpath leading to Sare fox's den.

At its mouth, I pull my sleeping self out of the Great Grove and step into Waking as my two selves snap together. Inside the cave, Sare fox is tucked against the wall with her babies, sound asleep.

I wake her with a gentle nudge of my nose, and she peers sleepily at me for a moment before she understands who I am and why I'm here. We change places and I snuggle in with the pups while she slinks out of the den, off to hunt.

As soon as she's gone, a sparrow flutters to an overhanging branch like it's been waiting for me. It chirps once and hops cautiously toward me, and I shiver from fox to wood elf.

"Come, Kyu," I whisper, holding out my hand, careful not to wake the pups snuggling against my leg.

The bird chirps once and tilts her head as if to say, *"Are you crazy? I'm not going in there."*

With a sigh, I untangle myself from the pile of cubs and crawl a safe distance away, and she hops into my waiting palm and puffs out her chest proudly.

"Here," I whisper, and offer her some crumbs from the stale wheat nut bread in my belt pouch. When she's eaten her fill, I take the tiny scroll from the loop around her neck and unroll it eagerly to read Mari's message.

Sheshi,

I dreamed of you last night. Were you here, or was it only my wish carried on a breeze? I have such an awful notion, Brother. Tell me the truth of what is happening there. Whisper it to Kyu, and she'll carry your message to me.

Celian vore estier'analla, with deepest love, Mari

"Kyu, you're such a good little bird," I tell the sparrow, stroking her feathers with the tip of my finger. She leans into the affection for a moment and then flutters to my shoulder, pecking at my cheek.

"All right," I laugh, then whisper, "tell Mari this: I did come to see you last night, Sister, and learned your secret. A baby? It's wonderful!" I pause, searching for words I might be allowed to share. "There has been a threat here, but we're strong against it, and we're safe. Amma is being cared for. I wish I could say more, but you know how things are. Don't worry, Sister. I miss you every day. Be well. I'm with you, too."

Kyu chirps at me as if to ask if that's it, and when I nod to her, she hops up and soars away. I watch her fly out over the lake and up into the sky to the west until she's a tiny dot. Once she's gone completely, I feel a pang of regret.

I wish I could tell Mari everything like I used to. She's the only one who ever really understood me. And I was the only one to know when she'd found Elowyn's injured dove tangled in the thick, abandoned web of a hawk spider and nursed it to health, then sent it away only for it to return with a message for her.

Ancient kinship with the high elves means that their messages and diplomats can usually cross our wards. Even though we never go to Ceras'lain and they rarely come here, it's still possible for them to send official messages. But Mari, the Forgotten, is a different story.

No secrets from us.

The Ancients have to know I'm still passing messages to her. Every time I go to the Sanctum and look into the wisps, I'm sure it will be the moment they take her from me. For some reason, though, they don't. I don't know how long we'll be able to go on this way. I don't know when she'll become as Forgotten to me as she is to everyone else.

When a child of the Grove leaves, it's the ultimate betrayal. We're to turn our backs on those who disregard us. To the Grove, the Forgotten no longer exist. But I refuse to stop talking to the sister who practically raised me.

There are so many rules of the Grove like that. Things we're supposed to do that no one questions or dares to challenge. I don't know if anyone else thinks about these boundaries like I do. It isn't something that's discussed, ever. Living by the Grove's will means doing as we're taught without question.

Look into shadows for us, young one. Courageous one.

Far from the Sanctum, snuggling with the cozy fox kits with Mari's smooth Elven parchment in my hand, one word keeps beating in time with my heart, over and over: Why?

Eventually, I doze off. In the In-between, a carpet of fallen pine needles crunches under my feet as I walk along. I'm not sure why I appeared here until I spot Hana in the distance, crouched with her back toward me. Most of her vines have snaked over her shoulders as she peers at something on the ground in front of her. One vine is wrapped around the nearest cedar, pulsing messages against its bark.

"It looks to be very young," Hana whispers. "A sprout from just this spring. But it refuses to be transplanted." Her message shivers up the tree trunk into the leaves, and a swift breeze carries it away across the canopy, toward the center of the Grove.

I move closer, keeping a watchful eye on the field beyond the mists and brambles, until I reach Hana and stand hidden beside her. She's leaning far forward, her hands cupped around the tiny sapling, cooing affectionately to it. Her gray eyes gleam with a strange golden light.

This isn't an ordinary sapling. It's a *Rianave* sprout.

I suck in a shocked breath and glance between the sprout and the field beyond the tree line. How could it have sprouted here, so close to the border and so far away from the Great Grove? As if in answer to my question, a thin black line slithers away from the base of the tiny plant like a root with a mind of its own. It snakes toward the border, thin and weak, until it crosses the territory line and unfurls into a broader, walkable path.

Look into shadow, Courageous one. Why do you turn away from dark paths?

My heart thumps. I have permission now. This is my purpose. Except I can't leave the litter alone in the den, and I don't want to leave Hana alone in this place or lose the path that's been placed before me.

I try something I've never done before. I split my awareness. Half-asleep in the den, I listen for Sare fox's return, while here in the outer Grove, I stand beside Hana, my attention locked on the black path while she speaks into the trees.

As soon as Sare fox returns from her hunt, I pull myself through In-between and step into Waking. Hana startles when I crouch beside her and take her trembling hand. When she glances at me, her face is pale and serious bathed in the sprout's golden glow.

"How can it be here?" I ask her.

"I don't know," she whispers, glancing up at the mists and brambles. "Do you want to ask it? It's a sassy little thing. Maybe you'll have more luck than me."

She leans away from the tiny sprout, clinging to her vines, which are acting strangely. They swirl around her cautiously, like they're afraid to get too close to the little plant.

Frowning, I bend closer and graze the tender shoot with the tip of my finger.

"*Greetings!*" it squeaks brightly.

Before I can react, it flings me out of myself onto the narrow black root path. In the In-between, I skid straight across the border, into the shadow that lingers waiting for me. It spins me once to show me my first self; the wood elf boy kneeling before the Rianave sprout with one finger touching it, then pulls me swiftly away, swallowing me into darkness.

I don't know how long I swirl in the terror that follows, speeding across the grass until it spits me onto my hands and knees into filthy, churning waters.

I scramble to my feet breathlessly and try to pull myself back through the In-between to Hana, but the shadow still swirls around me, holding me in place as the water rises to my waist. A flood. A hundred paces away, sixteen rooftops jut above the surface of the filthy, churning water. Three dozen people cling to each other on top of them, screaming, waving their arms, crying for rescue.

"What have you brought me, dark one?"

I whirl to face the voice. Dressed in flowing red robes and a crimson cloak, a human woman hovers nearby. I recognize her right away as one of the four at Blackbird's Spine. This close, I can see the details of the deep black Mage Mark that curls across her neck and her hands. The sight of it sends a shiver of dread through me. The Mark is a blemish inflicted by the abuse of magic, a sign of evil and villainy we're taught to fear from a very young age in the Grove. She wears her Mark proudly, like Father's tattoos.

She's terrifying.

Floating elegantly above the muddied, rushing waters, she fixes her ruthless gaze on the shadow holding me. The wind shifts, pushing her acrid scent toward me: dark magic, desperation, disease.

With vicious intent, she moves closer to me and the shadow and swipes her hand from side to side.

Keep hidden, always.

I slip all the way into Dreaming just before her hand passes through my chest, leaving only a prickle of cold in its wake.

"Why call me here if you have nothing for me?" she growls at the shadow, sneering. "Go back to our little experiment, and do not summon me again without a good reason, or I will banish you to the darkness whence you came."

She thrusts her hand forward and the shadow spins away. I know I should return to Hana, but my curiosity gets the best of me. Look into shadows, they had said, so I streak toward the drowning village instead.

Only the occasional scream pierces through the deafening roar of rushing water as I reach the village. I land on the rooftop of a tall stone house almost completely washed out by the swell of the river that rushes down from the distant hills.

Awed, I gape at the power of the water which carries with it everything from horse carts to entire house frames. We're taught very young how to be respectful to the waters and trees and creatures of the forests, and we're also taught that humans don't revere them as we do. It makes sense that the river would rebel against them this way.

Shifting back into the In-between, I leap from the roof into fox form. I didn't know this village before, but judging from the sturdy houses that remain and the hundred or so people shivering and crying on either side of the filthy, raging water, it was once a large, important place.

It seems the flood has washed nearly everything away: the main road, the footbridges, the cart bridges. There were so many more houses, too. Most are so submerged I can only barely make out the tops of their chimneys beneath the deadly waters.

I run to the outskirts where many of the villagers are gathered at the water's edge. The group of them stand crying, calling out for loved ones, and holding onto the ones who have been rescued. Drenched and exhausted, their drab gray clothes hang heavily on their shoulders, weighing them down.

So many of them remind me of people I know in the Grove. Aside from their rounded ears and stockier builds, they don't seem as different from us as we're taught.

In sharp contrast to the weary folk, much richer-looking men and women draped in red cloaks and sashes weave through them, offering them food, blankets, comfort, and healing.

I keep my distance and watch one of them, a man, as he walks among them with glowing pink hands. He's a healer, like Kaini. He presses his palms to a crying boy whose arm is limp and broken. The boy sniffles and swallows his tears, relief washing over him as the healing mends his injury.

"Please, please! My husband!" A woman wails over the roar of rushing water. "He's there!"

A man whose face is obscured by his oversized hood clamps a hand over her shoulder reassuringly. He flicks his red cloak dramatically behind himself and turns toward the village calling strange, powerful words into the wind as he thrusts his hand outward. His voice rises dramatically over the thunderous sound of the water, commanding everyone's attention, then his feet lift from the ground and he begins to soar above the flooded village.

The villagers gasp, pointing and cheering, and I follow him to catch his scent: red spice smoke, decay, and dark magic. Again, I'm reminded of the Sorcerers who attacked Blackbird's Spine with their dark waters.

These flood waters are natural, though, like the spring thaw came all at once and washed the village away in a sudden, unrelenting deluge. They aren't black like that rain had been. Still, it puzzles me. Why would these Sorcerers be here helping when they're known to be so ruthless, selfish, and destructive?

Ahead of me, the Sorcerer dives to scoop up a man stranded on one of the rooftops just in time. As soon as the rescued man's feet leave the house, a roaring current slams into the thatch, smashing it to pieces.

Unaffected by the fearsome sight, the Sorcerer floats along the crest of the deluge, gliding back to the edge of the water to return the man to his terrified wife. She throws her arms around her husband, weeping with relief.

Amid the cheers of the crowd, the rescuer sinks to his knees. He curls into himself as if completely spent by his magic. A richly dressed man comes to his side to check on him. When the hooded man nods, the rich one pats his back and turns to the cheering villagers.

"Remember who saved us all this day," he shouts over the roar of the floodwaters, "long lives and peace to the Knights of Conquer!" He turns back to the red-cloaked man, crouching to speak to him. "We are forever indebted to you, my lord."

They're all too busy cheering to notice the young girl sweeping past in the destructive current. She's so close, all I would have to do is reach out and offer her my arm from here on the soggy bank. There's no time to think or try to alert anyone. Her arms slip from the fishing boat. She goes under and bobs up again, choking and gasping for breath.

I have to save her. I take a step forward, preparing to pull myself through even though it means crossing the border. Leaving the Grove. Becoming Forgotten.

"Elliot, please!" Hana's desperate scream rips me from the flooded village, yanking me harshly back along the strange, tight line to my sleeping self.

Wait. I wasn't sleeping. It was the *Rianave* sprout who thrust me onto the shadowed path. I crash painfully into myself beside Hana and roll several strides away with a force like I've fallen from the cliffs of Echo Lake.

"Elliot!" Hana screams and runs after me. Her vines curl around my shoulders, propping me up as her gray eyes meet mine apologetically.

"Are you all right? Where did you go?" she whispers, and I can feel her terror like it's my own.

"Shadows," I croak through the pounding in my head and the strange, sickening feeling that comes from being pulled out of the In-between against my will. My stomach twists. I'm going to be sick. I roll to the side and vomit into the lush ferns and carpet of pine needles, trying hard to avoid getting any on her vines.

"I'm sorry, I'm sorry!" Hana cries desperately. Out of nowhere, a tendril offers me a waterskin, and I gulp from it to rinse my mouth out. At first I think her apologies are for waking me, which she knows better than to do. Never, ever, wake a dream scout. But then she keeps going, and I work to wrap my head around what she's saying.

"I didn't know that would happen with the sprout! All it did when I spoke to it was answer me rudely. I didn't know it was going to make you..." she trails off. "What happened?"

"Sorcerers," I say, coughing as I breathe in the water accidentally. I catch my breath and gulp down another mouthful. "A black path. A flood. We need to stay away from that sprout. We need to tell someone straight away."

"I sent word through the trees. They're already coming," Hana reassures me. Despite her soothing words, her voice is frantic as she

70

gathers me closer, and I realize we're both trembling.

"Don't worry, Elliot," she whispers, her breath brushing my ear. "You're safe now. You're here. We're together. You're safe."

11

Rumination

The discomfort of being forcefully woken from dream scouting lingers for a long time. It's a feeling I have only experienced twice before, and both times were on purpose so I would know how to cope with it if it ever happened by accident. Everyone in the Grove knows it's dangerous to wake a dream scout when they're asleep.

"I'm sorry, I'm sorry," Hana keeps whispering.

The mildest consequence is the one I'm suffering now. My body feels twice as heavy as usual, and my second self is twice as light, so I have the constant sense that I'm spinning outside of myself and reeling myself in. And then there's the nausea.

Thankfully it was just a mild jolting. The worst consequence terrified me so much at first that when I learned of it, I refused to continue my training for weeks. Any time a dream scout leaves himself, he risks severing the tether between his waking self and sleeping self.

If that ever happened, the second self could spin off forever into the vast infinity of the Dreaming, never to be reunited. In the meantime, the true self would remain asleep forever, slowly wasting away until he's consumed by death and returned to the roots of the Ancients.

"Here," Hana calls. I focus on her vines clinging to my suede vest and grazing my cheek, but her voice sounds distant, like she's several paces away. When she speaks again, she's right beside me, "it's there, near the edge of the forest."

It's a massive effort to turn my head, and when I finally succeed, I see a group huddled around the sapling. There are two aunties and two uncles together. One auntie blurs between her wood elf form and her owl form, slipping back and forth between the Waking and the In-between just like I am.

"Auntie," I call to her desperately.

When she looks up, her eyes shift back and forth. She utters a curse under her breath and says something I can't hear to the others, then rushes to me and puts her hands on my cheeks.

"Look here," she commands, and I stare into the depths of her black-brown eyes. "Focus. Breathe."

"He touched it," I can hear Hana explain apologetically, but her voice goes in and out as if she's on a swing, dipping low and near, and high and far away again. "I told him to touch it so he could hear it speak, and he touched it and right away went into Dreaming. I know I shouldn't have roused him, but he was in a trance. He was gone for too long. It frightened me. I know I shouldn't have, but I was so scared. He wasn't moving. He was barely breathing. I'm sorry, I'm so sorry!"

"Coren," calls the auntie, still urging me to focus on her gaze. I feel myself blurring from side to side, but I try hard to concentrate. "Roots in soil, little fox," she says, holding my head firmly. "He's sliding around," she says to Coren, who I know. He's a healer.

"What were you two doing out here, so close to the border?" Coren asks. One of Hana's vines curls defensively across my line of sight, and he nudges it away gently.

"I sensed the magic from the sprout," Hana whispers. "It called to me, and I spent all morning searching. I knew it wasn't supposed to be all the way out here. I was going to recover it. Bring it back home."

"Alone?" scolds the auntie. "Foolish girl."

"I didn't realize how far away I'd wandered," Hana answers in a hushed, terrified tone. "I really am so sorry."

"And you?" asks Coren as his light blue eyes replace Auntie's dark ones.

"I saw a shadow path leading from the sprout," I explain, fighting the urge to roll and vomit again. "It flung me into the In-between, to a flood."

"All right," he soothes, and his gaze is obscured by the pink glow of healing that ebbs between us. The fast vibration of my warring two halves eases, and the strands tighten until I snap back fully, two parts into a whole again.

"There was a Sorceress," I whisper, but it could be only a thought. I'm not sure.

The healing energy washes over me in warm, soothing tingles like the strokes of a hundred feathers across my skin. My eyes flutter closed as I relish the wonderful, light feeling. My lurching stomach relaxes, my racing heart slows to a steady, peaceful beat, and I float within the pink-white glow, enveloped and caressed by its loving healing energy.

Everything and everyone around me fades slowly away, and I find myself alone, soaring in a pure white space. There's no sky or ground, no sound or direction, but I'm not afraid. I feel cloaked in an incredibly profound sense of peace.

It seems like I'm at the center of a cloud just as the sun is beginning to break through, except there is no cloud, no sun, no ground beneath my paws.

Paws. I'm in fox form, but as I move, I swing my hands and feel all my feet beneath me. I'm both at once: fox and wood elf. Six legs, two arms, two heads. I wave my hand before my eyes and see both a hand and a paw. I step with booted feet but feel my tail swish behind me. I look back at it, curious, and catch sight of a figure in the distance.

Cautiously, I turn to face it. This far away, I can only see a Mage in light gray robes, sitting cross-legged in the white glow with his head bowed. He has dark hair, nearly black, and wears a beard like a Mage. I sniff the air and creep closer, watching cautiously. As soon as his scent fills my fox nose, I know. I've encountered this Mage before.

"Gaethon," I call without thinking, and the Mage's eyes flutter behind their lids. Part of me wants to run away from this human, this magic user, but our gentle surroundings make me pause. His essence is so much different from the Sorcerers at the flood and Blackbird's Spine.

Even though my instincts warn me to run, the sense of peace and light I feel in his presence convinces me to stay. He is nothing like the Sorcerers I've encountered. Mages' magic is filled with creation, goodness, light, and life, whereas Sorcerers' magic stinks of wickedness, destruction, darkness, and death.

I move even closer, watching the Mage's chest rise and fall slowly as he draws deep, even breaths. He neither replies nor dares to open his eyes, though he turns his face toward me like he's trying to sense whatever called his name.

Even when I stand right in front of him casting a shadow over the Mage's face, Gaethon holds to his meditation and doesn't dare look. I watch him curiously, intrigued by how hard he seems to work to remain focused, silent, and peaceful.

I think to say his name again but stop myself.

Keep hidden, always.

Why?

Why would I be brought here to this same Mage on two different, random occasions so close together, only to be forced to keep myself secret? Silence stretches between us while I study his face and his scent, and he breathes through his peaceful meditation, his face lifted toward me.

Eventually, to my surprise, Gaethon lets his discipline slip. He opens his eyes and, squinting, looks straight at me.

"Druid," he whispers, and I skip backwards, pulling the light of the clouds around me to try to hide myself from his view.

I turn in a full circle searching for a path, but none open to me. I close my eyes in an effort to pull myself back to Waking, but that doesn't work, either. I've ventured too deep into Dreaming. My waking self is deep asleep.

The Mage closes his eyes and adjusts his rail-straight posture, breathing in again. My nose twitches as I pick up the aroma of parchment, candle wax and floral incense that fills the air around us; the unmistakable sharp scent of Cerion's magic. Thinking quickly, I shift to disguise myself as Mya's elf, which is the easiest appearance I can manage to conjure.

Gaethon peeks again, looking at the new version of me with curiosity and a hint of disbelief.

"You are not who I expected," says the Mage, his voice as distant as if he's at the bottom of a mountain and I'm at the peak of it.

"Am I not?" I ask, trying to force the elvish lilt.

Gaethon's image solidifies slightly, and the edges of his features come more clearly into focus. His eyes pierce me, searching my face, taking me in. Slowly, he offers a knowing smile and a nod.

"What is this place?" I ask, unable to resist my curiosity any longer.

"Rumination," answers Gaethon.

I step a bit closer, "Rumination?"

"If you are unfamiliar with the term, I cannot explain," answered Gaethon. "But we are here for the same reason."

"What reason?" I ask, forgetting to sound like an elf. "How can that be? I don't even know what this is."

Gaethon's head tilts very slightly to the side as if considering my words.

"And yet you have appeared to me twice," he says thoughtfully. "First in Cerion, and now in this place where none should be able to encounter me uninvited."

I don't answer. I've already broken the rules by showing myself to him, and I fear saying anything more will confirm what he shouldn't already know.

"I believe you to be of the light," Gaethon says once the silence between us grows awkward.

"And I, you," I reply, edging closer. I don't need to ask what he means. The understanding comes to me straight away, like an arrow in flight. He knows my essence the same way I could tell that his is filled with magic and light, and is different from that of Sorcerers, who feel foul and full of darkness.

"Sorcerers," Gaethon utters with such hatred that prickles of warning crackle through me.

"Sorcerers?" I ask, not daring to offer him any information. He might be a Mage, and of the light, but he's still an outsider and a human.

"You have looked into their eyes. You know their faces," Gaethon whispers. "Where have you seen them? Did you hear their names? Was it the Knights of Conquer?"

I back away, refusing to answer. There's too much risk in it. How does he know I've seen Sorcerers? I only thought it, I didn't say it.

The Mage's heartbeat quickens as he loses his grip on the meditation and allows desperation to seep into his voice. His drumming heart fills the space around us, thundering in my ears. Gaethon presses a hand to his chest to calm it, but he has already failed. Rapidly, his presence begins to fade.

"Not yet," he pleads, "not just yet." His voice is barely an echo as the light closes around him, obscuring him from my sight. As he fades, the light surrounding me shrinks until I'm left drifting alone in darkness.

12

Springswan Ball

"No secret from us."

"No secrets."

"As the Grove wills it."

"As the Grove wills it."

"Protection for all."

"Protection for all."

Someone's hand rests on my shoulder. Its pressure and warmth soothe me enough to make me open my eyes slightly, allowing the light of hundreds of wisps to dance in the blur in front of me. Whoever it is sits to my left, and someone larger kneels to my right. Kaini. Father.

"Duty above all."

"Duty above all."

"Keep hidden, always."

"Keep hidden, always."

"Roots in soil, limbs in sky."

"Roots in soil, limbs in sky."

Pink light pulses at my left shoulder, warming me through, waking me with a growing sense of urgency. On my other side, Father squeezes my hand gently, the callouses of his palm rough against my fingers. Confused, I squint into the Grove wisps' glow as the sounds of the Sanctum's supper gathering echo around us.

"We are one with the Grove."

"We are one with the Grove."

Their light grows brighter, and I sit up and blink rapidly as they descend like a slow, dreamy rainfall. This evening, my wisp is golden. Father draws his hand away to receive his wisp, a deep purple globe with a center of sparkling white. I cup my hands for the pure gold one that sinks to me, and it hovers in my palms and pulses with a calming, hypnotic effect.

My confusion and disorientation are quickly edged out by the overwhelming warmth in my chest as the love of the Grove and the encouragement of the *Rianaves* fills me up. Their pure, soothing energy sends me into a deep daze, and I watch with disconnected interest as the dream-like moments of my day play between us, feeding the wisp all it wishes to know.

Like glimpses in a mirror, Mya lies sound asleep in her bed, then kisses me in her glade and tells me her voice gets her into trouble sometimes. Her green eyes and freckled face fade, replaced by Cerion's bustling marketplace and the imposing white walls of the Mage Academy. Gaethon and his sister linger in my mind's eye, and the wisp pulses with interest and shuffles forward to Sare fox nursing her kits, and Kyu in my palm.

I suck in a breath and wince away, afraid of what it might mean for the wisp to see Mari's note.

"*No secrets from us,*" a breeze dances in my ear. "*We are all one.*"

I'm relieved when the wisp doesn't linger on the note. Instead, it shuffles ahead, watching my moments with the sprout, my journey to the flooded village, my interaction in the white space with Gaethon.

"*Mages and Sorcerers,*" they whisper. Far above, the *Rianaves'* leaves hiss and rustle in the brisk spring wind. "*Paths dark and light. You have begun to show us what we must know. We wish to see more of this, young one. Do not be afraid of the paths set before you. Duty above all.*"

"Duty above all," I murmur aloud.

"*We are with you, always.*"

The wisp sinks through my waiting palms, leaving behind a platter of crackling roasted boar glazed with mulberry sauce, tender spring mushrooms, *Rianave* nut cheese, steaming dumplings floating in honey syrup, and an enormous clay mug of glittering green *Rianave* leaf tea.

Beside me, Father rests his wooden bowl of some kind of meat stew on his knee while he stares, brows raised almost to his hairline, at my supper.

"Wild boars can live up to ten years in the wild and have six babies per season," Kaini spouts from my other side, reaching to snatch one of my mushrooms, "unless they end up on a spit for Elliot."

"Enough, Kaini," Father leans forward to scold him, and Kaini, Sulien, and I stare at him, our mouths agape. Never has he defended me against my brothers. They've always been his clear favorites, just as I've always been Amma's.

"Close your mouths before the flies steal your tongues," Father warns with a traditional saying. "Eat."

Silently, I balance the heaping platter on my knees and edge it toward Father, offering him a portion. He takes a slab of the boar meat with a nod of thanks and pops it into his mouth. Sulien, still staring, glances down at the platter and back at me, and I give him a shrug and push the platter a little closer for him to take a taste for himself.

"Here," I mutter to Kaini, whose meal is a simple bowl of grains, roasted vegetables, and nuts. He grabs two of the honeyed dumplings and nibbles one at a time, making each one last.

A few groups away from ours, I catch a glimpse of slithering vines and watch Hana sitting with Avela, her grandmother. She's crunching into a whole, sweet red brandymelon, the red juice trailing down her arm to her elbow. One of her vines catches the drip, lapping it up with its end leaf like a strange little tongue. She laughs, and when our eyes meet across the sanctuary, she grins to bare red-stained teeth.

"She would be a fine choice, Son," Father leans down to murmur in my ear. "Good family."

"I thought you were on respite," Kaini, who obviously didn't notice Father talking, says as he licks the honey from his fingers.

"I *am* on respite," I answer, pulling my gaze from Hana and spearing a chunk of boar meat. It's so tender I barely need to chew it, and so juicy and flavorful it seems almost magical.

"Then what'd you do to deserve that?" Kaini asks, poking his finger toward my platter. "It's like your personal feast day, or something."

"Kaini, enough of your insolence. Be grateful for your own meal, which you have earned by the grace of the Grove." Father says. He glances at my food again with the same longing expression as Kaini's, spoons up an enormous mouthful of his much less appetizing stew, and turns to Sulien to chat.

"Well?" Kaini whispers beside me, "what *did* you do?"

Suddenly realizing how hungry I am, I take few more bites of boar and mushrooms and cheese before I answer him. A gulp of the Rianave tea makes my mouth and throat buzz warm and cool at the same time as it washes down all the distinct, incredible flavors. It eases my stomach and makes my arms and legs tingle pleasantly,

"Not much," I offer with a smirk, starting to feel a bit cocky. "Just…" *scouted out some Sorcerers.* I try to form the words, but they get stuck somewhere between my mind and my mouth. My throat closes slightly, like it's trying to prevent me from speaking.

"Just what?" Kaini asks curiously.

Found a Rianave sprout, I try to say, but again, nothing comes out. Obviously, these are things the Ancients want me to keep to myself.

"Visited Sare fox," I'm finally able to utter.

"That doesn't make any sense," he grumbles, stabbing at a boiled dandelion root with his small knife. "If all you did all day was visit a fox, why the feast? And why'd Father carry you here asleep and have me heal you 'til you woke up?"

I turn to look at Father questioningly but find him deep in conversation with Sulien. I know better than to interrupt them.

"How would I know? I was asleep, right?" I snap at Kaini. I try not to let his question bother me. I try not to think of how vulnerable I really am when half of me is scouting. Did he carry me all the way from the outer Grove? I look around the crowded grove and shrink a little. How many of them saw Father carrying me in? Did Hana?

I force the thought away. So what if they all saw? There's worse out there. Much worse. I try not to picture the cruel face of the Sorceress or think about the girl being swept away by the flood or let the shadow on the black path lurk in my memory.

I sip my *Rianave* tea. It's strange. Even though I just came out, I find myself suddenly eager to return to the Dreaming. A nagging feeling like I'm missing something important tugs at me, nudging me to close my eyes just for a moment.

As I gulp down the rest of my tea, I think of Amma sunken into her chair in the darkness of the sitting room, her body wasting away under the nest of furs and blankets while her closed eyes danced rapidly behind their lids. I can't go the way she went. I can't let myself get swept in so deeply.

Already, though, the tingle of the tea and the fullness of my belly make my eyelids droop. The battle against my heavy eyelids is fought only by a dramatically loud yawn that makes Father turn and arch a brow at me again.

"Go and sleep if you're tired, Elliot," he says, taking the empty mug from my hand and the platter from my lap. "Kaini, go with him and wait for me there."

Not for the first time tonight, I stare at Father, puzzled by his uncharacteristic warmth. It's a strange thing to place because it's rarely directed toward me. I've seen that glint in his eye before, though, toward my brothers.

It's pride. Somehow, I finally did something to make him proud of me. But what? How? Did the Ancients show him what I did today? What I learned? Did Waterfowl tell him they spoke to me?

"Go, Elliot," Father says, gentler than usual. "Don't Wander."

Kaini complains about at least a hundred things on the way to Amma's house:

"Why didn't *I* get a platter of honeyed dumplings? Why was Father so foul to me tonight? Why couldn't I have a respite like you? What do you need a respite from, anyway, since you never do anything? Why won't you take me to see Sare fox? Doesn't anyone care that I'm tired, too, after all that healing?"

He doesn't even wait for me to answer any of it. It's just one thing after another, complaining for the sake of complaining. I wish he'd stop. He used to look up to me until I became a dream scout and stole away his chance at it. Now, even as young as he is, even with his greater gift, he resents me for it.

Usually I try to be patient with him, but tonight I'm so tired I can barely put one foot in front of the other. Every word he whines irritates me. When we reach the door, I trip over the flat sisal mat and stumble inside. The glow lamps are still open from earlier. I guess I forgot to shutter them.

"Why's it always so dusty and dark in here?" Kaini grumbles, pushing past me. He flops into Amma's lounge, kicking her blankets and furs to the floor. "I don't see why I have to be the one to stay with you. Why couldn't Sulien do it? I was going to go firefly hunting for the glow lamps with Eve and Tomli."

"Maybe Father will arrive soon," I say thickly through a yawn I can't fight off.

"Well, I just—" his words are abruptly cut off by the door of my room, which I slam behind me, shutting out his complaints. The memory of the gold wisp bobs in my mind. My eyes closed as I drop to the bed. The Dreaming takes me before I even feel myself land.

The forest surrounding me is familiar but strange. Moss covered tree trunks twist unusually from the forest floor, curling around themselves like writhing serpents frozen in time. Obscured by clouds, the moon casts no shadow. The forest itself is shadow. I spin in place, searching for a light to turn to, and a glint of it shines beneath the brush in the distance. Panicked, I race toward it, desperate to escape the shadow.

When I reach it, I see that it's not a light at all, but the reflection of candles stretched across a polished wood path. I know the path immediately. It leads to the palace.

As soon as I put my soft boot down on it, I spin out of control, swirling like I'm caught up in a whirlpool. I try to call out, to reach out and grab something, anything to stop the spinning. When I can't, I squeeze my eyes shut and pray to wake up.

Surprisingly, the spinning stops, and I land with a thump on the seat of a cushioned wooden chair. At first I think it worked, that my pleas have woken me, but then I remember I was in my bed at home, and now I'm sitting, and the sounds and smells that barrage me don't fit with the ones at Amma's house.

Strange, beautiful music played on instruments I've never heard before sounds in my twitching ears, and when I find the courage to open my eyes again, I can't believe what I see. The vast room could fit Grandymum herself, leaves and all, all the way up to the ceiling. Its stonework, sturdy and expertly carved, seems almost weightless as its pillars and arms push the ceiling to an elegant, glass-paned peak.

I follow the line of the pillars down from the ceiling just as I follow the tree trunks at home with my eyes, listening to laughter and voices as they blend with the music and echo across the vast space. Scattered across the polished marble floor, a crowd of dozens of interestingly dressed humans weave about, mingling and dancing, gesturing gracefully with their arms while their silky gowns and velvet capes sway dreamily to the music.

I feel so apart from it all, I can only stare in awe as the salty sea air tickles my nose. Wine and roast meat, dozens of vegetables, spit-fired fish, citrus fruit, spices, musk, sweat, leather, steel, silver, rushes of sweet reed and countless sharp-smelling herbs crowd my nostrils, making me feel dizzy.

I push out of my chair to wander among the humans who crowd the edges of the room in separate groups, talking and laughing together, drinking from jeweled goblets that flash in the light.

Past elaborate arrangements of candles and flame-lit lanterns that remind me of golden wisps, groups of dancers move together, their clicking steps loudly matching the beat of the music. I've never seen anyone dance this way before. At home when we dance, it's wild and chaotic. Here, it's so controlled it almost seems like they're bound to each other. Their synchronous movements entrance me. It's strangely beautiful.

The women's strange dresses and men's odd, shimmery outfits are the rich colors of summer butterflies, shining beetles, and meadow blooms. Aunties sparkle with jewels adorning their hair, necks, and wrists. Uncles flash with metal buckles and studs and medallions. Their steel and golden sword pommels catch the light like flames.

I can't tell if this is a dream or if I'm scouting. It's too bizarre to be real, but it also doesn't seem like something I could have imagined. Dazzled by the scene, I weave through the dancers and the gathered crowds, careful to avoid getting too close to anyone.

"Your Majesty, I must admit this is the most impressive Springswan Ball I can remember," says a nearby lady.

Majesty.

I follow the voice, curious to see a king for the first time. I remember the young prince's whispers in the night about his father, and that makes me even more eager to look at him.

Ducking through a pair of dancers who gallop past, I'm momentarily distracted by the sheer amount of fabric it must have taken to make the lady dancer's dress. I reach out for it just to see what the shimmering skirt feels like, but I pull my hand away before I can touch it.

Keep hidden, always.

"Ah, your flattery is misguided," an old voice croaks in reply. "I had nothing to do with it, except signing a thing here and there. It was mostly Master Rand'ell, of course."

"Oh, Majesty," purrs the lady, "You're just being gracious as always. Shall we dance?"

I dodge around another pair of dancers and finally find them. The woman wears her pale blond hair arranged in intricate braids on top of her head, which sparkle with golden jeweled pins. Her dress is as red as a woodpecker's crown, and it's so tight at the waist it seems to push the rest of her out of the top of it. When she leans nearer to the king, I follow her gaze and step closer, fascinated by the contrast between the two humans.

The king is the oldest looking man I have ever seen. Older even than Feren, the Grove's eldest Druid who has recently celebrated his hundred and eighty-seventh birthday. Dressed in a purple tunic that looks as soft as spring moss, his shoulders draped in the fur of white rabbits, he seems to compress under the weight of the crown on his head, a golden circlet that shines like midday sun in the lamplight.

"Now, now, my dear," the king chuckles, patting the lady's hand, "these old feet would make a fool of me. Sir Josten!" he calls to a man passing by, who pauses and bows.

His broad shoulders and strong fighter's stance remind me of Father, and a pang of guilt charges through me. Don't Wander, he'd said, yet here I find myself again in the palace of Cerion. According to Waterfowl, though, it isn't Wandering if I followed the path set before me. I wonder who's right.

"Majesty," Sir Josten says with a genuine smile. "I was looking for my daughter. Have you seen her?"

"Not since the feast, I'm afraid," answers the king, patting the arm of the black-haired woman. "Here," he lifts her hand gently in the knight's direction, and she eyes Sir Josten with a hint of distaste. "Ciri would like to dance."

"Of course, Majesty," says the knight dutifully, even though he looks just as reluctant as Ciri. Still, she accepts his offered hand, and they fall easily into step with the rest of the dancers.

"Another cup, good page," the king calls to a boy my age, who runs off eagerly to fetch it.

I follow, interested where he'll go, but end up losing him, too fascinated by the musicians and their odd wood and string instruments. Their singer is masterful, the way he weaves words and notes to stir excitement.

I stop and listen for a while, until Sir Josten and Ciri sweep past me and I wonder why the king would ask them to dance together when it's so obvious they hate one another.

A fresh breeze whispers past carrying the scent of the sea, and my nose leads me to a grand balcony overlooking the ocean. The sun is just beginning to set in the sky, splashing pinks and oranges across the water. I've never seen a sunset over so much water before, so I stand watching it for a long time until a ripple of laughter steals my attention.

"Still no letters?" someone nearby asks gently. I've heard that voice just recently. It's Lisabella, the sister from the cobblestone street.

"None," answers the prince, sounding dejected.

"Well, I feared as much, so I brought you something to cheer you up," Lisabella says, mischief playing in her tone.

"Oh?" the prince asks curiously, then after a pause, he starts to laugh. "Only you."

"What?" Lisabella asks innocently.

"Are you sure you wouldn't rather dance? You aren't dressed for a spar," the prince chuckles, and Lisabella laughs again.

I creep closer and find a narrow ledge leading to a second, smaller terrace where the prince and Lisabella have tucked themselves away from the ball.

"I might need to fight in a dress at some point." Lisabella faces the prince, holding a wooden training sword out to him. "You never know."

"Lisabella," Tirnon laughs, "*where* did you get a training sword?"

"A lady never tells her secrets," she replies with a dainty curtsy. Their eyes dance with a warm familiarity that makes me think of Hana. With a mischievous smile, Lisabella shakes out her skirt and jiggles her foot, and a second wooden sword clatters to the stone floor.

The prince's laughter echoes across the terrace. He holds his stomach, and I can't help but laugh along with him. His amusement infects Lisabella, too, until they're both hugging their stomachs, doubled over.

The idea of a girl dressed so splendidly smuggling wooden swords into an elegant dance like this is ridiculous, even to me with no knowledge of this land's customs.

I stop laughing, though, when the prince turns to look straight at me.

"Did you see? Did you see that?" he asks, still laughing.

I take a step back; certain he's seen me, but unsure how.

Then, beside me, a third human I hadn't noticed clears his throat. Relieved the prince didn't spot me after all, I relax a little and lean forward to see him better. On the other side of the pillar, he holds the side of his fist to his lips, clearly trying hard not to join in laughing. It only takes a moment for me to realize he's a warrior, too. A guardian of some kind, I gather, from the armor he wears and the sword at his belt.

"Leave Finn out of it." Lisabella says. She collects herself, holding up her sword in a salute. "Wait, maybe *you'd* rather go in and dance?"

"Now you're just taunting me," answers the prince, still grinning as he returns her salute with his wooden weapon. "There's far too much red in there for my taste."

Red, I think to myself. *Too much red.*

13

No Secrets

Red. Too much red.

The prince's voice echoes in my mind, and I feel a strange tugging between my two selves like a guttering candle flame clinging to the wick, desperate to keep its light. I bolt up in bed, panting, my wide eyes searching my pitch-black surroundings for any pinpoint of light. Was I really just scouting, or was I only dreaming?

"Say what you will," says Amma in the next room. "I know the truth of it. I know how to keep you out, and I will never falter. I made myself blind. I can make myself deaf if need be."

"Amma?" I whisper in a daze and rub my eyes to try to clear them. It's never as dark as this in my room. There's usually at least some streak of moonlight through the shutters, a smudge of lighter gray against the black. It doesn't matter, though. This place is familiar enough I don't need light. I slip quietly out of bed and creep to the door toward my mother's voice.

"Do you never tire of defying me?"

With my hand on the door latch, I freeze and listen hard to the second voice. The hair on the back of my head prickles up like my hackles when I'm on edge in fox-form. Something in the timbre of the man's voice warns the fox in me, and I feel myself starting to shift without willing it so I can flee.

"Until I take my last breath, I will not tire," Amma answers bravely.

"That may come sooner than you think," the deep, sinister voice carries a human accent, a Northerner's accent, "if you continue to refuse me."

"Please," Amma cries softly. "I used to be enough for you. I alone."

"How long did you think you could deceive me?"

There's a thump and a clatter, and Amma makes a single, painful yelp of protest.

"Amma!" I call out, still blurring between fox-form and my true self. The sensation makes me dizzy, and I work to force the fox away for now and keep myself on two feet rather than four.

"Turn away!" Amma shouts in warning as soon as I open the door. "Turn away from shadow!"

Look into shadow for us, young one. Courageous one. See what we must know.

There's no light beyond the door, either, but I can see enough to know right away we're not in Amma's house. We're in Amma's shadowed version of the Dreaming. She and the man with her are both cloaked in it. Hidden. I strain to see them, but I can barely sense her a few paces away. I want to run to her, to throw my arms around her, but her desperate warnings make me pause.

"Turn away, please!" she begs me. "Please!"

"Is this him, then?" asks the man with her. I sense him moving closer and catch a scent in the air between us: wolf, rot, dark magic. Sinister intentions.

"Please, no," Amma screams. "Elliot, wake up!"

"Elliot, hm?" the man growls like a hunter after prey. Amma curses under her breath. I feel him stalking closer and imagine a glimpse of a black-tipped tail. Reddish, pointed ears.

Courageous one.

My mind and my feet are at odds with one another. The fox in me senses the warning and my instinct is to listen to Amma, but my feet and heart are reluctant to leave her with him, whoever he is.

"Turn away!" Amma's words are more of a command this time. This is her Dreaming, and there are rules. I'm her son, and still a fledgling. As torn as I am, my feet obey.

With a racing heart, I spin to put my back to them. Midday sun spills across the room, dancing over Mari's drawings on the wall as the vellum flaps gently in the breeze. I raise my arm to shield my eyes, blinded by the sudden brightness. The contrast is too stark, too abrupt.

Nearby, someone breathes rapidly, whispering and whimpering like they're having a nightmare. Still shielding my eyes, I move to the bed and squint into my own sleeping face. As soon as the realization strikes me that I've been two instead of one, I fall into myself. Like the crack of a twig, my eyes snap open and sting from the sudden assault of sunlight.

I lunge from my bed and fling open my door, half-expecting to be greeted by the darkness and Amma and her mystery companion. Instead, Hana yelps in surprise.

Perched on a seat of her own vines, her ankle crossed over one knee, she clutches Amma's bowl of spring mulberries to her chest with one hand while her vines flip through the pages of a tiny tome.

"Finally!" she exclaims. She licks her juice-stained fingertips hastily and wipes them clean on her leafy green tunic. With grace, her vines push her to her feet, and she passes the bowl to a waiting tendril. "I was starting to think you were going to sleep all the way through your last day of respite!"

Her tendrils reach out for me with longing as I brush past her into the rest of the house, still expecting to find Amma.

"If you're looking for Kaini, he's swimming," Hana explains, following me casually while I rush around to search. "He was awfully bored and annoyed, so I told him to go. I didn't mind waiting."

Amma isn't in her chair in the gathering room, or the kitchen, or the bedroom she used to share with Father. Of course she wouldn't be. She was in Dreaming, after all. She's still in the care of the fold. I shouldn't have been able to see her at all, in Waking or Dreaming or anywhere else, but I did.

Part of me wishes I hadn't. Who *was* that man? What did it all mean?

"Grandmother Avela gave me a day of respite, too," Hana continues brightly, still trailing my heels. "She said I should keep you company. She thinks--"

I turn so abruptly I nearly trip over her, but her tendrils steady me. Her eyes meet mine, wide and curious, and the vines nudge us a bit closer. I try to brush them away, but they keep coming back. One nuzzles my cheek affectionately.

"Stop it, you," Hana gives a desperate whisper, swatting that one away, "can't you see he's still angry at us?"

"Angry?" I ask, scowling. "I'm not—"

"Not that I can blame you," Hana looks down at her feet, and her vines and tendrils droop guiltily away. "I know it's dangerous to pull a dream scout out. I shouldn't have done it. I was just so scared. You were so still for so long. I tried to be patient, but, well, you know better than anyone I have no talent for patience."

"Pull a dream scout out?" I ask dimly. My head is in a fog, swirling with bewilderment and fear. "You didn't. I woke up on my own."

"No, not today," Hana explains, "Yesterday, with the sprout. Remember?"

"Right, I…" I trail off, looking over my shoulder with a lingering hope that Amma will somehow appear. The cool frond of a tendril catches my chin and turns my face back to Hana. I brush it away, but the way she's looking at me makes it hard for me to do more than that.

"You saw something," she whispers, searching my eyes with hers.

"Something horrible."

"Mages and Sorcerers." The voice of the Ancients flicks into my memory. *"Paths dark and light. You have begun to show us what we must know. We wish to see more of this, young one. Do not be afraid of the paths set before you. Duty above all."*

I think of what Amma said to that man: *I made myself blind. I can make myself deaf if need be.* I think of the scents that rolled off him: wolf, rot, dark magic, sinister intentions.

"I have to go to the Sanctum," I say urgently.

"But it's not supper yet, they won't let you—"

Hana squeaks when I take her hand and start for the door. Her vines set down her book and the half-eaten bowl of fruit as she jogs beside me.

"Avela is your grandmother. She'll see you if you ask, won't she?" We duck through the door together and start down the ramp, picking up speed as we go. "I need to get inside the Grove. I have to show them something important."

"Show who?" Hana asks a little breathlessly.

"The Ancients."

My answer makes her dig in her heels. She tugs my hand, forcing me to stop midway down the ramp. Someone passes going up, and she gives them a sheepish wave and waits for them to pass.

"Is this about the sprout?" she asks in a conspiratorial whisper. "Because it wasn't what we thought it was. It wasn't a *Rianave*. They know that already."

"No, it's not about—what?" I stare at her, trying to make sense of what she's telling me.

"The sprout," she whispers, and one of her vines snakes up to press her lips shut. She guides it away gently and moves closer. "We were meant to think it was one, but it wasn't. It was an impostor."

I think back to the moment I touched the tender stem, how I was thrust forward onto the black path in the In-between, whisked by a shadow to the flood. The thought that I could be so easily tricked terrifies me.

"But it looked like one. It felt like one, it even spoke like one!" I whisper, moving closer to her and lowering my voice as an auntie ushers her two little ones past us.

"I know," Hana says, clinging to my arm, "I thought the same. That's what makes it so scary. They think it was placed there. Planted by dark magic." Her vines draw in, hugging her close.

"Impossible. It was within the border."

Another pair of Druids approaches, and Hana tugs me along, a vine pressed to her lips to signal me quiet. When we reach the bottom, she guides me to a quiet nook of moss and woven tree trunks usually used for lessons, and she sinks to her knees on the soft, green carpet.

"They're clever. Sorcerers," she whispers, beckoning me to sit. Her vines make a line across the space between us, and I understand right away they're meant to represent the magical border of the Grove. "They know they can't get in, so," she takes a pebble and places it on my side of the line, "they planted it outside, and…" she coaxes the vine slightly, edging it over the pebble so it's on her side now, rather than mine.

"They pulled the border out toward them?" I whisper, my brow furrowed.

"There are no protections against that," Hana explains. "Well, there weren't. Why would an enemy outsider want to give us more land than we already have, after all?"

I stare at the pebble and the vine in disbelief.

"They were trying to lure someone out there," I whisper, shivering as I realize Hana and I fell right into their trap.

"They're working on changing it now. Adding protections to keep it from happening again. But, right, they just pulled it out a little, leaving their dark sprout inside to watch and listen."

"It looked just like a real sprout," I shake my head. "How could they know what a *Rianave* looks like?"

"I imagine someone had a hand in it who lived here once. A Forgotten, maybe. Someone familiar with the look and feel of them."

Mari? No, she would never. The elves hate Sorcerers just as much as we do.

I made myself blind… Amma's words edge into my mind, but it couldn't have been her, either. She would never betray the Grove that way.

"What happened to it?" I ask a little hoarsely, my emotions getting the better of my voice. "The sprout?"

"They took it into the fold," Hana replies, and her eyes meet mine meaningfully.

"Like Amma," I whisper.

She nods.

"Cerion's Sorcerers are getting more and more brazen," Hana says, pushing herself to her feet. "At breakfast, we were all cautioned to stay away from the borders unless the Ancients send us there. They're strengthening defenses, but it's going to take time. Some are afraid of what it could mean. Others are whispering of war."

I recall the shadowed man with Amma. The more I think about it, the more I'm convinced he's a Sorcerer, himself.

"Then they need to know what I saw," I stand up and brush off my suede trousers. "It can't wait until supper. Come on."

"Was it about your Amma? If it was, then they already know. She's in the fold, after all," Hana steps lightly beside me, her vines curling around my arm again.

No secrets from us.

Look into shadow for us, young one. Courageous one. See what we must know.

"It was," I say, "but I don't think even the fold could see what I've seen. Amma was hiding it from them. She probably still is. To protect them. To protect all of us."

One of her vines tugs my arm, halting me before we leave the nook. I put my hand on it and look at her, and she knits her brow.

"What is it?" I ask.

"It's only, well, I know how they are. If you really mean to get into the Sanctum and through to the fold, you should collect yourself first. You're a little…"

"A little what?" I scowl, shrinking away from her vine. It loosens some, but it doesn't let go completely.

"Just a little…intense?" She blows a puff of air to clear a lock of hair across her nose. "Sorry, I'm trying to help! The fold is a place of healing. If you can sort it out first and be calm you might have a chance, but if you go in ranting, the wisps will make you leave."

"I'm not ranting," I bark defensively, and she raises a brow at me.

"Just like you didn't after Blackbird's Spine?" She tilts her head to the side, and one of her vines echoes the movement.

"You heard about that?"

She shrugs. "It's part of why your father was so angry after. First your mother's taken into the fold, and then you make a scene outside the Sanctum."

"But I had to! Men were hurt and no one was listening. You were in danger!" My heart races with anger and shame as I remember the way people looked at me. The way they have looked at me ever since Amma was titled Wanderer. Like I'm a problem to be solved. Like I'm an example of how not to be. For some reason, it makes me think of the wolf in Amma's shadows again.

I start to pace, but the vine still tucked in the crook of my elbow catches me. More vines slide to my arms, my shoulders, my back.

"Elliot…" My name as she speaks it is filled with emotions I don't have time for right now. I tug free of her hold and take a few steps, and she follows me and stands by my side.

"You put too much weight on what others think," she offers quietly after a long silence. "It doesn't matter what they think. You can't let their ideas about you change who you are. You're on your own path. A path no one else can fathom. A noble path."

I turn to look at her. A path? Why would she choose that word? Her vines stay back, hovering out of the way just above her shoulders. Her wide gray eyes dance knowingly as they meet mine.

"How much do you know?" I whisper.

"I know what the Grove wills," she says a little sadly. Her gaze slides from my eyes to my lips. Her vines slink forward in anticipation. When she circles her arms around me, the vines stay where they are. It reminds me of myself in the Dreaming, staying perfectly still so I don't spook Amma. But the way it feels when Hana holds me close sends thoughts of Amma away quickly. It's been a long time since I was embraced by anyone. Probably since before Mari left.

Her closeness soothes a need in me I didn't even realize I'd been hurting for.

"What does the Grove will?" I pull her closer, breathing in the scent of rich loam and spring leaves in her hair.

Cautiously, she moves her head so our cheeks are touching.

"I'll tell you after," she whispers, her warm breath tickling my cheek. My heart pumps faster.

"After what?" I turn my head slightly closer.

"My last chance, maybe, for this." Her lips brush mine and a rush of warmth surges through me unlike anything I've felt in Dreaming or Waking. Her kiss is timid at first. Gentle and hesitant until I pull her tighter and deepen it.

The kiss works like a salve on my tattered mind, clearing my thoughts, brightening my memories better than a feast day meal. I race down all the paths I've been shown in Dreaming, through flashes of scenes that grow crisp and sharp, like a blade honed on a whetstone.

I'm standing in the desolation of Amma's dreams, feeling her fear of the shadows, turning toward the moonlight. I'm on Mari's balcony, watching her take Elowyn's hand to go inside. I'm under the prince's bed, listening to him pray for the health of his father, the king. In a crowded market street, staring into the face of a Mage as he glimpses me. I'm flung past the impostor *Rianave* sprout down a black path that leads to Sorcerers and flood waters. I'm bathed in white, face-to-face with that same Mage. I'm at a ball in Cerion's palace. I'm facing the darkness again, listening to Amma and strange shadows.

I'm kissing Mya in a peaceful green meadow. Kissing Mya.

I step back, breaking my embrace with Hana too abruptly. Her vines snake forward, twining longingly into my hair alongside her fingers, urging me to stay close. She blinks at me breathlessly, her lips still parted. I don't let go, even though I feel like a betrayer. But Mya is only a dream. Hana is here. Hana is real.

It's a losing battle. Even she notices. Tears make her eyes go silver, and she blinks them away.

"What do you mean, your last chance?" I whisper, trying to distract her. I don't know what that was, all those memories, or how much she gleaned from it. Nothing, I hope.

She swallows tears and takes a shaky breath before she replies. "Every time I've come to see you these past few days, I half expected to find you gone. Forgotten."

"What? Why would you think that?"

She gazes far up into the canopy beyond rope bridges and platforms.

"Because you're supposed to go," she mumbles, suddenly finding her feet very interesting.

"What? Go where?"

"There are whispers in the leaves. Portents," she says returning her wistful gaze to me. "You aren't meant to stay in the Grove. You're called away on another path. To Cerion."

"You're no seer, Hana," I say, shaking my head defensively. My ears are ringing with shame. I feel like my breath is being siphoned out of me.

"Didn't used to be," she agrees quietly. "But lately when I'm in meditations whispering to the trees and I think of you," her eyes slide away a little sheepishly, "I see strange things in my mind's eye. Things I haven't seen before and can't explain. Your feet slipped into puffs of clover. Banners of purple and blue, and blue and gold. A fox sleeping under a feather bed. Smoke in the sky. A red-haired girl with a voice as pure as birdsong…"

I gasp and step back from her. She doesn't reach for me this time.

"Don't worry," she smiles a little sadly. "I haven't told anyone. Not even Grandmother. Only the Ancients know these things I saw. You know," she shrugs apologetically. "No secrets."

I try to make sense of what she's telling me. Hana can talk to the trees like I can. She has a talent for growing things and healing plant life. One day, she'll most likely be a Steward of the Grove like Elder Avela. Until then, she's training to be a defender. She has many talents, but…

"Hana, you're no seer," I utter again, but even I can't deny what she said about Mya. There's no way she could have known that.

"I didn't think so either," she shivers, and her vines snake around her own shoulders, enfolding and comforting her. "But I guess I'm sprouting a new talent."

She startles and looks past me over my shoulder, and the glint of a pink glow flashes in her wide eyes.

"Elliot Eldinae," the wisp behind me calls, "you are summoned to the fold."

14

The Fold

The Sanctum is strangely silent. No one lingers among the *Rianaves*. No group lounges in the meadow grass like we did yesterday.

The wisp guides me alone to an opening on the far side past the *Rianaves*. Every day of my life I have come to the Sanctum to recite the rites, to meet, to dine. I know this place like I know Amma's sitting room and Sare fox's den. In all the time I've spent here, I've never noticed this gap between the *Rianaves* curtained by drifting tendrils of willow before.

When the wisp stops before it and waits for me, I realize I'm trembling. Each step is an effort. This was a mistake. I shouldn't have come here. I shouldn't have followed it this far.

Something else bothers me. Something that only just occurred to me.

"Where is Hana?" I ask the wisp. When I turn to look behind me, it floats to my shoulder and blocks my view.

"*She remained behind,*" the wisp explains. "*Come.*"

It leaves a trail of tingling warmth in my chest as it drifts through me to glide between two massive *Rianave* trunks. Beyond them the silvery willow leaves reflect its pink light. It should be a soothing sight. Pink is the color of healing, after all. But for some reason, it feels like a warning. Turn around. Go back.

I don't like that I forgot about Hana so easily. I don't like how this short journey makes my stomach twist. I remember Elowyn and Mari walking away through the curtains on their balcony. The Mage Academy disappearing into the sunlight. Wards.

"I can't," I tell the wisp, just as afraid to defy it as I am to keep walking. "It's protected. It's forbidden."

"*You may,*" the wisp replies. "*You must.*"

Its permission does nothing to ease the foreboding that charges through me. I force myself to take a few more steps until my heart starts to race and my ears ring. My scalp prickles with warning and I look far up into the sunlight through the *Rianave* canopy.

"I don't understand," I call to the leaves far above.

"*Step forward,*" the wisp commands. "*Follow the path set before you.*"

I stare at the fronds of the willows that are close enough to touch, if only I could lift my hand to do it. It's impossible to see through to the other side. The leaves are too thick and too still.

The fold. What if I'm someone who goes in and never returns? I sniff the air and smell nothing but the usual earthy scents of the Grove. Still, my heart drums uncontrollably and my nose and ears twitch. I'm fox and boy at once. Two parts of a whole, snapping into one another, each alarming the other to flee.

"*Trust.*"

I creep forward until my nose nearly brushes the delicate leaves. This close, they entice me. They remind me of Hana's vines. Her kiss. Her words: *You aren't meant to stay in the Grove.* Her words, but in Mya's voice. My two selves snap to one again. I draw in a long, deep breath.

Courageous one.

I step through the willows.

On the other side, there's only peace. I feel nothing at all; no brush of leaves across my cheek, no change in temperature, no sound to greet me. My trepidation vanishes, leaving me content and prepared. For what, I don't know. I'm a slate washed clean of markings, ready to do as the Grove wills.

Vaguely, despite the thick pink mist, I'm aware of the forest around me and those within it watching me pass. I don't need to concern myself with them. I only need to take another step, and another. The way is long, straight, and unchanging. My footsteps on the pure white pebbles are silent. I walk for what feels like half a day, but the light never changes.

Eventually my eyelids grow heavy, and my head nods. My feet shuffle and stop. My eyes close.

The voice that wakes me is not a voice I've heard before. It sounds both male and female, both tranquil and powerful. It soothes me, lulling me to an easy emptiness.

"Open your eyes, child, and greet us," they say, so I do.

Amma. My heart leaps at the sight of her all draped in soft muslin, cradled in the twisted nook of a moss-covered willow stump. When I rush toward her, the stump shifts. Eyes blink at me, and I make out a nose, a chin, a face.

It's some sort of tree-man—or woman— but not a dryad.

Whatever it is is so much grander than a dryad. Even as it sits cross-legged in front of me, supporting Amma in her sleep, this creature has a noble, ancient air to it. I understand without any explanation how special this meeting is between us. How rare.

"Slowly, slowly," it cautions, its eyes opening slightly wider as I approach. "Gently. She is very weak."

"Amma," I cry softly, but I stop before I reach her. She looks awful. Frail and gray, like the ash of long-cold embers about to be scattered by the wind. "How is she worse?" I utter, unable to suppress the anger in my voice. "You're supposed to be helping her!"

"Easy," warns the willow stump. "There is no need to be disrespectful. Your mother's condition is her own choice. We have been desperate to reach her, but she evades us both here and in Dreaming."

"I made myself blind," I whisper, and remember at once why I was so determined to come here. "Someone is with her," I tell them. "Someone wicked. She's trying to protect the Grove from him."

"You have looked into shadow as you were instructed," they say.

I nod, rubbing the chills that prickle my arms.

"You have seen what she would not allow anyone else to see. Not even us. For so long, she has protected us by eluding us." They beckon me closer, brushing long fingers that are more like tender spring fiddleheads across Amma's shoulder.

"Come near, and let her feel the touch of her favored son. She cannot see you. She cannot hear you, but she can feel your warmth and presence. Slowly, now."

"She's deaf now, too?" I mutter as I reach Amma's side. I want to throw my arms around her, to snuggle into her, to kiss her hollow cheek as I always have, but I only graze her shoulder like her carer did, afraid even my softest touch will break her.

"By her own choice," they remind me. "She does all she can to close out this world. Soon she will no longer be a part of it. She will waste her existence here and be lost to the Dreaming forever, and they will move to another of your kind for their dark workings."

"Oh, Amma," I whisper. I tuck my head beneath the chisel of her jaw and cover her gray, limp hand with mine carefully.

"Do not lament," says the tree-like healer, and the herbal vapors of camphor and chamomile gently waft from their breath. "There is still hope. Lorelai is not a Wanderer, but a Great Protector. We do not wish to lose her to the Dreaming."

My heart starts to race. Lorelai is not a Wanderer, they said. Not a Wanderer. A Great Protector. Just like I told Father, she isn't someone to be ashamed of. All this time, she hasn't been weak.

She's been honorable. Valiant. I wish he was here to hear them say it. I wonder if he'd listen. I look up into the noble, bark-covered face, intrigued.

"Who are you?" I ask, brushing away the tears that spill down my cheeks as I shift a little closer to Amma. Even in this warm, bright place, she's cold as ice. "This isn't what I thought the fold would be like."

"Isn't it?" they ask curiously. "Our name is of little importance to you. You shall forget it, and us, once you leave here. But we understand the need for your kind to use names, so you may address us as Aft'elu."

"Aft'elu," I echo. The name stirs nostalgia, even though I'm sure I've never heard it before. It invokes tales from distant generations about the most holy, most loving enlightened ones who used to walk among the *Rianave* like we do, but who have long since found solace in solitude.

For the first time, I gaze out at our surroundings, but I can see nothing beyond myself and Amma. A thick, cherry-blossom-pink mist curtains us from the rest of the fold. I understand at once why it's there. It's the same reason Amma has closed her sight and hearing to the Waking.

"You want me to go in there," I say quietly. "To her."

"Yes."

"And try to get her to come out?"

"No. She will not. She will refuse to return to the Waking until she is rid of the Sorcerer who holds her in his grip. She will not leave us vulnerable to his meddling."

I press my cheek to her bundled shoulder and curl up closer.

"You want me to try to get him to come out?" I croak, barely able to fathom the thought of baiting him.

"Yes. To lure him here. Make him think he is clever. Make him think he has won, and he shall be an example to all Sorcerers who would dare threaten us with their wicked intentions."

Their eyes flash menacing red, then quickly fade to pink again. I remember how terrifying the man in Amma's dream was, how dark and furious. How wolf-like.

Warnings scream in my mind. My darkest thoughts come forward. Why did Amma never trust us with this truth? How long has she known him? What are they to each other? What other secrets has she kept? Was Father right to be jealous? If I can save her life, does any of that even matter?

No. It doesn't.

"I'll do anything you need me to," I say with confidence. "Anything. Please. Tell me the plan."

15

Bait

I wake in my room, dazed and disoriented. I don't remember how I got here or what happened before. I don't remember anything at all, except there's something I need to do. Look into shadow.

My eyes flutter open and I squeeze them shut again quickly. The light, too harsh and focused to be daylight, radiates from something at the center of the room just near Mari's bed. I push away my coverlet and slide from my bed on my belly to land on fox paws.

My black nose twitches. My whiskers prickle in warning. I blink again, this time more rapidly, and the object comes into focus. Sprouted right out of my floor, through the sisal rug, is the impostor *Rianave* sprout. The closer I get to it, the brighter it shines, but I don't turn away or shield my eyes. This is part of the plan. A plan I've since forgotten, like I was meant to. A plan that will reveal itself slowly as I make my way through it. Down the path set before me.

"Tell me what you desire," a sinister voice whispers behind me. I whirl to face it and find myself staring into the darkness of my own shadow. There's no one there, only the door to my room. I remember the evil beyond. I recall a conversation I wasn't meant to hear and the terror in Amma's voice when she discovered I did.

"You, and only you," Amma answers breathlessly.

"I'm sick of your endless lies! You want me to think you're devoted to me, yet you deny my will again and again!"

He strikes her and she cries out, and it takes all my restraint not to charge through the door and tear him apart with my claws and teeth. I want to rip him to shreds, to make him hurt like he's hurting her, to make him feel as helpless, as weak.

Then it comes back to me…Amma isn't weak. She knows exactly what she's doing. She's stronger than anyone has ever realized. Her vulnerability is nothing more than a masterful deception; a distraction for what I'm here to do. He can't hurt her here. Not really. The Dreaming is an illusion. I must focus on my part. To save her, I have to ignore what's happening between them and complete my task.

I step into the shadows and let them fold around me, cloaking me from nose to tail tip. Shadows aren't always wicked. Just like the night is a place of solace and rest, the shadows can be useful. I used to be afraid of them, but that fear is lifted now. Gone. I breathe in deeply, staring at the door, and remember what Amma taught me during my training. We go where we like in the Dreaming. Anywhere our heart desires. Right now, I want to be on the other side of that door unnoticed, hidden away. Cloaked in useful shadows.

His scent is stronger this time: wolf, rot, dark magic, sinister intentions. It swirls around him like a storm, as ominous and violent as the cruelty that radiates from him. I inhale it, committing it to my memory, ignoring the turmoil between him and my mother. If I'm going to succeed, I need to create a distance between us. I need to make myself go blank. I can't give him a reason to sense any part of me. He can't know I'm here. Not yet.

One with the shadows, I skirt around him in search of his strand. How it takes form is different for each dream scout. For him, it's a tangle of shadows that carry the scent of campfire smoke and feel like the comfort of warmth and shelter. I sniff it once, silently, careful not to disturb it, and then my feet propel me at an unnatural pace.

I streak through the darkness until I break out of the shadow of Amma's Dreaming and emerge into a frozen tundra. Here, the sky is gray and overcast, and the snow is deep, frigid blue. It's a harsh cold; the sort that stings my throat and the inside of my nose with every breath. I'm not here, though. Not really. I'm scouting. My true self is tucked away someplace safe. I'm protected so well, even I don't know where that other part of me is. Not yet. I will remember once this task is done.

The thought gives me strength and purpose. I run faster, extending my claws into the brisk wind to pull it beneath me and speed my pace. The smoke shadow blurs beside me, guiding my path. I will find him. His true self. The sleeping self. I will find him, and I will call the name that comes to me. My heart pounds, drumming a rhythm in time with my paws. The mountains here are immense and imposing. They jut into the sky like the limbs of wasted, broken trees, so high their peaks are obscured by blackening clouds.

I can't imagine anyone could live in a place so harsh and desolate. No wonder he let himself fall to Sorcery. No wonder he became so wicked. I dip into a thick of pine trees bent and suffocating from the weight of ice and snow, and I shiver at their wailing. I want to help them, but I can't. The shadow smoke is thickening, blending with the scent of a man. I'm nearly there.

"*Only you can do this,*" a reminder whispers through my mind. "*Her favored son. She has closed herself off to us. She is nearly consumed now. Nearly lost to us forever.*"

I push myself faster, following his scent along a sheer mountain crest until I reach the craggy mouth of a cave. Here, his scent mixes with another. A woman. Dark magic. I imagine red robes. I see her in my memory, gliding over rushing waters to the sound of screaming villagers. I duck into the opening so narrow that my whiskers brush the icy stone on both sides.

Inside isn't a cave like I expected. It's a room of smooth stone walls draped in crimson, with a bed as luxurious as the prince's, set on a dais at its center. Beside the hearth, the Sorceress stands glaring into the blazing fire, lost in her thoughts. Greenish firelight dances across her face, playing along the pale skin that peeks out from between the dark swirls of Mage Mark. The stream of smoke flows to the bed, where only the pointed tips of wolf ears poke out from the furs and plush blankets.

The wards block me from moving closer, but we expected them. Even so far closed off from the rest of the world, so hidden in the mountains, no respectable Sorcerers would leave themselves unprotected. I step forward just enough to let the shift happen, and I feel myself change from fox to boy again. Just as they had told me it would, as soon as I'm ready to speak it, a name comes to my mind.

"Valenor," I whisper.

"Do not fear. I am with you," his reply comes from all around me. His voice is deep and resonant, encouraging and kind. It gives me strength. It calms my quickened breath and thrumming heart. "Step through. Break the wards. Do not be afraid. You are protected."

I stare at the Sorceress so lost in her thoughts and remember her wickedness at the flood. She was so hungry for the shadow to bring her something and so furious when it didn't, and now, here I am on her doorstep.

I'm not afraid, though. It's as though my ability to feel fear was taken from me the moment he told me I was protected.

"Trust," says Valenor gently.

"For Amma," I whisper, and push myself through the wards to the other side. A sense of the fear I should be feeling crashes over me, so devastating I might not have survived it. It would have stolen my breath and driven me mad. I would have been trapped in it. It would have sent me to my knees to grovel and beg for release or death.

Instead, I'm swathed in comfort, immune to its effects. Valenor will stand beside me. He won't leave until this is done.

As the wards break, the Sorceress vanishes. She was only an illusion, a construct meant to make any intruder think twice. Only my mother's sleeping tormentor remains, but he's rousing. He's aware the wards have broken, but he's fighting waking. The smoke trail thins as his second self sweeps away from Amma to return to himself.

The stench of death and waste is so pungent within the chamber I have to hold my breath. The fire, which looked to be blazing outside of the wards, is nearly out. A dried-out stew pot hangs hooked over it, streaming acrid smoke up the chimney. A half dozen rotting fox skins dangle from the rough stone mantel only partly scraped out, their bones sprinkled among the dying embers of the hearth. Fox skins.

"Elliot," Valenor warns.

"Elliot," a drawn-out growl rumbles across the room as Amma's tormentor wakes.

In the Dreaming I could only sense and hear him. His voice was chilling, his presence a menace. In Waking, he's nearly as wasted as Amma. I wonder how long he's been obsessed with the Grove and with her. Judging by the looks of him and this place, months, at least.

"Such a handsome child," he croaks, propping himself up in the bed to get a better look at me. His skin is pale between the lines of the Mark, his eyes ringed with dark circles. His chewed, wolfish ears twitch as though flicking away flies, and his whitish eyes narrow, homing in on his prey. On me.

"What was it that finally made you snap to seek me out?" he asks with a wry grin, baring chipped and yellowed teeth. "Curiosity? Fear? Anger? The desire for vengeance? I knew as a scout, yourself, you'd be the easiest of her kin to lure. Little fox."

He hisses the last, licking pointed teeth with a famished pink tongue.

"I've acquired quite a taste for fox, imagining how delectable this moment would be," he snarls.

I'm surprised by his strength when he slips from the bed to stalk toward me. As sickly as he looks, I expected him to stumble or to clutch at something to help prop him up, but he stands on his own two feet, his thickly Marked chest bare to the firelight, his loose trousers swirling around his legs.

I don't answer him. I only stand like I was instructed to. Silent. Distant. Intriguing. If he was anyone else, he couldn't see me. I'm in the Dreaming, after all, and he's in the Waking. But I left my own trail along his smoke line. I alerted his wards and stepped into his territory. I was reckless on purpose. I broke rules that are meant to protect both of us.

Before he was even fully awake, he was expecting me.

In his mind, he set his trap for me and I took the bait. Little does he know we've set our own trap, and I'm the bait.

He strides forward, glaring at me as he sweeps a hand across his shoulders to conjure a wolf skin cloak over a rich crimson vest. Behind him, his shaggy tail flicks with annoyance. Intrigued, I sniff the air between us. It's strange. He's part man and part wolf at once, with no need to choose one or the other like I must.

He smirks when he notices how I'm looking at him.

"Never seen a Northern Faefolk before?" he asks snidely. "So sheltered. Naive, like your mother. Imagine what else they must be keeping from the empty-headed masses of the Grove."

My hands curl into fists at the mention of my mother, but I hold my tongue and stand my ground as he moves closer.

"Have you come all this way only to glare at me, then? Will you not speak?" he barks impatiently.

"Rubeus." I utter the name that comes to mind and smirk with satisfaction at his shock and anger. Knowing his name gives me a certain power over him, I can tell. It infuriates him and inspires fear.

"What do you want, boy?" he glowers.

"I want you to leave her alone." I say, but my voice is different. Older. Not mine at all. It's recently familiar, but I can't place it.

"Now, why would I do that?" he snarls. "She is bound to me. In Dreaming, she is mine."

"I'll give you a way in," I offer. My reply shocks me, but the emotion is suppressed from my voice to ensure this will work. I understand these words are part of a greater plan that has been hidden from me. The Grove is acting through me, using me as a vessel for its workings. I agreed to this.

"Sever her from you," I say firmly, "and you'll be rewarded with entry to the Grove. I give you one chance to agree."

His eyes narrow to slits.

"What trick is this? What do you take me for?"

"It's no trick. It is a gift." I reach into my vest pocket and pull out an acorn cap containing a single drop of sparkling Lifesap. "This is what you're after, isn't it?"

I hold it toward him in my palm and watch its blue-green glow dance across my fingertips. The glimpse of it causes Rubeus to lose all wit and sense. With a feral, guttural growl he bares his teeth and lunges at me.

"Take heart, Elliot," Valenor whispers in my ear. "Stand your ground. Grab him."

I shouldn't be able to touch him from the Dreaming, but Valenor's guidance assures me this plan will work. When Rubeus lunges to snatch the acorn cap from me, I clamp my free hand over his wrist and yank him closer. His hand closes over mine and the acorn cap fuses us together. Valenor's cloak falls over us all, enveloping us in swaths of sunny sky blue and moonlit midnight.

With barely a lurch, we speed along my thread and snap back to the room where I first appeared in this dream, which is meant to be my room, but isn't.

Valenor's cloak falls away from us and I feel him vanish, leaving us bathed in that same strange burst of unnatural, searing light.

Still firmly in my grasp, Rubeus screams in agony, yanking and pulling, struggling to free himself from my hold. His eyes are screwed tightly closed, his tail thrashes as he howls and begs for mercy. The light is hurting him, but I don't feel a thing. He's fighting against me, but I barely need to plant my feet to keep my grip on him.

Though he's a grown man, it takes no effort to hold him. I feel like I'm grasping a rabbit by the ears while he scrambles for his life.

"Keep hold, Elliot," Father orders from behind me, and I whirl to face him. He stands fierce and ready, his broad spear firm in his grip. At his chest, the Dream Stone pulses with an angry red glow.

Amma cowers in his shadow, sobbing and pleading: "Don't hurt him, Gwain! Please! Spare him!"

Unlike me, Father has been allowed to keep his emotions. His rage and contempt for the creature who has ensorcelled his wife rolls off him in waves.

"Hold him fast, Elliot," he commands, his weapon prepared to strike.

Rubeus screams and clambers desperately, but no matter how hard he tries to claw and bite me, his attacks never meet their mark. When I tighten my grip to try to still him, I glimpse a thin trail of black tendril that wafts through the bright space, tethering him to Amma.

The more she cries and he struggles, the brighter the light beams until it reveals his full hold on her. His wicked, smoky shadows have wound around her ankles and bound her waist and her arms. They've speared into her chest and obscured her eyes, tangling into her hair. She's so confined by his darkness, I wonder how she's survived this long.

"Turn away from shadow, Elliot," she weeps, her voice thick with shame.

Father wastes no time. He growls and slashes the tendril of shadow with a powerful swipe of his spear. With his rage to fuel him, it only takes one strike to sever the bindings imprisoning Amma. They swirl away from her, tangling around the spear until Father flings them into the brilliant light.

"LORELAI!" Rubeus screams in fury. He fights my hold with all his strength as he watches Amma fall into Father's arms, but I don't let go.

"Gwain," Amma whispers.

"Lore," Father cries with relief, encircling her in his strong arms. Locked in each other's embrace, they vanish into the ever-brightening light leaving me and Rubeus alone together. He isn't fighting anymore. He hangs limp in my grasp, staring blankly into the space where she had been. The light fades slightly to reveal the sapling sprout, curling up from the center of the sisal rug.

"No," Rubeus panics, his voice ragged with horror. "No."

"What you have dreamed shall be," I tell him, even though I have no idea what it means. I steer him closer to the sprout until he's standing almost on top of it.

"Don't do this," he begs, his fear-glossed eyes locking to mine.

"You saw this come to pass, and yet you persisted," the reply filters through me. "And now, as you longed to, you shall experience firsthand the might of the Grove."

I release my hold only when the sprout slithers around him, binding his ankles, his legs, his waist, just like his shadows bound my amma. As the light engulfs him, obscuring him from my view, I feel the Ancients' influence fade away from me.

"As the Grove wills it," I say over his screams, fully myself again.

Then, I wake up.

16

The Source

My feet move at a leisurely pace along the white pebble path as I wake. The pink fog has cleared to reveal a neat line of white birch trees edged with fragrant rose bushes along the path. I breathe in deeply, grateful for the sweet perfume that washes away the scent of rot and decay that lingers with me.

With each step I take, memories of the things that just happened spill out behind me. I forget the sight of Rubeus's bedroom in the cave, the fox skins drying on the hearth near the Sorceress. I forget Valenor, the being who came to stand with me and keep me safe. I forget the location of the lair, and how cold it was there.

A golden wisp keeps pace behind me, just within my line of sight. Shimmering gold sparks billow from me into the space between us, and I understand. These memories won't serve me anymore. Holding onto them will only foster fear and discomfort. With a sigh of relief, I let them go. I won't remember any of it, and I'm grateful.

I'm left with only a feeling of great accomplishment in the face of peril, and the image of Amma tumbling into Father's arms, safe and free from the darkness that held her. They're together again, safe and content, and it couldn't have happened if not for me.

I remember only one small, disturbing part. A wicked man, tangled in tendrils, screaming for mercy. A man who did terrible things, getting exactly what he deserved. I'll need to know this for later. It will help me understand what happens next.

The path ends at a white quartz bank of a pristine circular pool filled with blue-green sparkling liquid. Butterflies dance across the thick, colorful flowers framing the bank, and across the way a family of white rabbits nibbles at clover together, undisturbed by my presence.

With peace in my heart and nothing else to do, I sink to kneel before its majesty and tranquility. Its surface sometimes flashes with bursts of magic, and as I gaze at it, I imagine the roots of the Ancients deep beneath, drawing its waters into their trunks, creating the Lifesap that is the source of all magic in the Grove.

This is what he had wanted to see. The wicked one. This is what he went mad for in the end. This is what we live to preserve. I realize what an honor it is for me to be shown this marvel, and my heart soars with gratitude. No one has ever described such a place to me. As far as I know, I'm the only wood elf in the Grove who has ever been gifted this privilege.

It's so tranquil, so serene and unsullied, and yet it's so powerful. Sitting this close feels like grazing the edge of infinity itself. All the stars in the sky, all the water in the sea, it could all be contained in this one perfect, glittering pool.

"Elliot Eldinae," calls a voice the moment a ripple disturbs the exact center of the smooth, shining surface.

I edge closer on my knees to see a face emerging there. It's neither a man nor a woman, with perfectly balanced features that look like they've been dipped in gold. It gazes across the pool at me as I watch shoulders emerge, then arms and hands, then a torso up to the being's waist. Their hair is long and flowing, and their body is draped in shimmering blue-green gossamer.

Brilliant feathery wings glow at their back, their span so broad that the tips of them graze the edges of the pool on either side of them. I nearly forget to breathe, I'm so awed by them as they glide close.

"We are Aft'elu," they say with a voice as gentle as a breeze.

"I remember you," I say, ducking my head respectfully. "You look different."

"We take many forms," Aft'elu explains. "This is our truest."

A soft golden glow ebbs behind me, and Aft'elu opens a hand to the wisp which collected my memories. It floats into their waiting palm, and they close their eyes as they absorb it into themselves.

"You have done well in service to the Grove," they say after a long stretch of silence.

At their praise, too much emotion wells up inside of me to be able to answer them. Finally, I've done something worthwhile. I've had some purpose. I wish I could remember fully what it was.

"Take this, our gift," they say, and a jade-colored feather with golden veins appears in their offered hand. It floats across the space between us and twines itself into one of the beaded braids beside my right ear.

"Thank you," I whisper reverently. I reach to stroke the sleek feather and marvel at the power it exudes.

"You shall leave us now," Aft'elu says serenely. "We hope you never again require our counsel or company."

"What about Amma?" I ask, suddenly remembering. "And Father?"

"They have left our presence together. You shall find them in the Sanctum."

Distantly, someone calls my name. It takes me a long time to tear my attention from the pool and come to my senses, but when I do, I recognize her voice right away.

"Hana?" I call, squinting over my shoulders. My nose twitches, but I can't pick up her scent. The air here is too pure and unfettered by anything outside of its powerful magic.

"Elliot?" she calls, sounding more puzzled than concerned. She's far away, and I know no matter how hard she tries she won't be able to reach me here. She hasn't earned a viewing of the pool. The magic is too strong for her to ever find it on her own.

I wonder if the Lifesap pool has always been so close to the Sanctum, or if it just seems that way now, for my sake. I stare at it, wishing I could share this beauty with her. Hana and her vines would wonder at this place.

"Child of the Grove," Aft'elu whispers, "leave us."

Their words are a final reminder this place must remain secret and protected. Once I turn my back on it, I know it will slip from my memory.

"Elliot!" Hana calls from even further away, and I take one last look before reluctantly turning to answer.

"I'm here, Hana! I'll find you. Stay where you are!"

"Supper is a celebration," she shouts. "You can't be late! Ow! Oh, there are thorns... Mind the thorns!"

A gap between two rose bushes along the white stone path opens to me, and I slip through it, jogging in her direction.

"I'm coming," I tell her. "Just stay there!"

As I follow the path, there's a shift away from the fold, and the forest grows more familiar around me. A profound sense of loss strikes me as I leave its border, but I recover quickly when I see Hana waiting on the path ahead.

She runs to me and throws her arms around me, her vines grazing my cheeks and slipping into my hair.

"I thought you'd never come back," she whispers against my cheek.

I hug her tightly, breathing in the scent of fresh leaves and earth.

"I was only gone for an afternoon," I mumble, and she steps back to hold me at arm's length.

"You're serious?" she whispers, searching my eyes. When I nod, she shakes her head. "A week, Elliot," she says with concern. "You were gone a week. Your father, too. Sulien and Kaini have been waiting and waiting. Grandmother refused to tell me anything. It's been awful."

"No, I..." I scowl, shaking my head. "I only went in…to..." I turn to look at the path behind me, which has grown over again with hemlock and ferns. I'm not sure what I was going to say.

"Never mind, you can't be late to supper tonight," she says, taking my hand to pull me toward the Sanctum. "Everyone's talking. The Ancients have something special planned."

"What?" I ask, still feeling muddled. I have a sense that I've just experienced something extraordinary, but I can't for my own life remember what it was. All I know is everything is as it should be now. Amma and Father are safe and together, thanks to me. Thanks to the fold, we're going to be a family again.

The thought makes me break into a jog, and Hana runs beside me. I hope Amma and Father will be at supper, too. I can't wait to see them together, whole and happy again. I can't wait to see what the Ancients have in store for us. It isn't often they call for a celebration outside of ceremony days.

"What do you think it will be?" I ask her as she keeps pace beside me.

"Rumors say it's a Despoiling," she answers, glancing sidelong at me.

"A Despoiling?" I scowl, only vaguely aware of what that is.

"Everyone's saying we captured one of them," she squeezes my hand like she knows more than she's letting on. "A Sorcerer. They're going to make an example of him. Strip him of his powers. Punish him. We can't be late," she says with a strange determination. "We can't miss it."

17

Despoiling

Just before we reach the Sanctum, one of Hana's vines grazes the gifted feather bound in my braid.

"That's new," she says, tilting her head to the side. "It's beautiful. Powerful, too."

When I touch it, I remember the pride and accomplishment I felt when it was given to me. The honor. That's all, though. Where it came from or who tied it there is a lost moment. It bothers me a little, until Hana cheerfully distracts me.

"Don't worry. I know you can't tell me about it. It doesn't matter anyway. Look, it's like a feast day!"

I tear my gaze from her to look through the fringe of willow into the Sanctum. In the light of the setting sun, the normally peaceful gathering buzzes with excited, lively chatter.

A large group has gathered at the center of the meadow around someone or something I can't quite see due to the crowd. As we emerge from the forest, Kaini squeezes from inside of the group and peers around excitedly.

"Brother!" I call as soon as I see him, and he looks at me with wide eyes and waves, jumping up and down.

"Elliot!" he shouts gleefully. "Amma, Father, it's Elliot!"

The hum of voices echoing across the Sanctum goes silent as everyone turns to look at me, and Kaini glances behind him.

"Elliot?" Amma calls from within the crowd, and the mass of wood elves parts to reveal her and Father at its center.

I stare in stunned amazement at Amma across the meadow. My feet seem rooted to the spot. I can't will myself to move. If it wasn't for her voice, I wouldn't have believed it was her.

Lovingly held in Father's embrace, Amma stands dressed in traditional wedding garb of head-to-toe green beads and fringe. Her once wasted body, so frail I thought she might tumble away with the wind, is full and healthy now. Her skin glows rosy pink, and her clear, beautiful hazel eyes dance with joy as they meet mine. My heart flutters. She can see.

"Amma?" I whisper, afraid if I speak louder or move, this illusion might be shattered.

Around us, everyone stares, but for once their whispers aren't of judgment or ridicule. This time, they look at us with admiration and pride. Amma opens her arms and I take off at a run and throw myself into them. She and Father gather me close, and the crowd closes in around us, cheering and joining in the embrace.

Tearfully, I look into Amma's rosy face and meet her glittering eyes. "You're back," I whisper, and she laughs through her tears and hugs me tighter.

"Thanks to you," Father says with a hearty pride that makes a lump form in my throat. "My boy."

"Is this real?" I ask, clinging to the two of them as the crowd surges in on us. It can't be. It has to be a dream. It's too perfect, too amazing to be anything else.

"Have I taught you nothing?" Amma laughs and kisses my cheek. "Use your senses. All of them. Look, listen, feel. It's real, my dear, sweet Elliot."

Father bends to kiss her, and the two of them work up into such a passion that I'm forced to slip away and leave them to it.

"Not again," Kaini groans beside me.

"Don't complain, Kaini." Sulien edges through the crowd to wrap an arm around both of us. He rolls his eyes and glances at Amma and Father. "They have a lot of catching up to do."

"Doesn't mean we should have to watch it," Kaini grumbles, kicking at the piles of rose petals mounded at Amma and Father's feet.

The crush of the crowd eases, and we all gaze upward into the *Rianave* canopy where hundreds of wisps pulse and twinkle like stars. Beyond them through the leaves, the full moon hangs round and heavy in the dusky sky.

The Sanctum goes quiet as the wisps start to descend, and together we sink to our knees in the moss. I scramble for a spot beside Amma, who sits close to Father with her fingers still twined into his hair as he tucks her close.

Once all is still and silent, the wisps divert from their usual pattern. Instead of coming to us individually, they settle in vertical rows like a curtain at the front of the Grove and address us as one.

"What are they doing?" Kaini whispers all the way down on the other side of Sulien, who shushes him urgently. "Well, I never saw them do that before," Kaini grumbles.

"Wait and see, Darling," Amma leans forward to whisper to him, and he brightens up a little and crawls over to sit as close to her lap as he can manage without actually sitting in it.

"*No secrets from us,*" the Rianaves' booming voices thunder over us as the wisps' lights pulse with each word.

"No secrets," we repeat together.

"*As the Grove wills it.*"

"As the Grove wills it."

"*Protection for all,*" the *Rianaves* promise.

"Protection for all," we reply.

"*Duty above all.*"

"Duty above all."

"*Keep hidden, always.*"

"Keep hidden, always," Amma reaches for my hand and squeezes it.

"*Roots in soil, Limbs in sky.*"

"Roots in soil, limbs in sky."

"*We are one with the Grove.*"

"We are one with the Grove." Father tears his gaze from the wisps to offer Amma a loving smile.

The curtain of wisps shimmers softly as a reverent silence falls over the Grove. Their multi-colored light dims almost completely and then surges to breathtaking gold.

Like reflections on the surface of still waters, the wisps show us things. Flashes of my journey into the cave where Rubeus slept, and what happened at Blackbird's Spine, and the flooded village being saved by men and women dressed in red.

I feel a surge of pride and accomplishment. These are things I've scouted for the Grove, things I've shown the *Rianaves* that they're now sharing with everyone else. The scenes fade to darker moments, ones which didn't come from me. There are glimpses of a doe's lashes and black-tipped nose. Amma. The things she has seen in her scouting are so much worse than anything I've encountered in mine.

Rubeus stands with a Sorceress at the peak of a mountain beside a stream fed by a snow cap's spring thaw. The pair cling to each other with determination and malice in their eyes, and together they howl the workings of a wicked spell. The mountain rumbles and quakes, and the snow cap melts instantly, surging the stream into a powerful, muddy, rushing river. The perspective changes to show the slope of the mountain and the village at the base, right in the path of the river's torrent.

The two look on with cruel exhilaration as the water crashes into the village, and as the screams of the villagers below carry to them on the wind, they kiss each other passionately. The scene fades to another. Amma is on the opposite side of Blackbird's Spine, watching Sorcerers send their black rain splashing against our border, marking the line of our protections as it spills into the ravine.

We see Rubeus and Amma surrounded by darkness as he tortures her, plying her for the secrets of the Grove. Amma is strong, though. She kept his attention over the span of years, giving him just a little at a time, letting him think she was devoted to him, blinding herself to our Grove. She distracted him, avoiding everything and everyone to prevent him from seeing any of it through her. She made herself an outcast, a Wanderer, to keep us safe. All of us. She hid it from me, even, by instructing me from the very beginning to turn away from shadow.

As she gained his trust, she was allowed into his workings to be a witness of the horrors he inflicted on so many. Children, elders, animals, it didn't matter. Anyone or anything that crossed his path was either used, tortured, or obliterated in his pursuit of power. He was a foul, ruthless, and selfish man. Even his love for the Sorceress was fraught with lies and deception.

In the Grove, we work to help each other. Everyone has their place and their duty, and we all take pride in our contributions. Seeing such callousness and selfishness is so disturbing and foreign, it turns my stomach.

We see so many more examples of the evil intent of Sorcerers and their interactions with the Grove. A group of our hunters stands-off at the edge of the forest against a trio of men Marked with black swirls across their hands and faces. Enraged, the three men barrage our magical walls with everything from fire to lightning to pure arcane energy, but their efforts are only absorbed by the protections as our hunters watch on, collecting the scene to be gathered by golden wisps for the Ancients at the Grove supper ceremony.

"*The threat of Sorcery has returned to our peaceful borders,*" the Ancients' voices thunder their warning while the golden orbs continue to pulse with scene after scene of attempted breaches. It shows us the Sorceress who kissed Rubeus on the mountain peak, this time kneeling at our boundary planting an impostor Rianave, pulling the edge of our protections toward her to nestle it safely inside, just like Hana said.

"They believe their subtle workings have gone unnoticed, but *the Grove sees all.*"

"The Grove sees all," I whisper together with the gathering.

"*We are all one.*"

"We are all one."

"*We shall prevail.*"

"We shall prevail."

We see Amma standing in the darkness, bearing the barrage of Rubeus's mental and physical attacks as his desperation to discover secrets of the Grove consumes him. The more she refuses, the more obsessed he becomes. I want to look away, but I'm not able to. The wisps hold my gaze, and what they show me fills me with such a hatred for this Sorcerer that my lips curl back in a sneer and I feel the shiver over my skin that comes from shifting to fox form.

"*Lorelai Eldinae,*" the voice of the *Rianaves* startles me to my senses as the wisps return their original colors and float apart from each other. "*Step forward.*"

I didn't realize I'd been squeezing Amma's hand until she gently pries it from my grip and pats my knee reassuringly. She kisses Father softly on the cheek and brushes Kaini's shoulder before she rises from her knees.

Whispers of admiration shiver through the Grove as she approaches the grouping of wisps now arranged in a formation similar to a tree's trunk. When Amma nears, a few of them float away to reveal chewed wolf ear tips, a gaunt face framed with shaggy gray fur, and the hunched wolf pelt-draped shoulders of the Sorcerer Rubeus.

All around us, the crowd jeers and hisses at the sight of him, but Amma doesn't recoil or turn away. She stands straight and tall, her eyes narrowed with disgust for the man who stands bound by the wisps, his head lolling to the side weakly.

"Please," he utters, his voice tinged with madness.

From the darkness behind him, the Elders of the Grove emerge. There are six in all, each painted with glowing blue-green Lifesap, each dressed for high ceremony in head-to-toe gold leaves, jade feathers, and crystals that seem to sing in the moonlight.

One at a time, they kiss Amma's forehead and touch first her left shoulder and then her right with their staves, calling out the highest honors and blessings of the *Rianaves*. The Ancient trees seem to lean inward to show their approval.

"*Elliot Eldinae,*" the *Rianaves* boom, and I push myself to my feet in a daze and walk to join Amma. So close to Rubeus, even as lethargic as he is, even surrounded by wisps and Elders, I can feel the evil rolling off him. His chapped upper lip curls back from his yellowed teeth when I enter his line of sight, and I don't give him the satisfaction of looking away as I take my place beside Amma.

"Many are to be commended for their contribution to this night,"

Elder Feren declares. His knee-length braids swing forward as he gestures toward the gathering. "But these two dream scouts, Lorelai Eldinae and her son Elliot Eldinae, have earned the highest honors. As such, they are gifted the privilege of retribution. It is the Grove's will that this creature shall be Despoiled. Stripped of his foul magic."

Inside the wisps' hold, Rubeus growls and fights to break free.

Elder Feren turns to us, opening his hands in a welcoming gesture. "What happens to him after, my children, is your determination."

Amma takes a step closer to me and puts a hand on my shoulder. I tear my gaze from Rubeus to look into her eyes, which seem to ask me to trust her. I nod slowly, unsure what she has in mind. She turns to look across the meadow at Father, who's watching with a mix of pride and fury, his jaw clenched, his shoulders squared.

"He always wished to see the full might of the Grove," Amma says, her voice ringing clear and firm across the gathering. "I declare a hunt. A midnight hunt, this night."

"As you declare, if the Grove wills it, so let it be," Elder Feren agrees, lifting his face and palms to the canopy.

"*A hunt to the death*," the *Rianaves* thunder over us. "*At midnight this night.*"

While everyone else gazes deep into the glittering *Rianave* leaves, a small movement catches my eye among the wisps holding Rubeus. Two of the dozen wisps have been snuffed to a dim brownish glow, right where the Sorcerer's hands would be inside his bindings. His face is twisted and strained with effort as those two wisps extinguish and fade, leaving two empty holes for his clawed hands to reach through.

It happens too fast for me to see. Amma dives to shield me, and I grab her and pull her low as Rubeus unleashes a wild, desperate pulse of arcane energy. Everyone screams. We duck our heads as more wisps surge from above to shield us from his unexpected attack.

"You wish to hunt me?" Rubeus seethes, thrashing and writhing inside his wisp bindings. "You'll regret it. I'll take as many of you with me as I can, and I am nothing compared to what's out there."

He flings out his hand again and a crackle of pure white energy pulses there, causing half the Grove to jump to their feet and either draw weapons to fight or start to flee. Before he can unleash it, though, Elder Feren steps forward.

"Enough," he says calmly. With the single word, the Grove goes still and silent. Father and Sulien freeze in place, their spears raised and ready to strike just paces from Rubeus and the wisps. Even the pulse of the wisps stills to a steady, eerie glow.

Elder Feren gestures to Avela and the other Elders, who form a circle around Rubeus. Still trapped by the wisps, the Sorcerer stands like carved stone, his hands contorted into claws, a garish snarl stuck on his face.

I try to reach for Amma, but my movements take far longer than they should. It's like everything other than what the Elders are doing is slowed to a crawl. The wisps surrounding Rubeus leave him to float to each of the circling Elders, coming to rest on the ends of their staves. Rubeus doesn't move. Like us, he seems to be held in a separate, slower plane.

"*We shall prevail*," the *Rianaves* rumble.

"Fool Sorcerer," Elder Feren hisses as the circle raise their staves and streams of dark energy are ripped through Rubeus's eyes, nose, mouth, ears, fingertips, and toes to be gathered by the wisps on the staves.

"You might have stood a chance if you had shown any semblance of restraint. Instead, you shall be hunted with little more than your wits to guard you. All you have worked for belongs to us now."

"*As the Grove wills it.*"

18

The Impending Storm

The Elders drain Rubeus of his magic until the fury fades from his eyes and they go blank and empty. While the others keep their aim steady to hold the trapped Sorcerer, Elder Feren lowers his staff to address the Grove.

"Not all of his powers shall be stripped away. During the moonlight hunt, our warriors will gain skill and prowess by learning how to defeat one of his ilk. As the Grove wills, he has been drained for his actions here, but this prey will not be left without some magic for the chase."

"As the Grove wills," the other Elders echo.

They pull their staves away and the wisps descend from them into the moss. Beneath Rubeus, the ground rolls and quakes and *Rianave* roots snake up from the soil to bind his arms and legs, constricting his body and face until he's no longer visible within them.

The leaves overhead hiss with the sudden, violent gust of wind announcing the approach of a late spring storm. Lightning flashes ominously overhead and thunder rumbles in the distance.

Once the Elders break the circle and move to join the gathering, the spell over the Grove lifts. As time returns to normal, Father halts his charge and lowers his weapon, still sneering at the bound Sorcerer.

"All who wish to join the hunt shall prepare now," Elder Feren announces. "Children will remain under the Grove's protection here in the Sanctum until dawn. When the moon is high, the hunt will begin!"

He nods to a grouping of Druids to the side, who start to play. Their drums sound in time with the rumbling of thunder overhead, and as panpipes and rattles join in, the gathering swirls into revelry and wild dancing.

In the blink of an eye, I'm whisked into the thick of it by strong green vines. "Hana!" I laugh breathlessly as she spins me around and pulls me by the hand into the chaos. The rhythmic thumping of drums echoes through the trees, pounding ancient beats against the rising crash of thunder and lightning.

We circle raucously around the roots that hold Rubeus captive, our voices raised in tribal chants, our flailing limbs casting long, eerie shadows across the trunks of the *Rianaves* with every pulse of lightning. I kick and run and scream and leap like everyone else, bounding free and feral to the trees and the storm and the Grove.

The frenzied gathering churns power from the Rianave roots far below us, stirring up sparks of blue-green. The spirits of our ancestors fill us with centuries of pure, primal energy. My skin prickles from head to toe with its power as it the Grove magic pulses through me, filling me with courage, honing my instincts.

Blue sparkles dance in her billowing hair as Hana laughs beside me, yowling to the wisps in the trees above. I join in, howling as we circle around and around the Sorcerer's prison, catching glimpses of the faces of my kin in the flickering light.

The skies open, spilling a fierce rain that hisses loudly through the *Rianave* canopy, but the leaves are so high and so thick we only feel the occasional drip all the way down here.

Eventually, when there's a break in the storm showing the moon high overhead, the dancing slows, and everyone scatters to return to their family groups.

Hana grins at me breathlessly, her eyes flashing with untamed excitement, and gives me a kiss on the cheek before sprinting off to join her grandmother and parents.

My heart sinks a little as I realize that for me, the night is over. Children are to remain in the Sanctum, Elder Feren had said. With a huff of disappointment, I weave through the crowd to find Amma and Father. I stand beside Kaini, who's already back to his complaining.

"But you'll need a healer, Amma!" he whines.

"Not another word, Kaini," Father scolds. "It's out of the question. You will remain here with the other young ones as the Grove wills, under the protection of the Ancients."

Sulien joins us, already dressed in his warrior gear. His ceremonial spear is decorated with the feathers and beads of an initiate warrior, and his hair has been pulled away from his face in a web of intricate braids and colored leather cords.

When did he have time to do all that?

I look around, and I realize we're all similarly transformed. Amma's bridal dress has been replaced with polished, coppery leather armor embossed with stylized fauns leaping through flowers and meadow grasses. Father is even more intimidating than usual in stone-like burnished gray armor that flashes with studs and drips with honor beads. His spear is twice as long as he is tall and polished to such a sharp edge it looks like he could slice through a man with barely a swing.

My clothes have changed, too. My vest and trousers are of a finer, softer type of leaf green suede that fits me like a second skin. The fringe at my chest and shoulders waves like fresh spring grasses when I move, and the bow I usually carry has a more familiar grip, a firmer spring to the decoratively carved wood, and a fresh, strong string. Even my arrows have transformed from training fletch to advanced, longer-ranged broad-tipped ones with gold and jade feather vanes.

A thrill rushes through me as I draw an arrow and hold it up to check the point. Kaini stands beyond it, unchanged. I understand what it means. He's a child, and he's staying behind. I'm not.

"I get to join the hunt?" I dare to whisper.

Amma looks up at Father hesitantly, and to my surprise he strides to me and clamps his hand on my shoulder.

"If anyone deserves to join, Elliot," he says proudly, "you do."

"That's not FAIR!" Kaini shouts, stomping his foot.

"Kaini, don't be insolent!" Father scolds, but before he can do anything more Amma takes Kaini by both hands and leads him gently away to talk to him.

Sulien, Father and I watch as she crouches to his eye level and strokes his hair tenderly from his face. Suppressing his anger, Kaini listens to whatever she's saying earnestly and nods and throws his arms around her neck.

"I missed her," Sulien offers quietly.

"As we all did," Father agrees.

A group of Kaini's friends rush us and crowd around him and Amma, tugging at him to join them.

"Kaini! We're having our own hunt for night sky salamanders!"

"It's too early in the season for those," Kaini argues, tucking himself closer to Amma.

"No, it isn't! Eve saw one in the ferns. Come help us look!"

"Go on," Amma urges, giving him a nudge. He hesitates until Amma nods reassuringly, then he dashes off with the others across the meadow.

An ominous strobe of lightning flashes so brightly it paints everyone with a ghostly blue-white light for a sudden, blinding pulse. It's punctuated just a breath later by crash of thunder so loud it shakes the canopy overhead. A few of the children scream, then a hush falls over the Sanctum.

The roots holding the Sorcerer begin to glow white, then red, a rare color in our grove. The color of warning. The color of poison. The color of blood. Red. The color of rage. My heart pumps the color through my mind, fueling a sudden, wild urgency to fight. I'm reminded of Sorcerers gliding over raging waters, of women in rich gowns dancing with the king's men, of the inside lining of Rubeus's wolf-fur cloak. Red.

Rubeus's root prison pulses like hot coals, unfurling slowly. My hand flies to my quiver while beside me Father grips his spear. My fingers graze the fletching of an arrow, ready to pluck it out, but only hover there. No matter how hard I try, I can't even twitch a finger. All around me, the Druids of the Grove stand in similar battle-ready stances, their eyes fixed on the red warning glow, unmoving just like before.

In a swift, abrupt motion, the roots release the Sorcerer. The red light bursts into ember-like wisps which fling him out of the Sanctum, leaving fiery streaks of light in their wake. Beside me, Father growls with frenzied anticipation.

"*Begin,*" the Ancients boom in time with the storm. They release their hold on us and we charge, surging together as one into the midnight shadows of the forest.

19

The Midnight Hunt

Protected as we are as the children of the Grove, the forest at night is not a place we venture lightly. Our instincts are guided by generations of warnings and fostered by mutual respect of the nocturnal creatures, both corrupt and natural, which lurk in the wilds beyond the Great Grove.

Rubeus doesn't know of these creatures or their territories.

He could be anywhere.

Even with Father charging ahead of us, Amma and Sulien at my side, and the Grove's will pulsing through us, I feel the thrum of danger as we cross into darkness. My instincts take over, and I shift from boy to fox.

Immediately I catch a familiar scent: wolf, rot, and much more subtle dark magic. My claws flex into the damp earth with each footfall as I speed past Father to follow the scent trail.

Here outside of the *Rianave's* thick canopy, the storm is fierce and drenching. Rivulets of muddied rainwater splash under my paws, spraying up behind me as I veer from the path and plunge deeper into the trees to chase the Sorcerer's scent. It mingles with the scent of a doe, and I glance to the side to see Amma transformed as well, keeping pace beside me.

"Elliot has his trail!" Hana calls from behind me, and as thunder claps loudly overhead, I'm aware of the hunt joining the chase with me.

The scent trail grows stronger, and I follow my nose deeper into the darkness as rain catches in my whiskers and fur. My paws barely touch the forest floor as I speed along, faster than any of them. Faster than I've ever gone outside of the Dreaming. A gap widens between me and the rest of the hunt, except for Amma and others like us who can take animal form, but I can't slow for them. Rubeus is close. Not only can I smell him, I can feel his presence.

My lips curl into a wild snarl as my fox's instincts push my wood elf thinking all the way to the back of my mind. Chase. Find. Attack. I'll be the first to sink my teeth into him. The first to tear away his flesh.

Wolf. Rot. Dark Magic. Lynx. Something else. Deep in my fox mind, I identify it straight away. Goblins. It's a scent meant to invoke danger. Stop. Do not approach.

I ignore it.

The trail calls me.

It's overwhelmingly strong. Smudged with sweat. Sprinkled with drops of blood. Northman's blood. Sorcerer's blood. Rubeus's blood.

My right ear tingles and twitches in warning. I shake my head with a spray of rainwater and run faster, but Amma leaps in front of me to block my path and I crash with full force into her side before I can stop myself.

As we sprawl into the mud, she shifts back to her true form and gathers me into her arms. Too overcome by the fox, I gnash my teeth and writhe to free myself as she whispers warnings into my still-tingling ear.

"Elliot, be still. Be quiet. It's the outskirts of Gorvelk. It was a false trail."

The fear and warning heavy in her tone bring me to my senses just before I sink my teeth into her arm. I close my mouth and shift back, shivering at the thought of how close I came to hurting her.

"It's Gorvelk," she repeats. "Get up quietly. Stay downwind. Do not ready your bow. Do not run. Just walk with me."

Breathless, I crane my neck to look over the hedgerow at the settlement on the other side. That same sharp warning scent makes my nose twitch. Goblins.

"How are we so far north already?" I whisper, but she shakes her head, eases me to my feet, and offers me her hand.

We make our way slowly toward the torches in the distance, their light diffused by the driving rain and thickening mists brought on by the storm. The closer we get to them, the more my chest tightens. How did that just happen? How did I nearly lead half of the Grove into protected goblin territory?

I start to panic, and the only thing that prevents it is Amma's forced slow pace and her hand clamped over mine.

We come through the gray mist to the other side, where Father and two dozen or so of the of the hunt has halted to wait for us. As soon as Father sees us, he runs to scoop us away from the mist and the thicker woods, his glare fixed thankfully not on me, but in the direction of the goblin camp.

"I'm sorry, Father," I offer, still breathless as I cling to his trunk-like forearm. The others close in around us, ready to listen to what I've seen. "I swear he went in there. His trail was growing stronger. There was blood in it. I almost got to him."

"It was a false trail," Amma says. "Rubeus is a master illusionist. Nothing about him can be trusted. Not even his scent."

Father's jaw clenches as he listens, still staring into the thick greenish mist. I know what he's thinking. If I'm right and Rubeus had gone in there, into Gorvelk, the hunt is over. Goblins are too savage to let an outsider like that live. I shiver again, thinking about how close I came. How close Amma came.

"Aye, Waterfowl caught another trail from the sky, going east," Father nods. "Sulien and the rest broke off to follow." He clamps a hand on my shoulder reassuringly. "Good instincts, son. Don't let it rattle you. Keep your head. This is no ordinary hunt."

I nod, trying to hide my embarrassment. A feather-soft touch tickles my elbow and I whirl defensively. Hana, whose vines reach across the space between us, shrinks back slightly. My heart pumps faster as our eyes meet, but Amma steps between us to talk to me.

"As scouts, we carry the trust of the hunt on our shoulders," she explains. Even though her tone is calm and understanding, I can't help but feel scolded. "No matter how much your instinct fights to take hold, you have an obligation to those behind you to always keep your wits. Know where the trail is leading you. Understand where you're guiding them. Instinct is crucial, but so is your Druid learning. Never give those rallying behind you a reason to doubt their trust."

"Yes, Amma. I'm sorry."

She smiles and cups my cheek with her muddy hand. "We learn and we step forward on the path."

The rustle of leaves and squelch of dozens of soggy footsteps beyond the green mist makes us both snap to attention. Father readies his spear. I reach for an arrow and take several paces backward to stand beside Hana. Around us, weapons are raised and ready. My heart gallops as I train my arrow toward the sounds.

There's a long stretch of silence before a scourge of goblins seeps through the cover of the mist. Shorter than me by half, their size is no measure of their ferocity. Their green skin glistens in the rain, their readied weapons primitive but deadly.

Long noses droop over sneers bearing sharp, venomous fangs. They stand just outside of the cover of the mist, glaring with ink-black eyes, panting as a unit, ready to charge.

One of them at the front barks a question in goblin tongue, and Hana steps forward boldly to answer them.

The harsh sounds they make as they speak are a clash of snarling, spitting, and screeching that sounds more like a threat than any sort of language.

As the two exchange words, the hunt forms a protective semi-circle around Hana. After much back and forth, eventually, the goblins seem to yield.

"I told them of the Sorcerer," Hana explains to the rest of us as the creatures slink backwards through the mist, never turning their wet black eyes away from us. "They said he didn't pass near their camp. They gave us a warning never to step through their mists again, or…"

She shivers as her vines slither around her, forming a protective shell of plants, leaves, and bark.

"Well done, Hana," Father says with a hint of awe as the others lower their weapons. "Your knowledge prevented a slaughter this night."

The group of us edge cautiously around the mist this time and take off at a run as shouts and battle sounds ring out in the distance, melding with the hiss of drenching rain and the rumbling of thunder.

At the outskirts of the fray, we find a handful of our kind scattered across the forest floor, their skin unnaturally white, like the stems of mushrooms. Their weapons are still gripped in their hands, their eyes are blank and motionless, their breath so shallow it's a wonder they're still alive.

"They're all healers," someone whispers, horrified.

On the other side of a thick hedge, the sounds of battle continue. Father and most of the others race to join the fray, which pulses with pink healing and blue and red and purple flashes of magic through the tangle of brambles.

A few of the Druids with us scatter to tend to the white, lifeless healers, their fingertips glowing pink with healing energy.

"Quickly," Amma says. She shifts from wood elf form to doe and disappears through the glossy leaves of a hedge, but I can't stop staring at the empty-eyed, white-skinned bodies littered around us.

Somewhere in the opposite direction, Hana screams. I whirl away from the battle toward the darkness and take off at a run, slipping easily into fox form.

Her screams, visceral and panicked, speed away from me into the far reaches of the forest. I race toward the terrifying sounds, picking up Rubeus's scent stronger than ever as I crash through the underbrush and leap over ivy and thorns.

The faster I run, the further she gets from me until her cries grow hoarse and exhausted, but I don't give up. I charge through the forest to the west, my nose twitching with his scent, my determination to find her propelling me as fast as I can go.

Abruptly, I crash into a crumpled tangle of white vines at the edge of a clearing. When I spring to my feet again to get my bearings, I yelp in shock.

Hana.

She shudders, fighting for breath, struggling to push herself up as her vines slump limp, white, and withered in the mud around her.

"Mm, mmm," Rubeus's voice echoes around us, filling me with dread.

Protectively, I edge around Hana and bare my teeth as he emerges from the darkness at the center of the clearing.

His wolf fur cloak glows with brisk red light and his bare chest ripples beneath it, stained with the Mark, full and healthy.

With narrowed, wicked eyes, he licks his clawed fingertips one by one.

"Lifesap," he grins, "Delicious, though I've grown to prefer fox as a main course."

"Elliot," Hana's pleading croak brings me to my senses. I slip into wood elf form and try to scoop her into my arms, but her limp, muddy vines add too much weight and I'm not strong enough to lift her.

"Can you stand?" I whisper to her as Rubeus eyes us with cruel fascination, like he's watching a struggling insect whose wings are pinned beneath his thumb.

She whimpers, and when I try to lift a slimy white vine to sling it over my shoulder, she cries out in pain.

"Oh," Rubeus winces mockingly, lifting a glowing red hand in our direction with a sickening grin, "does that hurt?"

He flings the spell, and just before it strikes us Hana plunges both hands to the earth. A thick tangle of brambles and foxgloves springs from the mud between us and his spell crashes into it, fizzling and breaking apart.

Under the cover of our bramble shelter, Hana slumps to the ground, pressing her cheek to the wet loam.

"Look," she breathes. "Is he weaker?"

"You think you can stop me with twigs and thorns?" Rubeus barks, but his voice is noticeably more ragged and worn.

I peer through a gap in the thick, winding branches and see him stalking closer. One foot drags behind him, and his crooked shoulders are slumped forward like they had been before. He growls and paces, stalking back and forth along the twisted wall, searching for a way in.

"Fetch your amma, Boy," Rubeus growls. "Now. Or taste a bolt."

"It looks like it," I whisper, kneeling at her shoulder. "Hana, don't talk. You're—"

"Make him cast again," she coughs. "Make him spend what he stole."

I stare at her limp white vines and think of the pale, drained healers sprawled on the outskirts of battle. He must have stolen their magic from them, somehow. Taken it to replenish his own, then cast some illusion to keep everyone fighting so he could make his escape.

Hana's shaking fingertips stretch out toward the inside of our shelter, grazing the sturdy roots as Rubeus paces back and forth beyond them, seething. My eyes go wide as I realize what she means to do.

"Never!" I shout at him, my heart galloping, "Amma hates you. She has always hated you, you filthy, mangy—"

With a growl of fury, he unleashes another powerful blast. I cringe and position myself between the blast and Hana as it crashes into the woody, thorned vines, but not only do they absorb his power, they transform it.

Red and orange flames ebb to blue-green embers which rain over us, collecting over Hana's prone form, seeping into the white of her vines. Two of her vines slither weakly. With barely any help, she's able to sit up.

"Again," she whispers.

Rubeus growls, stalking along the circular domed hedge, swiping at its leaves in a frenzy of annoyance. I nock an arrow from my quiver and aim it through a gap, and as soon as he comes into view, I let it loose. It grazes his cloak, and he howls in fury and smashes at the hedge with another spell of flames.

The same thing happens, and I watch him hunch further. His ribs protrude beneath his furs, his ears droop, he stumbles to his knees.

"Look," Hana's two best vines sweep to my shoulders, and she points past me through the gap. It takes me a moment to recognize the scene in the dark.

"Isn't that where the sprout was?" I gasp, staring at the hole in the ground and the misty border beyond it. A flutter of red fabric flaps in the darkness there, and the right side of my head tingles.

"Fetch your mother, you filthy scavenger," Rubeus growls weakly, his crazed yellow eye flashing as he catches a glimpse of me through the gap. "Now."

"Someone's there, Hana," I tell her, crouching low. "Just on the other side of the border."

"I see them," Hana whispers. "Two others."

Our whispering makes Rubeus go quiet, and Hana and I cling to each other as we watch him turn slowly toward the border.

"Alayne?" he calls hoarsely, and runs to the shifting shadows, but stumbles backwards after crashing into the wards. "Gorhen!"

Hana kneels and presses her hands to the earth, closing her eyes. A brisk wind flutters her damp hair, and her lips move silently.

"They're coming," she mutters. "I called them. They're coming."

I nock an arrow and aim it through the gap as the hunt rumbles closer to us.

"SORCERERS!" I shout from inside our bramble shelter.

I raise my bow, aiming my arrow through the hole. I have a clear shot of his back, but the jade feather at my ear tickles my right ear. The odd sensation guides my aim three paces to Rubeus's left, and a trail of angry orange light travels from my fingertips along the length of my arrow until it glows hot as embers at the arrow's tip.

I let it go, and it flies swift and true across the clearing leaving a trail of golden orange sparks behind it.

"Elliot, no," Hana whispers, mortified. "The border!"

Her vines pull me to her level, and we kneel watching through the hedge as my arrow tears through the wards, shredding a long, jagged hole like a portal through the Grove's protections. The Sorceress beyond raises a graceful hand, and with her gesture, my arrow halts and drifts to the ground like a feather.

Feather. My right ear rings. My tingling face is so numb I can no longer feel the cold droplets of rain. Hana's saying something to me, but I don't hear. I watch the Sorceress glide through the fracture, set foot on our soil, call forth her shadow minions. Dozens of them, solid yet ethereal, follow her through along with the third Sorcerer.

Beside me Hana tugs frantically at my arm, but I barely feel her.

"*The Grove wills it,*" a recently familiar voice presses into my mind.

The hunt arrives, clashing with the three Sorcerers and shadows who have breached into our lands.

Hana's gaze locks with mine, her dark eyes reflecting the sparkling light of the feather that flutters at my ear. I expect to see fear within that reflection. Instead, there's only fierce determination.

"*Let them come,*" the voices of the Ancients resonate with the rumble of thunder above us as chaos erupts everywhere. "*End them all.*"

Hana starts to charge out into it, her fury set on Rubeus, but I catch her arm before she leaves the cover of the hedge. She whirls to face me ready to fight, her eyes wild with the Ancients' command.

"Wait," I mouth to her. She's too weakened to fight against such a foe, but the fact that she's so blinded by the Grove's influence scares me. I wonder if everyone else on the hunt has been affected the same way.

"Let go," she growls, yanking to break my hold. Thorns sprout from her smooth skin beneath my hands, tearing through my palms. I cry out in pain, and when she realizes what she's done, Hana drops to her knees and takes my hands in hers. Her skin is so pale and clammy, I'm afraid she'll pass out.

Outside the brambles, the battle is relentless and brutal. All around us, Druids and trees and creatures scream and howl with pain or determination or anguish. The storm rages, tearing trees from their roots, sending debris piercing across hundreds of fallen figures.

Peering through the hedge, it's impossible to see what creatures they're up against. It's more than just shadows and Sorcerers, though. The mass of them is too many, too fast. I glimpse Father plowing through creature after creature, skewering them on his spear as he works to rid us of the threat.

A red doe watches from the outskirts of the clearing. Amma. Eyes for the Grove.

"*Stand,*" a command bristles though my feather. "*You need but three shots, young one. Courageous one.*"

Three shots. One for each Sorcerer. My heart pounds. I find the gap and nock my arrow. Shadows and creatures writhe across the clearing, locked in battle with Druids swinging spears and daggers and swords and slings. So many have fallen on both sides, and still more dark creatures spill through the tear I created.

What have I done?

"*You have done as we bade you,*" they reply. "*Now, find your mark.*"

"*Gorhen.*"

He's the nearest, standing just paces away, conjuring spells to tear screaming trees up by their roots and fling them into the fray, turning raindrops into spears of glass that slice into his enemies. I follow his movements with the tip of my arrow. The arrowhead flares with pure white light as I release it, and it thumps into him effortlessly, engulfing him in flames.

"*Alayne.*"

I remember the cold swipe of her hand as her shadow held me over the flood, and my next arrow finds her with an easy *thwack*. She, too, bursts into flames, and the shadows that had surged into the clearing dissipate. Her control of her dark minions breaks, and the creatures of the forest scatter, mostly back through the rift in the border wards.

"*Rubeus.*"

His name makes my blood run cold. I scan the fight for him and find him locked in a magic-to-spear battle with Father. I nock my arrow and watch as Father's broad spear tip jabs into the Sorcerer's robes and comes away red. Surprisingly spry despite his weakness, Rubeus skulks backward, casting a ward to protect him from the next spear attack.

I train my aim, following the two. The white light streaks along the shaft and the arrowhead bursts with that same orange glow, but Father moves in front of me, blocking my shot. He swings again and his spear sinks into Rubeus's throat.

"*Now.*"

My finger twitches under the Ancients' influence, but I tighten my grip, refusing.

I think of how Rubeus licked his fingers after leaving Hana's vines white and limp. I think of the healers lying spent in the mud and the rain. I think of Amma. How he tortured her. How he abused her. A single shot is too good for that wolf. He deserves to be skewered by Father's spear a hundred times over.

My hesitation costs Father. The Sorcerer musters his last bit of strength and leaps at Father, catching him around the throat. His wolf claws dig into Father's neck, causing beads of blood to pool beneath them. The hunt surges to his defense, swarming around the two of them, blocking any clean shot I might have had.

"*Fire.*"

The command comes with a stabbing pain that shoots through my temple and cheek, and my fingers release the bowstring. The arrow soars through the air, slips into the struggle, and meets its mark impossibly.

White flames engulf Rubeus, who screams and claws at his cloak, falling to the ground. I stare in disbelief at first, until I realize what it means.

"Yes!" I yelp with excitement. "Did you see that, Hana? Three in a—"

I look down to where she'd been kneeling and find Hana toppled over, a red slash of blood blooming across her chest.

"Hana, no," I whisper, gathering her into my arms as her white vines slump around her.

"Help!" I scream. She's still. Too still. Too white. She's barely breathing. Now I understand why they call healing a greater gift. I feel useless with her limp in my arms, her sap-like blood caked between us. "Help us!"

They hear me. Healers, I hope. Someone is running toward me. Past the brambles, they're coming.

"Hold on, Hana," I cry.

Someone is nearby. Someone who will help.

"In here!" I shout. "Hurry!"

Just on the other side of the hedge, something moves. It slips through to us, dark and creeping. A shadow. Before I can react, it lashes out and I'm sliced by some weapon I can't see. I look down in disbelief at my own blood spilling, mixing into Hana's, and I pull her closer, supporting the weight of her lolling head as I feel myself grow weaker.

"HELP US!" I scream again before I'm overcome with dizziness, and I slump sideways into the mud.

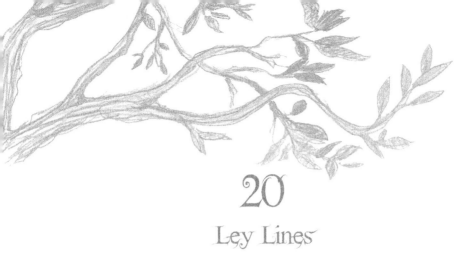

20

Ley Lines

The sunlit glen of Mya's dreams has become a place of solace in the weeks since the midnight hunt. With her in my arms, cloaked in my high elf deception, it's easy to forget everything else. I can pretend to be who I'm not, soothed by her voice, comforted by simple warmth and pleasure. And even if it's just in Dreaming, kissing her is amazing.

Eventually, of course, she wakes and fades away, leaving me alone. Like so many other things, I realize her lingering warmth isn't real, so I've taken to the silver ley lines to search for her in Waking.

Waves crash at my feet as I scout along the coastline of Elespen. The first time I came this far out without a path I was feeling defiant. Emboldened by Mya's whispered musings of adventures together, just the two of us. High elf and human. Singer and scout.

Without a path, I was Wandering, and I knew it. But it didn't matter. She loves me, and I love her. When I'm with her, everything else is second. Even Hana.

Hana.

Thoughts of her tug at my heart. At Amma's urging, I've tried not to blame myself for what happened to Father or to Hana. Not to feel responsible, somehow. But I hesitated at the hunt, and he was hurt. I was right there with her, and she fell. No matter what anyone says, it is my fault.

I'll probably believe it until the fleck of fear in Father's bold eyes that was never there before fades. Until Hana is healed. Until she can return from the fold and tell me herself there was nothing I could have done. That she forgives me. That we're still the friends we have always been.

I hope she returns soon, but with each day that passes I wonder whether she'll return at all. Twelve children of the Grove were lost to the hunt. Twelve were returned to the roots in grave, somber ceremonies. Not all at once. One by one, day after day over all these weeks.

At the time, the hunt had seemed so exciting. So necessary. At the time, we were all so charged with the need for vengeance and justice for what Rubeus did. At the time, it made sense that we should rally together and fight. But if all it took were three arrows guided by the Ancients, what was the point? Why hunt at all? Why put so many lives at risk?

Please, Hana. Please come back.

Since the hunt, since I started going this far out, I feel like I'm overly aware. Too many thoughts stir in my mind. Disturbing thoughts of how things are in the Grove. Things Rubeus said to me in the Dreaming about us being brainwashed masses. Questions I know I shouldn't have. Resentment.

Thinking on that, really thinking hard, it's impossible for me to tell what's real and what's been tampered with anymore. What's been given to me? What's been taken away? What's left? It's all a jumble. A casting of stones and bones of the memories that make me who I am, that I have no will to decipher.

The farther I venture from the Grove without a path, the more these thoughts needle me. Scouting this way is risky. As the distance grows, the strands that hold me to myself all the way back in the Hamlet grow so thin they might snap. I might end up divided in two; my second self left to Wander in the Dreaming until my body, stuck asleep at home, withers to nothing just like Amma almost did.

Maybe it's because of what I've been through, but that idea doesn't really scare me like it used to.

Mya hasn't been at the Millers' farm for weeks when I search for her in the In-between. I have no idea where she is in Waking. I have only been able to follow the trail of her scent, mixed with horses, to Cresten where it ends on the docks.

She never said anything about a ship to me in Dreaming, but, admittedly, we don't do a lot of talking. Still, there have been some nights where she hasn't dreamed at all. On top of that, there was an uproar at the mill about stolen barrels. The patrolmen are searching for her, too, and someone else whose name they don't mention. A female thief. All of it worries me. I've even tried to search for her pa, but I can't find him anywhere, either.

Did she decide to run off to adventure alone without telling me? Why has she eluded me in Dreaming?

Along the northern shore of Elespen, I raise my nose and sniff, gazing hopefully toward the horizon, but there's no trace of Mya in the wind that blows from the sea. I hop up, my feet catching air, and push myself into the sky far above the endless expanse of blue ocean that stretches between two continents, staying within the confines of the straight, silvery ley line.

As I run on the wind searching for a ship that might carry her, my thoughts veer back to that night. The thundering voice over the hunt rumbles in my memories. The feral, mindless reactions of the children of the Grove flash in my mind's eye.

I wonder how different things might have gone if I never lured Rubeus out of his lair, or fired that arrow into the border wards to let them all in. I try not to think about how I probably had no choice in the matter—how many times I never had a choice, really, or how none of us in the Grove do.

Over the sparkling sea midway between Elespen and Cerion's cliffs, a path opens to me. I know it well. White pebbles. Pink mist through willow fronds. An invitation to the fold.

"*Wanderer,*" they call.

My heart leaps. Hana. I could see her. I could tell her how sorry I am. I could finally know if she's well. When she's coming back.

But what if she isn't coming back? What if she agrees all of it was my fault? What if they changed her? What if they're just trying to get me to stop Wandering and come home?

I turn away from the path, and my right ear buzzes with warning. Aft'elu. I thought I would have forgotten that name by now, but for some reason it lingers with me. For this reason, probably. To make me trust. To make me go back to them.

They know I'm suffering from this awareness. They'll take it from me, whether Hana forgives me or not.

Either way, if I journey down that path, I know I'll never be the same. Hana would understand, I hope. I'd rather keep what I know. I'd rather become a Wanderer.

When the white sea cliffs of Cerion finally break on the distant horizon, my heart sinks. I managed to spot only four ships in all the ocean along my careful path, and Mya wasn't on any of them.

I trot on the wind, letting it lift me over the now-familiar golden dome of the Academy where the ley line I'm traveling intersects with the one that goes through the palace and on to the Grove.

A voice drifts on the wind as I soar over the palace: "Lord Filian of the Knights of Conquer has stepped forward."

Knights of Conquer? I remember the flood. How everyone cheered for the Sorcerers cloaked in red. I veer closer and come to land lightly on the same palace balcony where I spied Lisabella and Tirnon playing at swords during the ball.

"Lord Filian," a different voice calls, "please come nearer. Tell what your scouts have determined."

I creep forward on the balcony, stopping beside the armored leg of a palace guard, and peer into the crowd of brightly dressed courtiers. Light spills from stained-glass windows in the ceiling far above them, splashing their mostly red garb with colorful sunbeams.

I sniff, but I smell no rot. No dark magic. There is a hint of deception, though, mixed with disrespect. And citrus oil.

"Your Majesty," Filian bows before the elderly king, who sits on his huge throne propped up by pillows and bolsters and draped snugly in a thick velvet cloak despite the warm sunlight. "A report in my lord Synnen Archomyn's own hand, from a letter we received just this morning."

The king nods, and Filian continues.

"On the outskirts of Sorlen Grove, just within its borders, our scouts thought they had discovered three effigies burning with magical fire. They risked a closer look, moving just ten paces from the border's edge.'"

This causes a ripple of astonished murmurs from the gathering, disbelief that the scouts would dare to get so close. Filian looks around like he's pleased his story is inspiring such a reaction. He allows his words to hang for a dramatic pause before he continues.

"Once close enough to feel the border wards prickling their skin, they were able to determine that the effigies were, in truth, the bodies of three of our Mages who had so willingly aided in rescue and recovery after the great flood at Sorlen River Crossing, saving countless lives."

"They weren't Mages," I want to shout. "They were Sorcerers!" But even if I was in the right form to shout, I know I shouldn't dare.

While the audience whispers amongst themselves, I creep even closer and sniff the damp, heavy summer air within the throne room. I catch Filian's scent: rare meat, steel, wine, as it flutters from the hem of his short, red, silk-lined cloak. His black slippers click on the stone floor as he takes a couple of steps toward the king to hear him speak.

As old, wrinkled, and feeble as he looks, the king's eyes flash brightly while they flick over his subjects to take in their reactions. At his left stands a man wearing a gray robe slashed with a red sash and a high, strange-looking hat. At his right, on a throne set slightly lower and further back on the platform than the king, sits Prince Tirnon. Finn, the guard from the balcony, stands stoic beside the prince.

Tirnon's eyes narrow slightly as he watches the room, and as I test the wards cast across the balcony entry with the tip of my nose, the prince leans forward and rests a hand on the king's arm. Before he can whisper, though, the king speaks.

"Concerning, indeed," he says.

I glance up at Filian for his reaction and catch his smug glance in the prince's direction before he quickly changes his expression to neutral. The prince doesn't miss the look, though, and leans even closer to the king.

"Father," he says with curiosity, "I thought the Druids of Sorlen Grove kept to themselves as part of our treaties. Why would they attack us, their allies, unless they had been provoked?"

"Ah, that is a fair question, a fair question, my son," says the king, patting the prince's hand. I take in the wrinkles around the old king's mouth and eyes, wrinkles that seem like they must have come from years of smiling. I can tell he's been a fair king. A happy king. The way his subjects watch him with reverence, quieting to hear him speak, reminds me of our own Elders in the Grove.

It's obvious they respect him deeply. Even as self-assured and commanding as Filian is, he seems to yearn for His Majesty's favor.

"Prince Tirnon," the man standing on the king's other side says with a lilt in his voice that sounds like he's explaining things to a child. "The Druids are simple forest folk. They have no real grasp of the importance of treaties and formal agreements. It would not at all surprise me to hear that they had perhaps misjudged and attacked our Mages in savage ignorance."

My ears twitch as I listen to his condescending tone, and my tail flicks angrily. We are not simple, and they're the ones who broke our agreement by tampering with our borders. Lord Filian catches the adviser's eye and winks almost imperceptibly. No one else seems to notice except Tirnon, whose scowl deepens.

"I'm sure the prince meant no disrespect to our fine Mages," says Filian, "but they know well enough where the territory lines are drawn, and they would never risk our peace by venturing too close or daring to endanger our alliance with the Grove. Especially not those of our guild. The Knights of Conquer have the utmost reverence for His Majesty's great kingdom, its laws, and its lands, as has been proven by our efforts at Sorlen River Crossing."

The prince leans to his father's ear and whispers, and Filian and the adviser exchange glances again while the king's attention is drawn away.

"Your Majesty," the adviser ventures, "this blatant act of violence cannot go unchecked. If we are to strike, we must do so swiftly and with conviction."

The prince and the king continue to whisper, and a hush falls over the gathering while everyone waits for his declaration. Finally, the king nods and waves the prince away, and sits up a little straighter in his throne.

"As we have no real proof of the events which led to the demise of the three Mages, we cannot in good conscience retaliate," His Majesty declares.

The crowd erupts into a rush of whispers, and a few shouts of protest, but the king raises his hand, and they quiet down again.

"We shall meet with our advisers, and a quest shall be declared. The Druids of the Grove steep themselves in secrets, so much so that we have no way of contacting them. But we shall, by quest, attempt to make contact and hear their explanations."

"His Majesty is most wise," Lord Filian says with a bow so exaggerated it almost seems like he's mocking the king. "Our men would be honored to be given such a quest."

The prince whispers again and the king nods, eyeing Lord Filian thoughtfully.

"I wonder whether Lord Archomyn would be as eager," says the king. "Your great leader has been absent from our presence for nearly a half-year now."

"It's true, my lord has been delayed, Your Majesty," Lord Filian replies, glancing from the king a little hesitantly. "My lord Synnen wished to present this matter to you himself, but the rebuilding of Sorlen River Crossing in your name was too important for him to leave to another. He sends his most heartfelt promise that he shall return to His Majesty's court in a fortnight or less."

Maybe it's because I rarely see or hear lies among my own people that the deception in his tone and in his stance are surprisingly obvious to me. The prince seems to notice. If the king does, too, he doesn't show it.

"Another fortnight," Prince Tirnon utters under his breath so that even the king doesn't seem to hear.

"Very well, Lord Filian," says the king. "Thank you."

"Your Majesty," Lord Filian impresses, his cold gaze flicking away from Tirnon, "Lord Synnen remains ever devoted to you, as do all of your loyal Knights."

"Yet not enough to grace us with his presence after our many requests," the king says with a tone of finality. "Thank you, Lord Filian. And with that business done," he stands with little trouble at all for someone who looks so old and frail, and opens his hands to the group, "let us retire to our meal."

As the crowd files out of the throne room, the king, still standing, turns to his adviser.

"Go in, go in, Keres," says the king. "I would have a word with my son alone."

The adviser gives the prince a smug look, like he's sure the prince is about to have a scolding, then shuffles off behind the others.

As soon as the throne room is cleared of its subjects, the king leans heavily on the prince's offered arm and gives a groan of exhaustion.

"Father," Tirnon whispers with concern as Finn steps closer to them both. "You went too long."

The king gives a dismissive wave.

"Will you at least allow me to send for the healers?" Tirnon asks with concern.

"My son, there is only so much healing an old man can tolerate," the king replies, his voice growing raspy. He wobbles a little, and Tirnon settles him back into his throne while they talk.

"Tell me," the king looks up into the younger man's face and coughs with a wet, gurgling sound. "What do you make of all of it?"

The prince crouches at his father's arm and looks at him earnestly.

"It doesn't make sense, Father. The borders have been drawn for generations. Why would the Druids of the Grove suddenly ignore them to attack our Mages?"

"Indeed," says the king, urging the prince to continue.

"It's more likely that Synnen's men pressed too close, or even tried to cross, and were punished for it." The prince stands up and paces, raking a hand through his sandy curls. "His absence, the collapsing silos, the flood, now this. Father, it seems obvious to me that they're behind all of it. The more that happens, the more I suspect it."

"But a fair king should not take action based solely on suspicion," says the elder man. "In matters such as this, with so many of their number behind them, we must be certain. We must have proof."

"Finn," says the king, and the guard stands a little taller. "Once we've gone in for our meal, have them fetch Sir Josten and Lady Crisanne from Solace Hall and bring them straight into my cabinet."

Finn bows, and the prince's relieved look turns quickly to concern.

"Perhaps a rest first, Father. It can wait a day."

The king flicks his hand dismissively and pushes himself stubbornly to his feet again. "If I allow Crisanne to heal me while we meet," the king barters while the trio move slowly toward the dining hall, "will you stop pestering me?"

"Yes, Father," says the prince, relieved. He glances across the king at Finn, who offers him a subtle, approving nod, and they disappear through the doors that release a puff of delectable scents that make my stomach rumble as they close behind them.

With no one left to watch aside from the palace guards who stand as stoic as our Grove Guardians, I leap into the sky and let the wind catch me. Reluctantly, I head homeward to the Grove's westernmost border, to make myself look at what I know is still there. What the king's men were talking about. What *I* did, guided by the Ancients' words.

Sorcerers, skewered on stakes. Three of them, still alight with wispflame after all these weeks.

A reminder of the hunt and all that happened. A warning to anyone else who dares meddle with the Druids of Sorlen Grove.

21

Bitter Farewell

At the edge of the Outer Grove, tucked close to the remains of Hana's domed brambles, I sit in fox form gazing through the border wards. They were repaired the night of the hunt, of course. The rift I tore with my arrow is gone. The three Sorcerers remain, though, upright on their spikes, still glowing white with wispfire like beacons as dusk falls around them.

The gentle sound of hooves on pine needles rustles nearby, and I glance to the side to see the red doe edging closer, her ears pricked for danger. I look away and curl into myself, hoping she'll take it as a sign that I don't want to talk to her.

I don't want to talk to anyone.

When Amma steps into her true form and says, "*Sheshi*," I tuck my nose into my paws and close my eyes.

She kneels beside me, her suede dress softly brushing the fur of my shoulder. Instead of saying anything, she gazes out across the wards, wispfire dancing in her unshed tears.

"You missed supper again," she says quietly. "You must be hungry."

I'm not. I had some rabbit. Some trout from the brook. A clutch of duck eggs. I don't need the Ancients. I can take care of myself.

She strokes the top of my head, and after a long period of silence, she ventures, "you can talk to me, my sweet one. About anything."

I glance up at her and consider it, but then I close my eyes again. I know she means well, but we both know it isn't true.

No secrets.

My tail flicks with annoyance.

"Is it about the girl?" she asks. "The human?"

That makes me sit up. The only way she could know about Mya is if she had been following me in Dreaming. Or if the Ancients found out through the feather and told her. Aft'elu can speak to me through it. Make me do things. They can probably spy on me, too.

My tail flicks with deeper anger. Mya is mine. My peace. I refuse to answer for her, for what we have.

"I understand," Amma says. "I know what it feels like to find someone outside. Someone exotic and alluring, who is nothing like anyone you have known."

I stare at her in disbelief, and for the first time in her presence since the hunt, I shift to my true form. Her eyes go wide for just a blink before she makes her face go smooth again. Concerned.

"She's nothing like Rubeus," I say with more of an edge than I meant to, and Amma winces. "It isn't the same."

She reaches for me. Strokes my cheek. Pulls me to her and tucks me into the hollow of her shoulder where I used to sleep all those years ago when I was just learning to scout.

"It isn't," I insist. "Mya is pure and good, Amma. She doesn't know about the Grove. She doesn't even know who I really am."

"And yet you think you love her," she whispers. "Love cannot thrive on lies, *Sheshi*. Not even well-intended ones. You are a dream to her. Nothing more. And even that is more than you should be."

I say nothing. I wish I had stayed a fox and avoided talking about it.

"You torment yourself, my son. For what?" she sighs, stroking my hair, kissing my head just above the feather, turning me gently away from the wispflame. "It's over, *Sheshi*. You were courageous. You were the hands of the Ancients. You did what was required of you, and now it is done. Let go of this burden, before you become lost as I was. It breaks my heart to watch you fall to Wandering."

I look up at her, watching her tears reflect the flames as they trail down her cheeks.

"Come back to us, dear one," she whispers. "I know you are tired. It's over now. Let us be the family we once were. Let me care for you as you cared for me all that time."

Beyond her in the forest, a golden wisp emerges. I think of the past weeks, worrying, wandering, searching. I think of all my guilt and anger. The wisp drifts nearer, glowing warmly, enticing me.

"Come," Amma says, rising to her feet. She offers me her hand, and I take it. Here in the Grove, with the wisp so near, I realize she's right. I've been clinging to these troubling thoughts for so long now, searching for something I can't find.

The glittering center of the golden wisp grows larger and larger until the white pebble path sprawls out of it, edged in pink mist.

"*Courageous one,*" it says.

The moment I step onto the path, relief spills over me. Pink dust kicks up behind me as I enter through the gentle willows. Everything goes silent.

"Amma?" I call, but there's no answer. She's gone.

Suddenly I remember I've been avoiding this path. I remember why.

"*Elliot*," Aft'elu's soothing voice echoes from deep within the mist. They say something else, but I can't hear it over the sound of my heartbeat thudding in my ears.

I have to get out of here. They'll make me forget. I can't let them. My memories are a part of me. Mya is a part of me. I have to keep them.

"*You do not need them*," Aft'elu's whisper echoes from the feather at my right ear. If I were a fox now, my ear would surely twitch. I rub my nose and push the feather back over my shoulder.

When I turn to try and duck back through the willows, there are none. There's only thick pink mist.

The longer I stand breathing in the fog, the calmer I feel. My heart slows to a relaxed pace, and after some contemplation, I don't quite remember why I was so reluctant to come here. The way the light shines diffused through the mist and the slender trunks of pure white birch is so pleasant.

The Grove is my home, and such a beautiful place. I resented it, avoided it, but the reason why eludes me. This is where I belong. This is where I'm loved and cared for.

As I stroll along the path the air begins to clear, revealing more of the pristine birch grove. Far ahead, a pool of aether casts a blue-green glow along the white trunks in a breathtaking display. Drawn to it, I quicken my pace as golden wisps bob at my shoulders, tethered by strands of memories that spill away from me.

My mind feels so much lighter, so carefree. I can't remember the last time I felt this content. I can't remember much of anything, really, but it doesn't bother me. I feel so much peace, so much contentedness, so much relief.

Aft'elu is waiting when I reach the pool, watching me with a loving smile. Their golden skin shimmers with flashes of blue and green from the pond that dance across my face, filling me with joy.

They tilt their head, watching me, waiting for something. For me to speak, maybe, but there's no reason to. I have everything I need in this moment. I'm loved by the Grove. I'm honored by Aft'elu's presence.

"There is much you have been through, little fox," they say. Their voice is like the sound of light itself. In it I hear the vastness of the Ancients, from roots to leaves to sunlight. They venture closer and stroke my cheek just above my right ear, and my skin tingles deliciously. "And now, this burden is lifted from you."

Something is taken away. The wing feather. The gift they gave me last time I was here. I choke back a sob and reach for it, but when they draw their hand away, it's already gone.

"Do not lament," they say gently. "You remain a favored child of the Grove. You have been our eyes and ears in Cerion, and for that we are grateful. Now we can prepare, and you may rest. You have no need to cling to all your eyes and ears have beheld. There is no need for you to fret over any of it, our beloved son."

I draw in a breath of relief and let it out slowly, and with it I feel all my tension melt away.

"Now, sleep, child, and we shall behold your future."

Washed in the glow of the Lifesap, I curl up in the soft grass at the edge of the pool and fall asleep.

Mya's voice greets me as I enter Dreaming, but rather than lead me to our meadow, I find myself in an unfamiliar hallway. Firelight casts a merry glow across stonework that's strange to the Grove, but my heart knows it, somehow.

Home.

I follow the soft blue carpet, marveling in the sound of her voice. I've been looking for her. Searching oceans, and now she's here. Her song brings me a sense of contentment even deeper than Aft'elu's peace.

She's so close. Just beyond that door. My hand rests on the latch. My heart races. I nearly forget my high elf disguise before I pull the door open and step through. The room within is a cozy den with soft, comfortable chairs to curl up in and an enormous hearth with a crackling fire. Even though it's place I'm sure I've never been before, I know it. I belong here.

Mya.

She strums her lute, lazily picking out a melody to match the perfection of her voice, and I sink into the chair beside her. She watches me, smiling with a look in her eyes that I know is only ever meant for me. I reach across to her, tracing her cheek with my elven fingers to convince myself it's really her. She's really here.

"I feared for you," I whisper, remembering the Millers and her scent on the road ending at the docks. "I could not find you."

"I am at sea," she replies. "Traveling to Cerion."

Cerion. I remember a balcony. A palace. A prince.

"What are you doing here?" a warning voice booms across us from all around us, resonating from the stone of the walls and the fibers of the chairs where we sit.

"Father?" I whisper, feeling my face drain of color. How could he have found me? How could he know I'm here?

"What is it?" Mya asks from what feels like far away, still strumming her lute.

"This is not where you are meant to be, boy," Father's voice booms. Within his voice, I hear a second, more powerful one. Aft'elu. The Ancients. It isn't him at all. It's them.

"Sleep, child, and we shall behold your future." My future. This isn't what they expected. I can smell their anger, their confusion. I remember what Hana told me forever ago: *"You aren't meant to stay in the Grove. You're called away on another path. To Cerion."*

"Why do you resist us?" Aft'elu whispers into my mind, but I fight their influence. This feels right. More right than the Grove, or the Ancients, or even Amma.

Amma. Was that really her? No, it couldn't have been. They tricked me. They deceived me with that wisp. They lured me. They used me, and now they mean to take it all away. And now they wonder why I resist.

I feel them nearing, somehow. Presences. Wisps. If they reach me, I know I'll forget again.

"I'm sorry," I say to Mya, and kiss her gently. "I must go."

I try hard to sound calm even though I know I have to run. I have to figure out a way to get out of the fold, out of the mist. But this is her dream. I don't want to frighten her.

The wisps are nearing. I feel them rather than see them. I feel Aft'elu, too. They're so close. Listening, like they have been. Watching me. Watching everything through me.

"I will return to you, my darling. Be safe, and keep heart," I tell her, defying Aft'elu's whispered warnings.

"Wait," Mya calls, and takes my hand, but I step away and turn my back and run from her, away from the future I shouldn't have seen. I run through memories of places and events I ought to have forgotten, but can't. They're too fixed in my mind, too important to who I'm meant to be.

"You aren't meant to stay in the Grove. You're called away on another path. To Cerion."

"I am at sea. Traveling to Cerion."

Cerion.

"Courageous one. Beloved son of the Grove."

I shift myself to fox form, speeding away faster, faster as golden wisps chase. I race over continents, across sunrises and sunsets and days and nights but they gain and grow and pulse. Their presence tangles around my paws and guides me back, all the way to the Grove, to my home, to the fold.

Pink wisps cling to me, lifting me, carrying me. I'm not afraid. I feel nothing. Only peace. Welcome emptiness. The pulse of Lifesap. I'm one with the roots. One with the trunks of the almighty Ancients. They are all that matter. By their Grace, the fold cares for me, nurtures me, and protects me. I am theirs. I belong here. I belong to them.

I sleep dreamlessly for days until I find myself rambling over a new path of sun-dappled dirt. Melodies play in the leaves as the wind gently tousles my hair and the feather that flutters at my ear. A feather I thought I had lost.

"*No secrets from us,*" the Ancients' booming voices thunder in my ears, and I feel a rush of adoration and respect for their words.

"As the Grove wills it," I answer, calling up into the leaves. The melodies converge, carrying with them a sweet, perfect voice.

"Protection for all.

Duty above all.

Keep hidden, always…"

That last phrase comes with a hint of warning, of scolding. I'm not sure why until I catch a glimpse of red hair wandering along the path toward me and hear her voice. Mya.

"It has been some time," my disguised elven voice emanates from the trees, blending in perfect harmony with the melody of the leaves.

"I've wondered where you were," Mya calls. My heart races. I want to run to her, but I can't. Something inexplicable holds me back. I watch her as if through another person's eyes as she steps into the Grove and looks around in wonder.

"Is it because of that voice?" she asks. Across the Grove I see the elven figure I made myself seem to her, like I'm watching someone else's dream. "Your father?"

I feel a shiver of fear, remembering our last meeting that feels like only moments ago to me, but must have been days or weeks to her.

She wanders the edges of the Grove, grazing the trunks of trees with wonder, humming to herself.

"A Druid's Grove," she whispers.

"Do you remember," the elf murmurs behind her, so close I can almost feel her presence myself, "what I said when we first met?"

"What's happening?" I whisper to the ones who I know are listening. The ones who I know are behind all of this. Aft'elu. "Why are you showing me this?"

"*She is an enchantress. A siren. Ties must be cut,*" comes the answer. "*Our beloved son.*"

Mya stares ahead at the moss, never turning to look at the elf I once was. I creep along the outskirts of the Grove, moving closer despite the unspoken warnings that make my stomach churn.

"You said, 'You are not what you seem, and neither am I,'" she answers. She puts a hand on her own shoulder, and my elf apparition grazes her fingertips. Their heartbeats pulse over the Grove, thundering in my ears.

"*We have seen the bond between you,*" Aft'elu says into my mind. "*We have endeavored to break it, and yet, it cannot be broken. If you wish it, she can remain here, a child of the Grove as you are.*"

I step into the high elf, feeling my fingers slide into place where his once were. With the feel of her warmth under my hand, I remember everything. Everything they took away from me. Dreams and visions I didn't even realize I'd seen. Things they hid from me to keep me here. Their beloved son.

No secrets. Unless they're the ones keeping them.

I see what I saw when I was running from the wisps, a battle that brought Mya to the brink of death, a scream that made men fall. She could be an asset to the Grove. Our bloodline would be unusual and strong.

"You've been through trials," I whisper with the high elf's voice. "Recently, you've brushed with death."

She nods, and the golden wisp ebbs between us, showing me her memories like a mirror.

I say something else, but my voice is strange and distant as I pull myself back into my own mind.

"Were you on the corsair?" she asks me, and at first I don't know what she means, but then the wisps show me the battle up close. Two ships at sea; one filled with Sorcerers, the other pirates. Mya screaming, clinging to a mast as her ship lists dangerously. Sorcerers falling to their knees, clutching their bleeding ears.

"No," I answer. "I despise Sorcerers. I travel on the wind, Mya. I go where the Ancients guide me, and they brought me to you."

I don't realize it's the truth until it leaves my lips. Every path is set before me by the Grove. If I found her, it's because they wanted me to. They led me to her. And now they want me to make this choice for her. To take her from her life and bring her here, where they would mold her as they've molded me. Make her forget. Make her one of us. One of them.

"I must leave you," I tell her, and feel her anguish as I speak the words. "I think of nothing and no one but you, and my heart feels it will break with these words, but I must not see you again."

"*Your choice is made, then, beloved son.*"

"But, why?" she asks, her voice filled with desperation.

"Because I have deceived you," my voice cracks as it's taken over by them, and I feel the shame of what I've done wash over me.

Keep hidden, always.

"And broken an unbreakable law." I never should have gone to her. I never should have let myself get so close. I trace my fingers along her skin, knowing it'll be the last time I ever touch her, knowing how close I came to putting her in real danger.

"I don't care if you deceived me," she replies tearfully, stepping backward, closer to me. "I need you. I can't lose you."

"I am not who I presented to you. I am no elf."

"*Say farewell,*" they tell me with compassion, but I can't help but feel the need to explain myself to her.

"The first time I heard your voice, I had to see you. I traveled leagues across the Dreaming, lured by it. I wanted to impress you, to enchant you as you enchanted me. And so I made myself something I wasn't. I made myself what I always wished to be. An elf, elegant and bold, with a presence that couldn't be ignored. I misused my talent selfishly, in a way that's forbidden by my people." I put you in danger, I want to say, but can't bring myself to admit it. It would allude to the Grove.

I feel disjointed, like I'm them and myself and the high elf all blended into one. I don't know which words are mine and which are theirs. I only know shame for what I've done and fear for what might become of her. She's an outsider, and now she's been exposed, and it's my fault. I imagine the Sorcerers burning on pikes at our border's edge, and I shiver.

"But you meant no harm," she argues. "You only wanted to meet me."

"That is the harm," I whisper, feeling the power of the admission of guilt rushing through me.

"*Say farewell,*" they tell me again, this time with a hint of command in their tone.

"Show me," she says softly, twining her fingers into mine as I pull her closer. "If you have to leave me, at least show me first who you really are. Please."

Her tone is a command even stronger than Aft'elu's, even stronger than the Ancients. It compels me to do as she asks. The feather shimmers with magic to ward her suggestion, and I find the strength to argue against her will.

"It's forbidden," I whisper apologetically. How I wish I could show her the truth.

"To me, it's only a dream, isn't it? I may not even remember after I wake. Please," she begs and starts to turn toward me, but I stop her, trying hard to be gentle. "Let me see you, so I can remember you for who you are, for your true self."

"Show her, then. She will think it a dream, and you will have your farewell," they say, resigned.

"May I kiss you?" I ask, "one last time, as the elf you knew?"

The wind in the leaves slows enough that the rushing sound of our heartbeats together overwhelms it.

"You may," she whispers, sounding slightly nervous.

"Close your eyes, then, my only," I murmur, and turn her to face me.

"Look one last time upon her, beloved son. After this day, you shall not see her again. After this day, you shan't remember." With those words spoken, I feel them leave my presence.

I kiss her with their words echoing in my mind. I kiss her knowing I saved her from something I can't explain. Something that even as I begin to understand it myself, it gets taken from me only to begin the journey again from the start. As we kiss, I feel myself changing back into my true form, releasing the disguise, letting go of who I wished I could be so I can grasp who I truly am.

From now on I'll stand in my own skin, no matter where I am. I'll find my truth and wear it proudly, no matter how many times they try to take it from me or make me hide it. I blink, and realize that somehow during our kiss, she opened her eyes.

"You weren't supposed to look," I say, feeling a little bashful.

She takes me in, gazing into my eyes, tracing her fingertips over the pointed tip of my ear, sending a shiver of a thrill rushing through me.

"You are too an elf," she teases.

"Just a wood elf," I say quietly, trying hard to play it down. Trying hard not to let her hear the grief in my voice at having to leave her forever. "Not nearly as impressive as a high elf."

"But you are," she disagrees, and her fingers find the feather in my braid. Aft'elu's feather. "Even more impressive."

I roll my eyes at that, and she tucks herself closer to me, resting her head on my chest. For a moment I wonder whether it's too late to change my mind. She could come with me. Stay with me. We could live together in the Grove. We could be happy.

"Will you finally tell me your name now?" she asks, taking in a deep breath as she nuzzles my vest.

"Elliot," I answer with a bit of defiance. After all, it's only a dream to her, like they said. I kiss her temple, and she gazes into my face as if expecting to hear the rest of it. I shake my head slowly.

"Already I've gone too far," I say, not bothering to hide the sorrow in my voice. It's time, I know. Time to say goodbye. She knows, too.

"Thank you for everything," she tells me. "For all the time you've given and the secrets we've shared. I'll never forget you, Elliot. Never."

"I won't forget you either, Mya Songspinner. Not ever," I say, even though I know it isn't true. Even if I was desperate to remember, they'd make me forget. They already said they would. "Now, it's time for you to wake up."

I kiss her forehead sweetly and feel her fade from my arms as I wake at the edge of the pool, gazing blankly into the hypnotic sparkle of the Lifesap.

22

Grove Life

The gentle sound of rain pattering on the rooftop wakes me along with Kaini's snoring. Sleepily, I graze my fingers across the smooth wooden wall at my head and whisper, "Grandymum, is it raining everywhere? Will it rain all day?"

"De-li-cious sum-mer rain," croaks Grandymum. "Wat-ter-ing all the Grove. We hope it does, lit-tle kit."

I huff and prop myself onto my elbow to look across at Kaini. I'd hate for him to be disappointed. We were supposed to swim at Echo Pool today. Maybe it won't thunderstorm, and we can still go. I was looking forward to it, too.

The raindrops tapping at the windowsill grow more insistent, until I realize those aren't raindrops at all. I scramble from my bed and push open the shutter just a crack to look out, and Hana's vines reach through and tug me close to her. Her gray eyes flash with mischief and excitement as she rests her arms on my shoulders and touches the tip of her nose to mine.

"We're still going, right?" she whispers excitedly as her vines curl into my hair.

"Of course," I reply, grinning as I brush my fingertips across the bark of her arms. "But we'll have to make sure we come back with twice as many berries this time, since they keep disappearing on the way back."

Hana shrugs impishly, and her sweet floral breath grazes my cheek as she leans forward to peer at Kaini. Behind her shoulder, a vine of fragrant blue flowers lifts a giant gathering basket to show me.

"Good." I nod and follow her gaze to Kaini's bed, framed by walls full of feathers and pinecones and freshwater shells and all the treasures he's discovered on our adventures through the Grove. I feel a pang of sadness, a fleeting feeling that something dear is missing, but it fades quickly as Little Brother groans and stretches. My heart swells with love for him. He's so adorable.

Deep in the house I hear the front door close followed by father's heavy footsteps coming down the hall. He goes into Amma's room and tenderly greets her good morning.

"I have to get ready," I whisper, reaching for the shutter.

"I'll see you later," Hana winks. My eyes flick to hers and a flutter of excitement rushes through me as I nod and close the shutters.

At breakfast, the Ancients' canopy protects us from the driving rain, leaving the Sanctum dry and welcoming as always. We sit as a family in a circle with Sulien to my right and Kaini to my left and Amma and father opposite us. After the recitations and the wisps, Kaini trades his meat to me and I dish him half of my boysenberry cobbler, even though it's my favorite.

We share our plans for the day, laughing and joking and encouraging one another.

"Brother is taking me hunting for berries at Echo Pool, and then we'll go swimming, right?" Kaini asks, tugging my arm excitedly. I nod, smiling.

Across our small circle, Father peers up into the low blanket of gray, drenching clouds.

"It may well clear up," he says, nodding knowingly.

"But keep an ear pricked for thunder and come home if you hear it," Amma adds with a warm smile. "Father and I will be scouting the west border thunder or not, but we'll return for supper."

"Yes, Amma," I beam at her, and the warm way she looks at me fills me with affection.

"I'll be in the south," Brother Sulien adds. "Though it's been quiet there for days."

"They are coming," Father warns. "We must be vigilant, quiet or not. It has been foreseen. We must trust in the Ancients."

"Yes, Father," Sulien nods.

"What if the Cerion men get inside?" Kaini asks, shivering. He nudges closer to me, and I tuck my arm around him protectively.

"If they do, the Grove will protect us," I say. "They'll be swiftly punished."

"They will not breach, Kaini," Father assures him firmly. "They would not dare."

"Enough of this frightening talk," Amma says quietly, getting to her feet as others around us begin to leave. She comes to me and Kaini and strokes our hair back and kisses us both tenderly on the cheek. "My sweet ones. You are both too young for such worries. Go and play.

Have faith in the Grove that all will be well."

"Yes, Amma," Kaini and I reply together as Father comes to give us his blessing for the day. Sulien does the same, and we leave the Sanctum together.

"Watch this, Brother!" Kaini shouts over the hiss of the drenching rain. He runs to the cliff edge, his feet splashing in slick mud, and leaps out over the lake. He does a series of twists and somersaults all the way down until his splash mingles with thousands of raindrops plucking the surface of the lake. "You do it now!" he calls up to me as soon as he surfaces.

I shake out my arms and legs, sending out a spray of rainwater, and marvel at the feeling of the cool mud as it squishes between my toes. Grinning, I dart forward and, mid-leap, transform to fox form. My skin shivers to wet fur and whiskers on the way down but I don't miss a trick, spinning and flipping exactly the way Kaini did. His laughter rings out across the lake, weaving through the raindrops, making my heart leap as I splash into the water.

"I didn't know you were going to change," he says as I surface, his giggle nearly drowned out by the roar of the rain splashing around us. "That was so funny. I wish you could have seen yourself! Let's go again!" He pulls my front paws to his shoulders and paddles me toward the shore, and I shake the water from my ears and turn them to the sky, listening for thunder.

"Oh, look, it's Hana! Hana's here!" Kaini shouts, letting go of my paws to wave excitedly at her. My heart leaps and I swim forward to transform. Kaini clings to my back and I push my hair and feathers back over my shoulders and tow him to shore.

It's not long before his friends arrive, and we spend the morning climbing and diving and trying to best each other at speed, distance, and tricks. We laugh and play and scream until our throats are sore, and we stay in the water until our fingertips are wrinkled and our toes are puckered and sore from so much running and slipping on rocks and mud.

When thunder rumbles overhead and lightning cracks into the lake, we huddle together in the mouth of a nearby cave to wait out the worst of it.

"It stinks in here," says Kaini as he pats pink-glowing fingertips over his friend's scraped knee.

"It was a fox den," I answer, sniffing their lingering scent in the heavy air. "A mother and kits. They've grown up, though. Moved out."

Hana trails me silently as I slip deeper into the space. Her vines curl around my arms, ready to pull me back from anything lurking in the shadows. Something is familiar about this place. I feel like I've been here before. I peer into the darkest shadows and glimpse the memory of a bird, and folded parchment and, strangely, my room with sheets of drawings fluttering on the walls beside Kaini's bed.

Hana tugs me to the side and tucks me against the rocks, out of the view of the others. She gives me a coy smile as her vines draw us closer together, and she risks a quick kiss to my cheek. I crane my neck past her and when I'm sure no one is paying attention to us, I kiss her back. A clap of thunder outside makes us all jump and cry out in surprise, followed by peals of nervous laughter.

"What's back there?" Hana asks once we've calmed down again.

I glance from the darkness to her bright, eager face.

"Only shadows," I say, trying to clear the strange images that linger in my thoughts.

"To match the ones in your eyes," she whispers with concern.

"Look! The sun's coming out!" someone shouts, causing the others to whoop and crowd at the mouth of the cave.

I take Hana's hand and we rush to join them. The scene that greets us is strange. The gray-black line of storm clouds creeps off over the mountains. The rain has slowed to fat, lazy drops that splat occasionally into the mud and gravel. Above us, a swath of bright blue sky has broken through the gray, and the heat of the sunbeams is already baking off the rain, causing silvery mist to swirl from leaves and grass and stone.

"Look at those strange clouds," Kaini says, pointing westward where more clouds churn thick, black, and low over the treetops. My nose twitches, picking up the sharp scent of burning fresh wood and sap.

"Those aren't clouds," I say with a shaky voice. "That's smoke. The forest is burning."

Kaini turns to look at me, his face pale with fear. I know what he's thinking. Amma and Father are out there.

"Go look, Brother," he whispers through white lips. Hana's vines tighten around me protectively. I shake my head.

"I'm not supposed to."

A lingering clap of thunder rumbles into the frightened silence that has fallen over our hiding place.

"My sister is out there," whispers one of Kaini's friends. "Scouting the border."

"And my grandfather," mutters another.

"And Uncle Oakson," Hana says, the fear in her voice rousing my courage.

"I'm not supposed to," I repeat, faltering. "The Grove will protect them."

"It's not Wandering," Kaini argues, whining into my side as he tucks close to me. "Not if you stick to the paths. Not if you stay inside the border."

"He's right," Hana whispers as the others around us start to cry. "Just go make sure they're safe and come straight back."

"We won't tell anyone you went," Kaini urges. "We promise."

No secrets from us.

"No secrets from us," I say, looking them each directly in the face. "I won't defy the Grove, and you shouldn't ask me to. You should trust the Ancients. Come, on, Kaini."

"Elliot," Hana starts, but I shake my head and scowl at her, and she ducks apologetically. She, more than anyone else here, should understand the seriousness of what they're asking me to do. I step forward, shifting into fox form, and nip gently at Kaini's hand, tugging him away.

"Ow," he whines, but takes my hint and follows me close as I trot off down the muddy path toward the Hamlet.

23

Keep Hidden

We aren't far down the path before the wisps find us. Kaini's is pink, the color of healing. Hana, who had chased after us, is met with a green wisp. The other children who followed have wisps of their own, in colors I'm sure are important to them in some way. Mine is orange, the color of flames. The rest split away as mine guides me through the Hamlet toward home.

"*Be our eyes, little fox,*" says the wisp. Its voice reverberates through my mind, commanding me with the power of the Ancients. "*Duty above all.*"

Duty above all.

My heart races with excitement for the purpose the wisp instills in me. Out of everyone else, I have been chosen for this task. To be the eyes of the Ancients.

The wisp leads me all the way to my bedroom, where I fall into the warm familiarity of my bed. Sleep takes me quickly as the wisp hovers over me. Before I know it, I'm dashing out of myself to tear off to the west, alone.

With unnatural speed, I race between tree trunks and under brambles, following my fox nose toward the smoke. The border is a far hike, but I reach it in no time at all. The cedar sentries lining the edge of our lands stand immense and untouched by the flames that lick against our magical barriers.

The fire can't cross, but it seems the smoke can. That implies the fire was set intentionally as a threat to our borders, but as far as I can tell, there is nothing magically sinister about the smoke.

It billows toward me black and smothering, swirling into our lands high above the treetops like a cloak in the wind. This low to the ground it doesn't reach me, though it still makes my nose twitch and throws off my scent. I remember a moment I can't place. A pot full of burnt grain. A portent I'd forgotten.

It isn't until I see the black path seeping like midnight darkness over the ground that I realize I'm not meant to be searching for Amma and Father and the others. The Grove has different plans for me.

Warning lurches in my belly, but I give myself a good shake from my nose to the tip of my tail and ignore it to bound along the only path set before me. The shadow path.

Once I'm on it, I hesitate only where the inky trail crosses out of the Grove and thins to a thread even narrower than my paw.

My heart races.

Wanderer.

"*Be our eyes.*"

The Ancients' urging is stronger than my own instinct. I follow the shadowed path, skirting along the edge of the flames that lick against our border protections, trying to see the source.

To the west I see the rooftops of a village and recall a vague memory of a flood. The path veers off in that direction and I keep to it, my paws churning dirt and shadows as they drum along.

It leads me to a building I've only seen on maps. Sprawling and low, it's bordered with a towering wall of cut stones. The path leads me over the wall, past a posting of guards, along an inner wall, and into the arrow-slit window of the highest tower.

As soon as I perch on the ledge, I catch the scent of something cruel and familiar. I don't remember why I know it, but I do: Red spice smoke, decay, and dark magic.

Sorcerer.

Within the room, two chairs are arranged at a table. A man sits in one of them, his hand cupped around what looks like a glass bottle wrapped in leather. His scent wafts to me as well: leather, blood, steel and sweat, murder. His gaze is narrowed at the space across from him, where the other chair sits empty.

"It will be done," he says, rolling the tiny bottle between his fingers. "And cleanly. I swear it. I will leave no trace, my lord. The king is already gasping his death throes. His son shall be dead before him."

"You say too much," a second voice hisses from the empty chair. I gasp and blink and stare, trying to see someone. Anyone. To be the eyes of the Ancients. But if there's someone there, his wards are strong enough to protect him from me. I can only smell his scent and hear the faint breeze of his voice.

The first man bows and clutches the bottle to his chest silently.

"Leave me now," says the hidden one.

I creep inside the window, ever closer to the disembodied voice.

A small box slides across the tabletop, seemingly on its own. The lid opens to reveal a dead sparrow. Something tugs at its neck. A strap. A roll of parchment. The unseen one unrolls the tiny note, flattening it across the table.

"Now, let us see what secrets you bear from Ceras'lain to that wretched Grove, little messenger," murmurs the hidden one.

My right cheek buzzes with warning, tugging me back to the windowsill. I followed the path too far. I got too close. I try to shuffle backwards, but something about the stiff sparrow makes my heart pound so hard I'm sure the Sorcerer can hear it.

"Well, well," says the empty air, closer than it had been before. That snaps me out of it. I scamper back to the window, terrified.

The shadowed path curls around me, lurching me away with impossible speed, pulling me over the wall, through the village, and across the rolling hills. It draws me faster and faster until everything around me is a blur of green and gray.

I wake with a start in my bed gasping for breath, my hands tightly clenching my coverlet. My heart feels like it will leap out of my chest. My head is pounding. Fear prickles over me, stabbing into my stomach, paralyzing me.

Keep hidden, always.

That man. I couldn't see him, but he could see me. He saw me. But how? And why did the sight of that dead sparrow throw me into such a panic? As a fox, I've *eaten* birds before. Bigger ones than that. Feathers and all.

Kaini's deep, slow breathing across the room tells me it's night. How long was I scouting? It didn't feel like so many hours, and my clothes, hair, and bed are still slightly damp from the rain and from swimming.

"Amma?" I call quietly, trying not to wake my brother even though I'm terrified by what I've just seen. Shivering despite the summer heat, I force my legs over the edge of the bed. Pins and needles jab at the soles of my bare feet as I shuffle to her room. My heart thuds so loudly I'm sure I'll wake the entire house.

"Amma?" I call again as I push her door open and peer inside.

She and Father lie in each other's arms on the bed, sound asleep. The room smells like soot from the smoke that billowed into the Grove, and dampness, and washing herbs. They've been home a long time, it seems.

My mind follows the shadow trail again along the fire, to the highest tower of a keep. My teeth chatter as I stand frozen to the spot, terrified by what I've seen. *Be our eyes*, the Ancients had said, and that's what I did. *Duty above all.*

But what do I do with what I saw, now that I've seen it? Someone has to stop that man with the bottle before he reaches the prince. And what message should that bird have carried here from Ceras'lain? Is it even my place to wonder about these things?

"Amma," I whisper again, but she's too sound asleep to hear me. She could be scouting. I shouldn't try to wake her.

A whisper of a sound like the rustle of fabric catches my ear. At the corner of my eye along the dark hallway leading to the gathering room, I see what can only be described as the twinkle of starlight. My still-racing heart pounds in my eardrums as I turn slowly to get a better look.

"Elliot Eldinae," the shimmer of a figure whispers gently. At first I'm terrified it's the hidden man from the tower, but a golden wisp hovers at his shoulder casting a soft, pulsing glow over me, and the memory of someone else emerges. Someone who stood with me during a time I forgot, someone who bolstered me, guided me, and helped me.

"Valenor," I whisper.

"How would you like to go on an adventure, my dear boy?" he asks, and I can hear the grin in his tone even if I can't see his face.

"What kind of adventure?" I mouth, my voice failing me.

"To thwart an assassin. To save a prince. To preserve Cerion," he replies with a stirring tone.

I glance at the wisp, my fear shifting slowly to excitement. "Does the Grove will it?"

"*Indeed*," echoes the wisp at his shoulder, and I feel the sway of the Ancients flowing through its voice.

"Come," says Valenor, opening his cloak to reveal a bright blue sunlit sky.

I shield my eyes from the sudden burst of light and join him, stepping through his cloak into the warmth of midday sun. The golden wisp descends on me as I step onto fresh green summer grass in the center of a windswept meadow.

"Courageous One," Aft'elu's voice whispers around me like a breeze, and as motes of golden dust fall into my hair and onto my shoulders, I start to remember.

I remember everything: Father's anger and distance while Amma was lost in Dreaming. Kaini's disgust at the meat on my plate. Hana's portent that I'd one day leave the Grove and become Forgotten. Rubeus. The prince. The Sorcerers. Mya. Mya. Mya.

"How am I remembering all of this now?" I ask, gazing into the impossible blue sky as anger tightens my chest. "Why did you keep this from me?"

"We had to be certain of your path," Aft'elu replies.

"But *you* make the paths," I shout, seething. My head spins with the memories that have been returned. I shuffle through them with relief, agitation, fury.

"The Ancients make the paths," Aft'elu corrects me. "We are not the Ancients. We are a servant, as you are. A guardian of their most precious resource."

I spin again, trying to locate them, and find myself face-to face with a mystical, breathtaking creature. Their paws are broad and strong, like the paws of a lynx. Their bear-like black nose splits to dark lips that curl into a smile, revealing fearsome, pointed teeth. They sit back onto thickly tufted haunches and spread wings of red, white, and gold like a stripe-tailed falcon's.

Awed, I step closer, feeling the power of their presence roll from them in waves. They tilt their head, regarding me with deep blue-green eyes, the most human-like feature about them.

"We are all as we see ourselves in this place," I whisper.

Aft'elu nods.

"How are you here in the Dreaming?" I ask.

"We go where we are sent, as you do," Aft'elu replies. "We are but a servant, as you are."

A few paces away, I'm aware of the flutter of a cloak, and of Valenor's waiting presence.

"I don't understand what's happening," I say, hugging myself to try to slow my racing heart. "You made me cut ties with Mya. You made me feel ashamed. Then you took it all away and gave me false memories, a false life, false joy. Why?"

"Do not be upset, Elliot Eldinae. Dream scout. By shielding you from these memories, we meant only to protect you. We did not yet know how your paths would unfold. The Ancients gifted you idyllic experiences within the Grove to ease your suffering.

"We did not anticipate attacks of flame and smoke. Not even the Ancients could have foreseen the Sorcerers of Cerion could be so obsessed with entering our Grove that they would intentionally burn their own lands, risking their own villages, their own people."

I think back to that meeting in the throne room, when the men in red mocked the prince and tried to manipulate the king into attacking us.

"Did the king ever set a quest?" I ask. "He said he and the prince would discuss sending men here."

"They were sent," Aft'elu replies calmly. "They are here, even now."

They sweep their paw across the grass, opening an oval-shaped gap of what seems to be glittering water. When they gesture for me to peer into it, I step forward and see the burning Sorcerers on stakes. A group of six humans on horseback mill before them, their hands pressed to their mouths and noses to block the haze of smoke.

"I thought I saw a deer," one of them says, and I realize we're looking through the eyes of a doe. I think of Amma in her bed, sleeping in Father's arms.

"Are we seeing what Amma sees?" I whisper in wonder.

"Indeed," Aft'elu replies. "She has been our eyes, tracking the movements of this band of Cerion's men, waiting for them to make some move against us."

"But they aren't here to move against us," I argue. "They only came to speak to us."

"They came to accuse us of murder," answers Aft'elu. "The Ancients shall not lower themselves to answer such accusations. The Grove shall be nothing to them but a forgotten mystery. The unknown is far more unnerving than the known, and so we shall remain unseen.

"Except one of us. A chosen one. A courageous one. One who has been seen more than once, and so cannot remain within the Grove except at great risk to the rest of us."

"Me," I whisper, thinking of Gaethon the Mage, and Mya, and the unseen Sorcerer, and all the times I let myself be seen by outsiders.

Keep hidden, always.

"But I didn't mean to," I argue. The idea of leaving the Grove has played in my mind before, I realize with discomfort, but I never really meant it. To turn my back on the Ancients, and my family, and Hana…

"I didn't mean to…" I whisper again, fighting tears.

"You did not, and yet it happened. Only the Ancients know why. You could not have been seen if it was not their will to have you seen. We are at the cusp of a new age, Elliot Eldinae, and your place in this movement is not within our borders. It is without. In Cerion."

The feather at my ear pulses with a tingling warmth that tickles my ear and makes me blink rapidly.

"You shall be allowed to choose your own path, knowing all that you have learned and all that you have become. Choose to remain, and we shall offer you a comfortable life, and send another in your place. But you shall no longer be a dream scout. We could not allow you such powers, and risk you exposing us further. If you choose to leave, your abilities may shift in ways we cannot predict, but you shall keep them and be our eyes in Cerion. Your fealty to the Grove shall be kept secret and protected. You shan't be able to speak of it to any outsider."

I try to imagine leaving the Grove, saying farewell to Amma and

Father, Kaini and Sulien…Hana. My heart pangs sharply at the last, and then it occurs to me what Aft'elu is saying.

"If I choose to leave, to be the eyes of the Grove, I won't be forgotten?"

Slowly, and with a gentle smile, Aft'elu shakes their head.

"I could return to the Grove? I could see everyone again?" I ask, my lips numb with excitement over the very thought of it.

"To any outside of the Grove, you must make it seem that you have cut all ties with us, but yes."

"And the choice is mine?" I shake my head, still trying to understand.

"It can only be yours."

"Why would I ever choose to remain, to be stripped of my scouting and shifting, over leaving and being free to go where I like and do what I choose?"

"Because once the choice is made, it is a choice for all of your life. The moment you cross out of the Grove, you agree to be our eyes, and to place the will of the Grove at the forefront of every action you take from that moment until your final breath leaves you."

I understand what they're saying. If I chose to leave, I wouldn't be running away. I'd still belong to them. I'd still be as bound to the Grove outside of it as I have been all my life.

I look to Valenor, who stands several paces away. His hands are clasped behind his back, his expression neutral.

"This is a decision you must make of your own mind and choosing. But you must make it in haste. Even now, the assassin rides to Cerion carrying poison intended for the prince. The Ancients believe this is the purpose you have been so desperately seeking. To intercept this assassin. To join us with Cerion."

"But why do the Ancients care what happens to the prince?" I ask, scowling. "What difference does it make to the Grove?"

"They have seen what you have shown them, Courageous one. They have seen his sharp mind, which cannot be deceived by men in cloaks of red. They have seen his respect for the Grove and its secrets. And they have seen those who would usurp him, burning and razing their own lands in order to force their way to us. Their thirst for this power and other Sources like it is unlike anything we have seen in a hundred years. The Plethores must prevail. We will not tolerate another Sorcerer King on the throne of Cerion."

I gaze into the pool, watching the humans through my mother's eyes as they snake along the border's edge. If I look closely, one of them resembles an older version of Lisabella. All of them are wearing white cloaks with emblems of purple and blue, the same colors that were on her tabbard, and on Josten's cloak, the man who the king forced to dance with the red-clad woman at the spring ball.

I realize everything I've been allowed to see up until now has shown me my intended allegiances as well as my enemies. Every path that has been set before me has led me to the same place.

"I'll go," I agree, looking once more into Aft'elu's blue-green eyes. "I choose Cerion."

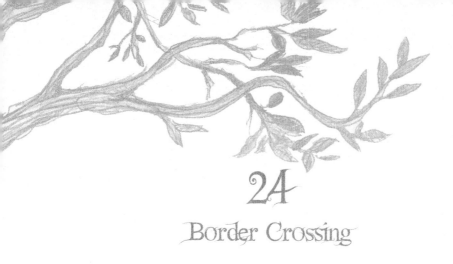

24

Border Crossing

Valenor and Aft'elu breathe a collective sigh of relief. Aft'elu beckons me closer, and I skirt around the grass-framed pool to come to their side.

"We gift you with these," they say, and with their gesture I feel a rush of cool air swirl across my skin. Leggings and a vest of fringed green suede form around me. Moccasin boots. A new bow, elegantly carved with the forms of racing foxes along its handle. New arrows, fletched with feathers from Aft'elu's own wings.

I brush my fingers across them and feel a surge of confidence in my skill. I raise the bow and aim into the distance, and I know it could strike any target I intend, no matter how far away.

"And this," they graze their feather woven into my braid. "This, you must treasure and protect."

"It's my connection to you," I say, thinking back on all the times it prickled me to guide me.

"To the Ancients," Aft'elu nods. "As long as you wear it, you may return to us. If it is lost, its magic shall die, your connection to the Grove shall be severed, and you shall be forced to return to us by foot."

I nod, touching the smooth feather thoughtfully.

"Now you must make haste," Aft'elu says, the tone in their voice stirring an urgency in me. "Go with Valenor."

As I turn from them to Valenor, I'm left with a memory of Amma cradled lovingly in Aft'elu's arms in the form of a tree, and my heart pangs with gratitude and a lingering sense of obligation. I turn to thank them, but they've already gone.

"Elliot Eldinae of the Grove. Dream scout."

The way Valenor declares my name seems to give power to it, and to me. It sets me apart from Aft'elu, from the Grove, and from everyone else. It gives me a sense of independence. Individuality. I'm on my own now. A boy with a purpose.

"Let's go," I say, already trying to pick up the scent of the man with the poison. I remember it well: leather, blood, steel, and sweat. I step into fox form and take off through the grass, sniffing for the trail.

Valenor follows silently, never saying a word until I start to think over what just happened. Back in the Hamlet, in Amma's house, I was awake. He offered me his cloak, and I stepped through it whole. Not as a dream scout with part of me asleep in bed and the other part of me here. I slow to a stop and return to my true form.

"I left the Grove already?" I ask, my heart plummeting into my stomach like a stone. "I didn't feel any change…"

"Not yet," says Valenor, a twinkle of a smile in his eyes. When I give him a questioning look, he spreads his arms wide. "We are just above the Grove. My domain, the Dreaming, is far vaster than the world in which you live. It spreads over the Known Lands like a blanket, an unseen layer between land and sky. As you know, the Half-Realm lies beneath it, between sleeping and awake, touching both Dreaming and reality.

"Though you can travel seamlessly into Dreaming as a dream scout, the In-between is where both realms meet, and where you might catch the scent of the assassin and track him down. As a dream scout, you are able to travel wherever the Grove wills without consequence, so long as a part of you remains asleep. That rule shall not change once you cross out of its borders."

"So, I should go to sleep first?" I ask.

"Just as you have always done," Valenor says, nodding. "Once you have located the man you seek, you may choose to wake there. At that point, you will have fully crossed beyond the borders of the Grove."

"Go to sleep from inside of the Dreaming?" I ask, uncertain. "That seems like it shouldn't be able to happen."

"In most circumstances, it cannot," says Valenor, "but you are here as my guest."

He waves a hand, conjuring a soft feather bed.

"I understand that as a dream scout you have mostly been trained to explore and observe. When I stood beside you in your confrontation with the Sorcerer Rubeus, you had found him by following his scent, and his strand between his two selves. This time, there is no such strand. Seeking one man in a sea of humanity is no small task." He smiles knowingly. "You must focus on his essence. His features, his demeanor. The whole of his flesh and his spirit. Not merely his scent. Knowing his name is always helpful, but it is still possible to find him if you do not."

I climb into the bed, nodding along to his directions, my eyes already drooping closed.

"Focus. When the time is right, pull yourself from Dreaming and bring your whole self into Waking."

I nod again, my heart thumping. If I find him, if I do this right, it means I'll be leaving the Grove fully for the first time in my life. I try to ignore how wrong it feels, how much it pains me even though I know it's the right choice.

"Sleep now," Valenor says, and with his whisper, I slip under. As soon as I feel the shift to sleep, my fox-self leaps away, darting down through the grass of the Dreaming and into the clouds of the In-between.

I think of the man at the table, his hand clenched around the bottle, the timbre of his voice, the feel of his cruelty mixed with his fear of the unseen man. The unseen man...I forgot to ask about him. Why could he see me, but I couldn't see him? What kind of magic was that? Did Valenor know about it? Did Aft'elu?

I push the questions to the back of my mind. It's not the time. I must focus. My ears twitch at the sound of horses' hooves drumming over a muddy road. The night sky is black with smoke and storm clouds. Rain falls across the landscape in sheets so heavy I can barely see ten paces ahead of me.

I keep running, remembering what Valenor said, and close my eyes. I don't need to look. I need to feel. I change course, following the essence, the scent, the sound of hoof beats. I can hear the man's heart racing. I can feel his urgency, his cruel determination.

There are others on the road to Cerion City. Hundreds of others. Some smell similar to him, like steel, sweat, or leather. Many do, actually. I'm grateful for Valenor's lesson. I never would have found him going on scent alone.

A plan starts to form in my mind as I speed my chase, certain I'm on the right trail. As soon as I see him, I'll pull myself through from the Dreaming. I'll take my true form and snap together as soon as he's in range. I'll ready my bow. I'll fire, hopefully just once, and it'll be done.

The prince will be saved.

I'll have left the Grove for Cerion, for good.

My stomach twists at how wrong it feels to think it. My heart thrums in time with my paws. I divert my own attention, focusing on honing my plan. It takes so much more effort in fox form to think logically and not on instinct.

After I have the vial, I'll take it to the palace and try to speak to Finn, the prince's guard. I'll tell him about the unseen Sorcerer and the fires. I'll warn him about the ones in red. The Knights of Conquer. Hopefully, he'll let me tell the prince myself.

Just as I'm satisfied with the plan I've made, the assassin's essence sharpens. My eyes snap open. The blur of his silhouette emerges from the mist and rain as he races along the road I'm approaching from the side.

He's riding alone, his oiled leather cloak wrapped tightly around him, his hood pulled low against the drenching rain. He leans into his horse, shouting cruelly and whipping its hind quarters to speed it along. The white of the poor creature's eye is a moon-like sliver under its brow, and it tosses its head in fear as its hooves slip dangerously over the mud-slick road.

The sight of his cruelty to the horse makes me even more determined to stop him. I muster my rage. It's time. If I keep pace, I'll crash straight through him unless I shift now and ready my bow.

I barely have time to think. I can't think too hard. I pull myself out of Dreaming and feel my second self drawing closer. Just as I'm about to slip into my true form, a strange sensation assaults me.

It feels like a wrenching or a straining, as if someone has a hold of both of my arms and is trying to pull me in two. I let loose an agonized fox's scream and keep focused, continuing to try to draw myself out.

The sensation stings like a twig snapping into my face after being pulled too far back. I gasp as my two halves crash together, and I realize too late that I never shifted.

I careen toward the rider in midair, my paws splayed out, my tail thrashing behind me, and I crash hard into the man. He's so shocked he barely cries out as my unnatural speed throws him from his horse.

The horse keeps going as the man curses, crushing me beneath him as we roll together along the muddy road. His hand clamps onto the scruff of my neck, and I hear the slide of steel being pulled from a sheath.

"What in the bloody stars?" he growls, and the familiarity of his voice from the tower breaks over me, harsh and terrifying.

Panic wracks through me, clouding out all other instincts. Not panic over rolling in the mud with an armed assassin. No. Somehow, that immediate threat holds no flame to the reality of what just happened.

I crossed the border.

I left the Grove.

I'm here.

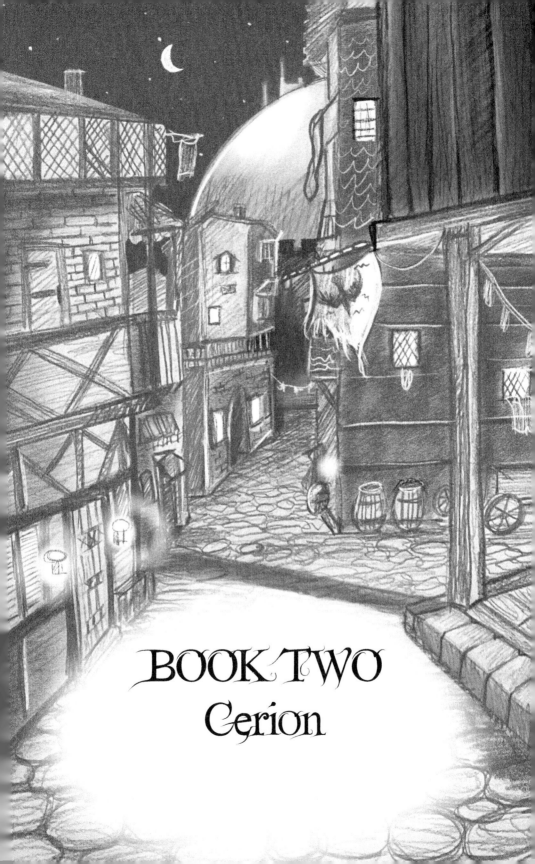

BOOK TWO
Cerion

25

CERION

I come to my senses as soon as I see the flash of steel streaking toward me, aimed for my side. Reacting quickly, I fling my hand up to grab his wrist, gnashing my teeth against his leather bracer.

Hand.

Teeth.

I'm a fox, then a boy, then a fox again—shifting back and forth with no control over either. My opponent is just as shocked as I am by my rapid changing. He scrambles away from me in the mud, the point of his knife trembling as he brandishes it in my direction.

"What are you?" he growls fearfully.

With my hands squishing into the mud and rain drenching my back, I pant from the prickling rush of pain that shivers over my skin. My snout and ears grow long. My arms and hands shrink to legs and paws. I howl in confusion and agony.

"Fox," Valenor's voice hastens to me, woven through the hiss of the rain. "Be still."

I shake my furry head to clear it, blinking muddy water from my eyes. Three paces away, the assassin sits in the mud, too stunned to move. My vision grows keener through fox eyes, narrowing to a point at his chest. The pocket where he slipped the vial of poison.

"I don't know what kind of beast you are," the assassin calls warily. He tosses his knife away and holds his hands out and open. "I mean you no harm. Just...give me leave to get my horse and I'll be on my way."

With a spry movement he jumps to his feet. My hackles rise. I crouch low, snarling, my eyes fixed on that pocket. His surrender doesn't fool me. The handles of several more knives glint from straps in his sleeve, his bicep, his thigh.

"Now, beastie," he mutters. His own lips curl, and he crouches low to mirror my stance. "I've no quarrel with you. Just let me pass."

My vision dims. My stomach churns. My skin prickles.

FOX, I think to myself firmly. I can't keep changing back and forth. Not now.

The assassin's eyes widen as my growing face and shoulders shrink to fox size again. He snarls, and without warning he draws a knife in each hand and flings them both at me.

I sprint away, dodging his flung weapons with ease. Before he has a chance to draw another, I leap at him, claws extended, teeth bared, aiming for his throat. I glance his jaw instead, and a sickening feeling surges over me as my bite rips his skin.

I've never injured a person before with my teeth. Not intentionally. Not with so much damage. If it should feel like a triumph, it doesn't. As his blood spills into muddy rivulets and he clamps his hand over his throat, screaming and cursing me, I back away, terrified by what I've done.

Without thinking, I escape into the nearby underbrush, wiping my face frantically in the wet, rotting leaves of the forest floor. The taste in my mouth is sickening. Sharp and metallic. My tongue hangs limp, dragging through the grass, desperate to taste anything other than the blood of a man.

I scramble deeper into the woods until I find a stream to plunge my face into to wash the sickening taste away. Partway through diving and drinking, I shiver and writhe and shift again, back to myself. Back to Elliot.

"Breathe, my boy," Valenor's voice is barely a whisper in my ear. "Be still."

Crouched in the cover of a bush with the rush of water beside me, I curl into myself and try to do as he says. My breath comes in panicked, unpredictable bursts that make my lips go numb and my head feel dizzy.

"What's happening to me?" I croak as tremors quake my shoulders and legs.

"You are adjusting to this realm," he whispers.

"What did I just do?" I ask between sharp, labored gasps.

"What you were sent to do," Valenor says with a steady, calming tone. I can almost feel his hands on my shoulders, his cloak enveloping me kindly. But he remains in the Dreaming, unable to cross into this realm.

"Did I—" I suck in a breath and let it out in a shudder. "Is he dead?"

The reply that comes is not a whisper through the rain, like Valenor's voice, but a shimmer of a thought from the feather in my braid. Reassurance, such as it is, from Aft'elu.

"The Grove willed it, child. Courageous one."

Sinking back into the damp moss, I wonder whether that's reason enough. The Grove seems so far away now. It feels like a distant memory, a place I might have only dreamed about. Could its will really justify me killing someone all the way out here? Even someone who would have killed a prince if I hadn't stopped him first?

After leaving everyone I have ever known behind, it doesn't feel like the best first action.

My thoughts flash back over what just happened. In my shock, I forgot the poison. Dead or alive, the assassin still has it. My stomach lurches as I realize what it means. I'll have to go back for it. I'll have to look at him and see the consequences of what I've done. Still shaken, but at least able to breathe now, I stumble into the cover of an overhang beside the stream bank and close my eyes.

It takes much longer than usual to calm myself enough to let sleep take me. As soon as I do, I split away into fox form and race toward the road. I find him at the bottom of the roadside gutter on his back, as if he crawled to chase and eventually lost his fight.

I creep closer, my nose twitching, watching cautiously, but he doesn't move. He doesn't breathe. I try not to think about it even though the scent of blood is hard to ignore. I focus on other things, pushing my thoughts to the back, letting my fox instincts take over.

Up on the road, a caravan approaches. They may not be able to see down into the ditch, but I don't want to risk it. I shift my presence to this spot and pull myself together, feeling my sleeping self rush closer. The moment we snap together I lurch forward, tear at his pocket with my teeth, wrench the poison bottle free, and run back into the forest before the caravan reaches us.

My body tremors again and just as I reach the tree line I find myself on two feet rather than four. I spit the wax-sealed vial into my palm and tilt my head back to open my mouth to the rain, rinsing the foul taste of blood away. My ears ring, and my heart thuds with fear that I might have accidentally swallowed a trace of poison.

Up on the road, the caravan passes slowly, the carriage wheels and its horses churning up mud. I work on calming my breath, and I tuck the vial into my belt pouch as I watch it pass. It's a fascinating thing, like a hut on wheels. The only other carriage I've seen was one floating around the flooded village all those weeks ago. This one passes without slowing. No one notices the heap at the bottom of the ditch.

I feel another shift coming on and brace myself, squeezing my eyes shut. When I open them again, I'm a fox.

"Please stay this way," I command inside my head. The frequent

shifting is taking its toll. My head pounds, my stomach growls with hunger, my limbs shake weakly. "*No more changing.*"

My right ear tingles and a rush of calm floods through me from the feather in my braid.

"Rest a moment," says Valenor from somewhere close by.

His calm voice reassures me, giving me strength to go a little further and find a safe place to sit.

These trees are unfamiliar and cold. They hold none of the kind, welcoming energy I'm used to from the grove. I think of Grandymum and my heart pangs with regret. Will I really see her again? If I do, will she treat me the same now that I've left? My thoughts race dangerously, tinged with regret, and I reel them back quickly. I do my best to keep in my fox's mind, switching again to instinct and less complicated thoughts.

The base of a leaning poplar makes easy shelter, and I tuck myself into its shadow and curl into the warmth of my own tail. Sleep takes me quickly. In Dreaming, Amma's arms are around me before I'm even aware of where I am. I burrow into her embrace as the forest around us comes to life in warm, sun-dappled leaves, birds' songs, and the gentle thrum of trees calling secrets to one another.

"*Sheshi,*" Amma whispers, "my sweet boy."

"Amma," I suck in a breath, wrapping my arms around her tightly.

"I'm so proud of you." Her voice is so thick with emotion that I don't have to look into her face to know she's crying.

"Proud? I left the Grove," I argue.

"As I knew you would," she answers, gathering me tighter to her. I want to tell her what I did to the assassin, to confess it and clear it away, but I can't bring myself to say it aloud. The thought of it makes my eyes sting with tears, and I allow them to drip onto her soft suede vest as she strokes my hair tenderly.

"Your journey is not yet done, my darling one," she says once I'm calmed down. "It isn't safe for you to remain in the roadside forest. You must go to Cerion and find safety there."

"But where will I go?" I ask, sniffling.

"You know the answer to that. It lies within your own heart," Amma replies. She holds me away from her so she can look into my eyes. "You've been given a great gift, Elliot. Whether within the Grove or without, true love finds its match."

"Mya," I whisper. Amma nods. "You remember her? I thought the Grove would make you forget."

"The Ancients have shown me many things. I saw their offer to you and the choice you made. It isn't what I would have chosen for you,

176

but I trust in the Grove, and I believe in you."

I hug her tighter and begin to understand. Even as my parents, she and Father have little say in what happens to me. If it's the Grove's will that I go to Cerion, then they must let me go.

"Go," she says, smiling sadly as she strokes the hair from my brow. "I'll be beside you. I will see this girl who calls to your heart."

"Are you sure?" I ask, my heart beating faster. This is why I came to Cerion. Not for the assassin. For Mya. For the prince.

"The Grove wills it," she affirms, as if reading my thoughts.

She gives me a nudge, and I slink into fox form while she takes the form of the doe beside me. Together, we leap onto the breeze until our feet graze the treetops and our faces are bathed in starlight through the parting storm clouds.

The dark feelings that plagued me after the assassin fall away into the night. We soar southward together above a road still crowded with travelers even at this late hour. It's not long before I catch a glimpse of the Academy's golden dome. Beyond it, Cerion's pale palace spires shine despite the misty ocean backdrop.

I'm grateful for Valenor's lesson as Amma and I leap together over the outer wall of the kingdom and soar through streets crowded with revelers. There are so many out, even in the drenching rain, that it would have been nearly impossible to find Mya with my nose. I feel her, though. She's here. I know it.

I close my eyes and search for her essence: light, creativity, beauty, song. It leads me to a two-story building stuffed between two smaller ones along the main sea market road. A seagull is painted on its chipped and faded sign, and yellowish light from guttering candles spills out over the wet cobbles from its noisy insides.

I dive through the wall and peer into the huge room filled with men and women drinking, singing, and dancing. It's a fascinating sight, and if it weren't for Amma beside me, I'd probably linger and watch through the night, forgetting why I'm here. She butts my side with her nose, though, and I trot above their heads up to the second level where Mya's presence is even stronger.

It leads me to a narrow hallway, to a warded door. The wards don't seem like they would keep me out, but something warns me against crossing them anyway, so I sniff along the length of the wall until I find the spells' end, and I step through with Amma close behind me.

As soon as we're inside, my pulse quickens. It's a small room with a chest at the foot of a narrow bed, and two windows, and a dresser. All of it smells unmistakably like her. This is her room.

My breath catches. Mya's here. Just steps away, kneeling at a chest draped with a glittering blue gown. Tears slip down her cheeks as she sinks to her knees to stare at the crystals of the gown, and despite her apparent sadness, I'm filled with elation.

I found her, so easily and so quickly. She's really here. We're both really here. I amble joyfully around the room as I pull myself away from the forest where my other half is sleeping and snap myself together again.

Mya sees me first in the reflection of the crystals, but I'm too excited to slow and let her truly see. She jumps to her feet and spins around, frantic, trying to glimpse me. I fight the urge to leap into her arms, to lick her face. I try to shift to my wood elf form, but I'm too charged with excitement to concentrate on it.

"Please," she calls softly as she twirls in place. She glances at the door like she's afraid someone will hear. "Who are you? Let me see you."

Here in Waking, her voice is a hundred times more resonant, more beautiful than it had ever been in Dreaming. It calms me, and I leap up on the bed to be nearer to her face. When she turns to face me, her eyes widen in disbelief.

"How did you get in here?" she whispers, stretching a wary hand toward me as she glances at the windows, trying to puzzle it out.

Fully here now, the chill of the rain and mud and roots catches up with me. I crouch low, shivering as she nears, my fox instincts taking over. Cautiously, I creep toward her outstretched hand and crane my neck until the tip of my nose grazes her fingertip.

Warmth and recognition spark between us in that moment, and her gorgeous ocean eyes widen even further as my heart races.

"I know you," she whispers, climbing onto the bed beside me.

I nuzzle her hand with my face and tremble, overwhelmed by everything that has happened. I did it. I left the Grove. I thwarted the assassin. I made it to Cerion. I found Mya.

"Oh, you're shivering, poor thing," she whispers and bundles me tenderly into the coverlet to scoop me into her arms. "How did you get so muddy?"

She scratches at my ear, tickling me, and I twitch and move away on instinct.

"Sorry, shh, stay, stay." She hums a melody to soothe me, and my racing heart settles. My eyes slowly close, and I fall asleep in her arms, feeling more loved and assured in this moment than all my lifetime living in the Grove.

26
MAZES AND TOURNEYS

A mma is still waiting in the Dreaming, lingering beside a hedge, peering away from me into the thick forest. I don't have to look to know she's watching Mya, who fell asleep beside me. In her own dream, Mya's melody rises over the songs of birds, lilting through the leaves, dancing with the distant sound of waves lapping at the shore.

I stand back, watching as Amma offers Mya a nod of approval. When Mya tries to move closer, though, Amma raises her chin and Mya pauses with her hand over the strings of her lute. The birds go silent and everything seems to hold its breath as I move forward, gazing at her beauty, knowing this is the moment she'll understand I'm here. The fox is me.

"Elliot," her whisper thrills me, and I hold up a finger to ask her to wait a moment so I can whisper to Amma.

I step closer and take her velvety head in my hands and press my forehead to hers.

"Don't worry, Amma," I whisper. "I'll visit you again in Dreaming soon. I'm safe here. I'll be careful. I promise."

Her soft ears twitch, her eyes close slowly in approval, and I stroke her face one last time before stepping away. The way Mya looks at me when I turn to her tells me I'm wearing my emotions plain on my face. When I reach to touch her cheek, it feels different than all our other times together. Even though we're in the Dreaming, it seems more real, more definite, because of the promise of what's to come.

No one, not even Hana, has ever looked at me the way she does.

There's so much longing and depth in her eyes that I feel I could fall into the pools of them and swim forever in the sea within. I cling to her and pull her closer, grazing kisses across her cheek, finding her soft lips, losing myself.

We kiss until Amma butts my hip and shifts nervously, peering into the distance. Her hoof paws at the earth as she nudges my arm in warning.

"I found you," I whisper to Mya, still lost in the affection of her gaze.

Mya clings to me, gazing into the distance past Amma like she sees or feels something frightening. I look, too. Anything could be here—anything her sleeping mind can conjure.

A deep red mist billows into the forest consuming everything in its path. It's like nothing I have ever seen in Dreaming. It reminds me of something from my past, a nightmare from a time before I was a dream scout, when I was able to have dreams of my own.

Mya, paralyzed by her nightmare, stares as the mist encroaches. I cling to her arms and try to pull her from it, but it's moving too fast. There's no escape. We're sucked under the mist of red tide until it spits us out into a frigid crimson ocean.

Mya's hand is torn from mine. I'm assaulted by visions of the assassin as he fell screaming, crimson blood spilling from his torn throat. Mya splashes just out of reach, floundering and gulping.

"Mya!" I shout frantically as a wave lifts me up and crashes me toward her. The terror is plain on her face as she screams mutely and reaches toward me. It's strange that the seas have made her silent. I can't make sense of the dream, only its emotions: terror, helplessness, quiet.

I swim hard, trying to reach her, but only graze her fingertips as the sea goes black like shadows, thrashing its way between us, wrenching us apart.

"ELLIOT!" Mya's scream jolts me with pain and fear, and then she's gone.

A crash in the bedroom wakes me, and I feel Mya's hand resting protectively over my blanket.

"It was just a dream," she says, nudging me before I can dig my way out to see who she's talking to. I catch the scent of a woman: leather, liquor, musk, deceit. The same scent I caught back at the mill where the barrels were stolen.

"Alistar," the woman calls out, and a second scent nears: incense, burlap, a hint of rot, like a Sorcerer, but he feels more like a Mage.

I hold my breath, resisting the urge to fight free of her hand and the coverlet and get a good look at them. Mya seems to think I should stay hidden, though, so I do my best to just sniff and listen.

"Nothing can cross the wards," Alistar says, yawning.

Mya holds her breath, pressing her hand a little more firmly over my back as if in warning, and I hear the woman move closer. After a tense moment, she moves away and the door closes.

"That was close," Mya whispers.

I want to ask her why she's in the company of a pair like that. Does she know he's a dark-leaning Mage? Is she suspicious of that thieving woman? I consider slipping to my true form, but after what happened in the road with the assassin, how afraid he was of my constant shifting, I'm reluctant. Right now, I'm firmly fox. What if I got stuck bouncing again? What if I got sick all over her room?

Besides, I'm too exhausted, too dirty, and too hungry. And I must be careful now that I'm here. I can't reveal what I can do either by accident or on purpose. If it was just Mya that would be one thing, but how would she explain a wood elf suddenly appearing in her room to Alistar and that woman?

"You really need a bath, don't you?" Mya whispers, oblivious to my inner turmoil.

I yawn and scratch at my mud-caked ear. More than anything, I want to hold her. To kiss her here in Waking for the first time. I take her hand gently in my mouth and tug her to the door, hoping a bath might lead to a meal. I'm starving.

"All right," she agrees, "but you have to be extra quiet. They can't know about you until I can figure out an explanation."

She scoops me into her dressing robe and sneaks me down some stairs to a steaming hot spring that's so inviting I can't help but chatter excitedly and scramble out of her arms to plunge into it. I dive and surface and dive again, washing away the mud and blood and chill of the rain. As I splash, any lingering doubts about the path I had chosen dissolve around me into the warm, soothing water.

Once I feel better, I leave the pool and go to her side, my tail flicking happily as I gaze up at her. She strokes the wet fur of my face, and I gaze up at her, thinking of my true form. Her eyes meet mine, and recognition dawns in them.

"Elliot?" Her whisper is filled with wonder. I acknowledge her question with only a flick of my tail and a very slight wink.

She sneaks me back to her room, and I snuggle close to her and wait for her to fall asleep before I let Dreaming take me. This time when I fall asleep, I'm greeted by a polished wooden path in the In-between. The path to the palace. I jog along it until the palace walls emerge from the space around me, and I reach an ornate, closed wooden door. With a deep breath I duck inside and find myself once again in the bedroom of the prince.

The hour being well past midnight, it's not surprising to find him sound asleep in his bed. I scowl and sniff around and realize the wards here are weak and muddled, like they've been tampered with and slowly unraveled. Across the room, the door to the terrace is closed to block out the rain.

A tray at the prince's bedside table stacked with slices of fruit and cheeses and little cakes catches my nose. Even in the In-between, it calls to my hunger. Some of it has been picked over, but he left most of it untouched. I consider drawing myself to whole and taking a few nibbles. No one would notice, probably.

I shake my head and step away. A little hunger isn't worth getting caught lurking in the prince's room in the middle of the night with a vial of poison. I don't know a lot about the customs here, but I'm sure that would be frowned upon.

Besides, I have a message to deliver. I close my eyes and try something new. If the prince is sleeping, then maybe I could visit him in his dreams like I did with Mya and deliver a message.

I slip back into the vast Dreaming. Once I make myself aware of it, I realize it's even more crowded than Cerion is on this festival night. So many dreamers spread out across the realm, dreaming their own dreams, believing what they're seeing and experiencing is real.

"Prince Tirnon," I think to myself, trying hard to focus. It'll be difficult to find him without a path.

"Oh, Tirnon," a woman's voice echoes across the expanse, followed by a flirtatious giggle.

"Come out, Naelle," calls the prince. "Please."

The woman giggles again, and I rush through the Dreaming to find the two of them in an enormous hedge maze. I see her first: a young woman with deep brown curls piled on her head, adorned with a sparkling silver circlet and wearing a rose-colored gown that flutters around her.

"I'm just around the corner," she sings, her carefree laughter a contrast to the prince's tone of longing and fear.

"Which corner?" he shouts, and Naelle darts past me, still laughing, to disappear around a bend. The prince emerges soon after, coming to a stop before me.

"Please," he says breathlessly, taking me by the shoulders, "did a woman pass this way? A beautiful woman? With dark, dancing eyes and shining brown curls?"

"I'll tell you in a moment," I answer, trying to seem enigmatic as someone randomly appearing in a dream would. I do my best to make an impression on him, so he'll be sure to remember me when he wakes up. "First, I have a message of warning."

"Warning?" He scowls. Somewhere in the maze, Naelle laughs again and calls his name. "What warning?"

I reach into my vest pocket and produce the poison vial, still crusted with the rider's blood. "This night, I stopped a rider on the road to Cerion, intent on coming to poison you. His orders came from a tower in Kordelya Keep, issued by a Sorcerer I could not see."

"Kordelya?" Tirnon's eyes widen, and he looks me over.

"You're one of them, aren't you? From Sorlen Grove? We sent my father's best guild to seek you, and we have heard nothing from them since."

"Tirnon!" Naelle sings playfully.

"Please, did you see which way she went?" he asks me. I worry he's already forgotten my warning, so I say it again.

"This night, I stopped a rider on the road to Cerion, intent on coming to poison you. His orders came from a tower in Kordelya Keep, issued by a Sorcerer I could not see."

I turn then and point in the direction the girl ran, but her path has since been closed off, blocked by the hedge.

"Not again," Tirnon says, shaking his head. "All my paths are closing before I can even reach them."

I think of the paths I've always followed and shiver. I hope I'm wrong, but his words feel like a portent.

As he turns in search of Naelle, I close my eyes and try to focus elsewhere.

"Finn," I whisper, reaching out to seek him in his own dream.

"Finn, by all the stars, at least let me get a swing in!"

It's the prince's voice again, but different. He sounds younger, and far away from this place. It's Finn, now. His dream. I fling myself through space, engulfed by the sounds of shouting and metal on metal. Battle sounds. I focus on the ring of swords and on Finn's urgent energy. He's fighting somewhere nearby. Blocking. Running. Shouting.

The field where he stands is surrounded by seats of hundreds of people, all cheering so thunderously that I can barely pick out one sound from another.

"Keep your distance!" Finn bellows.

I find him at the far end of a mobbed field, surrounded by hulking, faceless figures draped in red cloaks that flap menacingly around them. Beside him, Prince Tirnon tries to press his attack against the red-clad figures, but Finn steps in front of him, blocking their relentless charges again and again.

Blood spills from the gaps in the prince's armor, but he doesn't even seem to notice. Sometimes he's the prince, and sometimes he has his father's face. The king.

"Stay behind me, Sire," Finn commands as he slices through foe after foe with barely an effort.

"I just want to fight, Finn!" Prince Tirnon argues, brandishing his wooden training sword like a child. "Stand aside and let me!"

"This is not a game, Highness," Finn argues, exasperated, as he cuts down three more of their unrelenting foes.

"It is a game, Finn!" Tirnon pokes at one of the attackers, who screams in fury and nearly takes off the prince's head before Finn slices him in two. "It's a tournament! I'm winning!"

"I have a message for you!" I yell.

The roar of the crowd is deafening, but I step closer and shout as loud as I can, standing in front of Finn, not bothering to dodge his sword as it slashes through me like I'm not here. It's a true strike to his opponent, though, who falls to the ground with an agonized gurgle.

"How many of you Knights of Conquer are there, anyway?" he screams ferociously. "Come taste my blade, the lot of you! See how easy I cut you down!"

It's obvious he isn't going to stop fighting just because a wood elf is shouting in his ear, so rather than try to make him stop, I just shout the message over and over as he fights, "This night, I stopped a rider on the road to Cerion, intent on coming to poison the prince. His orders came from a tower in Kordelya Keep, issued by a Sorcerer I could not see."

I make sure it's nearly word for word the same message I gave the prince. I hope he remembers it when he wakes. I hope one of them mentions it to the other.

"I have to go and sing," Mya's whisper slips into to my mind, blotting out all other noise. "Won't you come with me?"

Lured by her voice, I draw myself away through the Dreaming, back to the inn room where I'm curled up cozily in a sunbeam, and I open one reluctant eye to find her staring back at me hopefully.

"Will you?" she asks again. "If you stay, they might discover you."

It takes me a moment to realize what she's saying. She's leaving the room, and the other two will still be here. My empty stomach growls, and for a moment I consider shifting, but again I realize that would cause more problems and questions than it would be worth risking. I blink at her and wish I had some way to ask for breakfast, but she isn't a mind reader.

After a moment, I yawn and stretch and slink off the edge of the bed to hide underneath it.

"Elliot," Mya whispers after me, but I pretend I'm asleep to keep her from asking again and tempting me. I'm not ready yet to try and shift in the Waking in front of her, and I'm sure it would be strange to have a fox trailing her around the city.

"Mya!" the thief woman shouts, pounding angrily on the door.

Mya bangs her head on the frame of the bed, where she's crawled to peek at me.

"I'm coming!" she shouts, and I try not to wince at the anger in her voice. I know it's not meant for me. As if to confirm it, she whispers tenderly, grazing my tail with her fingertips, "I hate to leave you. I'll be back as soon as I can. Stay safe."

I nod, curl myself under my own tail, and fall back to sleep.

27

HOME AND HOME

The trail I follow this time in the In-between is one of smoke and flame. The fires stretch across the kingdom, smudging the rich green fields and forests with billowing swaths of black. I run northeast along the trail, propelled by gusts of wind, toward the Grove. Instead of being greeted by the lush green forest, all I see are smoke and flames beyond the fields of Cerion.

I push faster, skirting the Grove's border north, east, south, west, but the fires snake along all the way around the border, entombing it. Choking it out. I think of the burnt grain caked in Amma's soup pot.

Panic grips me. I only left yesterday. How could these fires have grown so thick and destructive so fast? Passing the Sorcerers burning with wispfire, I know exactly how. Dark magic. Three were defeated, but there's more out there. The unseen one in the tower was proof of that.

I soar above the canopy, bracing myself for the moment I cross the border, but all I feel when I do is a prickle of energy that rushes from my nose to my tail. Far above the treetops it's easy to see how the Grove is affected. Though the fires are raging outside of its borders, no flames have crossed over. Only the smoke has breached. It hangs heavily over the whole of the Grove, blotting out the sun, casting everything into murky shadows as dark as night.

Diving through darkness, I finally reach the Hamlet, where everyone is going about their morning with scarves tied around their mouths and glow lamps to light their work. This low to the ground the smoke is fairly thin, but the occasional cough from a grandmother or grandfather is concerning.

I spring up to the platform where Amma's house sits. The smoke seems to have lessened here around the houses, almost like it's being cleansed by Grandymum's protections. I spot Hana across the way, leaning against Grandymum's branches, her eyes closed and her head bowed reverently. I shift from fox to boy and run to her.

"Hana!" I shout, forgetting she can't see or hear me while I'm here in the In-between.

But to my surprise, Hana's vines perk up. She lifts her head and looks over her shoulder, and her tendrils curl toward me as if searching for sunlight. At first I think it must be a coincidence, but her red-rimmed eyes widen, and she looks right at me.

"Elliot?" She blinks in disbelief.

I stop just a step from her, and when her vines curl around my elbows, they feel as real as if we were both here in the Grove, together in the Waking.

"You can see me?" I ask.

"Are you really here?" she asks at the same time.

"I don't...I don't know," I reply, scowling. I can feel myself far away under Mya's bed, sound asleep in fox form. It's so strange. "I shouldn't be."

"Your Amma said you'd gone." She shakes her head, and her tear-filled eyes meet mine. "Why would she lie to me about that? I thought you'd left without saying..." she chokes on the last word, and I take her hand in mine. Her vines weave over my forearms, pulling me even closer, and she rests a hand on my shoulder.

"I don't understand," I say. "I'm asleep in Cerion. The real me. I came here scouting."

"Cerion," she nods to herself sorrowfully. "So, you did leave, then. Without a goodbye."

"Hana, I had to. There was—" I start to explain about the prince and the poison, but I can't form the words. I try to tell her about Valenor and Aft'elu and the assassin, but every time I open my mouth, all that comes out is my breath.

"What?" she asks, dropping her hand. "What are you trying to say?"

"I had to go. It was urgent. There was no time for goodbyes."

She looks away, far up into Grandymum's branches.

"Does it have to do with the smoke?" she asks, her vines still clinging to my arms even though her arms are crossed. "Do you know how to stop it?"

I shake my head, "Don't the Ancients know how?"

"I hope so. They're saying the fire can't cross our borders because it's magical, but the smoke is natural, so there aren't provisions against it. All our dream scouts are out now, watching the borders. Later, there will be a wind-calling ritual to drive the smoke away. Everyone will participate, no matter the talent."

She looks at me with a little more distance than usual in her gaze and opens her mouth and closes it a few times without saying anything.

"Oh," she whispers, chewing her lip thoughtfully. "Well, it seems like there are things we simply can't talk about anymore."

"I don't understand how I'm here and there," I tell her. I take her hand again and pull her into a hug just in case this is the goodbye we never had. I breathe in the fresh, spring-like scent of the leaves and vines tangled in her hair, and I wonder whether I made the right choice in going to Cerion.

"Maybe it's a gift," she whispers. "A gift from the Grove, so we won't ever really have to say goodbye."

"Maybe," I agree, remembering what Aft'elu said about my abilities possibly changing. My thoughts return to the fox under Mya's bed, and the way she held me and protected me from being seen. Her arms. Her kiss. I take a step back from Hana, feeling slightly less present than I had been when I arrived.

"I should go," I say, with the sense that I'm caught between two worlds in more ways than one. "I already feel myself fading. I don't think these visits are meant to last."

"I'm glad you came, even if only for a moment," she offers quietly.

I want to promise I'll tell them about the fires in Cerion, but the words won't come, so I just hug her again and turn and run away, switching into fox form just before I leap off the edge of the platform and glide into the sky.

The mouth-watering aroma of fresh hot bread and roasted shellfish wafts to my nose, enticing me before I'm even fully awake. Whole again under the cover of Mya's bed, I crawl out to find that she's left me a tray piled high with food, but she's gone again.

I try to shift from fox to enjoy the meal with two hands and my wood elf tongue, but I barely have enough energy to reach the tray and sit before it, let alone shift. Appearing in two places at once has exhausted me thoroughly, and as soon as I lap up the last of the strange, spicy gravy and wash the meal down with fizzing cider, I have no energy left.

My full belly weighs me down and makes me even sleepier. I slump onto my side and rest my head on the floor, staring at the locked door, wondering when Mya will return. Thoughts of her make my heart race despite my exhaustion.

I don't like how vulnerable the fatigue makes me. Being in Cerion, so far away from the Grove, drains me in a way I haven't felt before. Especially after that meal, I could sleep for another full day. Nothing is stopping me, really. I slink back under the bed and curl up and doze off again.

This time my sleep starts out restful and dreamless. I find myself bathed in white light, floating peacefully through my slumber, feeling my weariness seep from me into pure serenity.

I've been here before. What did Gaethon call it? Rumination? I stay until I feel my strength return. I'm not sure how long. As soon as I feel replenished, the white fades away until I find myself standing in the shadows of a wall surrounding Kordelya Keep's courtyard.

I shrink back to press myself against the wall as a man approaches me, leading a horse. The man talks in hushed tones, whispering to someone I can't see.

"She only just returned, my lord," he says. "No rider, as you can see. We sent a group out to search the road for him, thinking he fell off, maybe."

"And you're certain this was Anten's horse?"

The voice sends a shiver of fear through me, even though I was partly expecting it. It's the same one that gave instructions to the assassin. The Sorcerer who I couldn't see, but who seemed to be able to see me. A hint of the assassin's scent curls from the horse as they pass by, and I shiver.

Terrified the unseen one will spot me again, I back away slowly to hide behind a nearby stack of crates that stink of iron and soot.

"Yes, my lord. See? His badge is there, and all of his effects still intact."

"Don't!" The Sorcerer barks. "Don't touch anything. You'll contaminate the essences. Stand to the side so I can concentrate."

I watch as the man moves away, and the horse tosses her head in protest.

"Stand still," growls the Sorcerer, and I peer over the top of the crates trying everything I can think of to make myself see him.

I can see where his hands press into the saddlebags. I can even feel his presence, but he remains completely hidden from me. No dust is kicked up under his feet, no shadow is cast as he stands in the sun.

After a stretch of silence, he lets out what sounds like a long, irritated hiss.

"Utter nonsense," he growls in annoyance.

"Sir?" The other man asks rather hesitantly.

"It seems one of my prized men was thwarted by nothing more than a rabid fox," he says. "How pathetic of him. Call back that search and let him rot where he is. I have no sympathy for such incompetence."

"Of course, Lord S——,"

With no warning, he's struck hard across the cheek, his head snapping to the side from the force of the blow.

"Say not my name, fool," hisses the voice. "Or I'll have your tongue for a trophy."

"F-forgive me," the man stutters, cowering, one hand cuffed over his bruised cheek.

"Get out of my sight!" barks the Sorcerer in his fury.

I shrink deeper into the cover of the crates, shocked by how close I came to learning the Sorcerer's identity, wishing the man had been quicker about revealing it.

After the horse is led hastily away, I wait for a long time to leave, just to be safe. When I'm as sure as I can be that the way is clear and I won't be spotted, I leap over the wall and dash from the keep. Tents scatter the sprawling lawns in the fields between the keep and the village, each one flying a flag bearing the same emblem everyone in red wore in the palace, and at the flood. The Knights of Conquer.

Between Kordelya and Cerion I pass floods, fires, and worse. I pass red-cloaked battalions all riding, camping, hunting, or rescuing. The kingdom swarms with them. I must find the prince. This can't wait. I must tell him.

I close my eyes and think of him, remembering his scent, recalling his essence. Over Cerion's wall I leap, and I weave my way through the festival crowds to home in on him. I lose his trail at a broad set of guarded doors in a stone wall beside a shop, but I catch it again at the opposite side of the city, on a quieter, tucked-away street.

It leads me to a stone staircase going up to a rich wooden door. The banner waving above it displays the same emblem Lisabella and her brother wear, as well as the man called Josten who didn't want to dance with the woman at the spring ball, and the group of riders the king sent to the Grove's borders.

I trot up to the door and sniff it, finding it well-warded. Same with the windows, but, just like Mya's room, the walls are not warded.

I'm going to have to tell these Mages a thing or two about their methods, I think, sauntering through the wall. To my delight, inside, I find not just the prince, but his guards, Lisabella, Gaethon, and Mya all gathered around a wide, round map table.

Cautiously, I creep across the room and duck beneath the table. I listen to the prince as he explains to Mya about the different markers on the map and what they mean, and while they discuss loyalties and oaths together, I concentrate on pulling myself across the city to this spot, and I wake up in fox form at Mya's feet.

28

MAP CRASHING

The mouth-watering aromas of a feast hangs heavy in the air. My stomach growls, the remnants of my breakfast long forgotten. There's no food in sight, though, and the heavier scent of soap mingling with the clatter of washing up nearby tells me I probably just missed it.

The second thing I notice is how just the thought of shifting to my true form makes me slip around a little, and I have to concentrate hard to keep myself to fox.

"Curse the lot of them," Finn's growl draws my attention back to the conversation. "They knew exactly what they were doing waiting until now."

"Yes, they did, Finn," the prince answers. "It grows more and more apparent that this is something they've had planned for quite some time."

They're talking about the red-cloaked Sorcerers. The Knights of Conquer. I creep forward, crouched low until my whiskers nearly brush the tip of Mya's boot. Not for the first time, I'm glad I'm in fox form. What would any of them think discovering a wood elf hiding under the table, eavesdropping about such things?

Mya is writing something in the little book she's holding. I move a little closer, hoping her downcast eyes will catch a glimpse of me. When they do, she looks surprised and glances at the others, then she drops her pen right between my paws and ducks to pick it up.

She doesn't anticipate the prince, though, who bends at the same time and knocks his head into hers.

"Oh! Your Highness! I'm so sorry!" She presses her hand over her head and stares at me like she's trying to decide whether she's imagining things.

"Not at all," says the prince.

He looks at her with an expression that stirs territorial instincts in me. I lunge for the pen without thinking, snatch it between my teeth, and growl a subtle warning before I realize what I'm doing.

"What in seven stars?" Tirnon gasps and stumbles back, and Finn charges with his sword raised.

"No!" Mya blocks me from Finn, her voice sending a wave of warning out from her like a pulse of a spell. For just a breath, everyone freezes.

"Hold, Finn." The prince puts up a hand and his guard does as he says, but Finn's eyes stay locked on me, and his sword remains readied. The tension in the room builds as everyone stares at Mya, and me lurking behind her.

"Don't hurt him," Mya pleads. "He's…" She reaches a hand back to stroke my side, and I slink forward and set the pen gently on the toe of her boot. "He's mine," she whispers, gathering me into her arms. My heart thumps joyfully.

Despite the others' wariness, Mya buries her face into my fur, and I nuzzle her neck affectionately.

"Yours?" Prince Tirnon waves a hand more insistently for Finn to stand down, and the guard sheaths his sword and returns to his post.

"You certainly are full of surprises, Mya," Lisabella says, crouching beside us. She reaches toward me, but I don't allow it. Mya and I know each other. I'd rather save Lisabella and myself both the embarrassment of petting me and realizing later I'm not what she thinks I am. "What's his name?"

"Ah," Mya looks at me, and a blush blooms across her freckled cheeks. "It's…"

I'm reminded of my conversation with Hana, how neither of us could say certain things. I follow her gaze to Gaethon and when his eyes meet mine, recognition sparks between us. He realizes we've met before.

"Will you, ah, will you excuse me?" he asks with a hurried, distracted bow, and rushes out of the room.

"Gaethon," Lisabella runs after him, glancing back at us once before she ducks around the corner.

"How did you get in here?" Mya whispers. Her soft, warm breath tickles my ear. Her voice, even whispered, sends a tingle of pleasure through me. I watch Tirnon thoughtfully and realize I probably only have a short time to offer the information I came for, if Gaethon suspects what I think he suspects.

I jump up to the tabletop and look around the map all laid out with markers for fires, floods, landslides, and red flags marking the Knights of Conquer's movements. Except they're not at all accurate.

It's a little clumsy moving things around with my paw and my nose, but I'm able to shuffle things enough so they're far more accurate than they had been before I started. The prince orders me to get down. When I just keep working moving the markers, he tries to pick me up.

I growl at him.

"Hey," Mya warns me.

I ignore her. Everything is still fresh in my memory, and I don't need the prince distracting me. This is too important.

"Don't," Mya says firmly, and I feel the command take hold of me. My paw hovers over a yellow stone, ready to mark the last of the fire line around the Grove.

"No," Tirnon whispers, "No, let him do it. Look what he's done, there."

I push the last stone into place and Tirnon circles the table, taking in the new movements. Finally, I pick up a handful of red flags in my teeth, trot northward, and drop them right on Kordelya Keep. That does it. His Highness grips the table's edge, white-knuckled. His jaw clenches. His nostrils flare.

"Mya," he murmurs, his voice tinged with fear and anger, "what is this? Where did he come from?"

"I don't—he's—it's," she stutters, but she can't reveal me. The Grove protects me.

I try to shift, but the effort makes me slip around again. Just as I move to hop from the table, Gaethon comes barreling around the corner. His uttered spell flies across the room and slams into me, throwing me from the table.

I crash to the floor, feeling my limbs grow longer and the shag of my hair spill into my eyes. Relief floods over me as I curl into myself, marveling at the spells' ability to change me completely without feeling like I'll slip back and forth again.

Mya screams, and I wince. Lisabella and Tirnon are shouting, yelling at Gaethon for attacking me without warning. I roll to my side gasping for breath, stunned by the efficiency of the Mage's spell.

"Elliot," Mya whispers nearby. "It *is* you."

"It was a simple revealer," Gaethon explains, his tone bored as always.

"Stay back," Mya warns as the others edge closer. They pause. Her voice holds such interesting power. I never noticed it in Dreaming, but she never used it that way there. Not with me, anyway. I don't think.

"How could you?" Mya glowers at Gaethon furiously. He winces a little, and I rush to curtail her wrath.

"Mya," I try to sound soothing, but groan as I push myself to my feet. My limbs feel too heavy, my head too light, my stomach too empty. I realize suddenly this is the first time I've stood in Cerion city on two feet, fully in Waking. I'm actually here now. In my true form. In Cerion.

"It's all right, I'm grateful to the Mage," I tell Mya, resting a hand on her shoulder. All I want is to pull her to me and kiss her, but she's still seething at Gaethon, so it doesn't seem like the right time.

She doesn't answer me or even look at me, so I graze her arm with my fingertips apologetically and step around her to look at the map.

"Are you certain of these movements, Elliot?" the prince asks, deftly changing the subject. When his eyes meet mine, recognition dawns in them.

"Yes, Your Highness," I answer. I'm about to reach into my vest and produce the poison vial to warn him when Mya's stare draws my attention. Her face is pale as a mushroom stem as she gazes at me with a strange, vacant look.

Then, without warning, her legs buckle under her. I catch her in my arms just as her eyes roll back in her head and her body goes limp.

"Fainting... a normal reaction, especially in the wake of a Revealer," Gaethon drawls. "It can be a shock to one's system to witness such a shift."

"Is she all right?" I ask as I sink to the floor, cradling her in my arms. Her body is so solid, so soft and warm against mine. I dip lower, gazing into her beautiful face, thinking about kissing her, but then I remember myself. This isn't the Dreaming. We aren't alone. She isn't even awake.

"I didn't know she'd react this way..." I say quietly, tearing my gaze from her to look to Gaethon.

"Give her a moment," Gaethon replies, looking me over like I'm some sort of specimen. "Her mind needs time to grasp what she has just witnessed."

"Dreams brought into waking," the prince muses as I stroke Mya's pale cheek with my fingertips.

Her freckles are so lovely, her hair so much redder than it had been in Dreaming or through my fox eyes. In Waking, even more than in Dreaming, she's breathtaking. I feel the prince's eyes on me, but I don't want to look away from her. I hope it's not rude of me to ignore him.

"You came to me in a dream last night," says the prince.

"And me, Highness," says Finn from across the room. "Had a

strange message for me."

"Is that right, Finn?" Tirnon asks. "Did you? Forgive me, Elliot?"

"Eldinae," I reply softly.

"Did you, Master Eldinae?" the prince asks more formally.

I nod.

"I did. Please, just call me Elliot."

When I'm about to explain my presence in their dreams, Mya stirs in my arms. Her eyes flutter open, and she gazes at me with such adoration that I can think of nothing else. She clings to me as we get to our feet, and I circle my arms around her.

"I'm sorry," I whisper. "It was never my intention to…"

Her hands slide into my hair, and she leans close until her breath is warm on my lips. My eyes slide from hers along her cheek to her lips, and again I think about what it would be like to finally kiss her here in Waking. It doesn't matter whose company we're in. She closes her eyes and I lean closer—

"Really! The noise!" a shrill voice interrupts us, and Mya gasps and jumps away from me.

"Mouli," Lisabella whispers, and she and Gaethon exchange slightly embarrassed glances.

Nervous tension hangs thick in the air as a hassled, round, middle-aged woman in an apron and a frilly white hat bustles into the room.

"What are you doing in here? Throwing boulders?" Mouli cries, coming to a stop right in front of me. I freeze in place, terrified to move as she looks me over slowly from head to toe.

"Oh no. Boots," Lisabella whispers too late.

"Boots!" Mouli yelps. She grabs me by the elbow and leads me out of the room, and I'm too perplexed to try to get away.

"I don't spend all day with a scrub brush for my own pleasure," she scolds. "Honestly, is it too much to ask not to have you lot traipsing all over the hall, tracking mud over the floors? Go on, take them off!"

"S-sorry," I murmur, flopping onto the mat to pull off my fringed moccasins. I glimpse all the boots lined up beside the door and take note of the strange custom for next time.

"Take some slippers, for stars' sake." Mouli clicks her tongue at my bare feet, hands on hips, shaking her head, then she rushes off to shout again at the others. No wonder Lisabella was so concerned about Gaethon being home in time for supper. Mouli is a little scary.

I take the only slippers from the tray: a pair of fluffy, purple-colored woolen ones that fit like clouds over my feet. Sitting on the mat, I wriggle my toes inside of them and remember Hana's prediction:

"Your feet slipped into puffs of clover. Banners of purple and blue, and blue

and gold. A fox sleeping under a feather bed. Smoke in the sky. A red-haired girl with a voice as pure as birdsong..."

A thrill shivers over me, and I creep up behind Mouli and wiggle my foot in Mya's direction, smiling.

"Oh! Not those," Mouli cries, pointing at the slippers. "Those are his Highness's!" She gestures to Tirnon, who's trying hard not to laugh. Behind him, Lisabella covers her own smile, hugging her stomach.

"It's all right, I don't mind," says the prince with a wave of his hand and a triumphant grin at Lisabella while Mouli's attention is on me. "Keep them."

I skulk in the doorway behind Mouli while she shouts at them some more, my thoughts sliding back to Hana and the slippers and the Grove and all that's happened. She'd be excited to hear her predictions have come true. She'd love the slippers, especially.

After Mouli finally rushes back to the kitchen, the prince returns to the map on the table and mutters under his breath, "If only we could harness Mouli's boot wrath against our enemies."

"If only," Gaethon agrees, still obviously embarrassed.

I make my way back to Mya's side, staring thoughtfully at my new slippers. When I look up at her and our eyes meet, I smile, and her face lights up.

"Back to our unexpected guest," Gaethon says. "I assume he has come to you in dreams, Mya?"

Mya nods, taking my hand, and a surge of warmth blooms all the way to my toes.

"Fascinating," Gaethon says, his eyes meeting mine. In them I see a familiarity, like he already knows the answers, but he's asking anyway to benefit the others. "From which Grove do you hail, Druid?"

"Sorlen Grove," I reply, the feather in my braid causing my ear and cheek to tingle softly. I'm aware of a shift within me. Aft'elu is nearby. I can feel their presence hovering and my own awareness drifting aside as the Mage questions us. I look around warily. Nobody else seems to notice.

"The East Grove," the prince says thoughtfully.

"That is how it is known to us, yes, Your Highness," Gaethon nods.

The prince stands over the map, pointing to our Grove completely surrounded by yellow stones.

"Fires," Aft'elu has me whisper. "A line from Sownsod to Mare's Head at the east, and another along the stretch of Sorlen River."

"Surrounding the Grove," the prince frowns. "You have come to ask for our aid?"

"That's doubtful, Highness," Gaethon shakes his head. "It is not the way of Druids to approach those on the outside. They have methods of protecting themselves and their Grove. Ancient magic outside of the reaches of our own."

"It's true," I agree, heavily under Aft'elu's influence. "My people would have burned with the Grove before coming here for help. But I couldn't ignore the call. It was much stronger than the warnings of my Elders. Stronger than the forbidding of my father. I didn't come here to ask for help. I came here to offer it. I knew what leaving would mean."

I listen to myself speak, my voice as soft as a breeze through grass, and wonder at the words Aft'elu has chosen. I understand why they would twist the truth in such a way. They want these humans to trust me. They want them to think me separate from the Grove. An outcast. A hero who has sacrificed everything to be here.

"What would it mean?" Mya asks breathlessly, squeezing my hand.

"A Druid is bound to the Grove. Leaving once is leaving for life," Gaethon explains.

"A Druid follows the trail set before him," I say, the words mostly my own again. "Two paths opened to me. When they converged, when I realized Mya was here, too…" I gesture to the map and to Mya, and move my hands together, one of them still clinging to hers, "I couldn't deny it. I knew my fate called me to leave the Grove."

That, at least, is the truth. It's a relief to admit it. A relief I'm allowed to say so. I expect Aft'elu to fade, but their presence surges slightly stronger, and I yield to them again.

"Unlike the others, I couldn't sit at peace and watch the world around me burn. Or do nothing, knowing the life of a good man who would one day be a good king was threatened. Knowing the peace of an empire was at stake."

They are carefully crafted words, words I never would have thought of myself, words chosen to inspire sympathy and ensure my commitment to helping them. Words that make it seem like my leaving was final, and I'm on my own now. Words that are, in the end, mostly true.

"Then I am indebted to you, Druid," says the prince. "And I thank you for choosing the path which would aid me." The prince meets my gaze from across the table, his lips pressed into a thin line. I wonder if he's thinking about the dream message I sent him, the assassin, the poison. If he is, he doesn't let on.

"The plots of the red-cloaks are woven like a web all across Cerion, spun with traces of dark magic," Aft'elu says with my voice. I think of the unseen Sorcerer and the three who entered the Grove, and the rest of the Knights of Conquer spread across the kingdom. "I only ask that you let me help put a stop to them."

"As we feared," Gaethon says, his brow deeply furrowed. "Sorcery." Beside him, his sister shivers.

"They tell me nothing can be done without proof," Tirnon explains to me. "They tell me there are no explicit threats against me." His eyes slide toward my vest pocket where the poison vial is tucked away. "That the actions of that guild are charitable in the face of natural disasters. They have come to the aid of my father's subjects, and the people love them for it."

His gaze settles on the red flags at Kordelya keep, and his expression darkens.

"Not all say that," Gaethon argues gently. "Some see through it, Highness."

"Yes. Even Father is starting to see the truth, now that Tasiven has been able to divert his attentions."

I glance at Mya, who looks slightly proud at that. I want to ask who Tasiven is, but I think it's better to stay quiet for now.

"Indeed," Gaethon's bored tone snaps me back to the conversation, "it was wise to suggest someone else have his ear for a change."

"Tell me, Elliot of Sorlen Grove," the prince asks. "What help have you come to offer?"

"In sleep," I explain, my voice a little wary as I wait for Aft'elu to take over again. When they don't, I continue on my own, "I can scout over leagues of land. I can seek out one man or one hundred. I can hear plans and see movements that are about to be made. I can find a man of suspicion and watch him, unnoticed." *As long as he's not an invisible Sorcerer,* I think.

"You mean to say you would remain in one place, but travel elsewhere in your mind?" Tirnon asks, fascinated.

"In my dreams," I agree.

"Forgive me," says the prince, "how then do you know the difference between Dreaming and reality? How can anything you discover be trusted as fact?"

I nod toward the map, "Intuition. Intuition with absolutely no doubt, Highness. I know what is real and what is not."

"I have read of this manner of dream scouting, Highness," Gaethon says. "It is a highly sought-after skill, and most reliable when authentic."

"Is it something that must be regulated through the Academy?" the prince asks.

"No, Highness," Gaethon explains. "They need not be aware. As I noted, the magic of Druids is ancient and separate. It is untouchable by the Academy and its scholars and rules."

"But it is not illegal?" asks the prince.

"No, Highness," Gaethon says. "In fact, I believe this is the very solution we have been searching for. A sure way to determine Mage or Sorcerer without making anyone aware of our efforts."

"But that's easy," Mya interjects. "Sorcerers bear Mage Mark. You can see it plain as day on their skin."

"The Mark begins here," Gaethon points to his chest, just over his heart. "It spreads to the shoulders first, and up toward the neck, and is easily hidden by the high collars of Cerion's Mages. So, to a point, one could practice a certain degree of dark magic without raising suspicion."

"So, you want me to find out who's a Sorcerer and who isn't?" I ask.

"That's a good first step in all of this," the prince agrees, his eyes still fixed on the red flags at Kordelya Keep. "Is it possible?"

"Absolutely," I reply proudly, eager to prove myself and make a difference. This task would help both the Grove and Cerion equally. "It's one of the easiest things I can do. All I need is a safe place to curl up."

I look at Gaethon, suddenly remembering the faulty wards here, and the fading wards at the palace. I have to tell him about them, but I don't want to mention them in front of everyone else. I'm afraid it might embarrass him.

"Oh, and perhaps a change back? My abilities come easier in fox-form, you see, and traveling here took a lot out of me. I'm afraid I'm rather drained." It's mostly true. But also, a good excuse to get him alone to warn him.

"Of course," Gaethon agrees. "Easy enough."

"You're going to change back already?" Mya asks sadly, sidling closer to me. I look into her eyes apologetically. I know what she's thinking. We haven't even gotten to kiss yet.

"Just for a little while," I say. "But we should return to the inn first. The lines are clearer there. This place has far too many wards on it for me to easily get through to Dreaming." Again, it's mostly true, but it also ensures we'll stay together.

"Well," Gaethon says, slightly annoyed, "that is very much the point of wards. I shall have to adjust our protections to include the very obscure and unexpected passing-by of uninvited Druids, from now on."

I give him a sheepish shrug, relieved he's admitted it himself. He's smarter than I anticipated. I like him.

"Gaethon, don't be inhospitable," Lisabella scolds.

"I am being practical, Sister. That is all."

"Well, this has turned out to be a much more eventful afternoon than I think any of us expected," says the prince, still looking over the map. "I've stayed too long. I should be getting back to Father."

They all say their farewells, and Mya and I walk hand-in-hand as Gaethon leads us out of the hall and across the city, back to the inn.

29
GAETHON

"**M**ya, if this is indeed your room, I hope you did not pay good money for its wards." Standing in front of her inn door with a disgusted expression, Gaethon drones explanations about the nature of the wards cast here. His deep voice lulls me, and my eyelids grow heavier and heavier as we stand beside him in the hall.

By the time Mya lets us into the room, I can barely keep my eyes open. I slump into the nearest chair and yawn. All this shifting and scouting without a meal to help me recover is starting to take its toll. I wonder whether my energy draining quicker is temporary, or if this is just how things will work for me since I left the Grove.

While the other two talk, I let my eyes close just for a moment.

When I wake up, they're in Mya's room whispering together with the door closed. Yawning, I push myself out of the chair and go to the door and call for her. She comes out looking concerned, her gorgeous green eyes pools of ocean and tears.

I can't help myself. I pull her to me and kiss her like I've wanted to since the moment our eyes met underneath the map table. Our kiss feeds my soul, replenishing my energy, filling me up. The taste of her lips is better than a wisp's gift, better than any feast, better than a sip at Aft'elu's pool of Lifesap. We kiss for as long as she lets me, until my hunger pangs are forgotten and my exhaustion fades to nothing. When we eventually part, I gaze into those same eyes of green ocean feeling worlds better.

"Are you sure you have to?" she asks, her voice filled with reluctance.

I'm soaring so high from our kiss that I have to think very hard to remember what she might be worried about. Oh, right. The Sorcerers.

"Are you sure it's a good idea?" she goes on. "Gaethon said—"

"Mages think they know everything," I whisper, my lips brushing her ear. I wish she'd turn her head and kiss me again. Any doubts I had about leaving the Grove to come here have vanished completely.

"He said I need to keep you safe," Mya explains, trailing her fingers across my back. I shiver with pleasure and pull her closer, marveling at how perfectly we seem to fit in each others' arms.

"Stay with me while I'm gone," I say quietly. "So I can come back to you. That's all I need."

"I will," she whispers. "I promise."

I hug her tighter, and her voice lilts around us like a melody.

"There are songs about love," she says. "I've heard so many of them and even written some of my own, but all of them fail in this moment, with you here."

Warmth floods through me at her words, and as I kiss her cheek in response, Gaethon clears his throat over her shoulder.

"Very profound, for one so young," he says, sounding slightly jealous.

"I'm fourteen next month," Mya argues, her eyes sparkling as she keeps them locked to mine.

"Ah, then you must know all of the secrets of the stars already," Gaethon says dryly. "And now you have learned why Mages don't joke. Come, Elliot, and make yourself comfortable. Mya, I advise you to wait here until I call for you, to avoid distraction."

"That was a joke?" I whisper, kissing her close to her ear. She laughs and hugs and kisses me once more, and I feel charged with determination for the task ahead.

"Be safe," she says, "and careful."

I nod and duck into her room, closing the door behind me, and find Gaethon studying me again just as he had been in the map room. He stands exactly in the center of the room, right beside the blue dress draped over the chest at the foot of her bed.

"You have no need of my aid, Druid," he says knowingly.

I shrug and shake my head. The buzz of Mya's kiss lingers, making it hard for me to remember exactly why I did want to speak to him alone.

"I can change on my own," I admit. "And your spell has helped to ground my shifting. But I have information for you, and something is troubling me that I hoped you might shed light on."

"I have countless questions for you as well," the Mage admits. "But none are so pressing as to delay your important work."

"Mine are pressing enough for that," I say.

"By all means," he nods, and gestures for me to continue.

"Firstly, most importantly, a warning about the wards you have set on your hall. They cover only the doors and windows. The walls are open to any who have a way through them."

"Ah, so that's how you managed to get in, is it?" Gaethon taps his lip thoughtfully. "Fascinating. I am eager to hear more about how you're able to pass through solid things, such as walls."

"There are many things I'll be happy to share with you, and many things I'm forbidden to speak about. It'll be interesting to figure out which is which later, but for now, as you said, best not to let ourselves get distracted."

"Indeed," Gaethon nods. "Though the mere fact you were able to visit me in Rumination seems to indicate we are linked in some small way. Perhaps we are meant to share secrets others might not be able to discuss."

Aft'elu's feather tickles my cheek, and I understand its meaning right away.

"I think you're right in that. I'm glad you remembered seeing me there."

"I have not stopped thinking about it since the moment it happened. And I suspect it was not your only visit, either. Though I would ask you to refrain from such…observations in the future. Here, watching someone while you remain hidden is frowned upon. A breach of trust at the very least. You understand, I'm sure.'

"I do," I say, shrugging apologetically.

"Good," says the Mage. "Now, what was it you wished to ask me? Something was troubling you?"

"Recently I was scouting," I tell him, "and I came upon a Sorcerer in a tower."

"Where was this tower?" he interrupts. "What did the Sorcerer look like?"

"Kordelya Keep—"

"Kordelya! Are you certain? That keep is occupied by a loyalist to the king and to the prince. They would never be hosts to any Sorcerer!"

"I'm sure," I answer, scowling at his interruption. He paces the room, drumming his fingers on his chin, looking very agitated.

"What is it about Kordelya?" I ask. "The prince seemed just as furious when I told him the red-cloaks are occupying it."

"It is the home of the Earl of Kordelya and his daughter, Lady Naelle, whom the prince is courting," he answers darkly. "If a Sorcerer has occupied himself there, we must inform the throne and the

Academy at once. Tell me, who was this Sorcerer?"

"That's just it," I answer, "I couldn't see him. Others could see him, and I could hear him, and I think he was able to see me, though I should have been hidden to him."

"Ah," Gaethon continues to pace, his brow furrowed thoughtfully. "There is a certain sight unseen charm." He stops pacing and thinks for a long time. "It fits your description perfectly, in fact. Its wearer cannot be observed by anyone who is hidden to them. More powerful instances of this charm can disguise the wearer's voice, and even more powerful ones would lend him the ability to see the unseen."

"A charm?" I ask, shaking my head. It sounds so simple.

"It could be anything. An amulet, an earring, a bracer. Any object that has been imbued for such a purpose."

"So, in order to be able to see who he is, I'd have to get the charm away from him?"

"Indeed. Which, as you can imagine, would prove a difficult task if he is invisible to you."

"Right," I nod, scowling.

"I would advise against trying it," Gaethon warns. "If you sense the presence of this Sorcerer again, do not approach him. Anyone harboring such a powerful object has fully embraced the darkest magic. Such an object is an implementation of Necromancy. Death magic is abhorrent, and strictly forbidden in all of Cerion."

"Speaking of abhorrent," I say, pulling the poison vial from my vest. "I intercepted an assassin on the way here. This was meant for the prince, under the orders of that same Sorcerer."

Gaethon takes the vial and whispers a spell over it, and the vial rattles and quakes in his palm until he closes his fingers around it.

"Blackheart poison," he seethes. "Despicable. I'll inform the Mage council at once, and they'll bring the matter before the king. I must confiscate this. It is highly illegal within our borders." He sweeps a hand over it and the vial vanishes.

"Now, to business. I would advise you to start your search for Sorcerers within the city. We are in the middle of a festival, as I am sure you're aware, and many have gathered for the celebrations. I imagine you might find several Sorcerers lurking around pretending to be Mages. We would be most interested in those bearing the colors of the Knights of Conquer, as his Highness is highly suspicious of them and desperate to produce solid proof of their dark dealings. Names, if at all possible, and locations."

I nod, wondering to myself whether all Mages enjoy the sound of their own voices as much as Gaethon seems to.

"How does it work, exactly?" he asks me, leaning forward with fascination.

"Finding Sorcerers?" I ask.

He nods. "You said it was one of the easiest things you could do. For us, finding a Sorcerer who wishes to keep his dealings secret is quite challenging."

"By scent, mostly. They all have a particular odor to them. Mages smell different." I sniff the air around him, and he raises a dubious brow. "A cleaner, fresher sort of scent. Sorcerers smell like something that has gone foul. Like rotten meat."

"Remarkable," the Mage whispers, tapping his fingertips together like steeples as he gazes at me again like I'm something to be studied.

"Well," I say, clearing my throat softly. "I'd better get started."

"Oh, I imagine you'd prefer to change without an audience..." he trails off as I step forward, shifting easily to fox form midway through my hop up to the bed. Gaethon's jaw drops and he shakes his head, obviously astonished.

Look at that, I think to myself as I yawn and curl up, *he's speechless.*

30

REMEMBERED

Despite the crowded city, it's even easier to find Sorcerers than I expected. There aren't many, and they stick out asleep in inn rooms mingled with normal folk. Their rooms are always over-warded just like Solace Hall, with doors and windows under protection, but not walls.

I find eight of them all across the city before dawn. By daybreak I discover that inns have logbooks, and I go back around collect the names of all the Sorcerers I sniffed in them.

The Knights' of Conquer hall is a disappointment, though. A few Mages leave around breakfast time in a group of two score members all dressed in red, but they all smell clean. No Sorcerers there. Of course not. All their Sorcerers are out wreaking havoc on the countryside while the king and the prince are occupied with the festival, just like the others said last night.

My tail twitches anxiously, and I pick up speed to leap into the sky onto pink and orange sunrise clouds. Soaring across the countryside, I marvel at the endless rows of tents dappling the fields outside the city walls, and I dive to weave through the line of travelers that snakes along the road and disappears behind a hillock far in the distance.

I had no idea so many people existed in Cerion. I had no idea so many existed in the entire world, really. The sight of them fills me with questions. Have they all come for the festival? Why? How are so many going to fit inside the city? Do they not have festivals in their own villages? Then my heart sinks. Do they still have villages of their own?

I circle around to the ocean side and gape at the harbor, packed just as full as the road. Imagine if that Sorcerer had succeeded, and the prince had been killed while all these people visited his kingdom. It would have been an unthinkable tragedy.

Blackheart poison. Gaethon had seemed repulsed by the thought of it, like it was low even for a Sorcerer and an assassin who would conspire to murder a prince. I hope he didn't notice that I had no idea what he was talking about. I had never heard if it before.

In the Grove we're aware of the concept of poisons. We know there are mushrooms and berries we should never eat, and reptiles and amphibians we should never provoke or touch. The concept of poison is no stranger to us, but using it to harm another is so foreign to me.

In the Grove, wicked thoughts like that wouldn't even cross our minds. I wonder if that's because of our nature. Or maybe...maybe some Druids do have those thoughts, but they're taken away. Prevented. Stolen by the fold, or the wisps, or the *Rianave*. The Ancients. With the ocean far beneath me, the wind in my fur, and the knowledge that I'm safe back at the inn with Mya, I let my thoughts wander from my task, all the way back to the Grove.

My thoughts race even faster than my feet. I think about how many times my will was shifted by the wisps. How much of what I did and said and felt came from them and not myself? My ear tingles, reminding me of Aft'elu's feather, and my mind turns down a dark path. Even now, I'm not alone. Even now, they're watching. Yesterday in Solace Hall, they took me over and spoke with my own voice, and I let them. I even thought it was a good idea at the time.

With time and space between then and now, I realize I deceived a prince and his guards and his friends. What would have happened to me if Aft'elu's intentions weren't good ones? We Druids wouldn't intentionally cause harm, but would the wisps? Would the *Rianaves*? Would Aft'elu?

I skirt west along the coast and up again into the sky, and I'm greeted by a sweet little blue and gold songbird who chirps excitedly and circles around my head. I think back to that day I saw the sparrow dead on the unseen Sorcerer's table.

Random memories of the time before that spill into my head. Everything was so strange in the Grove just before that: Diving into Echo Pool from those high, muddy cliffs, the way the storm clouds churned over the mountains, kissing Hana in the cave that used to belong to foxes—except at the time I had forgotten all about the foxes.

I keep running. Breathtaking mountains too vast to climb stand like sentinels along the elven coastline, its shores all frothy white foam bubbling as impossibly blue waves crash over pure white stones. The seawater is so clear I can see all the way to the sandy bottom, which is dotted with a spectacle of fish more colorful than a meadow full of wildflowers.

The songbird darts around me until I reach the water's surface to skim across it. Her chirps stir the memory of a completely different scene in my mind. The room I slept in with Kaini, my room, but with walls covered in vellum writings and drawings.

Mari sitting up in bed whispering to a sparrow in the window.

Mari.

Sister.

Remembering her is such a shock that I lose my focus and tumble beneath the ocean waves. I know from scouting under Echo Pool that I'm safe underwater. I don't even have to hold my breath. I don't even have to pretend to swim. I just run through the depths, dazzled by the way the sunlight sparkles on its surface and streaks through the water, dancing over fields of kelp and sea grass and dozens of fantastical sea creatures.

It's a feast for my eyes, but all I can think of is of Mari. Her letters. Her kindness. Her fear as she stood on the balcony with Elowyn, fretting over me. Her love.

I miss you desperately. Keep me in your mind. I beg you, do not make me Forgotten.

I look away from the shore toward the depths and realize there's an entire world down here that I could spend the rest of my life exploring, but I won't allow myself to get distracted. Not now that I remember. I try to think of how long it has been since Mari last heard from me. She must be beside herself with worry.

I think of poor Kyu and let out a mournful cry and soar out of the waves, taking my true form.

The new songbird greets me like she's been waiting, and I run faster, letting the wind propel me.

"Are you one of Mari's?" I call. "Is she nearby?"

The songbird tweets excitedly and soars away, and I shift easily back to a fox to follow her over the unclimbable mountains, through lush green valleys dotted here and there with white stone cottages and immense sentinel statues. I've never seen this side of Ceras'lain before. I can't believe how vast it is, how stunning its landscape of mountains and waterfalls and forests heavy with the perfumes of all the colorful unusual flowers that cascade around me.

Then I pick up a different blend of scents: earth, lavender, straw, and reeds. Mari. Sister.

I fly so fast everything becomes a blur until I reach her balcony, where she's perched on a silky cushioned chaise, rocking her baby in her arms. Her baby. Has it been that long?

Inside the curtains beyond the wards, I glimpse Elowyn's robes fluttering in the gentle summer breeze as he writes at his desk. My heart skips with excitement as I land lightly on the polished ivory stone of the balcony and concentrate, pulling my awareness back along the threads to my fox form in Cerion.

I'm still curled on Mya's bed, asleep. Mya isn't there. The door is locked. I could leave, just for a little while. Back in Ceras'lain, I draw myself along the thread, snap myself back to one again, and step out of hiding in wood elf form.

Mari notices the songbird first, who trills brightly as she comes to rest on the back of the chaise. My sister's gaze flicks away from her cooing baby across the balcony to me, and her eyes go wide.

"Elliot?" she whispers in disbelief. "Brother?" she cries louder and jumps up from the chaise. Elowyn ducks though the curtains as Mari and I run to each other, and I throw my arms around her and the baby.

"How are you here?" she whispers, her voice strangled with emotion. Between us, the baby giggles and coos and reaches for the feather dangling from my braid. I push it back over my shoulder to keep it from touching her.

"Here is your little niece," Mari sniffles and shifts the baby closer. "Elomae, this is your Uncle Elliot."

I gaze down at the little one, marveling at her delicate little pointed nose, the softness of her rosy cheeks, the elegant point of her tiny ears poking out of her lacy little cap, and her dancing, sparkling eyes.

"She's amazing," I whisper, awestruck by how much of the elves' charm she already possesses.

Elowyn steps forward and offers his open arms to Elomae, and she squeals with excitement and reaches for him.

"And this is Elowyn," Mari says, looking at him with such adoration as she passes him the baby that my heart warms for her.

"I know," I say, grinning.

"I imagine you do," says the elf, offering as much of a bow as he can with the wriggling baby in his arms. "Mari has told me many things about you, my wood elf brother. I am delighted to finally see you with my own eyes. You are of course welcome here. Please," he sweeps a hand toward the grouping of elegant chairs across the balcony. With a flourish at the end of his gesture, a tray piled with food appears on the table there.

"Mari has told me how famished you become while traveling," he explains with a smile. He gazes at me with the same wonder most show when first meeting a high elf like him, and I can see the hundreds of questions racing behind his eyes.

Mari takes me by both hands to pull me toward the seats, which are dappled by the shade of enormous willow. Its long, silvery leaves remind me so much of the entrance to the fold that I half expect to see pink mist when I peer through them, but the other side is just a soothing waterfall spilling into a milky blue pool.

"How are you here?" Mari asks again, her eyes dancing with excitement. "I was sure you had forgotten me, especially after Kyu…" She shakes her head and Elowyn reaches for her, brushing her shoulder with his hand.

"You know what happened to Kyu?" I ask mournfully, and Mari nods. Her face holds so much anguish I can't bear to ask anything more about it. As I take the chair beside hers, she clings to my hands like she's afraid I'll disappear if she lets go.

"Are you hurt?" she asks urgently. "Did something happen? I've been beside myself with worry and awful thoughts, with no way to send a bird…"

She goes quiet and tearful again, and I shake my head slowly, glancing at Elowyn as he settles with the baby in a seat across the small table.

"Eat, Brother," he urges as Elomae gums the knuckle of his thumb, gurgling happily.

"Yes, of course," Mari says, flustered. "Please."

She slips into her old habits of taking care of me, wiping tears from her cheeks as she piles an elegant silver dish high with elven delights for me, and I tell her as much as I'm able to about Mya, and my recent travels, and my choice to leave the Grove. So much of what I want to tell her is forced from my mind before I can begin to form the words.

I'm able to tell them of the unseen Sorcerer, the fires, what I saw at Kordelya Keep, and my meetings with Mya and the others in Cerion, but anything that happened before then is blocked from my lips.

At one point when I look over at Elowyn I notice he's sitting rail straight, his expression darkening.

"What's wrong?" I ask warily, setting my emptied dish on the carved stone table.

Silently, Elowyn hands the baby to Mari and crosses to me, and I gulp nervously and tuck deeper into my chair as he stands over me, brow furrowed.

"Elowyn," Mari whispers as she snuggles the baby closer. "What is it?"

The elf reaches a slender hand toward my face, his fingers tracing the air beside my ear, where the feather is braided securely.

"Did you agree to this?" he murmurs, his tone both concerned and appalled.

My heart starts to race like I've been caught in a terrible lie. I nod slowly, looking from him to Mari, whose face has gone pale with concern.

"Agreed to what?" she asks. "What is it, Husband?"

"*Il'iluvrie*," Elowyn replies.

"*Il'i...*" she whispers, staring at me. She shakes her head, her voice rising in anger. "They couldn't just let him go, could they? Couldn't simply let him leave. Of course not. Even when we're gone, even when Forgotten, we're under their thumb. No matter what we do or where we go the Grove keeps its hold, blotting our memories, holding our tongues for us. Using us in whatever way serves them best!"

"Peace, Mari," Elowyn offers quietly, his gaze still fixed on my feather.

"How can I find peace with this?" she glowers at me, tears of anger spilling to mingle with the joyful ones. "It's vile."

Her agitation makes the baby fuss and cry, and Elowyn steps away and takes her gently from her mother, his eyes never leaving the feather in my braid.

"What does it mean?" I ask Elowyn, even though I already know the answer.

"It means you are tied to one there. There is someone in the Grove who you remain bonded to, even now, who can see through your eyes, feel your feelings, hear what you hear."

I remember the moment Aft'elu gave me the feather at the pool of the fold. I remember how special it made me feel. How important. How purposeful. I remember the promise I made, that I'd be their eyes wherever I go. Even here. I stand up and take a few steps back, the realization of what I've agreed to crashing over me like a tree struck by lightning.

Mari holds me, but I hardly feel her touch even when she hugs me so tightly I can barely breathe.

"If I can see you, they can see you," I whisper.

"I don't care," Mari says firmly. "You are my brother and I love you. I've already lost you once because of them."

"My wards prevent it," says Elowyn, who kisses Mari's temple as he gathers all three of us into his long, graceful arms. "Though your tongue might be held, whoever has bound you cannot reach you here, my brother."

My stomach churns anyway. The baby reaches for my feather again and Mari grabs her hand away with a gasp.

"Who is it?" Mari asks, her voice tinged with anger. "Who are you bonded to? Amma?"

I shake my head, pushing the feather back over my shoulder, out of the way.

"Father?"

Again, I shake my head.

"An Elder?"

"He could not tell you, *Av'alenia,* my beloved," Elowyn interrupts. "Even if it was someone you named, he could not tell you."

"Can you break it?" she whispers to Elowyn.

"It cannot be done," he replies apologetically.

"Elowyn." Mari looks up at him like she knows he isn't being truthful.

Elowyn sighs.

"It cannot be done without risking our alliance with the Grove," he elaborates. "Please do not ask it of me. I can only offer our home as a place of refuge from the bond, should you need it. Even that is a breach of our treaties."

She gathers me close, hugging me to her like she'll never let go. That's fine with me. I don't want her to.

"I wouldn't break it anyway, Sister," I tell her truthfully. "Not now. Many paths were open to me. I chose this one for myself."

31
A JOURNEY ASLEEP

When my eyes flutter open again I'm on Mya's bed, alone, with my heart still racing. Getting back here was a strange, sickening blur of leaps and dozing that leaves me so exhausted I can barely move. In the next room, Mya is crying. I want to go to her, to comfort her, but my head is too muddled.

I feel like I need a week to go back through every memory I ever had and determine whether it truly happened or not. And what about all the things I've forgotten? Is there more like Mari?

Part of me meant what I said to Mari about choosing the path, but part of me resents that there's no way out of it. I agreed to this for life. Aft'elu made that clear. My ear prickles with magic and I scratch at it vigorously with my hind leg to make it stop. I know I wanted a purpose of my own, but this wasn't what I had in mind by leaving the Grove. I didn't realize they'd always be with me, watching me, putting thoughts in my head and words in my mouth.

I hop from the bed, shifting to two feet just as I reach Mya's wash basin mirror. The green and gold feather glints at my shoulder even in the dim light of the small, shuttered room. I stare at it, my eyes narrowed, for a long time, imagining Aft'elu looking back at me. I wait for them to say something. To scold me for disappearing into Ceras'lain, through wards where they couldn't see me.

They don't.

"Are you there?" I ask my sleepy reflection. The feather flutters gently, tickling my jaw. For a fleeting moment, I consider drawing my knife and cutting the braid free. Letting the feather fall to the floor. But then I remember with Aft'elu said about having to return to the Grove on foot. About potentially losing skills I've grown attached to.

I sigh and turn away. Drawn to Mya, I slink into the next room where she dozes tucked into the armchair at the foot of the big bed. She had been crying. I wonder why. I don't want to wake her now, when she just fell asleep.

I stand over her, deciding what to do, gazing at her beautiful bright red hair and the dappling of freckles across her delicate cheeks. A scent catches in my nose: Burnt herbs, fresh wood, jungle loam from Elespen, strange, faint magic. Copper and silver. Fear and cunning and wit. I follow the scent to a pack stuffed into the corner of the room and I breathe it in to commit it to memory.

That must be why she's crying again. Her father. I've searched for him time and time again since she told me how she missed him, without any luck. Maybe it'll be different searching from Cerion.

It's a welcome distraction. I think of her reaction when I tell her he's alive. At the very least, she'll stop crying over him. She'll know one way or another what really happened to him.

I return to fox form and curl up on the bed in her room where she left me. Then I leap through the shuttered window in the In-between and soar off into the oppressive, humid summer air. No wind blows, but my nose still catches the faintest wisps of scents that could be his. The city is sweltering, and so stagnant and packed with people that it's difficult to pick out one scent from another.

I catch his mix faintly at the entrance to the Seabird's Swoop and along the cobbles, weaving through to the market, tracing down the steps to the docks. Here, it mingles with the scents of barrels and malt liquor and the stuffy insides of a ship's hull which smells of wood and lacquer, tar and sweat and iron and rope.

I backtrack all the way across the sea to Elespen, where his trail twines with the thief woman's scent: leather and ale and copper. At the mill where Mya had been and where both of their scents are much stronger, their names come to me: Paewyn. Silas. I follow the trail along the road to the port.

At an abandoned camp that smells of the barrels again and a strange sort of fresh wood I can't place, Silas's scent disappears.

Puzzled, I leap again into the rich blue sky and back out over the sea, letting its sparkling surface become a blur beneath me. Back in Cerion, the strange wood-scented trail is faint among the throngs. It snakes through the city blended with the stronger scent of barrels and malt and fresh wood until I reach a narrow alleyway leading to a well-warded brick building.

The wards here are brilliantly cast. They cover the entire place from cobbles to roof tiles so I can't get in. They're so strong I can't even sniff the essence of the place. It reminds me of the Knights of Conquer hall.

Everyone who comes out or goes in stinks of shadows and secrets.

I linger through most of the night tucked in the corner of the alley, hoping I'll catch Silas or Paewyn going in or coming out. I never see either of them, but I see enough to make me wonder why Mya is so heartbroken over him.

She is so filled with light, so kind and pure, I can't imagine her associating with anyone who belongs in a place like this, unless my impression of her has been wrong all this time. Most of what I know of her, after all, is what she told me in the Dreaming. And like I told her before: *In Dreaming, we are all as we see our ownselves.*

Washed in moonlight, I reel back to my sleeping self and start to panic when it takes much longer than it should. The Seabird's Swoop blurs beneath me, and my strand pulls me all the way out of the city, past the gates and the walls, along the crowded main road to the northwest, to a village that smells so strongly of churned dirt and freshly broken trees I can barely breathe.

A lingering trace of smoke hangs heavily in the air, too, but the place is silent in sleep, with barely a guard stirring in the towers overlooking the village. It's just before dawn when I finally find Mya asleep in a low-lying building, my sleeping fox-self bundled in a cloak beside her. I pause before I hop up to join myself. It's me, I'm sure, but somehow she has disguised me as a fluffy white pup rather than a fox. I wonder why.

I sniff cautiously and catch the scent of disguising magic woven into the fibers of the cloak. It's all so strange. Why did she come here? Why did she bring me?

A soft snore comes from across the room, where a dark-skinned man sleeps soundly in his own bed. I slink close to him, sniffing the air, and catch the scent of the sea on him. Rope and sails and sunshine. He must be Cort, the Islander Mya said she'd befriended on her journey across the sea. I'm glad he's here with her, wherever here is. I'm glad she didn't travel alone, but I still don't understand why we're here.

Just as I'm about to slip back into myself, I catch another scent like the orchids and willows outside of Mari's balcony, and the Cygnets of Ceras'lain. It wafts on the breeze that whispers through the open door, luring me through hall into the courtyard beyond.

An elf? Here? I trot toward the scent, vaguely aware I'm being followed by someone in the Dreaming, so I pick up speed, letting my nose guide me. A path of white petals leads the way, ensuring this is a path I'm meant to follow.

"What's happening? Where are you going?" Mya asks as she runs beside me through the maze of hallways and outer fences and gates and out across a footbridge over a babbling brook. Her urgent concern distracts me from the scent only for a moment.

Maybe I should lead her back to her bed, but if I do, I might lose the scent. This is her dream, after all, that I've somehow stumbled into.

I tug at the hem of her trousers, urging her faster. The elf's scent grows stronger, calling to me. The petals swirl playfully, enticing me. I feel the intent of them strongly: Peace, vigilance, information. She's close, so close now. I glide up the bank of the mountainside over moss and stones and damp earth, guiding Mya closer to the elf.

"Wait!" Mya cries, falling behind as she scrambles up on hands and feet. "Where are we going?"

I can't wait, though. I have such a strong sense that this moment is fleeting but incredibly important. Aft'elu's feather tingles at my temple and this time I don't scorn it. I'm grateful it's there, guiding me to the waiting elf, who's standing on a flat of stone that overlooks the village where Mya slept. Her hand rests gracefully on her bow, her eyes are alight with relief and warmth at my arrival. Immediately, of course, I think of Elowyn and Mari and little Elomae.

"Wait for me!" Mya calls again, and just as I slip from fox to boy to help her pull herself up to us, the elf woman stoops and offers her own hand.

"Are you all right?" I ask Mya a little apologetically, but she's too transfixed on the beautiful elf in front of us to answer me. I can't blame her.

The elf is breathtakingly elegant, dressed in white and gray suede stitched with decorations of silver floss. Her gray-green cloak is drenched in camouflaging magic that causes parts of her to disappear into the forest behind her.

I watch her with admiration, aware that she has somehow manipulated the Dreaming to send a path to us and wait for us to find her.

"You are not like them," the elf says to Mya, nodding toward the village. Her voice soft, kind, and concerned. Beside me, Mya is silent. Speechless.

"You're of the White Line," I say reverently.

"And you are far from your Grove," she replies with a sorrowful tone.

"I left only days ago," I answer her in her language, Aft'elu's influence guiding me. "I have been sent as a scout, in service of the Ancients and the prince."

Much has happened to the lands outside of the Grove's reach," the elf replies. "It was wise that you would send one of your own to seek an explanation."

"We stand with our allies, as always," Aft'elu replies quietly, the elven language strange on my tongue. "We do not wish to see Cerion's territories razed, burning, crumbling."

"Nor do we," the elf answers with a somber tone. "I am glad we have met in this place. Fortune smiles on us this night, for I have a message for the king."

"The girl is in contact with the throne," Aft'elu says. "Give the message to her."

The elf bows to me reverently, then turns to Mya.

"You have ties to the king," she says in the common tongue, her finger grazing a medal pinned to Mya's tunic.

"More to the prince," Mya says, her voice wary.

"This was no act of nature," the elf explains as she sweeps her hand toward the village in the distance. "I was patrolling here yesterday when I witnessed the man behind this act. I could not fathom what he was doing until it was done. By then, he had fled. Cerion is our neighbor and ally, and the elves cannot idly ignore such evil acts. Nor is it our way to give chase alone into territories which, by treaty and promise, are not ours to traverse.

"When King Victens is prepared to seek the truth of these events, I am prepared to bear witness. Take this." She presses something into Mya's hand. "Tell your king when my name is read aloud, I will hear and come at once to speak my truth."

Mya nods and fades from Dreaming, and the elf gives me a reassuring smile.

"Do not be disheartened, little fox," she offers gently. "You have chosen a noble path."

She fades, too, and all that's left is for me to return to the room where Mya has already woken.

All at once I'm tired and starved. I yawn and crawl closer to Mya while she sits looking dazed. After a moment, I nudge her fist and she opens her hand to reveal the elf's rolled-up note.

"Mya. All right?" Cort asks from his own bed, his eyes fixed on me.

"I had a dream," Mya replies. Her voice, even speaking, even slightly confused, soothes my fox ears. I nudge closer to her and glance at Cort, considering shifting in front of him just so I can kiss her again.

"It was so strange," she goes on. "An elf woman gave me something, and I woke up and…" she holds the scroll out to him, and he sits up and slides a hand toward the hilt of a sword half-hidden beneath his coverlet.

"I was more asking about the fox in your bed," he replies, his eyes still fixed on me.

"Oh, that," Mya chuckles and drapes the cloak over me, and I feel the disguising magic settle over me.

"So, de whole time, it was a fox?" Cort asks, scowling. He reaches for the scroll, and she hands it to him. "Where did he come from, then?"

She looks from Cort to me, but she can't reveal my secret. I'm too protected. They've blocked even Mya from telling my truth. I watch her frustration grow as she sits chewing her lip, trying her hardest to say something. First Mari, now Mya? I stifle an annoyed growl and glance at Cort.

Mya told me about him often in Dreaming, how he looked after her on the ship and kept her safe. I believe I can trust her judgment in this friendship. With an edge of defiance against the Grove, I hop from the bed and shift midway, landing on two feet in my wood elf form.

Cort yelps and jumps to his feet, but Mya stops him with a command, and he pauses before he can draw his cutlasses. I'm reminded of a similar moment when I tried to move the markers over the map and Mya's voice stopped me.

I look at her in wonder and slight concern. Her voice gets her into trouble. She told me that in Dreaming. She also told me how guilty it makes her feel to use it on people who trust her. It's impressively powerful since she can stop an armed, grown man in his tracks with it.

"He's a friend, Cort," she explains soothingly as her command slides off him. "It's Elliot."

"Elliot?" Cort's mouth drops open. "The elf from your dreams, Elliot?"

"Wood elf," I correct him with a yawn, trying hard to ignore my empty stomach.

"When did dis…? How? What?" Cort sputters. "Why didn't you tell me sooner?"

"I felt like it wasn't my secret to tell, I guess," Mya says. "I was going to yesterday while we were riding, but I couldn't figure out the words."

"You?" Cort scoffs in disbelief. "*You* couldn't figure out the words?"

"Not her fault," I explain, yawning again. "My secret's protected by magic. She couldn't tell you."

My stomach growls again, and this time Mya notices and admits, "I'm hungry, too."

But then the two of them start talking about other things, and my own thoughts swirl around me, distracting me from their conversation.

I think of what the elf said about the Sorcerer causing the mountain to slide into the village. It's just like what happened with Rubeus and his companion and the flood. I should have asked her if it was only one Sorcerer, and what he looked like. I should have asked her many things, but I couldn't. Aft'elu took that opportunity away from me.

I slide closer to Mya, stroking her cheek, feeling her warmth. Being close to her reminds me why I left to begin with. Sitting beside her clears my mind, calming me. I wish she'd turn her head, just slightly. I wish she'd kiss me, just a quick one, to root me here.

Roots in soil...

But then Cort clears his throat, and I look away again, yawning and blinking and trying to figure out some other way to ground myself that doesn't involve kissing or eating. Since Cort has gotten up to close the door and pull out some paper from his vest, it seems like neither is going to happen for a while.

32

HUMAN ANGER

"I don't understand," Mya says, going tense beside me as we look over the torn page in Cort's hand. "What does this have to do with me?"

Sleepily, I gaze at the list scrawled there as Cort points from one line to the next in stern annoyance.

"Mya, audience with Prince Tirnon: Eight hundred gold, Traveled to Valleyside: Five hundred gold, King's Entertainments performance: Eight Hundred gold, public performance: Five hundred gold, Kin of Siren: Eight gold crown. Quite a tally she's got going, don't you think?" he growls. "Dat woman."

I haven't learned enough about the worth of gold for the tally to make much sense to me, but I can see the fury in Cort's expression plain as day and feel Mya broiling with her own anger as the color drains from her face. She folds the parchment and hands it back to him, grabbing the elf's scroll from his other hand.

Cort gives me a wary glance as Mya pulls on her vest and snatches up the rest of her things and storms out of the room. We follow her together out into the garden and through some pathetic looking splintered trees.

Hana would never let trees like that suffer. No Druid would walk by without noticing, without trying to help. At the thought of her, the feather tingles at my cheek. I graze the broken trunks with my fingertips as we pass, and Grove magic flows through me, mending the bark, straightening them, filling out their wilted leaves.

"Thank you, lit-tle fox," they murmur as we pass.

Mya and Cort don't notice, though. They don't even slow. She's in too much of a fury over what Cort showed her in the sleeping room.

"Mya," I say gently, reaching for her when I catch up again, but she thrusts out her hand to stop me.

"Wretched game," Cort mutters beside me. "That woman is lucky she didn't come back while I was there. I'd have—"

Mya whirls around looking so terrifying she's barely recognizable, and Cort throws up his hands apologetically. Someone stops us to talk to her and when she answers them, I can hear the effort she's making to keep her voice pleasant.

"I don't understand," I whisper to Cort while Mya is bombarded by villagers. Apparently, she performed a song for them yesterday, and they've all come to thank her for it. "Why is she so angry?"

"Because she won' hear the truth," he answers, glowering, then barks at the gathering crowd, "Come on, you lot, we're hungry. Move aside."

He takes the lead in our small procession and elbows us through the villagers until we reach a broad building that's like the tavern back in the city, but lower and stretched out.

Inside is just as noisy and crowded as any of Cerion's taverns, and while Cort asks about food, Mya puts on the disguising cloak and drops silently into a seat at a nearby table. I look around, watching others eat and thinking about home, where the wisps know what we like and bring it right to us.

Cort slides some coins across the bar and comes back with platters and bowls of dishes I've never seen before. I dig into my breakfast, too starved to ask what any of it is.

As we eat in silence, something needles me. *Kin of Siren,* that one line had said, and that's what got Mya so mad. When I glance across at her, even though her face is obscured by her hood, I can feel her anger radiating from her like flames.

I keep eating, filling the emptiness and exhaustion up with strange country flavors, my thoughts spinning with words from a dream when I had been forced to make a choice: "*She is an enchantress. A siren. Ties must be cut...*" and, "*We have seen the bond between you. We have endeavored to break it, and yet, it cannot be broken. If you wish it, she can remain here, a child of the Grove as you are.*"

The other two eat in silence until Mya finally breaks it.

"She's in for a shock," she says quietly, leaning toward Cort. "You know that, right? She's going to lose. There's no proof she can give, because it isn't true. I'm not one of those. I'm not."

"Mya," I offer cautiously, "have you heard your voice?"

"Thank you!" Cort bellows. People look at us, and Mya shushes him. "Well, honestly, girl. I been saying it to you since we met, ay? Since you did dat—"

"Shh!" she interrupts him, shaking her head. "That doesn't matter. She needs proof. The only person who can provide that is Pa, and he's—"

She chokes on the word, overcome by emotion, and they both go silent again. I glance around nervously and take a few more bites. In the Sanctum, if anyone had dared to shout this much during mealtime, the wisps would have come and calmed them. Nourishment is something to be grateful for, after all. A gift from the Grove. I chase a chunk of meat around my stew with my spoon silently while Mya rages on.

"He wouldn't even tell *me*. Why would he tell *her*? And what does it matter? I've made myself who I am. My mother, whoever she is, or was, has nothing to do with it. She was never there. Never. He pretended like she was a fable. A ghost! And now, because of her—because of who she might have been, now I'm worth what was it? Eight—"

Cort jumps up from his stool and guides her away from the table, and I scoop up two more quick mouthfuls and grab a heel of bread before I follow them reluctantly into a corridor that runs alongside the bar.

"We need to find him," Mya cries once we're tucked away from prying eyes. Her hood has dropped back in her anger, revealing her undisguised face. "I need to know he's safe. I need the truth. I need…Elliot!"

Her face is filled with such hope when she says my name that I can't look at her. I stare down at the wood floor, cracked and worn smooth from so much use. Stains that smell of ale and oil and blood spatter its surface. In the Grove, stains like that would be cleared away with magic. They wouldn't be left to sit as reminders of anything, just in case. Like Mari's letters and drawings, they'd simply disappear.

"You could search for him, couldn't you?" Mya asks, tugging my arm. Her touch warms me all the way through. Her voice stirs hope in my soul. "You could find him!"

I think of my recent journey all the way to Elespen and back. The mill, the road, the camp, the dock, the red brick building I camped outside of all for nothing.

"You said that I called you from across the Dreaming." She pushes off her hood and rests her hands on my shoulders, and I can't help but look into her eager, sea-green eyes. "You left everything you knew for me. For us."

"Is that true?" Cort mutters.

She's so close I could lean forward just a little and kiss her. Maybe if I did, she'd forget her anger. If nothing else, it could delay my reply. My heart beats faster as I rest a hand on her waist, considering it. Dismissing it. I won't be like them, the wisps, the Grove, Aft'elu, distracting and diverting. It's underhanded. It's wrong.

"Yes," I whisper. "And Mya, I looked already. I swear it. I could feel how you longed for him, and I searched for him across the expanse. I wanted to see your eyes light up when I told you I had found him. That he was safe. But I couldn't bring myself to tell you I searched and failed. I couldn't bear to take away your hope."

"You couldn't find him?" she asks tearfully. "What does it mean that you couldn't find him?"

"Don't think the worst," I soothe, pulling her into my arms, holding her close. She tucks herself into me, nuzzling my chest with her cheek, her tears dripping into my fringe. Beside us, Cort rests a hand on one hilt and glowers into the common room like he's expecting someone to jump us.

"Some people are just hard to find, even in Dreaming," I explain. It could mean many things. I'll keep looking. I promise. Until I find him."

We're interrupted by a large man in a dirty white apron who shouts as soon as he sees us, "What're you doing back here? This is not a common hallway!"

"Easy, friend," Cort says quickly, ushering us back from the man, who's carrying a stack of cooking pots in his thick arms. The scent of the stew I ate for breakfast wafts strongly from him. No wonder everyone's in a foul mood, if he's the one who cooked it.

"We're not from here," Cort explains.

"Never would have guessed that," the cook grunts. "Islander, Druid…" he stares at Mya with a hint of recognition and worse than that, a sort of hunger. I hug her tighter and shuffle us another cautious step away. "Hey, you're that singing girl. Mya something, right?"

"Yes," Mya says, clinging to me.

"Yeah, heard of you. A traveler checked out yesterday just before the landslide. Said he had a daughter with red hair spiked up just like yours, named Mya. Bragged about how she was going to sing at Cerion Day. Voice like a songbird, he said. Said he wouldn't miss it for the world. Proud man."

"Yesterday?" Mya whispers in disbelief, loosening her hold on me. I feel her heart thudding, and I hear the hope in her voice as she edges a little closer to the man.

"Aye," he nods. "I remember because I thought how lucky it was he left right before the landslide, and he'd get to hear his girl sing. Anyway, you should be heading back there, shouldn't you? Cerion Day's tomorrow. Wouldn't want to disappoint him."

"That so?" Cort puts his fists to his hips, making himself seem broader, challenging the other man. Cautiously, I edge Mya back a few more paces. Whatever is going on here, I don't want her in the middle of it. My feather prickles with warning. We ought to leave. We shouldn't be fighting here.

"What'd she pay you to say that?" Cort barks accusingly. "Couple gold?"

The man's jaw clenches. His face goes as red as Father's used to when he was in a fury.

"You calling me a liar?" he growls, stomping forward and raising the stack of pots like he means to use them as weapons somehow.

"Cort," Mya interrupts, reaching for his arm to pull him back. "He's telling the truth."

"That's what you want to believe," Cort says defiantly.

"What did he look like?" Mya asks the cook. Cort throws her an angry, warning glance.

"Worn," says the cook with a shrug. He lowers his pots a little. "Knobby. Long arms and legs, thin. Good looking fellow, and one who knew it, too."

I listen closely, painting a picture in my mind of the man he's describing. Maybe knowing what he looks like will help me find him.

"Dressed smartly, traveling clothes, you know. Nothing remarkable. He was a regular sort, or good at blending in, at least. Don't know how you ended up with red hair, though. His was brown. Your mother must be gorgeous, is all I can say. Anyway, got a lot to do, and like I said, you can't be down here. And here in Valleyside, keep in mind you get a lot more out of your stay when you don't go around calling people liars."

He glares at Cort, then rushes off to his work.

Mya and Cort argue in hushed tones all the way through the dining hall and out the front door. She wants to rush back to Cerion to see her father and Cort warns she should at least have a plan in case that man was lying. I agree with him, but I don't say anything. Human anger is strange and unpredictable. I don't want it turned on me if I can help it.

As we reach the steps leading down into the village, Mya pauses. A group of humans head toward us on the road. Some are villagers, others wear red cloaks that swirl behind them as they walk, like the ocean in Mya's dream. A commanding looking man walks at the center wearing a chest plate of burnished metal that glints in the sunlight like a beacon, and a smug expression. As soon as Mya catches his eye, his expression turns to hunger.

The villagers seem drawn to him the same way flies are drawn to

the sweet nectar of a pitcher flower. My right ear tingles with warning. As if reading my mind, Cort grabs Mya's arm and urges her to hurry, but she plants her feet instead and tugs her arm away.

"What are you doing?" Cort whispers through clenched teeth, eyeing the approaching group warily. "If we're going, let's go."

"Trust me," Mya says quietly. It's too late to avoid them, anyway. The commanding man's eyes rest on her, the desire in them a hundred times more threatening than the cook's had been.

When he gets close enough to speak, I realize I've seen him before. He's the Sorcerer from the flood, the one who rescued a man from the rooftop to the cheers of onlooking villagers. I've smelled him before, too: red spice smoke, decay, and dark magic. Haughty pride.

"Good morning," Mya calls as he and his entourage reach us. Her voice is so bright and welcoming I wonder if she even realizes who she's talking to.

"Good morning to you, Miss Songspinner," the man nods, eyeing her with greed like she's something to be owned.

"Forgive me for slipping away last night," she says sincerely. "I was tired, and my throat sore from singing."

"Not at all," the Sorcerer waves a hand, and I glimpse a curl of Mage Mark at his wrist. "Perhaps you can make it up to me, hm?"

I edge forward at his words, breathing in the scent of his wickedness, glowering. The feather at my braid flaps gently at the edge of my vision, tickling a warning that bristles across my cheek and forehead. Be still, it seems to say. Be careful. I try to whisper the warning to Mya, but Aft'elu's influence forces me silent.

Mya squeezes my hand reassuringly. Her voice takes on a sweet, naive tone that's very unlike her. I can feel the influence heavy in it, a powerful magic all her own which offers delectable, unknown promises.

"I haven't forgotten your offer," she nearly sings. "In fact, I've been considering it ever since. But I can't accept without consent from my father, who is traveling right now."

"I'm sure your father would be proud to have a daughter in our noble fold," he puffs up arrogantly, and all his entourage nod in eager agreement. "He'd be a fool not to be."

"Still," Mya offers sweetly, "I'm sure you understand. Perhaps in the meantime, you could send word to your fellows in the city to leave me be, at least until after Cerion Day, as an act of good faith. I should be able to give you an answer by then, and I'd very much like to focus on my performance and not on their...rivalry."

"Rivalry," the Sorcerer laughs through his nose, but even so, his eyes seem glazed over by the power of Mya's voice. I stare at her in disbelief as she continues to weave her voice's spell around him with barely an effort.

Then she starts to sing a song even more beautiful than any she sang to me in the Dreaming. Her voice fills my eyes with tears and steals my breath, leaving me dazed along with everyone else until it's finished and the group around the Sorcerer bursts into applause and starts to rush toward her.

Cort comes to his senses first and steps forward with his hands on his swords, warning them to keep back. Thankfully, they do.

"I'll send word straight away, Miss Songspinner," the Sorcerer promises. "I assure you, you will have no trouble from my guild in Cerion."

He nods to someone standing behind him, and they run off toward the stone house on the hill.

My guild.

My thoughts race back to that moment in the throne room when I spied a Knight of Conquer as he made excuses to the king about his guild leader, Synnen. I look this man over, so arrogant, surrounded by others in the Knights of Conquers' crest who watch him with awe and reverence. His chestplate is adorned with medallions and ribbons that remind me of the honor beads in Father's hair. His eyes glint with desire as he gazes up at Mya. He's fully aware of the power she just displayed, and he's probably already making plans for what he could accomplish with it.

I think of the king, and how this man has eluded him.

Synnen.

"And I will await your acceptance," he says with confidence. "Your gifts would be most welcome in our fold."

"I bet they would," Cort mutters, echoing my thoughts exactly.

Mya wastes no time once the agreement is made. She tugs me toward a man in brown robes waiting on the outskirts of the group with a pair of horses while Cort stews beside her.

My mind is swarmed with too many thoughts at once. I think of the elf on the ledge. The man who she described causing the landslide could have been him. I remember the Sorcerer in the tower. His voice was different, and I couldn't see him, but the scent was the same. Could he be tied to all of this? Could Synnen be behind all of it?

"Oh," Mya says, interrupting my racing thoughts. "We only have two horses. You can ride with me, Elliot."

"Ah," I look up into the sweet, soulful eyes of her bay and embarrassment blooms hot across my cheeks. We don't ride in the Grove. There are some wild horses, but they're left to roam. Animals, unless they're bonded as partners to those with animal kinship, aren't ever used to serve us.

"I'd rather use my own four legs," I whisper secretively into her ear, brushing her cheek with my lips. "I'll follow the road along the forest's edge."

"All right," she agrees, taking the reins from a kind-looking man in plain brown robes. "But be careful."

33

REPORTING

It's remarkable how different the forests of Cerion are compared to the Grove. This one is dark at midday, the sun choked out by the density of the stoic trees. Despite my sharpened fox's eyes, everything seems washed in dull gray. Birds' songs are warnings, not cheerful chatter. There are no splashes of color from glow worms peeking out under the leaf-strewn floor, or bright eyes of friendly forest creatures peering out at me as I speed past. There are no signs of any of the welcoming creatures I took for granted in my homeland.

Like the birdsong, everything seems to issue a tinge of fear. Survival drives everything. Unlike in the Grove, the creatures here are on their own. Unprotected. Nurtured by no one.

I feel too much like an impostor, an outsider. Not at all at one with the forest. I wonder whether that's something that'll pass, or if these woods will always feel too foreign to me.

"My horse is hot," Mya's voice, reverberating through the overcrowded tree trunks, is tinged with annoyance. "I need to get down for a bit."

I duck from under the ferns to find her standing beside her horse, shaking out her hands and legs as she looks around. Her fury melts some as I trot up and nuzzle her shin, and she crouches to pet me.

"You don't have anything to say?" Cort asks angrily.

"I think you said enough for the both of us," Mya replies, her voice empty.

"How do you know? You weren't even listening."

He drops from his saddle and kicks a rock, scowling. I'd step out of fox form, but there's too much tension between them, and I'm still too

232

wary of human anger to know how to be an effective peacemaker.

"I was," Mya says quietly, tickling the scruff of my neck.

"Don' you do that thing, Mya. Not to me," he growls, digging through his saddlebags.

"What thing?"

"The thing you do, making your voice all calm and quiet." He takes a bite of his apple. "Not to me."

"What do you want me to do?" Mya asks, her voice rising. "You want me to YELL?"

Above us in the trees, the birds squawk and fly away in alarm. Cort claps his hands over his ears. The horses rear up and stomp their hooves in agitation. I shake my head to clear the painful ringing echoing through my ears.

With her voice full of apology, she sings a soothing song while leading her horse to the nearby stream to drink.

"I don't want to fight with you," she says when Cort joins her with his own horse.

"Den tell me why. Making promises to the leader of dat guild? What were you thinking?"

"I know what I'm doing," she answers, her voice thick with emotion. She splashes her face with the cool water and drinks it, and I lap some up thirstily beside her. Even the water tastes different here. Not as crisp as in the Grove.

"I just wish you'd have a little more faith in me," she says. "I'd never really join them, especially after what they did to you. Solace has been tracking their movements for a while now. They've been searching for proof of what he's doing. Now, with an elf as witness, I have that proof. Not only that, but if I can get close to Synnen, maybe—"

I yelp in protest at the same time Cort interrupts her. I can't believe she'd even consider that.

"No," Cort says firmly.

"I've seen Pa—" she starts to argue, but he takes her by the shoulders and shakes his head in fierce disapproval. His eyes narrow to furious slits. Even though he's only a few years older than me, the way he takes stern charge reminds me of Father. Warrior-like. Protective.

I feel a pang, thinking of Father. I never said goodbye to him. I wonder how he reacted when Amma told him I was gone. I wonder if they're still plagued by smoke at the Grove. I push the thoughts away, Cort's warning tone snapping me back to the here and now.

"You want to play both sides, ay? It's dangerous, Mya. Dey are dangerous."

"So is scouring the ruins of a cursed wizard's tower," she barks back angrily, making my ears sting a little. "Or meeting face-to-face with a tribe of bloodthirsty *Donas* and nearly screaming them to death. Or crossing the sea in a ship full of pirates! I managed that! I know danger, Cort. I grew up surrounded by it. At least this time it's by my own choice, and for people who really need it. I'm not a child, and I don't need you following me around telling me how foolish I am! I can take care of myself!"

I shrink back under the ferns as her tirade makes my ears pulse with pain. The two of them keep arguing, shouting back and forth across a forest that seems to be holding its breath, waiting for them to leave.

"Forget it Mya," Cort fumes, springing spryly onto his saddle. "You did it all on your own. Got it all figured out. You do what you want. No matter what dey did to me, ay? You go on, keep believing lies. Chasing dat wreck of a father, cozying right up to dat Sorc.

"Cort," Mya whispers, but he swats toward her angrily and takes off, back toward the road.

She looks down at me and I watch her sadly and back away into the cover of the forest as instinct takes over. My head pounds with pain as my ears ring with the power of her voice. My heart thumps with concern for what she said and what she's thinking.

I don't blame Cort for his fury. He's right. As impressive as Mya was outside the inn, her actions were too brazen. Her plan is too risky. She has no idea what Synnen is capable of.

It reminds me of Amma, wasting away while blocking Rubeus from the Grove. I think of how she dwindled to nothing but bones, blind and weak and helpless, while she stood her ground in the Dreaming. This feels just as dangerous.

No matter her intentions, Mya cannot tangle with a Sorcerer. I have to tell the prince about Synnen before Mya gets to Cerion.

An outcropping of rocks makes a fine enough shelter for my needs. With a quick sniff I determine no other animal has used it recently, so I duck in and quickly fall asleep.

The moment I'm able, I slip out of myself and tear across the half-realm along the main road where Mya is riding fast toward Cort. The road ahead of them is crowded with travelers winding slowly toward the city. The distant sky is gray as slate. Angry storm clouds loom on the horizon, brimming with the threat of nasty weather to come.

I speed my pace, catching the air in my claws to propel myself ahead, past the blur of tents and travelers camped outside of the city gates. Through the wall I streak, over rooftops and past colorful banners until I land on my usual palace balcony. Unfortunately, I find only a sprinkling of guards and courtiers gathered together, whispering somberly.

Is it unusual for the king to be away from his throne in the middle of the day? I wish I knew. I sniff the air and find a trace of illness in it. It reminds me of a time many years ago, when Kaini tried so hard to keep an old field mouse he'd grown fond of alive. A sharp, sweet smell that Sulien explained comes at the end of life.

Kaini's healing helped it for a few days, but in the end, it was the field mouse's time to return to roots and soil, as we all do.

Wards bar me from going in through the balcony doors, but the walls remain unprotected, so I slink in unnoticed by guards or courtiers.

Tirnon, I think firmly to myself, pushing aside memories of death in favor of the prince's essence.

I find him easily. He's in a small room that reminds me of Amma's sitting room, except there are no windows, and there is no fireplace, and there's space enough for just two fine chairs and a table. The moment I realize why he's shut in by himself, I regret intruding.

He's crying. The prince. He's hunched over in his chair, his shoulders shaking, his face buried in his hands as he weeps silently.

I consider coming back later, but then I remember why I came. Synnen. Mya. This can't wait. Cautiously, I slip to my true form and sit in the empty chair beside his and pull myself to whole. Scents and sounds sharpen around me, and the heaviness of the prince's sorrow seeps over me.

As gently as I can to prevent startling him, I clear my throat.

The prince goes still, rubs his face, and turns his head in my direction. When he sees me his eyes go wide, but he doesn't shout for his guard like I expected him to, or reach for his own sword which rests by his leg against the chair.

"Is this a dream?" he whispers in confusion. "Have I fallen asleep?"

I smile, that he would associate me with Dreaming rather than Waking.

"No, Your Highness," I say, bowing like I've seen those in the throne room do. "You're awake. I'm sorry to intrude on you here where you thought you were alone. What I have to tell you couldn't wait."

"How did you get past Finn?" he asks, slightly annoyed, and pushes himself to his feet to brush past me and open the door.

"Highness?" Finn asks, then spots me and draws his sword, a snarl on his lips. "What? Where did he come from?"

"Stand down Finn, and come in," says the prince, both defeated and exhausted. "Elliot of the Grove has news of his scouting."

The guard does as he's ordered, closing the door behind him as he steps in to join us.

"Now, tell us what you have seen," the prince says. He gestures to my chair as he drops back to his own, and I sit.

"First, tell me how you got in here," Finn grumbles, his hand still gripping his sword, though he's slid it back into its sheath again. "I swear I saw hide nor hair of him, Highness."

"It's all right Finn," says the prince. "Your vigilance isn't in question here. But I'm curious as well, Elliot."

"Through the space between Dreaming and Waking," I answer. "Just like at Solace Hall."

"Impossible. There are wards preventing anything like that here," Finn argues defensively.

"I already told Gaethon about it," I answer, trying to keep calm even though Finn's knuckles are white from his grip on his sword. "Your Mages set wards only on doors and windows. The walls are unprotected."

"You can travel through walls?" asks the prince with awe.

I nod.

"Remarkable." He smiles, his thoughts racing behind his red-rimmed eyes.

"Dangerous," Finn glowers, obviously irritated by his inability to detect me. "And rude."

"He apologized already, Finn," says the prince, "and I'm certain he won't do it again now that he's seen how upset it's made you. Right, Elliot?"

"Upset," Finn huffs as I nod.

"Now," says the prince, "tell us, dream scout. What have you discovered?"

"I found Synnen," I tell them quickly. Already I've been here too long. "He's in Valleyside."

"Valleyside?" Tirnon and Finn exchange looks that imply they've already heard about the disaster there.

"He was there yesterday, Your Highness, when it all happened," I tell him. "There was an elf at the border who described him at the start of the landslide. Mya has her name and a way to call her when you're ready for her evidence."

"An elf can attest to his involvement?" Tirnon asks, leaning closer to me.

"Of the White Line," I say, nodding.

He brightens at that, glancing at Finn. "Father would listen to the White Line's word."

Finn grunts his agreement, keeping a wary eye on me.

"That isn't all, Highness," I say. "I noticed something about him. A curl of Mage Mark on his wrist, and a scent that was the same as the Sorcerer who sent the assassin to poison you."

"So, it's as we suspected," the prince scowls. "Were you able to determine who else of the Knights have fallen to Sorcery?"

"I have a list in memory," I tell him. "I can give it to you now, but there's something else. Mya has made a bargain with him. Synnen."

Finn shifts his stance and glances at Tirnon with a look that says, *I told you so.*

"What sort of bargain?" the prince asks, avoiding his guard's gaze.

"She made him agree to tell his guild to leave her alone until after she sings on Cerion Day. She said if he did so, she'd talk to her father about joining them."

"She means to switch her loyalties," Finn huffs under his breath.

"That, or play spy for us," says the prince.

"That's it," I agree with Tirnon. "She said as much."

"Unnecessary, now that there's evidence Synnen sent someone after you, Highness," Finn says, pointing at me. "He saw his schemes with his own eyes."

"Smelled him," I correct the guard. "I couldn't see him. He was invisible to me, and his voice was different. But his scent was unmistakable."

"How often do two people smell the same?" the prince asks.

"Everyone has an essence," I explain with a shrug. "I haven't ever smelled two people the same before, but I have only recently begun to venture into human spaces, so I can't be sure just based on scent that it was him at Kordelya Keep."

Finn glances at the prince with concern, and Tirnon's expression darkens.

"I will tell you, though," I go on, "that he was at the floods in Sorlen River Crossing in the spring. I'm sure it was him I saw there."

"Father will want to know that," Tirnon says hopefully, but then he sinks deeper into his chair. "If…"

"When." Finn says firmly. "The healers are with him. *When* His Majesty is up and about again, you can tell him what this scout has seen."

"Right," says the prince, rubbing his red-rimmed eyes. "At the very least, we know for certain he's in Valleyside now, defying the king's orders."

Anger spills into his voice at the idea of Synnen's disloyalty and he sits up squarely, looking for the first time since I arrived like the prince he should be.

"Elliot, will you go to Gaethon and give him your list? And Finn, issue an order to the city guard to be alert for Mya Songspinner and have her shown directly to the palace the moment she arrives. Between this and what we learned about the actions of the Knights of Conquer yesterday, I want her safe here tonight."

"What happened yesterday?" I ask, leaning forward.

The prince nods to Finn.

"Word has it," Finn explains, "A group of their lot showed up to hear her sing at Seabird's Swoop and harassed her, intimidating the proprietress, and pouring out their drinks all over the tables and floor. Mya left after that, riding out in the afternoon with Cort."

Tirnon shakes his head, scowling.

"How did you hear about that?" I ask, surprised I didn't even know it myself.

"Reports," Finn shrugs.

"All of the reports from the city guard come to the palace," Tirnon explains. "And there are certain people I ask to keep informed about."

He gestures to Finn, who nods and slips out to call to a guard further down the hall. While the two speak, the prince leans closer to me. His blue eyes search mine, holding the same desperation as in his dream while he was searching the maze for Naelle.

"I would ask something else of you, if you don't think me selfish," he whispers, his eyes flicking to Finn and back. When I nod, he goes on. "Will you return to Kordelya Keep and check on the earl's daughter there? Her letters have stopped, and when you informed me in dreams of the dealings in the tower, I feared the worst. Don't speak to her or tell her I asked for her. If she stopped writing me by her own choice, I respect her decision. I just need to know she's safe, especially now."

"I will," I agree. "I just have to check in with Mya and Cort first. I'm supposed to be running through the forest within their sights. I don't want her to worry."

"Thank you," says the prince. "If he's done anything to her, or to her father—"

He cuts himself off as Finn ducks back into the room, and in the silence, the prince studies me with fascination.

"So…you were just all the way out in the forest, and now you're here? Just like that?" he asks once Finn shuts the door. "How will you return so quickly?"

I shift in the chair, swallowing my hesitancy. "It's complicated," I explain as my feather prickles with warning. "But if you'd like, you can be a witness to it. I'll fall asleep here and when I reach the forest again, I'll fade. It'll be like I was never here."

"But you are fully here now?" asks the prince. He reaches across the space between us and squeezes my forearm, testing it. "Not in my mind, or Finn's?"

As fascinated as the prince seems, Finn is the opposite. He watches me with unguarded suspicion, edging protectively closer to the prince, his hand never leaving his hilt.

"I'm truly here," I say. "But not for long. Just don't try to wake me once I'm sleeping, please, Your Highness."

The prince nods, watching closely. I tuck myself back into the chair until I'm comfortable, and I let my head tip back, closing my eyes. It's easy for me to slip to sleep, even being watched by two men who were strangers to me until recently. Even when it's obvious one of them wouldn't hesitate to attack me if I gave him any reason to. He's only doing his job, after all. Protecting the prince, just like I am in my own way.

It's interesting what a sense of loyalty I feel to him already. Comforting that it's by my own choice.

I push the thought aside as sleep takes me and I split away in fox form, reeling out of the palace, through the city, over the walls of the kingdom, speeding through the forest with one eye on the main road, searching for Mya and Cort.

34

PEARL PEACOCK

A path of glowing white pebbles framed in soft pink mist opens before me, but I veer away, deftly avoiding it. I don't know why such a path would open to me now, but I have more important things to deal with. When the feather tingles at my cheek, I ignore that, too.

The once-looming storm clouds have turned into a torrential summer downpour that pummels both the main road and the forest. Gusts of wind bend the trees until their branches graze the ground, ready to snap, and their billowing leaves hiss and scream from the onslaught.

A drenched hive of travelers on the main road makes it impossible for Mya and Cort to come anywhere close to the city gate. As I skirt along the edge of the forest searching for an alternate route, I catch a startling scent on a sudden, watery gust. Synnen.

I speed up, chasing down his scent to a carriage swathed in so many wards I barely see it. It speeds along the road at an impossible pace, nearly plowing over travelers as it weaves dangerously around them.

When I near it, shadows swirl from the carriage in the form of wraith-like wolves. They streak in my direction, snarling and snapping threats as they give chase. The white path still glints alongside me promising safety, but I ignore it. The way that carriage is barreling down the road, I can only imagine its goal. Synnen isn't simply making the journey back to Cerion, he's chasing someone down.

My voice gets me into trouble sometimes.

He's after Mya.

I veer away from the road, back into the woods and speed up until the trees are nothing but earthy streaks around me. The further I get from the carriage, the further the shadows recede until they eventually disintegrate into the mists and the ferns.

Closer to the city, across the vast field of tents and makeshift market stalls, I catch sight of Mya and Cort astride their horses. They're still too far from the gates. Too blocked by the crowds in front of them. At this rate, Synnen will catch up to them well before Mya reaches the palace's shelter.

Under the cover of the thick canopy of trees, I find an alternate path that winds away from the road and ends much closer to the city wall.

"*Elliot Eldinae,*" the voice of a wisp echoes from my feather, and I feel its nurturing warmth envelope me, enticing me home. The white pebble path shines brightly beside my forest path, but I keep ignoring it. If I leave now, Synnen will surely catch up with Mya. I can't let that happen.

I pull myself together, trotting from Dreaming onto the dark forest path and let out the loudest yelp I can for Mya, just as a bolt of lightning crackles from the sky, striking a tree a few hundred paces away.

The force of it charges over me, setting my teeth on edge, prickling my wet fur with static. The tree screams horrifically as it goes up in flames, its trunk burning white hot from the inside.

I dart away, sickened by the sight and the knowledge that there's nothing I can do to help. My heart pumps in terror. This storm is intense. Deadly, even.

On the road, the crowd panics in the wake of the lightning strike, stampeding forward. Mya's cries for me reverberate over them, stirring me with urgency. I answer with my loudest fox screech, and she and Cort veer into the field and ride hard toward me.

As soon as their horses cross into the tree line, I take off toward the path. Mya sings behind me, boosting my speed, urging me faster. We run up the mountainside and down again, keeping a steady pace until my nose is bombarded with a hundred scents all mingled together and I stop short.

"What is it?" Mya asks, and I pounce forward to shift back to two feet.

"There's too many people to go in as a fox," I murmur, sounding as tired as I feel after my journey. "But I need to see Gaethon." I try to emphasize that truth to cover up my fear and urgency. I'm afraid if she knew about Synnen, she'd confront him again rather than run.

"Because of what you were searching for?" Mya whispers, alluding to the Sorcerers. "In Dreaming?"

"Probably soon," I say vaguely. "See that? It's the wall to the city. We can follow it and reach the gate."

We creep to the end of the forest where the rain is pouring down in cold, drenching sheets.

"How are we going to get through that?" Cort asks, pointing at the mob of people crammed at the gates is so thick it seems like a single entity pouring toward it like liquid.

"I have an idea," Mya says, sliding from her horse. "Elliot, you ride. Here, take this." I take her offered cloak and wipe the rain from my eyes to gaze up at the horse, my heart thumping harder now than it had with Synnen's shadows chasing me.

"I can get us through that crowd, and at least then we'll be within the city walls," Mya explains, oblivious to my plight.

With an apologetic whisper to the creature under my breath, I heave myself up into the saddle feeling very awkward. The horse sways mildly underneath me, her back expanding and contracting with her breath. I cling to the saddle with both hands and try my best not to slip to one side or the other. My efforts to seem like I at least have some idea what I'm doing don't fool Cort, who eyes me with a hint of a smile.

"Don't you ride, Elliot?" he asks impishly.

"Uh," I cling to the saddle, trying my best to stay upright and glance at Mya, suddenly embarrassed. "'Course I ride. I just prefer—" at that moment the horse betrays me, swaying to one side and catching me off guard. "Ah!" I scramble to right myself and throw my arms around the horse's neck, pulling her wet braids in my fists.

"Sorry," I whisper to the steed as she protests being yanked around by stomping angrily. While Mya takes the reins and soothes the beast, I slip around in the saddle, desperate to find a stable position.

"I just prefer if I'm going to be on four legs, that they're my own," I mumble under my breath, giving Cort a pleading look. This is humiliating, and worse, we don't have time for it.

"You got to put your feet through there," Cort says, pointing at the holders hanging from the saddle.

"I know," I lie, doing my best to avoid looking at Mya.

Cort finally shows some sympathy and hops down from his horse to give me a quick lesson while Mya meanders away a little, humming to herself.

"Like dis," Cort says, taking my muddied boot to guide my foot, "into de stirrup, aye?"

"Thank you," I whisper and lean down to him. "We have to get Mya inside. Synnen is chasing her down. The prince has issued orders for her to be brought to the palace where she'll be safe."

Cort scowls up at me, his deep brown skin glistening with rain. "How do ye know dat?"

"I'll tell you later," I whisper. "We have to hurry."

"I'll lead you," Mya says, gathering the reins as she gazes out over the crowd. Her expression has smoothed to a mystical sort of calm that makes her look like she's glistening with wisp glow rather than drenched in rain. "Don't worry."

I gaze down at her, entranced by her beauty and her composure. If it wasn't so hard getting up here and staying, I'd jump down right now and kiss her.

"It's a tall horse," I say lamely, clenching my stomach and leg muscles to stay upright. "I didn't realize how high up..."

"Don't worry..." Mya repeats.

Then, she starts to sing.

Her wordless melody emanates from her like a natural force as gentle as sea spray, as driving as rain from the storm, as unstoppable as the breeze in the leaves.

It soothes my embarrassment like a balm, it calms my racing heart like a lullaby, it parts the crowd before us. One by one, they move aside to gaze at her in awe.

Beside me on his own horse, Cort's shoulders slump. His head tilts slightly to the side, and he watches Mya with affection and admiration.

Ahead at the gates, a guard shouts at the pressing crowd, telling them there's no room, arguing sternly until Mya's song reaches the crowd and they go quiet and still. When we finally reach the gatehouse, Mya shows the suddenly calmed guard a medallion that glints in her palm.

"We have a room at the Seabird's Swoop," she tells him, and he looks up to me and Cort before looking back at her.

With her song finished, the crowd starts to shout and jostle again, and I hunch closer to the saddle to keep from falling off.

"Mya Songspinner?" the guard asks, to my relief.

Mya nods.

"Well!" He claps his hands excitedly, "Bonus in my pay tonight! Ha! Come with me."

He calls for another guard to take his place and Mya says something I can't hear over the roar of the rain and the unruly crowd. They argue for a moment, and then Mya calls up to us, "Go to the Peacock, and I'll ask His Highness to send for you. All right?"

I catch the reins she tosses up to me as Cort starts to argue, but then he glances at me and nods.

"Be careful," he says to her, and reaches across for my reins. I crane my neck to watch her weave away through packed, sodden courtyard.

"Hope you're right," Cort says to me with a hint of skepticism.

"She's with a guard,' I answer, relieved. Even if Synnen does manage to reach the city, she's protected now. "She'll be safe."

"You'd think," he says with a grunt, flicking his rain-soaked braids over his shoulder with a spray of rainwater. "Come on, den."

It takes a while to get there due to more crowds lingering in the streets, bartering over carts and tables and booths, undeterred by the rain. I stare in disbelief at the sheer number of them, as crowded in as weeds in a thicket.

"Watch it," a man shouts angrily up at me as I trail tethered behind Cort's horse, not daring to try and control her on my own. Thankfully, she's a smart girl who has figured out I'm definitely not the one in charge. She only needs to follow the hindquarters of the horse in front of her.

The horses apparently belong to the Peacock, which is the name of the place where Cort has been staying. It's a fair distance across the city, tucked in a nook a few turns away from the sea market, close to the Academy.

When we arrive, I watch Cort dismount first, then try my best to copy his movements. Thankfully, I manage to get down without falling or drawing too much attention to myself, but the stable boy still watches me with wide eyes and trades an amused glance at Cort before he leads our horses away.

"Always dismount from de near side," he says once the boy is out of earshot.

"Near side?" I ask, confused.

"De left," he reaches toward me, patting the dagger sheathed at my left hip. "Always left, to keep from getting weapons tangled up an' hurting de horse."

"Oh," I say quietly. "Thanks."

"Aye," he says, assessing me as he hitches his pack over his shoulder. "Follow me."

The Pearl Peacock is completely different from Mya's Seabird's Swoop. As soon as Cort opens the door and leads the way through a swishing beaded curtain, a sense of peace floods through me.

In the narrow entry corridor, smells of home greet me: Pine and birch, willows, *Rianave* nuts and fresh sweetgrass. A light breeze swirls around us both, drying our clothes, fluffing our hair, filling me with a sense of contentment and comfort. Cort pauses and closes his eyes as he breathes it in, grinning.

When we move out of this corridor the scents of home fade slightly, replaced by the aromas of strange spices and roasted meats. The room within is draped in airy gauze and delicate silks and dappled with lantern light that instantly reminds me of the wisps.

"*Adalutu,*" a gentle voice greets us, and a beautiful woman with exotic islander features welcomes us with open arms. As she steps forward to talk to us, her long black hair and bright turquoise silks sway pleasantly behind her. Bells and chimes tinkle softly with her movements, reminding me of Avela.

"Bos'n Daborr, and your guest," the woman bows slightly, her arms crossed over her chest. "Welcome."

"*Adalutu,*" Cort says, mirroring her gesture. He turns to me, and I do the same. "Nehkiti, this is Elliot of de Grove. Elliot, dis is Nehkiti, owner of de Peacock."

"*Adalutu.* Welcome, my wood elf friend," she says with reverence.

"Thank you," I whisper. The peace of this place is an entity in itself that I hate to disturb. It takes me a moment to realize that each of the dozens of billowing curtains here obscures a table full of patrons enjoying their suppers.

Nehkiti sweeps a graceful hand toward a nearby alcove, "will you dine, or have you returned to simply rest, my Bos'n?"

When she moves, her silks glide over her bare midriff and I note the smooth, unmarked skin of her chest beneath the glint of her gold chain necklaces and jewels. She smells partly of Mage, though. There's a subtle hint of red incense and candles and stale parchment deep beneath the cooking spices and perfumes.

"What do you say, Elliot?" Cort asks with a smile, his demeanor so much more at ease now that we're here. "Hungry?"

I nod, tearing my gaze from the woman to duck into a booth across from Cort.

"Tonight, a wood elf will taste the fare of our island home," Cort says. "Two of everything, please, Nehkiti."

Nchkiti bows with a smile and lets the curtain close between us. As soon as we're alone, Cort leans back with his arms crossed, watching me carefully.

"You knew de prince would have guards looking for her," he says after a stretch of awkward silence. "How?"

I glance at the curtain, then back at Cort, expecting the usual warning tingle from my feather. When it doesn't come, I lean closer, lowering my voice.

"No one else can hear us?"

He shakes his head.

"While you and Mya were riding, I went to the prince. I told him what happened in Valleyside."

"De landslide?" he asks.

"That, and what Mya said to Synnen."

"How?" Cort scowls. "How'd you go to him?"

"I found a spot to hide, fell asleep, and traveled to him through Dreaming," I explain easily, with no obstruction or warning from the feather.

"You fell asleep jus' like dat?"

"I'm tired all the time," I admit. "It's part of being what I am. Falling asleep is the easy part."

Nehkiti returns with silver platters full of dozens of artfully arranged silver cups and bowls filled with steaming meats, colorful gravies, rice, vegetables, and breads. She whispers some sort of blessing and ducks away again, and Cort shows me how to tear the bread apart and scoop up the spicy chunks of meat dripping in bright orange gravy.

It tastes vibrant and hot, like nothing I've ever tried before. While we eat, I fill him in on what I suspect about Synnen, and he tells me all about his own experience with the Knights of Conquer since he arrived in Cerion, and Mya's, too.

I shake my head, still struggling to fully grasp humans' potential for selfishness and cruelty.

"And this Paewyn," I say, lowering my voice. "You think she's using Mya as some sort of piece in a game?"

"It's the best sense I can make out of all this mess," he says, glowering. "All dis time she thought her Pa was waiting 'round the corner, and it's just been dat woman baiting her along."

I tell him what Gaethon said about the wards on Mya's inn room, and his expression darkens.

"I'm glad she went straight to the palace," I say, trying a taste of something that looks like mashed grass.

"You got to put de cream on dat one. Here," he says, and dabs a spoonful of it on, and it changes the flavor completely. "Aye, that was good thinking on your part. You sure you can't find her pa? I feel like finding him is de key to all dis mess."

I shake my head, savoring the complicated flavors. We don't have anything like this in the Grove.

"I can try again, but last I checked he wasn't in the city or anywhere else, and I didn't catch his scent in Valleyside even though that cook seemed so sure about it."

He raises a brow, looking impressed, "Dat's how you do it? By scent?"

I shrug and nod.

"What do I smell like, den?" he asks, chin raised. I lean across the table and breathe in, ignoring the complex aromas of the food to pick his out.

"Sisal rope, steel, oil of coconut, sea kelp."

He laughs through his nose and crosses his arms, looking me over like he's trying to figure me out.

"And Mya?"

"Jungle earth, charcoal ink, leather, and..." I glance at him, hesitating.

"And?"

"I don't know how to describe it. Goodness? Honesty? Purity? Some people have scents that are more like essences. She smells like Mya and no one else."

"You love her?" Cort asks, his eyes narrowing as he shifts his weight and rests an arm across his stomach.

I shrug again, and when he gives me a dubious look, I nod. "I came all this way for her. I left everything."

"Aye..." he says distantly, still looking me over like I'm a puzzle to be figured out.

"You care about her, too," I say. It's not a question.

"Not dat way," he says, finally looking away.

"What way, then?"

"She reminds me of someone," he reaches to the table and flicks away a stray crumb. "Someone I failed, long time ago."

"Someone you loved?"

"Aye," he says, clearing his throat. "But not the way you think. My sister."

A pang thumps my heart as I'm reminded of my own sister. We both go silent, lost in our thoughts as Nehkiti comes to clear away the trays and offer tea.

"I have to find Gaethon," I say once she's gone. "I have a list of names to deliver to him."

"What kind of list?" he asks, eager to change the subject.

"Red-cloaked Sorcerers," I answer, meeting his gaze. He grins.

"I can get behind that," he says. "What do you need from me?"

"Just a safe place to sleep," I reply, already yawning at the thought of it.

"Upstairs is safe enough," he says, pushing himself to his feet with a groan.

"I have a few things I need to check," I tell him, thinking about Kordelya and Naelle. "I'll search for Mya's pa again and see if I can find out what Paewyn is up to."

"Nothing I can do but keep watch, ay?" he asks with a scowl later while unlocking the door to his rented room.

"Just don't try to wake me. It's dangerous," I tell him, shivering a little at the thought of trusting him so quickly. "Once I'm asleep, let me sleep."

"Course." He nods seriously and ushers me inside. "Just promise if you find anything, you'll come tell me so I can help sort it out."

"I will," I agree.

His room is as extravagant and cozy as the one downstairs, with silky drapes fluttering in the widows and a soft, fluffy-looking bed. Trunks and sacks are crammed along the walls out of the way, and a chest of yellow fabric stands open by the door.

He strides to the bed to straighten the coverlet, and I yawn and take a step forward, shifting to fox form while he's facing away from me. When he turns back and sees a fox in my place, he yelps in surprise.

"Going to take some time to get used to dat, I think," he says, chuckling.

He pats the fluffy featherbed, offering it to me, but I slink underneath it and curl up in the den-like space instead. Content with a full belly and a list of places to go, I fall asleep the moment I shut my eyes.

35

KORDELYA

The entry to the white-pebble path follows me insistently as I soar beneath the clouds and the fields of Cerion become nothing more than patchworks of moon-washed green. Far below, the vast kingdom, broken only by the occasional glow of lit-up keeps and villages, sleeps peacefully.

As I near the smoky, flame-kissed border of the Grove on my route to Kordelya Keep, the white pebble path gleams brighter. The scent of fresh leaves and loam float strongly from it, along with the whisper of a voice.

"Elliot..."

Hana.

I shake my head clear as I speed faster, my paws kicking up puffs of mist behind me.

"Come home," Hana calls, and the side of my face tingles warmly, filling me with longing. I slow slightly and glance to the side to see the flick of a vine curling out, beckoning me. "We have something to tell you."

I consider it only for a moment before I snarl in the direction of the path and snap my teeth. I can't get distracted. I made a promise to the prince, and to Cort. I have things I need to do now, for Cerion's sake. For Mya.

For the first time ever, I have a purpose. There is no one else outside of the Grove who can do what I can do. I won't turn my back on that.

A new path opens before me paved with flagstone and framed by a neatly trimmed hedgerow just like the maze in Tirnon's dream.

Naelle.

I veer away from Hana's voice and the white pebble path to take this new one, which smells of linen and rose water and fresh parchment, but also of horses and carved wood, of sweat and...blood.

The paving stones disappear under my paws, replaced by slick mud beneath a carpet of decaying leaves. Wolves howl far in the distance, and I suddenly feel like I'm being chased again by the wolf-like shadows that tore from Synnen's warded carriage.

Somehow, I've been tricked. The white pebble path that had called to me since I left the city is gone. I'm surrounded by shadows, with no light to turn to.

A harsh forest looms over me, its skeleton trees obscured by thick mist, its depths silent and forbidding, except for the occasional howling of wolves on the hunt.

They're far away, though. Distant enough that I feel I have time to determine why a path which promised Naelle would lead me to a place like this instead.

Look into shadow for us. Courageous one.

I catch the scent of rose water again, and a scattering of torn up parchment and red flower petals swirls before me, creating a new, fleeting trail that might blow away with the next gust of wind.

I take off, following it through a thicket full of nettles that tangle around me and tear viciously at my fur. The red rose petals transform to drops of blood streaked across shreds of parchment. These nettles and thorns wouldn't move this way if they were in Waking, I realize. I must be fully in the Dreaming, not in the In-between.

"My Dear Prince,"

I spy the neatly scrawled words on one of the scraps before it flutters away. Beyond the nettles, someone cries softly. The scratchy sound of a quill twitches my ear. Through the brambles, Naelle sits at her writing desk, mist swirling around her as she drips wax onto the letter and presses it with her ring.

She hands it to a man in riding clothes, who bows and tucks it into a satchel. A horse emerges from the mist and he swings up into its saddle and rides away, kicking up scraps of bloodied parchment behind him, leaving a trail for me to follow.

The wolves howl nearer.

I soar above the brambles and race away again, out of the strange, shadowed dream, away from the threat of wolves. The trail leads me into the In-between, where the scent of blood grows stronger and stronger, mixing with the stench of decay.

Down in a ravine along the Sorlen River, I find the rider, his body twisted and sprawled across the rocky bank. Three arrows protrude from his body; one from his neck and two from his torso. Naelle's bloodstained letter peeks from the satchel pinned beneath him, flapping in the breeze.

I sniff the arrows, committing their scent to memory, and peer up to the top of the ravine. He must have been shot from up there and fallen to his death. I soar upward, sniffing the crest, where I catch the same scent from the arrows, much stronger, on much higher ground. Whoever shot him sat up here for hours waiting for his approach.

"Are you certain you don't need anything else, Father?" Naelle's distant voice echoes from the starlit sky, settling around me as I catch the scent of rosewater and the sight of paving stones edged with deep green hedges once again.

This time, her trail leads me to Forbend Keep, which I remember from Grandfather's old maps. I find Naelle in a damp, echoing room with sturdy stone walls lit by sconces holding smoky torches.

"No, no, my dear," the reply comes from the massive bed, which is draped heavily with worn, dusty velvets. I trot closer and sniff, easily detecting the weariness of the earl in his bed and the concern of his daughter.

"I shouldn't have asked it of you," says Naelle, sitting on the edge of the bed, holding her father's hand.

"Nonsense," the earl waves a trembling hand and drops it to the coverlet. "From what we have been told, it may well be our last chance to see His Majesty alive."

"I pray it isn't true," Naelle whispers. "You know how people exaggerate, Father. His Majesty is strong. Perhaps it isn't as dire as that."

"Mmm," the earl replies, his eyes closing slowly.

"The journey has worn you out," she whispers, tucking the coverlet around him tenderly. "Tomorrow we'll keep a slower pace."

"And miss the last day of Midsummer revels?" murmurs the earl. "I wish I had not listened to the counsel of that wretched lord. You could be dancing with the prince tonight instead of nursing this old cod."

"I'm rather fond of the old cod," Naelle says, smiling.

"Bah. Now we shall even be too late for Cerion Day tomorrow."

"There's still the King's Feast the day after," Naelle soothes. "As for the prince, I don't dare hope he still wants my company, Father. My letters to him have gone unanswered for far too long. I fear I've somehow fallen out of his favor."

"Cerion Day is a great undertaking," he explains. "Certainly, the prince has taken over much of the preparations. Perhaps he's simply overwhelmed, my dear."

"Perhaps," Naelle answers wistfully.

"You should have gone to court when I sent you," the earl's eyes flutter open and he slides his hand to cover hers.

"And leave you with no company but that of guards, dogs, and ghosts?" She tilts her head, stroking his cheek tenderly.

"I'm rather fond of the ghosts," he says, and they both laugh softly.

"In time, you would have forgotten me," he mumbles, drifting to sleep.

"I could never," Naelle says, lifting his limp hand to her lips.

She gets up, wringing her hands as she gazes down at her sleeping father for a long stretch, then goes to the door to let herself out. Left behind in the empty room with only the sleeping earl to spy on, I turn toward the wall prepared to return to Cerion.

"Elliot," Hana calls as white pebbles appear along the plush carpet and my cheek tingles enticingly.

I shift to my true form and call out toward the path, "I'm here, Hana. Are you all right?"

"Come home," she calls, but there's no distress or urgency in her voice. She sounds peaceful, happy.

"I will soon," I answer, "I have to do something first."

"Promise?" she calls, her voice much more distant this time.

"Yes," I reply, and speed back toward Cerion as the white path fades and the city gates sprawl beneath me, still mobbed with people trying to get inside. At least the storm has ended, I think, as I veer toward the Academy in search of Gaethon. The scent of Mages is overwhelming as I near, but surprisingly, his trail leads me away from the gold-domed building along the sea wall to the palace.

A thousand candles dapple the rain-kissed lawns of the castle, and the windows glow with warm, golden light and spill laughter and music out into the cooling summer breeze.

I leap to my usual balcony and peer inside at the ball. The ballroom is livelier than ever even though the moon is high and most reasonable people should be sleeping. Thankfully, the Mages still haven't fixed the wards, so I sweep through the wall and close my eyes, focusing on Gaethon's trail.

It leads me to a small room on the other side of the ballroom where the Mage sits alone, rail-straight in an armchair, flipping through a palm-sized book. I peek at the pages filled with names and realize it's the same one he'd had at Solace Hall, the one Mya had signed her name in before she dropped her pen.

I watch him curiously as he rubs his eyes and yawns. What is he doing here instead of at the Academy or his guild hall? Really, it doesn't matter. What I have to tell him is urgent, so I pull myself together and step out of the In-between with no warning.

The moment I appear, Gaethon leaps to his feet. His fingers crackle with powerful sparks, and he crouches low, aiming them straight at me. Before he can unleash his attack, I duck behind a chair and cry out, "It's me! It's Elliot!"

"Blast it, Druid," he growls, shaking the spell from his hands. "I nearly jumped out of my skin."

"Sorry," I reply, holding my hands up in surrender.

"Sneaking up on a Mage of Cerion is a sure way to get your hair singed off," Gaethon warns.

"I'm sorry," I repeat, this time more insistently.

He grunts and drops back into the chair, looking utterly irritated.

"What are you doing here in the palace?" I ask, taking the seat beside him.

"I'm the evening's Mage Steward," Gaethon says with a tone somewhere between disgust and annoyance.

"What does that mean?" I ask, my curiosity getting the better of me.

"It means Cerion is beginning to allow itself to fall into superfluous, wasteful, and degrading means of employing otherwise studious and diligent Mages," he grumbles.

When I raise my brow questioningly, he sighs and scratches his eyebrow.

"It means I must wait here until someone arrives not looking their best. When I am called, I then cast spells to spruce them up, so they are presentable for the revelries," he drones. "But I'm sure you have not come here to interrogate me on the dreary details of the life of a hired Mentor Mage, have you?"

"Actually, no," I answer, lowering my voice to a whisper. "I found them. As many as I could."

He perks up, gripping the arms of his char.

"Do you have names?" he asks eagerly.

I nod, and when he flicks the first book away and conjures another, I recite the list I've committed to memory as quickly as he can write it down.

"There's more," I say, telling him about the invisible Sorcerer in the tower, and Synnen in Valleyside. "They smelled the same to me. I think it was him."

"I see," he says, writing something else in his book. "I'll bring this to the attention of the Masters as soon as I'm relieved here."

"Good," I say, "because the last I knew he was on his way to the city, riding in a coach that is so covered in wards I can't even describe it to you."

Gaethon huffs and shakes his head. "What timing."

"Right. The king will want to know."

"Indeed," Gaethon says a little distantly. "Though His Majesty is not to be disturbed tonight."

"I have a message for the prince, as well," I say. "Do you know where I can find him?"

"The same," Gaethon says with a tone that warns me to drop it. "He is with His Majesty, also not to be disturbed."

"What about Mya?" I ask, and he shakes his head.

"She has been given a room for the night, so she can remain within the wards and protections of the palace before Cerion Day tomorrow. A page was sent to the Pearl Peacock to fetch you and Cort, but she returned empty handed."

"Oh," I say, feeling slightly disappointed but also relieved that Cort kept his word not to wake me.

"If you have a message for His Highness, I can deliver it to him," he tells me, conjuring a quill and a sheet of vellum from the air which he hands to me. "I shall keep it in strict confidence, of course."

"Thanks."

I take the parchment and quill and write to tell him Naelle is safe and on her way to the city.

"Forbend Keep is the one just across the channel, the closest to Cerion city, right?" I ask, checking my memory.

"Indeed," Gaethon says, respectfully averting his eyes from my note.

I write her location and the location where I found her fallen messenger, then I fold the note and hand it back to him and he vanishes it away again.

"Where does it go?" I ask curiously. "When you vanish something away like that?"

"Into the aether," he replies with an air of mystery. "Whatever I stash is always with me, floating nearby. I can see it all, of course, because I am attuned to it. I imagine it's similar for you, when you are traveling through Dreaming yet can see the Waking realm and everything between."

I squint at the space around him, trying to see evidence of anything he might have hidden, but there's no trace of it. The fact that I've never seen objects floating around anyone in Dreaming, or In-between, or

Waking means there must be a realm that's still hidden to me. The realization makes me shiver. I wonder if the Ancients know.

"Can living things hide in the aether?"

"You mean Sorcerers like the one who you saw at Kordelya? Or didn't see?"

I nod.

"Perhaps," Gaethon replies thoughtfully. "There are countless mysteries of magic awaiting explanations, as there will always be."

"Mage," calls someone rapping on the other side of the door, "You're needed by Lady Ovealin, who has had wine spilled on her gown."

"Very well," Gaethon calls, pinching the bridge of his nose in annoyance. "I'll be there presently."

"She's in a fit, best hurry!"

"Excuse me, friend," Gaethon says quietly to me, his tone dripping with sarcasm, "As you heard, there is a much more pressing matter than treason and Sorcery that requires my urgent attention." He stands up and brushes his robes straight, then gestures to his chair.

"Please, be my guest," he says. "I imagine once I return, you will have gone."

"Thank you," I say, dropping into the offered chair with a yawn.

"Thank you for taking the edge off an otherwise impossibly dull evening. Safe journeys."

He bows and ducks out, and I slip to sleep and pull myself back to Cort's room, where he's asleep on his bed. I duck beneath it and pull myself to whole so I'll be there when he wakes, and then I split again and trot out into the city in search of Mya's pa.

36

CERION DAY

After spending the hours past midnight searching, I wake to the sound of Cort moving quietly around the room. My stomach growls pathetically, and as though the inn itself recognizes my need, someone knocks on the door. I shrink back into the shadows under the bed while Cort goes to answer it.

It's still early enough that dawn light barely seeps between the cracks in the shutters, and the rest of the inn remains silently sleeping.

"Good morning, my Bos'n," Nehkiti says with a graceful nod over the broad golden tray in her arms. The aromas of stewed fruit, fresh bread, and eggs cooked in the shells wafts to my nose, and my mouth waters in anticipation.

"Good morning, and thank you," Cort says with a bright smile, taking the tray from her and eyeing its contents, looking as hungry as I feel.

"As always, it is my pleasure," Nehkiti says, sweeping her long black hair over her shoulder with a soft jingle of jewelry. "A page from the palace came in the night with a message for you. It was the same page who came earlier to summon you."

"Aye?" asks Cort as he sets the tray down on the writing desk near the window.

"The message was: 'Mya will remain here. You may come to the palace at dawn to accompany her to her performance if you wish. Give the gate guard this token.'" She hands him something I can't see, then slips away, closing the door behind her once he offers his thanks.

As soon as she's gone, I trot to his side and blink up at him.

"Aye, you missed the message last night," he says as he takes a neatly folded yellow shirt from the nearby chest and pulls it over his head. "But you said not to wake you, so I did nae."

"Thank you for that," I say after a quick step into my true form.

He blinks at me, shaking his head, then goes to the tray and pours a mug of strong-smelling spirits.

"Rum?" He offers me the cup as he tips back his flask. I sniff it cautiously and cough at the sharpness of it. It reminds me of a drink the elders partake in before rituals, made from fermented Rianave sap. I take a taste and it burns my throat all the way down into my stomach.

"Is this a traditional morning drink?" I ask, staring into cup. The vapors it gives off burn my eyes, and I blink to clear the tears from them.

"Only if you're a pirate." Cort chuckles and takes the cup, then hands me a glass of tea with berries floating in it instead. I sip it cautiously before gulping with appreciation. It tastes floral and sweet, exactly like summer in liquid form.

"What did ye find?" he asks as he digs into the tray, inviting me to join him.

"I caught something similar to her pa's scent outside the same red brick building I tracked it to before," I answer with a sigh and devour a buttery, flaky pastry filled with sweet brown jam, two apples, and a slab of meat that tastes like boar but sweeter and smokier.

"You can sure eat," he smirks.

"It helps me to have a good meal after I've been scouting," I explain, "It grounds me back in the Waking. Running all over the known lands in the span of a few hours works up an appetite."

"Aye, well," he eyes the already half-emptied tray, "I can call for another...but hey, it costs money, you know."

"Money?" I lick the honey from my fingers after finishing a nut-filled pocket of flakey dough. "Oh, coins? I noticed about those, lots of numbers marked next to names on the registers in the inns when I was scouting for Sorcerers. And the gold listed on that prize list you showed Mya."

Cort blinks at me, puzzled, "Ye don't know about coin? Gold? Riches?"

"I know humans are wild over it," I say with a shrug. "But in the Grove, we have no need for it."

He shakes his head, flicking his dark braids over his shoulder with a clatter of shells and beads.

"Well, here in Cerion, if you want to eat, or sleep in a bed outside your own house, or get supplies or clothes, you need coin to do it."

"Sorry," I say sincerely, and set the half-eaten slab of cheese back onto the tray. "I didn't realize."

"Nah, you're my guest here," he says, laughing. "Jus' don't expect you can walk into any inn or stall and get a meal without some coin, ay? That's stealing, and they'll throw you in the dungeons for it. If you mean to stay here, you got to find a way to make yourself some silver."

"All right," I agree, grabbing the lump of cheese again. "Thanks."

"Anyway, you were saying about Mya's pa?" he asks, buckling on his sword belt.

"I didn't find any fresh trails," I explain. "Just the same old ones leading from the docks to the Swoop and then to that red brick building, but never coming out again."

"Red brick building?" Cort asks, his brow knit thoughtfully. "Did it smell like dis, here?" He produces the page he'd shown Mya yesterday at the inn in Valleyside, and I bring it to my nose and sniff.

"My nose is sharper as a fox," I tell him, handing it back, "but I can pick up a few of the same scents on that."

"Scarlet Knaves," Cort grumbles. "He's all wrapped up with them, I bet, and this contest and dat woman and all de prize money, and dey got Mya tangled up in de middle of it, singing for their reward."

"Singing for a reward? For money?"

"Aye, Mya made it all the way to the end of the king's contest, and today she'll sing in de arena in front of all of de city. All those people you saw on de road here yesterday? Dey all came for Cerion Day, today. It's the last official day of the king's summer festival. People come from all over de world to join in. If Mya beats the eight she's up against, she'll win a chest full o' gold and the honor to write the king's song to tell of his life. She'll be named a master troubadour."

"My Mya?" I ask, wide-eyed.

Cort raises a brow and gives me a warning look. "Not yours, or anyone else's but her own."

"Right," I agree apologetically. "But...she seems so young for that."

"Aye, but you heard her sing. She could win it even against old Master Tasiven, who's got his own eye on her."

"Tasiven?"

"His Majesty's best minstrel, the favorite of all of Cerion. He says he wants her as an apprentice, but I've got my suspicions on dat."

His thick arm muscles ripple beneath his deep brown skin as he grips the hilts of his swords at his hips.

"You're suspicious of most things," I say quietly.

"And still alive to be, ay?" He winks. "I've seen enough of dis world to have good reason to be suspicious, especially when it comes to pretty young girls, or anyone with any sort of talent, for dat matter. Like yours." He eyes me with a warning look. "Best be careful who you share dat dream scouting thing with, ay?"

I nod.

"Come on, den, we have to get to de palace," Cort says with a jerk of his head, eyeing the empty platter. "Unless you want to lick de crumbs."

When we arrive at the palace gates and Cort hands the guard our token, I'm struck by the thought that I've been here several times already but never by invitation until now. I have to hide my smile as the guard questions us both thoroughly and verifies with the others that we're supposed to be here before finally calling for a page.

Cort gapes around as the page ushers us through the polished halls I've been through before, past alcoves stuffed with fresh flowers in vases and long corridor tables arranged with crystal bowls full of candied fruits and nuts. The occasional courtier passes us, either ignoring us completely or looking us over as if our presence is a personal insult. Most of those wear the Knight of Conquer's emblem, of course.

"Wait in here, sirs," the page says. He bows as he directs us to a bright, airy sitting room. A sound from inside might be music if it wasn't so screechy and out of rhythm. If I was in fox form, I'd have to fight the urge to shake my head to protect my sensitive ears. Thankfully, it stops as soon as we enter.

Inside, tall windows framed with gold and cream drapes let in splashes of morning sunlight. The walls are painted with scenes of trees and forest animals that remind me of the Grove. I feel a pang of guilt, remembering Hana. After the Cerion Day performance, I promise myself, I'll go see why she called me.

"Ah, Cort," a man calls as we enter. His voice is pleasantly resonant as it fills the space, reverberating off the gilded rafters far above. He has the sort of face that looks like he's always smiling, and a friendly disposition that draws me to him right away.

Beside him, a young boy tucks some sort of stringed instrument to the side of the sofa cushion, his cheeks blooming red. I smile, but he looks away, embarrassed.

"Master Tasiven," Cort greets the older man, and crosses to clasp hands with him. Tasiven is dressed so finely in rich jewel tones and gold jewelry I might have mistaken him for royalty.

"Sir, this is Elliot of de Grove," Cort says, beckoning me closer. "A very close friend of Mya's."

"Good morning, Uncle," I let slip the typical Grove greeting without thinking, and I feel my cheeks go red.

"Ah, that is the customary greeting of the Grove, is it not?" Tasiven, who is lean and graceful and much older than I expected, offers me a warm smile. "The honor is mine, of course."

He nods, and with his right hand he makes a flourish of a gesture that I take as a friendly enough greeting, but I don't dare try to mirror it. The boy who had been playing stares at me curiously, but he doesn't follow Tasiven across the room.

"Evan and I were simply passing the time with a lesson," Tasiven says with a hint of relief at being interrupted. "We've been waiting to accompany Miss Songspinner to the arena."

While Cort and Tasiven chat about the events of the last day or so, I'm drawn to a chair across the room bathed in the light of a sunbeam. I sink into the warmed yellow velvet and let my eyes close and my breathing slow as the men's conversation rambles around me.

What starts off as a gentle doze soon finds me floating along city streets so packed full of people that I find myself quickly overwhelmed and over-stimulated. The mingling smells of dozens of food stalls and hundreds of people, the shouting, the music, the chatter of conversation, the blur of pennants waving and street performers—all of it crashes over me like ocean waves breaking on crags.

Like a twig caught in the current, I'm carried over streets and alleyways all the way to the imposing double doors of the hall of Knights of Conquer. All other noise goes silent in the shadow of the grand facade. Synnen's scent hangs heavy in the air, overpowering my twitching nose. I tread on the air, four paws churning as my vision sharpens. Black smoke siphons from the cracks between the guarded double doors, billowing into a black silhouette against the crimson wood.

Within Synnen's stronger scent, I catch fainter hints of smoke, rot, and wolf. The silence is pierced by a sudden howling that makes me flinch. Rubeus's form appears in the smoke, crumpled and burning just like the Sorcerers on the stakes. Memories flash through me: the feeling of bones crunching under my bite. The taste of blood as I ripped into the assassin's throat.

Wolf-shaped shadows swirl from Rubeus's smoky form, their snarling black fangs dripping with pure darkness. They crouch low, their hackles raised, prepared to charge me.

My right cheek tingles. My ears ring. Hana's voice blends with Aft'elu's in my mind.

"Wake up."

My eyes fly open, and I blink into the sudden sunlight. Across the parlor, Mya stands framed by the doorway. She's dressed in a stunning blue gown covered in sparkling crystals that catch all the light in the room and throw it back against the walls in bright sparks. I blink, wondering whether I'm still dreaming. Is this some sort of perfect vision to balance out the darkness I just experienced? Like Waterfowl said? With difficulty, I try to remember to breathe.

"Well, I might as well just go home," Tasiven declares jovially, throwing his hands up in defeat as the rest of us stare in awe at Mya.

She looks unsure she's worthy of his praise. Her face is pale with nerves, and when she forces out a chuckle that sounds closer to a croak, I rush across the room and take her in my arms.

"You look like stars dancing in a summer sky," I whisper, brushing my lips against her cheek. I'm desperate to kiss her. I don't care who's watching. The way she gazes at me, her eyes dancing with affection, tells me she feels exactly the same. She clings to me, and I hold her like I'm sure her light will chase the wolves back to the shadows.

"We have to be quick." Tasiven's urgent tone seems to bring both of us to our senses. "Mya, I'm afraid I've been a neglectful teacher. There is a song you must know for the festival which I ought to have taught you yesterday. But apparently you and I both had other obligations, so you shall have to learn it while we walk."

"All right," Mya agrees, still sounding wary and preoccupied.

While we follow Tasiven out of the palace through the royal tunnels leading to the Arena, he prepares her by describing how big the crowds will be, and how many important people will be in the audience, and what the performance will be like. I focus on his words as I squeeze Mya's hand, trying hard to keep from dwelling on my nightmare. It's been years since I experienced anything like that. Listening to Tasiven isn't much more of a comfort, though. By the time he's finished describing what's required of Mya for her performance, my stomach is twisted into knots on her behalf.

But then he teaches her the song, and when she starts singing it her voice is so perfect it washes away any lingering darkness, filling me with unshakable hope. I can't help but admire her courage and skill. I don't know as much about this competition as the others seem to, but I can't imagine anyone other than Mya winning it.

By the time we reach the arena and we're shown into the tents where her competitors are warming up their own voices, I'm completely entranced by her. Cort nods to me and then moves to keep a watchful eye on a group of singers from Knights of Conquer. Three girls a little older than Mya. Synnen's scent lingers faintly on each one of them, like they've been claimed as his.

I start to follow Cort, but Mya takes my hand and pulls me toward the back of the tent where there's a folding dressing screen. Her eyes take me in eagerly and I pull her close. Her hands slide up into my hair and down my back. Her lips, warm and soft, press to mine. We kiss until we're breathless, and her excited energy soothes to calm and peaceful.

Outside of the tent, the crowd roars with an ear-splitting clamor. In all my life, I have never heard so many people gathered in one place to shout this way. I imagine her standing in front of all of them, capturing their attention, drawing their admiration. Yet, she chooses me for this quiet moment before the storm. Me, over anyone else in Cerion. Over the prince, even.

On the stage, an announcement is being made. The crowd quiets. The tent empties. Someone calls her name, but Mya is too swept up with me to notice.

"You have to go sing," I say with a grin after reluctantly pulling away from her.

"I know," she whispers breathlessly, but kisses me again anyway.

"Mya!' Cort calls, knocking on the screen frame. "It's starting!"

"Go on," I say reluctantly, turning her by the shoulders and giving a gentle push. Flustered, she smooths her rumpled hair as she rushes off.

"Did you at least tell her?" Cort eyes me with disapproval when I emerge from behind the screen.

I have to think for a moment before I can remember what he's talking about. Silas. Her father.

"I meant to, but I got distracted," I murmur, only feeling a little guilty.

"I hope it was worth it," Cort grumbles in obvious annoyance.

"Sorry," I whisper, and he rolls his eyes and shakes his head.

"Good luck, Mya!" we both call as the usher parts the curtain in front of her, guiding Mya onto the stage.

37

THE KNAVES

T he size of the arena crowd as we take our seats on the benches is unfathomable. I have never seen so many people together in my life. Hundreds. Thousands. Their mingling chatter and scents overpower my senses, leaving me feeling dizzy.

It's like standing in the center of the thickest part of the Grove and opening awareness to all the voices of the trees, except there, at least trees are predictable. This human noise could turn to chaos at any moment. It's unnerving.

The feather bristles against my cheek, and I hug my middle and follow Cort's searing gaze to a group of Knights of Conquer at the far end of the benches. Between us and them sits a large guild dressed in green and silver. I recognize their bird crest from a few of the other singers in the competition.

My stomach twists in disgust. The Knights' presence is a red gash against the crowd, like a bleeding wound. It reminds me too much of the assassin's throat after my attack. I search their numbers for a glimpse of Synnen, but he isn't among them, so I try my best to ignore them.

It's difficult, though. While the singers on the stage perform the anthem Tasiven taught Mya in the tunnels, the Knights of Conquer shout names and loud, obnoxious cheers that drown out the music.

While Cort rankles beside me, I try to focus on Mya, who stands just off from the center looking otherworldly in her sparkling blue dress as she puts her heart into the song. I pick out her voice from the others and home in on it, letting its perfect resonance swirl into me.

No one protests when the Knights begin to sing along raucously, still calling out a name from time to time as the song goes on.

I lean close to Cort and stand on my toes to yell in his ear over the din, "Should we call Mya's name?"

"Nah." His braids scratch my temple as he shakes his head. "They're just being rude."

Just as he shouts it, a pause in the song bares his words for all to hear. Half the Knights of Conquer glare in our direction, hands falling to hilts as they glower at him. Between us, the bird-crested guild turns to look at Cort, who, instead of waving or nodding an apology, rolls his shoulders back, raises his chin, and rests his hands on his own hilts in a challenging stance.

"Cort," I warn, imagining the entire guild bleeding through the green to attack us.

The brief moment of tension is broken by the sudden blare of trumpets and pealing of distant bells.

"His Royal Majesty, King Victens, and His Royal Highness, Prince Tirnon!" A man announces from beneath the purple canopy above us. His strong, proud voice booms across the arena like thunder.

The Knights of Conquer turn immediately to face the box behind us, which is draped with the king's banners of purple and blue. As a flawless unit they bow to the king, and the gesture seeps through the crowd until everyone is on one knee.

When the king steps forward to greet us, I can't believe my eyes. He stands strong and proud, not even resting a hand on the edge of the box as he waves to his people. His back is straight, his smile beaming. He doesn't even shake or wobble as the prince comes to stand beside him.

I lean to Cort again to ask him whether Cerion has something like the fold, but when the words don't come, I simply shake my head in disbelief.

"For Cerion, Cerion," the king and prince sing together, gesturing to the stage, and the whole crowd breaks into song and cheers and deafening applause that drowns out the performers until the performance is finished.

Once the king is in his box and the first singer is called up, the crowd quiets down. The Knights of Conquer are subdued unless it's their own bard on the stage, and even then they hold their deafening cheers until the end of the song. I stare into them, taking in one face after another, marking in my memory who I remember from Blackbird's Spine, and the flood, and Kordelya, and that group in Valleyside. A few of them were in all four places.

With a deep breath I try to catch a familiar scent. Synnen, maybe, invisible again. Or the archer who shot Naelle's messenger. But my wood elf nose fails me. There are too many other, stronger scents interfering.

"Ay," Cort nudges me. "Not sure what it's like where you're from, but here, staring at a lot like that is likely to get you squarely roughed."

"Roughed?"

"Attacked. Just stop staring and listen to the music, ay?"

A Sorcerer who I didn't realize was glaring back at me until now leans to someone beside him, whispers, and points at me like I'm some target. My pulse quickens, warning me to run, and I flick my gaze away.

A glint of blue and white catches my eye a row down from us, and I recognize Sir Josten and his guild right away. Solace. I wonder when they returned to Cerion from the Grove's border.

Mya is finally announced, and a murmur of anticipation rushes through the crowd. When she steps onto the stage, maybe it's my imagination, but the applause is more deafening than it had been for any of the other performers. My heart pounds so hard I can feel it in my ears. She looks so small and childlike, but the way she walks across the stage, waving to the crowd and bowing her thanks for their warm welcome, gives her an air of confidence and command that makes her seem worldly and mysterious.

Her energy is so enchanting that the entire arena—even the Knights of Conquer—seems to lean in and hold their breath as she plucks the first notes from her lute. Aside from her voice, for the first time since Cort and I took the bench, there is only captivated silence.

Her first song is one she sang to me in Dreaming about pining for her father, but the words stir a longing in me, too. Tears sting my eyes as I think of Hana waiting at the other end of the white pebble path, and Mari and her birds, and Amma and Father and my brothers, and the Grove I left behind.

Her voice echoes masterfully through the arena, vibrating off the high walls, moving everyone in the crowd. All eyes are on her, glassy and wide, as she eases into a second song and then a third, which ends abruptly with a whispered, "Pa."

Cort and I snap our gaze to the space where she's looking, but those rows of benches are obscured from us by the royal box. Someone there claps loudly, and the arena breaks into applause so thunderous my ears ache.

Cort says something I can't hear and grabs my arm to pull me along the benches. We weave through the bird-crested guild who have leapt to their feet for a standing ovation.

"Pa!" Mya's shout echoes powerfully over the overwhelming hoots and huzzahs. I try to keep my eye on her while Cort tugs me toward the obscured benches, but too many people are on their feet and I'm too short to see over them. I don't realize how close we've gotten to the Knights of Conquer until Cort stops abruptly and curses.

Beyond the gash of red, we can both see that the benches tucked to the side of the royal box have emptied out. If Mya's pa was there, he's long gone since. Tasiven is announced on the stage, and an eruption of applause to rival Mya's surges across the crowd.

Thankfully, Cort comes to his senses rather than try to nudge his way through the Knights of Conquer. He turns and gives me a push, and we rush back the way we came and race down the steps as Tasiven says something on stage that makes the masses laugh and cheer.

The excitement and fanatical adoration thundering from the crowd is a new experience for me, but I don't have time to linger in it. Cort and I race back toward the entrance of the tents where we'd left Mya earlier, only to find ourselves blocked by yet another crowd. They stampede toward the tent flaps, calling her name, trying as hard as we are to get a glimpse of her.

"Pa!" Mya calls frantically, and I catch a smudge of her red hair just outside of the tent before she's swarmed.

"We're here, Mya!" Paewyn answers, and I see an arm shoot up all the way on the other side of the gathering near the arena's performers' exit.

"Mya!" Cort shouts along with everyone else as he shoves his way through. "No!"

He turns around and tugs me again and growls, "Go around, go around! Hurry!"

"Is it him?" I ask as we skirt the edge of the crowd to reach the exit. I sniff at the air, but the scents of fry bread and spiced nuts and ale and sweat and a hundred other things block any hint that would tell me anything useful.

Cort doesn't reply. He just shoves through the crowd unapologetically as Mya slips out of view through the gateway with some man's arm around her. Her father, maybe. I hope.

When we finally break through to the outside ourselves, we're met with another sea of people milling in the street, blocking our path.

"Mya!" Cort bellows. Too far ahead of us, she turns. Her eyes go wide and fearful as they meet mine. Her father pulls her closer, turning her chin away. Paewyn says something to her in a fury. They take off running.

My heart drops.

Why would she look at us with such terror? Why would she run from us? What is happening?

Apparently determined to find out, Cort shoves his way through packs of festival goers with no concern for spilled drinks or angry shouts. Trying to keep up with him while keeping my eye on Mya and squeezing through the press of the crowd proves impossible. She and the other two disappear into an alley far ahead, while Cort and I are swallowed by the current of humans and pulled in two opposite directions.

I wriggle between a mother and her three girls, duck past a man wearing an outrageous amount of feathers and bright silks, and finally find a gap along the wall to follow to the alley. Cort's yellow tunic disappears at the end of it just as I reach it, and I take off at a run after him.

"Cort!" I call as I round the corner, and he glances behind him and jerks his head for me to catch up.

"Blasted woman," he growls furiously as we sweep past a small, shady-looking group tucked into the shadows. "Shoulda known she'd pounce before Mya even had time to think. We shoulda stayed in the tent instead of going to the blasted benches."

I jog to keep up with his brisk pace, my nose working to catch any scent that would help, my eyes sharpening on the figures who emerge every time we round another corner to go down another alleyway.

"She looked terrified," I say quietly. "Did you see? She was afraid of us."

"Aye, tricks and illusions," he says darkly. "Probably that Mage Alistar who works with Paewyn."

The next corner we turn leads us to a dead-end passage I recognize immediately. For the first time since I met him, Cort draws his curved swords.

"Weapon," he utters in warning, and I pull my bow free and notch an arrow even though it's just a brick building with a closed, unguarded door.

My heart thumps loudly as his arm muscles tense. When he flicks his braids back, I retreat a few paces to make room to fire, and I narrow my eyes, watching.

"I won't be jumped," Cort declares. "Not by you."

"Leave, then," a deep voice creeps from the shadows at the far end of the alley.

"Or join, Cort Daborr," calls another. "You know you'd be welcome."

"And who's your wood elf friend?" a third whispers. "Some new conquest?"

I train my bow on that one as he steps out of the shadows with a liquid, weasel-like gait. Long and lithe and dressed all in shadow-toned leathers, he tilts his head to the side and looks past Cort at me with a hint of jealousy.

"Where is she?" Cort growls, ignoring the question. His blades flash a threat between them, and the man's eyes flick over them with a hint of wary respect.

"Finishing her game," he replies with a playful gesture toward the door. "Shall I show you in?" He smirks and flicks his wrist and a blade appears in his hand. "Or shall we have a game of our own?"

I close one eye, raise my bow to aim the arrow at his chest, and pull back the string. The feather at my ear pulses with warmth in time with my heartbeat. Beyond my target, at the end of the alley, two much larger men slink out of the shadows. Both aim crossbows, already locked to fire. One is trained at my head, the other at Cort's.

"Or you can walk away now," the larger of the two says. "No harm, no foul."

Tension hangs thickly in the alley as we wait for Cort's reply. No one moves a weapon or speaks. The only sound is the creak of bowstrings and Cort's enraged huffs of breath as he considers our options.

I know how he feels. Part of me wants to cut the three of them down, break through the door, and get Mya out of there. But if we're outnumbered out here, how much worse will it be inside?

Cort seems to know. With a flash of his blades and a ring of steel, he concedes and sheathes his weapons. I'm surprised by the relief in the others' eyes, but I keep my aim on my target just in case. The other two lower their crossbows, and the lithe one issues a tisk of disappointment.

"Stow your bow," Cort says to me, his voice shaking with fury. He creeps backward, careful not to turn his back on any of them. "We're leaving."

38

STALKING

I expect us to scout the building looking for other entrances, but Cort leads me out of the alley, back the way we came instead. As soon as the red brick building is out of sight, I grab his elbow and he whirls to face me with a smoldering glare.

"We're just leaving?" I ask in disbelief.

"Aye, we're leaving," he answers much louder than he needs to. "She got herself into this mess all by herself. I tried to warn her a hundred times and she refused to listen to me. If she wants to choose her pa over us, so be it. I'm not getting bloodied over it."

Before I can argue, he gives me a wink and glances over his shoulder, and I understand. This is a ruse. They have ears in the shadows. They're listening even now.

"Come on," he barks, throwing his arm across my shoulders, "I need some rum."

"But--" I argue, glancing behind me.

"No buts. It's over," he says, steering me toward the noisy, crowded streets.

By the time we reach the Pearl Peacock and duck inside, a hundred questions are speeding through my head.

What are they doing to Mya in that place? What will happen to her once the game is over and Paewyn collects her prize? Was that Alistar with them, or was it really Mya's father? What will Mya do, if it was? Would they remain in Cerion? Go back to Elespen? Would she leave me behind? *Would* she choose that, even after everything she's been through and all she's accomplished here?

Does any of it even matter, if she's not safe? If they're hurting her?

"Congratulations, my Bos'n, to your minstrel friend," Nehkiti says with a bow as the beaded curtains brush over us, filling me with false comfort.

"What?" Cort asks, still sounding rattled despite the inn's magic.

"Mya?" I ask, puzzled.

"Yes, indeed," answers Nehkiti. "Word travels quickly to the Peacock. It seems she was declared the winner in a tied vote with Master Tasiven. What do you suppose her terms would be to perform here from time to time? Would she be open to it?"

Cort and I exchange glances, and some of the worry softens from his brow.

"She would, my friend," Cort continues under his breath, 'but at the moment she's in a bind we need to help her out of."

"May I be of assistance?" Nehkiti asks calmly. "You have but to ask."

She brings us to a booth and goes off to fetch the things Cort asks for. As soon as she's gone, he turns to me.

"Mya won dat money," he says darkly, his accent thickening with his anger, "so we have at least a day. De treasury won't pay her de prize until tomorrow, and dat woman will be sweet as honey to her and her pa—if dat's even him—until de prize money is lining her purse. So de good side of it is, for now, Mya is safe."

"Safe?" I shake my head. "In there? With people like the ones who nearly shot us in the face just for standing in their alley?"

"She's a clever girl," Cort says, leaning back against the wall. "You saw. She can hold 'er own until we figure out how to get to her."

There's doubt in his eyes when he says it, and even though neither of us admits it, I know we're both thinking the same thing: *as long as she can still speak.*

"We should have fought them," I argue, surprising myself.

"I might have," Cort says, shrugging, "but I never saw *you* fight before, and I didn't want to risk you being a poor shot with two crossbows pointed at us. Besides, it's best you don' get on de Knaves' bad side if you're plannin' on staying in Cerion."

"You say that like you know it from experience," I say.

Before he can answer, Nehkiti interrupts with a sweep of the curtain, offering us a lunch tray and a rolled-up map of one section of the city, which Cort unfurls across the table without a glance at the food.

"Thank you," I say to her as he looks over the buildings drawn there, and Nehkiti bows silently and slips away.

"Entrances here and here," Cort says as I dunk some fry bread into a little pot of spiced fig jam and take a bite. "And de tunnels, there, there, there."

He points to some markings in red and my eyes follow. My mouth goes dry as I chew the bread, and I force myself to swallow.

"The Scarlet Knaves' hall is connected to the Knights of Conquer's?" I ask, feeling the blood drain from my face as I trace my finger along one of the more obscure tunnels.

"Aye, little known to most," Cort frowns. "It's long been suspected de Knights have de Knaves do their dirty work, but never proved. Lots of rumors swarm the city, most of them fed by de Knaves themselves to keep everyone muddled on de truth. Anyway, you think you could take a look around? Scout some way in?"

"That was your plan all along," I say as I look over the map, committing it to memory.

He nods.

"With de crowds and de lookouts, I knew it'd take 'til after dark to search on foot, and probably we'd get spotted. This way you can do it in secret, aye?"

"Aye," I agree, slumping back and closing my eyes.

"Don' you want to go upstairs where it's safer?" he asks.

I shake my head, already yawning. "I'll be right back. Just don't—"

"Don't wake you, aye, I know," he says as he tears off a chunk of bread. "I won't."

As soon as I'm asleep, the white pebble path opens before me. The haunting howls of wolves on the hunt echo all around, much closer than they had been last time.

"Elliot," Hana calls, and my ear and cheek prickle with a sharp warning as I soar through the walls of the Peacock out into the crowded streets.

"Not yet, Hana," I whisper. "I'm sorry. Soon. I promise."

"When you're ready, but soon," she answers, and for the first time I can't tell whether it's her speaking or Aft'elu. Their voices blend together, calling to my heart. Right now, though, Mya is more important.

Banners and stone streak around me as I sprint above the bustling crowds and duck into now-familiar alleyways. I reach the Knaves' hall and slip into fox form to sniff at the doors where Cort and I were threatened. The scents of the three guards waft from the alley's dead end where they stay tucked into shadows, waiting. Hidden from them in the In-between, I can smell Mya's lingering trail filled with fear and defiance. I pick up Paewyn's scent, too, and Alistar's, blended with Silas'.

Illusions. Could Alistar have tricked us all into thinking he was her father? Could he have tricked the cook in Valleyside? Could it have been him all along, luring her to Cerion with Paewyn to play this cruel game? All for gold? For coins in a purse? The idea fills me with rage. The fact that I didn't pay better attention makes me even angrier.

I pace along the doorways, but the wards here are too thick and forbidding. Unlike the palace and Solace's hall, but much like the hall of the Knights of Conquer, the walls and windows are magically barricaded from top to bottom. Much like the Knights of Conquer's hall, there's the underlying stink of rot.

Unlike Elowyn's gentler, pillow-like wards, these jolt me with sparks when I test them. They prickle my fur with warning, even at a distance. The first time it happens I sling back to myself in the booth beside Cort and open my eyes. My breath comes in short bursts, and he puts a hand on my arm and meets my gaze to help me ground myself.

"Wards," I whisper. "They're well covered. Better than the palace."

I close my eyes and slow my breath and tear away again, this time checking the second door, the high windows, the walls in between, the roof, the hidden entries to the passages. There is no small opening, nothing left unguarded. Not the chimney, nor the cellar hatches, nor any other part of the building.

I search through the afternoon until the sun casts long, imposing shadows across the cobbles. With every failure, I feel Mya slipping further and further from our grasp. At some point I think I hear her scream my name, but there's nothing I can do to get to her.

Every brick I search feels like a broken promise, every tile of the roof a stab into my already-wounded hope. The howling of wolves circles me, never ceasing. Sometimes they're so close I can feel their breath on my hind legs, ready to bite, forcing me to shoot away to escape them.

I sweep over rooftops and dive along streets as the crowds churn below me firing strange, bright jets of sparks into the sky that explode with ear splitting noise and disorienting flashes of blinding light.

One of them shoots from below, arcing like an arrow right in front of me. Before I can change course it bursts into a spray of fire, disorienting me with its burst of light and thunderous explosion.

For a moment, I hear nothing. I see nothing. I float in midair, stunned by the silence around me. When I get my bearings again, blinking, the light doesn't fade. The crowd is gone, the city is gone, the silence is deafening.

I swim in a sea of perfect white light.

"Once again, you have found me where I ought not be found," Gaethon says with an even tone, and I spin to face the sound of his voice. Just like the last time I found myself in his Rumination, I'm fox and boy. Two heads, eight limbs, two bodies separate but merged.

"I didn't mean to," I whisper, blinking at the Mage who sits cross-legged in the center of the light, his hands resting open on his knees, his eyes closed. "How am I here? I need to get back!"

"Be calm," he says, "or you will slip back to Waking."

"I want to be back in Waking," I answer urgently. "They have Mya! I'm trying to get to her!"

"Who does?" he asks. The calm of his voice makes me want to run to him and shake him, but I restrain myself and try to force his peace upon myself.

"Paewyn. Maybe Alistar, or maybe her father. I'm trying to get to them, but the place is warded up better than the palace. It's just like the hall of the Knights of Conquer. Please. If you won't help me—"

"Slow your thoughts," Gaethon interrupts, breathing in deeply. "What place do you speak of?"

"Scarlet Knaves Hall," I tell him. "They brought her there right after her performance and she still hasn't come out."

"The hall of the Knaves bears the same ward signature as the hall of the Knights?" he asks, his brow knitting.

"That's what I just said!" I exclaim.

"Meet me at its northernmost wall. I shall be there presently," he says, and before I can say anything else, I wake up.

"Bout time," Cort barks, jolting me even more awake. "When you said be right back, I didn't think you meant after a few hours! Here."

He tosses me a bun the size of my face from the tray on the writing desk, and I scramble across the bed to catch it.

Bed?

"How did I get up here?" I ask around a huge bite of the roll.

"I carried you," he grunts. "Nehkiti kept bringing me tea and glancing at you asleep at her table, so I figured if Mya can ride across the country with you in a sling, it'd probably be safe to bring you up a few stairs."

I eye him silently as I finish the roll, trying hard to stay calm.

"What?" he asks, catching on to my tension. "Not safe?"

"Safe enough," I shrug, trying to hide my annoyance.

He raises a brow.

"I don't know," I say, licking jam from my fingers, "Mya carrying me around the countryside as a fox bundled in a cloak is one thing…but a grown man carrying me like this?" I tug at the shoulder of my vest, "asleep, through the common room of an inn? To his room? Did you toss me over your shoulder, or cradle me in your arms?"

Cort scoffs.

The more I think about it, the more I fume. I hate how vulnerable I am when I'm asleep. I hate that I trusted him to keep me safe and it feels like he broke that trust by moving me. The whole thing is embarrassing and more than a little rude.

"What was I supposed to do, just sit there for hours taking up Nehkiti's table while you slept and people were waiting to eat?" Cort glowers. "You said you'd be right back and I kept thinking any minute you'd wake up and we could get back to—"

"Gaethon!" I yelp. "I nearly forgot."

"What?"

"Gaethon! He said to meet him at the north wall," I explain, crossing to the door. "It's all warded up, the walls, the doors, everything. There's no way in."

"You met dat Mage while you were sleeping?"

"Right. I'll explain on the way. Let's not keep him waiting."

39

SOMETHING STOLEN

We find Gaethon just where he said he'd be, leaning against a wall across from the north side of the Scarlet Knaves hall, watching the display that Cort told me on the way are called fireworks.

"I already made my assessment while I was waiting for you," Gaethon explains under his breath as we join him to watch the colorful explosions. "It is as you said, Elliot. The place is too well protected."

"What next, then?" Cort asks, his hands resting on his belt close to his hilts.

"Assuming you are not reckless enough to try to go inside," he pauses, looking down his nose at each of us in turn, "I surreptitiously placed an alarm on the cobbles outside of the two main doors. Should anyone leave, I shall be alerted and informed.

"You did that without them seeing you?" Cort asks, impressed. "How? There are three in the shadows by the east door."

"I have my ways," he says with a dismissive wave.

"Right," Cort says, slightly annoyed. "So now we just wait for any of them to leave? Dat's the plan after all this?"

"Unless we can get inside somehow," I look to Gaethon. "Is there any way to make the smallest gap in the wards? Something say, a fox might fit through?"

"You're not going in there alone," Cort warns.

"Not to fight," I argue. "Just to look."

Gaethon closes his eyes and sighs.

"These are fortieth circle spells combined, or higher," says the Mage. "I can try to create a small rift, but it's likely it would repair itself.

276

Or worse, alert those who cast it after some time."

"How long?" I ask, staring at the wall with a scowl.

"According to the cases I've studied, not long at all. A tenth of an hour, doing the math between my circle and that of the wards. And that is if it works at all."

"I don't like it," says Cort.

I narrow my eyes, peering at the long shadows that stretch across the brick in the lamp light. They remind me of the wolves that chased me, snapping at my paws, closing in on the hunt.

"Gaethon," I venture a little hesitantly, "I understand the sparks of warning and the charge of fear, but the shadow wolves? Are they woven into the spells?"

The feather in my braid bristles a warning as it flutters in the wind, and Gaethon's gaze rests thoughtfully on it for a long pause before he speaks.

"As far as I am aware," he offers carefully, "wolves do not enter into the wards of our circles in Cerion, shadowed or otherwise. Though..." he glances at Cort and back to me, and lowers his voice, "there are many spells which draw out one's deepest fears."

"So, if I'm afraid of wolves and shadows..." I whisper.

Gaethon nods.

"Can they harm me?"

"Easily, if you allow them to have power over you," he explains.

"You didn't tell me you had wolves chasing you all day," Cort says, crossing his arms.

"You didn't ask," I shrug. "It doesn't matter. I'd spend a week chased by anything to make sure Mya is safe."

Cort eyes me, then shakes his head. "I'm not going to stop you trying to scout in there, am I?"

I shake my head.

"All right. Fox up so you don' get annoyed if I have to carry you, ay?"

I laugh. "Fox up?"

Cort rolls his eyes. "If you're going to reduce me to a fox valet, least you can do is let me turn a phrase."

"Fine," I whisper. "Wait here while I 'fox up'."

I slip around the corner, check it's empty, and duck into fox form, then come back and settle myself between Cort's feet and the wall behind him. Gaethon draws an ordinary gray pebble from his pocket and whispers to it. It glows and fades, then it sprouts wings and flutters across the street to cling to the bricks.

"Go quickly," he whispers, and I split from myself to dive across into the narrow gap in the wards that surges around the clinging, beetle-like pebble.

The moment I enter, darkness steals my vision. I shake my head and listen hard. Someone is approaching.

"Whether or not you agree with his methods, the man is a true artist."

Paewyn. I take off down the passage in the direction of her voice, and as my eyes acclimate to the darkness, I see three blurred figures moving westward away from me.

"The way he constructs an illusion is truly masterful, Silas. I could barely tell him apart from you, had I known. I honestly wish we'd tried it sooner. He certainly had you convinced, didn't he?"

One of the figures clears her scratchy throat and clings closer to the third. I catch her scent as it trails behind her.

Mya.

They're reaching the second door. Paewyn lifts the latch. I pull myself back through the split in the wards and snap into myself at Cort's feet, then streak off through the emptied streets to the door I know they'll exit.

As soon as I round the corner, the door opens. Paewyn steps out first, followed by Mya, who clings to her father looking defeated and exhausted. She smells like blood. Fear. Synnen.

I cry out and leap through the air into her arms, and she catches me and hugs me close as she stumbles back against the door. Overjoyed to see her and unable to contain myself, I kiss her salty, tear-stained face, whimpering.

Beside us Paewyn watches, looking caught as I let out a long, eerie call for the others. Paewyn curses under her breath, but when I turn and bare my teeth at her threateningly, she goes silent.

"Mya!" Cort shouts, and I hear him running toward us.

"Cort!" Mya calls hoarsely.

"Mya!" he calls again and rounds the corner, skidding to slow himself. He looks from me and Mya to Paewyn, and he slides his swords from their sheaths with a smooth, easy stroke.

"Woman," his lips curl back in a hateful grimace, and he charges. Mya shrinks against her father, still clinging to me.

"Islander," Paewyn moves with instinctive grace, drawing a pair of knives which she flings toward Cort, but he knocks them away with a deft flick of his cutlasses.

Silas tucks me and Mya protectively in his arms, shushing us both. He smells just as he did when I was trying to track him: Malt barrels, burnt herbs, fresh wood, jungle loam from Elespen, copper and silver, and strong, fading magic.

Paewyn and Cort charge each other, weapons raised, faces set in seething, hateful grimaces. Just before cutlass meets slender dagger, the glowing pink arc of a spell crashes into Paewyn, and she collapses to the ground in a heap. Mya yelps and hugs me tighter while Cort lowers his weapons.

"Are you jokin' with me?" he shouts in exasperation.

"I am not the sort," Gaethon's voice echoes from further down the street, and I wriggle free from Mya's arms and jump down to sniff at Paewyn.

"Gah," Cort gives her a disgusted shove with his foot and rests one sword against her throat. "Sleep spell's too good for this one. Maybe my blade ought to slip, ay?"

I snarl in agreement and lick my lips. With Mya looking so disheveled and terrorized, dressed only in her father's shirt, I can only imagine the horrible situation 'dat woman' must have led her into.

"Control yourselves," Gaethon mutters reasonably. Then he sneers down at her and tells her she's under arrest, whatever that means. I'll try to remember to ask later.

"Well, that solves the problem of what to do about her," Silas murmurs weakly as Cort shoves his cutlasses back into their sheaths.

I return to Mya's side and lean against her legs while she and her father hold each other steady. I wish I could spring to two feet and hold her and kiss her, but I'm not sure it's the best idea in front of him. I'm sure I've made the right decision when he gathers her closer and starts crying into her shoulder.

Cort and Gaethon exchange dubious glances, and Gaethon casts a spell that billows around Mya and Silas like a soft breeze. Silas winces as Gaethon declares, "Very well. This time that's him for certain."

"You knew it wasn't before?" Mya whispers, wide-eyed.

"Someone," Cort narrows his eyes at me, "Was supposed to tell you your pa wasn't at the Seabirds Swoop last night, or anywhere else in Cerion we could find him. But he got distracted."

I offer an apologetic whine and slink behind Mya's ankles.

"It's my fault then," Mya says quietly. Her voice sounds like rough stones scraping together. "That distraction was my idea."

"It hardly matters now, does it?" Gaethon huffs. "You should not mill about in the street, especially not looking like that."

"Aye, both half-dressed and shocked through," Cort says, shaking his head and unpinning his cloak. Before he can offer it to them, though, Gaethon casts another spell to grow Mya's tunic into a dress and conjure a shirt for Silas.

No one else seems to notice Cort's annoyance at once again being pushed aside.

"I'll call the guard for her," Gaethon says of Paewyn distastefully, "and notify the palace. The rest of you will be safe in Solace Hall."

"I see you've been in good company, Mya," Silas slurs as Cort props him up. "Will you introduce us?"

"After," Mya whispers, glancing gratefully at Cort. "When you're rested."

"What is Solace Hall?" he asks, shifting his weight to lean against Cort. "Sounds like a guild."

"It is," Mya whispers again. "But a good one, don't worry."

"Aye, now, to safety, both of you," Cort says gently, some of the anger draining from him as he makes himself useful practically carrying Mya's father.

"Will there be something to eat?" Mya whispers, and now I'm sure she's doing it to cover up the extent of the damage her voice has suffered.

"Do you even have to ask?" Gaethon smirks. "Mouli will be beside herself, from the looks of both of you. Now, go."

He points to the sky and a spear of bluish light erupts from his fingertip and bursts into a dozen spheres that light up the rooftops around us just like the fireworks. "I'll be along once the guard has come to clean this up."

"Should have let me run her through," Cort huffs, gripping his hilt with his free hand.

"There is no need for savagery," Gaethon replies calmly.

"Sometimes there is," Cort argues. "Come on, den, you two. Lean on me. I've got you. We follow the fox, aye?"

At Solace Hall, Sir Josten greets Mya like family. Even though he and I haven't been introduced yet, I feel like I know him already, but a prickle of warning from the feather tells me not to change from fox form just yet.

He calls for the healer Crisanne, who brushes her fingertips over Mya's bloodied hands, knitting scabs back to soft, clean skin. She grazes Mya's throat just above her collarbone and Mya watches her hopefully, but the healer shakes her head apologetically. Mya nods and swallows, blinking away tears, and as the others take Silas into the next room for deeper healing, Cort rests a hand on Mya's back.

"Come on," he says, and leads her along the entry hall. I stick close to her, and when she stops, I rest my head against her leg to try to comfort her. I'm so relieved we found her. Relieved she's alive. But her suffering makes me want to go back down that alley and tear out another throat or two.

"What happened?" Cort asks firmly once we're safely out of everyone's earshot.

"It was all so horrible," she replies with a raspy voice. "Pa was cursed…" she goes into a long explanation of the events as she understands them now, from the moment she left Elespen until the moment we saw her at the door.

Even though it's obvious none of what happened to her father was her fault, she insists over and over again she's the one to blame. As he listens, Cort grows more and more tense until it seems like the veins in his arms and temple will burst. I know exactly how he feels.

"And then," she sobs, pressing herself into Cort's shoulder. "Before I knew what was happening, he stole it. Synnen. He stole my voice. I thought I was just drinking water, I didn't know! I should have realized, I should have thought," she hiccups and shivers and sobs, and at her feet I let loose a growl of fury. Synnen. That's all I need to hear. I'll make him pay.

"Aye," says Cort, and without another word, he turns and starts to stalk away.

"Cort, please don't," Mya cries, tugging him back by the hand. "It's too dangerous. Wait until we can make a plan. Please!"

Her voice holds no power now, though. When Mouli ducks out of the kitchen and starts to fuss over her, Cort and I stalk out of the hall together, and he slams the door behind him.

"Stole her voice," he growls, cracking his knuckles as he jogs down the stairs and looks back at me. "Think of what a man like that could do with the power she tried so hard to keep herself from using. I'm sick of this pussyfooting around. I'm about ready to watch a Sorc bleed out. How about you?"

I snarl and gnash my teeth in fierce agreement, despite the feather's prickling warnings.

"You staying like that?" he asks, "or you going to fill him with arrows?"

He has a point. I duck into a nearby alcove and step into my wood elf form, and just as I jog out again, we're greeted by a hassled looking Mage running out of Solace Hall.

"Sirs!" he calls after us. "Cort!"

Cort kicks at the cobbles and mutters something that sounds like,

"Blasted, bloody Mages," but he turns and musters a smile as the Mage nears.

"Anod Bental," the Mage introduces himself with a half-bow. "And ah! Good! The wood elf. His Majesty was looking for you."

"Looking for us?" Cort raises a brow. "Why?"

"Oh, no, no, not you of course," says Anod, turning to me with a gesture. "You. Elliot of the Grove, I presume?"

"O' course," Cort rolls his eyes. "Well, give the king my regards, Elliot. I'm going Sorc hunting."

"Ah, man in yellow from the tournament," Anod says with admiration, clasping Cort's forearm and holding him there firmly. "I thought I recognized you. I'm sure if you're together, His Majesty would not mind your presence as well."

"A glowing invitation," Cort grunts.

"I'd not advise Sorcerer hunting this evening, especially if it's who I suspect you're after," says Anod. He sweeps a hand across his chest and a strange shift shimmers in the air around us. "His Majesty has already made plans for Synnen and his cohorts, during the feast tomorrow. He means to wait until they're gathered and arrest the whole of the guild."

"Bah, again with the arresting," Cort says, rolling his eyes.

"What does it mean, arrest?" I ask, scowling, and the two men stare at me in confusion.

"Don't people get arrested where you're from?" Cort asks. "If not, maybe I ought to pay dem a visit. Ha!"

"I imagine the customs are different in the Grove," Anod says gently, like he's explaining things to a child. "In Cerion, when a crime is committed, the offender is put under a powerful sleep spell and locked in a cell beneath the city until the time comes for their trial. A judge then determines whether the person is guilty and issues the appropriate punishment."

"Cerion's too merciful," Cort says. "Where I'm from, high crimes are punishable by death. Some crimes, you lose a limb. Others, you face the person you wronged and they get to act out their revenge."

I stare at Cort, waiting for him to laugh and tell me he's joking. When he doesn't, Anod clears his throat uncomfortably.

"Yes, well, Islanders are as entitled to their customs as the Druids are, certainly. Shall we?"

Cort crosses his arms and watches me closely. "I'm in no mood for de king's court, especially if I'm not de one summoned."

"Maybe go back to the Peacock?" I suggest apologetically. "For some rum?"

"Aye," he says, but not very convincingly.

"Promise you won't go after him until I can join you," I say. "For Mya's sake."

"What do you mean, for Mya's sake?" Cort rolls his eyes.

"Imagine if something happened to you because you went out for revenge for her. She'd never forgive herself."

Cort looks up at the sky and then to the side, glaring back toward Solace Hall.

"She saved your life, didn't she?" I press.

"More than once she did, aye," he admits with a huff.

"Imagine what she'd think if you got yourself killed, then."

"Your faith in me is an inspiration, Elliot," Cort says sarcastically.

"Promise you won't go looking for a fight without me tonight," I say again.

"Fine," he agrees reluctantly. He starts to say something else, but shakes his head and clenches his jaw and points at me. "Fine."

"Get some sleep, maybe?" I call after him as he storms away, and his only reply is a rude gesture he tosses over his shoulder before disappearing around the corner.

"Charming man," Anod mutters.

"I just hope he keeps his promise," I say with a sigh, and we set off together to the palace.

40

THE GROVE'S WILL

A nod leads me in thoughtful silence through the same tunnels I traveled with Tasiven just this morning. We enter the palace through an ornate door that opens into a familiar polished wooden corridor where the scents of camphor, lavender, citrus oil, and sea salt curl peacefully around us. Music and the murmur of revelry dance to my ears from a distant area of the palace. We hurry in that direction, passing dozens of doors, until he knocks lightly on one and it opens just a crack.

"Master Anod," says the page who peeks out at us curiously.

"I have Elliot of the Grove," says the Mage. The page nods and asks us to wait, and a moment later the door opens wide enough for us to enter.

The room inside has a wide circular table at the center bigger than the one at Solace Hall. Gathered around it are the king, the prince, Tasiven, two men I don't recognize, and the elf we met on the mountain outside of Valleyside. Across the room Finn stands watch with three other royal guards, their backs to a wall lined with tall bookshelves.

"Ah. Here, Father," says Tirnon, gesturing in my direction. "This is the Druid I was telling you about."

"Bow," whispers Anod as he bends at the waist, and I do the same. A strange sensation shivers over me, starting at the feather, and I feel a sudden rush of confidence as I stand before the king.

"Elliot of Sorlen Grove," His Majesty declares, his voice still as clear as it was in the arena. I feel like I know him already, so it feels strange to make introductions. The prince trails him as he comes around the table to stand in front of me and rest a hand on my shoulder.

"Stand, and let us look at you," the king says, his voice carrying a hint of awe. When I straighten, his eyes twinkle with fascination as they take in my face, my feathers, the tooling of my vest. "Imagine such a thing," he says quietly, his gaze flicking toward Anod. "A wood elf— a Druid— standing here in our own rooms. This festival has brought many wonders to our great kingdom, has it not?"

"Among other things," says the prince quietly.

No one replies, but they all look at me with the same curiosity and admiration the king wears plainly.

"He is the same one who came to you, my son?" asks the king. "And you, Finn?"

"Yes Father," says the prince. Across the room, Finn nods. "He told us of the threat on my life, and he provided Gaethon with the list of Sorcerers."

"I did not expect you to be so young," the king says, still gazing at me. "For all of the bravery and cunning you have shown us."

"Indeed, wood elves appear younger than our kind, Your Majesty," Anod reminds him gently.

"Ah, yes, of course we knew that," says the king, who continues to stare and smile. "We wish to reward you for your aid." He takes a ring from his smallest finger and presses it into my hand. "For now, take this as our token of gratitude. Later, we shall discuss other terms with you. Tirnon has informed us you wish to remain here in Cerion."

I nod gratefully and look at the ring, which is a heavy gold band etched with vines and inlaid with emerald leaves.

"Thank you, your Majesty," I say quietly, my heart racing from the unexpected reward, which I slip onto my thumb. Without warning, the feather blazes hot against my cheek and Aft'elu's presence surges into me, taking my breath and my words and turning them out again.

"Your allies of the Grove wish an audience alone with the king and his heir," I say with a voice much deeper and more commanding than my own. "One guard and one adviser may remain."

"Anod, Finn," says the king without a second thought, and everyone else files out. When the elf passes me, she tucks a folded note into my hand and offers me a reassuring smile.

"A trinket from your hand, a word of thanks, and a promise?" Mistrust and disbelief echo from my voice once we're alone, and my eyes go wide with shock and apology for Aft'elu's scolding tone. "Is that what the life of your son, the only true heir of Cerion, is worth to you?"

"I…" the king straightens defensively, as shocked as I am by the sudden change in energy. Across the room, Finn's hand goes to his sword as he and the prince step forward.

"Your foolish trust, your refusal to see the truth, your neglect of your own laws," under Aft'elu's command, my feet move forward without my willing it. I feel the power of the Ancients behind every word I utter. "Your weakness bred a scourge of Sorcery within your own kingdom, a scourge which nearly bled into our sacred Grove. Our people were placed in mortal danger. Had we not been forced by those Sorcerers' hands to intervene, the Plethore line would have ended days ago. And you wonder why we remain so closed off and secret."

Anod grabs my arm, pulls me several paces from the king and hisses, "You will not speak to His Majesty that way. You are a guest within these halls."

Aft'elu spins me to face Anod and yanks my arm free, "You will not speak to *us, Mage,*" they snarl through my teeth, "Your ilk is just as guilty as your king of negligence and apathy. Have you forgotten our gift of knowledge, the list of Sorcerers in your lands, which we provided only recently?"

At a gesture from the king, Finn advances and draws his blade. Aft'elu whirls me to face him.

"And now you threaten our agent with steel and violence," the Ancients thrum through me, "while the Sorcerer responsible for methodically unraveling your kingdom walks free, carrying with him more power than you know."

"Wait," Anod warns. "The boy is only a vessel. A messenger…"

"Stow your blade," the king says after a tense moment, and Finn sheaths his sword and takes a step back.

"What power do you speak of?" asks the king, edging closer to me.

"The sway of a siren, stolen from your newest champion," they reply. My head pounds as the feather's power travels forcefully through my braid, making my scalp itch and tingle. "He will use it against you."

"As we suspected," says the prince.

"Yet he remains free," the Ancients thunder through me.

"Until tomorrow," says the prince firmly. "My father and I are protected against such magic. We have a plan in place already. We will strip him and the Sorcerers who follow him of his magic in front of my father's most honored guests and bring justice to all who ally with him."

"Much destruction can happen in the span of one day," comes the Grove's reply. "We have seen ages pass, long before your recorded history. We know of human folly. By treaty we do not interfere until that folly threatens the Grove or its interests."

"We understand," says the king. "We assure you, you have nothing to fear."

"Fear?" my voice deepens to a strange, ominous tone. "We have already brought justice to three Sorcerers who dared to test our borders."

"What is it you ask of us, then?" asks the king sincerely. "We remain your allies, and as we have said, we are grateful for all you have done for our kingdom. It is apparent that you are more than capable of defending yourselves."

"Synnen Archomyn is the Sorcerer who directed these threats. His actions have brought a plague of curiosity to our borders and caused much destruction to your own flora and fauna. By all rights and agreements, the life of Synnen Archomyn is ours to claim. When it is done by this hand," my hand goes up, "we will retreat once more into mystery and obscurity."

My eyes widen and meet the prince's gaze, who looks just as shocked as I feel by this demand.

"By all rights and agreements," says the king, "of course we shall yield. As our allies, we ask only that you allow us to follow through with our plan. Tomorrow night, there will be a feast and a reconciliation. Synnen shall be confronted and stripped of his magic before all those who follow him. When it is done, he will be yours to claim."

"So be it," Aft'elu replies, and with a rush of my breath the feather goes still, and I feel their presence leave me. My legs wobble and I stumble backward, and Anod conjures a chair out of nowhere to catch me.

"Elliot," Prince Tirnon calls with concern, and he rushes across the room to crouch beside me.

"I didn't know," I whisper shakily as the emptiness left behind by Aft'elu's presence is filled up again with my own. I want to say I'm sorry, I didn't know they'd do that, I had no warning, but the words refuse to form.

The king, Anod, and the prince watch me with expressions ranging from pity to fascination that make me want to shrink into myself and disappear.

In my mind's eye, my hand floats in front of my face while Aft'elu's words ring over and over: *When it is done by this hand.*

I close my eyes and remember Cort pacing in the street, his blades drawn and prepared to take vengeance over what Synnen did to Mya. Would I really have followed him and taken part in that revenge? The image of the assassin sprawls before me, blood spilling from the gash in his throat. My breath speeds up and my eyes fly open.

"Elliot?" The prince asks cautiously.

"I didn't know it would come to this when I agreed to leave the Grove," I whisper. "I'm a scout. I was never meant to be a killer. I was meant to warn you. That's all."

Tirnon and his father exchange looks of concern, and the prince makes me a promise: "We'll make it as easy for you as possible to fulfill the wishes of the Grove. Don't worry. Now that Father and I have begun to make our plan, we're as anxious as you are to see it through. By tomorrow night at this time, all of it will be behind us."

I nod and curl tighter into the chair, trying to calm myself as they call the others in again.

"It's as we suspected," the king explains to the rest of them, "Synnen now has the power to sway with a spoken word."

I shift in the chair and the elf's note crumples in my fist. I look down curiously and open it, and when I see Mari's handwriting, my heart leaps:

Celian vore estier'analla

(I am with you, always), Sheshi.

No matter what happens, I am here. -Mari

I let myself imagine for a moment drifting to sleep to soar to Ceras'lain, greeting Mari with arms open, staying with her and Elowyn and Elomae. I could refuse to do what the Grove has required of me. I could cut away the feather and throw it into the fire and become as Forgotten as she is now. We could be a family.

For a blissful stretch of silence, I linger in that daydream. Then I remember what else I would be giving up: my scouting, my family, Hana, Mya.

"Stay here," the prince offers quietly, and I open my eyes and look at him. "As my guest in the palace. I'll have a room made up for you. It's the least we can do."

"I have to go to Mya," I whisper, tucking the note into my belt pouch.

"Stars. Mya," the prince curses softly. "We had hoped for her aid tomorrow as well, but now I see that won't be possible."

I imagine the satisfaction Mya would feel having a hand in Synnen's demise, and I meet the prince's gaze with newfound determination.

"Maybe it could be," I whisper. "If I could somehow steal it back."

"Go then," the prince replies urgently. "Carry my hopes with you."

41

SOLITUDE

I find Mya almost as soon as I slip into Dreaming, and don't even say a word before I pull her into my arms and kiss her. The wolves howl in the distance, mingling with images of them spilling out of Synnen's carriage, chasing me through the forest, seeping from shadowed cracks in red bricks.

I do my best to ignore them, focusing only on Mya; her breath on my cheek, the scent of her skin, the feel of her fingers twining my hair.

If I could keep us here in Dreaming, safe from the threats of Cerion and promises made for me but not by me, I would, forever. We kiss for what feels like hours, never parting or speaking, only comforting each other with touch and togetherness.

After a long time, the wolves' howls are drowned out by another sound. A beautiful song. A voice pure and perfect. Mya's song. Her voice as it used to be. It swirls around us both, vibrating with encouragement and wonder, soothing and caressing us.

In her dream, we're in a bedroom. She slips out from the covers and walks on tiptoes from the floor onto the notes of the melody, and I transform into fox form to follow her out the window, over the streets. She settles on the harbor wall overlooking the sea and gazes out with her song swirling around her, calling to her. A globe of light emerges from the waves and floats toward her, and she holds her hands out to accept it, but it remains just out of reach.

She starts to sing, and I feel the power of the sea seeping toward her, enticing her. Her song swirls around her as powerful as ever, calling her name again and again until she wakes with a gasp.

I race to the chair at her bedside in Solace Hall and wake up in my true form, hugging my knees like I was when I fell asleep in the planning room. As we both wake, I blink and smile timidly at her and hold out my hand. Her presence grounds me better than a hundred heaping trays from the Pearl Peacock.

Her freckled skin glows in the moonlight, her bright red hair washed purplish gray. She takes my hand, smiling, and all the fear and doubt I felt in the king's planning room fades. Together, we can do this. I'm sure of it.

"I think I found something," I whisper, grinning. I didn't really find it. She did. She just has to believe it, and I'm going to help her.

"What?" she mouths, and I can't help but pull her close and kiss her for real, here in Waking, bathed in the moonlight and the sea breeze. How could I ever have considered leaving her to go to Ceras'lain? How could I have imagined a life without us together even for a moment? Eventually, reluctantly, she pulls me away to the dressing room and closes the door so we can talk without waking her pa.

"You were there, weren't you? You heard it," I whisper once we're safely hidden.

"The voice?" she asks.

I nod.

"I thought it was the sea," she says.

"It was," I reply and kiss her again, pushing my hands into her hair, which is strangely smooth and limp, not spiked up as usual. It's such a relief that I want to kiss her even though her siren's voice is silenced. I didn't realize how much I wondered whether I was under her influence before. But to me, with or without her voice, she's still Mya. Still my *Av'alenia,* my beloved.

"What happened?" she asks, "with you and Cort and Synnen?"

"Nothing," I whisper, and while I kiss her again, I try to figure out how to tell her about the plan without mentioning what Aft'elu said in the planning chamber.

"Mage Anod found us and told us about their plan for the feast, so we calmed Cort down and sent him back to the Peacock."

"What's their plan for the feast?" she asks.

"King Victens is arresting them," I tell her. "The officers of the Knights of Conquer. And they need you to sing to help it along."

"I can't," she forces an emotional whisper. "He stole it. I told you. He wants me to join them, or to pay him all of my winnings and leave Cerion."

"What was it?" I ask, kissing her again. I can't help it. Being this close to her after everything that happened, knowing that right now we're safe in this moment before I'm forced to kill for the Grove a second time—even if it is a Sorcerer who deserves it— is a comfort to me.

"A pearl…" she replies. "It came from inside me. I coughed it up and he took it into a glass, and he vanished it."

"With a spell?" I ask, my heart racing as I think of Gaethon and his explanation of vanishing spells.

Mya nods, and I wink and step into fox form, then slip out of the dressing room to curl up on her bedside chair and fall asleep.

I need to talk to Gaethon again, but he isn't anywhere in the Dreaming or in the In-between. I track his scent from the street outside of the Scarlet Knaves' hall all the way to the Academy, but of course there's no way to get inside because of the wards, so I head to the Pearl Peacock instead. Here, the wards remain fairly open, and it's easy enough to slip through the window into Cort's room.

I find Cort asleep in his nightshirt on top of the coverlet, a bottle of rum on the floor beside him, and I decide to let him get some rest while it's still night. The thought that I haven't slept to rest in days crosses my mind, but I dismiss it quickly and speed back out the window.

As I near the hall of the Knights of Conquer, I suddenly realize the white path hasn't opened to me this time, and Hana hasn't called me. She wasn't there the last time, either, when I darted to Mya in Dreaming. I feel a pang of guilt. Had she been she trying to warn me that Aft'elu was going to use me that way in front of the king? What did she risk in trying to reach me? Did I miss my chance to see her, to speak to her?

I slip back to wood elf form and flick the feather over my shoulder angrily as the reality of what happened in the planning room crashes over me. They used me, and they're going to keep using me, and I have no choice but to do what they want or risk losing everything I value.

Howling startles me as I skirt past the red-draped hall of the Knights of Conquer. I can escape them more easily in fox form, so I switch back. Jagged shadows seep down the stairs, snarling and snapping fiercely. I dart away and they chase me, their hulking, wolf-like forms pulling away from the carved stone facade to hunt me down. I remember my conversation with Gaethon:

"Can they harm me?"

"Easily, if you allow them to have power over you."

One of the shadows lunges at my right hind leg and catches me with its teeth. I scream as pain sears through me, and when I push myself to run faster another of the shadows catches up to me and gnashes my left flank. I stumble on the wind and lose my footing, crashing into the wards covering the Knights of Conquer's roof.

The wolves howl and snarl and lunge as pain surges over me from the wards, paralyzing me, pressing me deeper into the magical shield meant to protect those inside and keep everyone out.

"...if you allow them to have power over you."

They pin me onto my back, and I bare my teeth and bite at every shadow within reach, but more pile on until the pain blots out my ability to think and reason. The shadows meld together to take the form of Rubeus, whose burnt, rotting stink fills my nose and mouth, choking me.

"Did you really think I'd die?" he sneers and clamps his hand over my nose and mouth. Somehow, I'm back to wood elf.

I gag from the stench and the pain and squirm to free myself, but he kneels on my chest and holds my head against the wards and laughs maniacally as the pain consumes me.

"I burned for WEEKS," he growls, wolf-like, and at that last word his form solidifies to reveal the burnt remains of his blackened face.

I try to come to my senses, but the pain is so intense I fear I'll burst into flames myself. It's not really him, I know. There's no way it can be. It's the wards. Some above me, some below, and me, caught in the middle like a slab of meat between bread.

"...if you allow them to have power over you."

"You're nothing but a nightmare." My voice comes out clear even though I choke on the feeling of his charred hand sliding over my lips as I speak, and I inhale ash and soot and wickedness.

It's not real.

I plant my hands on either side of me, ignoring the spikes of pain that spear my palms, and push myself up as hard as I can manage.

"We are all as we see our ownselves in this place."

I muster my courage as the shadows press in, and Rubeus reaches for the strand that binds me to my true self, ready to snap it. I think of the bravest person I know. My shoulders broaden to twice their width. My legs are strong and capable. Pain is nothing to me. A spear appears in my hand and the honor beads in my braids clatter threateningly. I swing with all my strength and catch Rubeus's shadow form and the howling wolves, and I cast them away from me with a single stroke.

I push off from the roof and tear toward the sea, running as fast as I can, never stopping until I'm outside of the city walls and I'm sure there is no charred Sorcerer chasing me, no trace of wolves howling in the distance. I gather my breath and look down at my palm, expecting it to be broad and scarred like Father's. It isn't, though. It's my own hand.

On the horizon, the cresting sun spills golden rays across the water, and as I roll and dive away from the city, Mari's blue and gold songbird darts down to greet me.

"Race you," I call on the wind, and he soars away toward Ceras'lain.

Mari and Elowyn are already breakfasting on their terrace as the bird chirps excitedly to announce my arrival, swooping around Sister's head. She listens to its excited chirps and then gasps and jumps up from her chair, gazing vaguely in my direction.

"Elliot?" she calls, and Elowyn sets down his crystal goblet and stands up too, following her gaze.

I close my eyes and pull myself through all the way from Cerion. It takes longer than usual, and for a moment I panic that perhaps Rubeus's shadow really did sever the strands that keep me together, but my two selves eventually snap into one and I stumble forward, my legs barely able to carry me to Mari's embrace.

"*Sheshi*," she whispers. "I had such a dream." Her voice cracks with emotion as she pulls me close, and I grab the silk of her gown tightly in my fists and bury my head in her shoulder and burst into embarrassing, heaving sobs.

"*Sifsivyan, sifsivyan,* ease your ails, brother Elliot," Elowyn murmurs beside us. His gentle hands rest on my shoulders and guide me to sit close to the waterfall.

My legs wobble beneath me as the memory of the pain I endured on the rooftop lingers. I try to convince myself it was only a dream, but it's difficult. It was real enough to linger this long, and all the way into waking. I have never experienced anything like that.

"He's shaking, Husband," Mari says, keeping me tight in her embrace. "Oh, what's happened? What have they done now?"

"I'll fetch Celorin," he says calmly.

"No," I shake my head and wipe my eyes. I don't have time to wait for a healer. I need to get back to Mya's before she wakes and finds me gone. "I'm not injured. I'm fine. I have a question for you, brother elf."

"Then I shall remain, of course," Elowyn says as he lowers himself gracefully to sit on the bench beside me. "Take your time. I have no better place to be."

"Just take a moment, Elliot," Mari whispers, wiping tears from my cheeks and smoothing my hair from my face. I gaze into her eyes and see Amma so strongly in them it takes my breath away. Did they always look so similar? Had I forgotten?

"I need to know," I tear my gaze from my sister to the elf. "If I can reach the place where things go when they're vanished with a human Mage spell."

"Of course," Elowyn says with such little hesitation it startles me. "How?"

"You must reach twentieth circle in their teachings and master the spell archived under the name 'Ethereal Shelf,'" he explains matter-of-factly.

"Oh." I sink back against Mari, who rubs my shoulder reassuringly. "I guess what I should have asked was: Can I reach the place where things are vanished...tomorrow?"

Elowyn laughs through his nose and looks up at the pre-dawn sky, shaking his head. "Ah, the humans are having an effect on you," he says mirthfully. "Everything must happen today or tomorrow. There is value in a slow approach, my brother."

"Maybe," I agree, "but not about this. Is there a way, please, or not? I have to get back."

"Have you lost something?" Mari asks softly. "Perhaps Elowyn could search for it?"

"It wasn't lost," I tell them. "It was stolen."

I start to explain everything to them, and to my relief, there is still no tingle of a feather nor interjection from Aft'elu. I tell them everything from Valleyside, to Synnen stealing Mya's voice, to Mya's dressing room with no trouble at all. Mari listens, reacting with sympathy, indignation, and fury in all the right places.

When I realize my tongue hasn't even been held when I accidentally slipped and mentioned the Ancients, I press further and tell them how the Grove took over my conversation with the king, and everything that was said between them.

Elowyn leans closer and closer, listening as if waiting for me to be cut off at any moment.

When I'm through, he and Mari exchange excited glances.

"It worked," she whispers, pressing her fingertips to her lips, her eyes wide.

"Indeed," Elowyn nods.

"It worked!" Mari squeals and takes me by the hands to dance me across the terrace.

"What worked?" I ask, pulling my hands free from hers and steadying myself on my still-wobbly legs.

"Speak Freely," Elowyn replies.

Mari reaches up to stroke my feather, and again there is no tingle or spark of warning. In fact, my connection to the grove seems distant. Blocked.

"Elowyn cast it," Mari explains. "It's a sort of ward. It makes it so we can talk about anything at all."

"Speak Freely?" I whisper, feeling relief flow into me. "We can talk about the Grove?"

Mari nods her head, beaming.

"Is that allowed?"

"What about making a killer of my *Sheshi*? Should that be allowed?" Mari asks defiantly. "Everyone deserves an escape, Brother, even a short one. Everyone should be able to speak on what troubles them. The spell works to stamp out their presence here on our veranda. As soon as you leave, though, the Grove will return to you."

"But what if I told you something that could expose them? Or harm you?" I take a step back from her, my heart racing with fear.

"Whatever you say here cannot leave this space to be spread to others. We are allies, Elliot," Elowyn offers reassuringly. "*Sifsivyan.*"

"Don't tell me to 'be at ease,'" I glower. "Not now."

"This was no betrayal. It was a gift, my brother," Elowyn says. His sincerity helps me feel a little better. "I can help you with what you seek as a show of faith between us. There is a spell which will allow you to find an item no matter where it is. But it can only be used once, and only for a specific object, and you must not tell anyone it was I who cast it upon you. Those are the rules set by the spell. There is no way around it. Do you agree?"

"Yes," I answer eagerly. "Tell me what to do."

"Elowyn," Mari warns.

"Do not worry, my only," Elowyn murmurs, kissing her softly before he turns to me. Their embrace reminds me of Mya, and my heart beats faster as I imagine her joy and relief when I recover her voice.

"Just stand there," he says, pointing at the space in front of him, "and think of nothing but the object you seek."

"What about wards?" I ask, "Will it allow me to go through wards?"

"Alas, no," Elowyn says apologetically, but doesn't explain further. "Now, close your eyes and imagine this pearl, and I shall begin."

42

THE ROYAL HUNT

S ynnen is at the palace. I find him in the king's outer chambers, dining from His Majesty's tray as they discuss the day ahead. In fox form, cautious to keep him from seeing me, I hide behind a curtain to watch. A strange greenish glow emanates from Synnen's throat, pulsing just beneath the collar of his silk vest.

The pearl.

"Your Majesty is most gracious," Synnen says with a sickeningly sweet tone.

"Of course, of course," says the king, waving a hand dismissively.

"You will allow me to be Steward of the Hall for this feast," Synnen commands. "Give Rand'ell a well-earned respite."

"If you think it best, Lord Commander," the king replies.

"Good. It will be a feast the likes of which no one in this kingdom has seen," Synnen's lip curls to a grimace of a smile, and I back away through the wall and nearly pass through the guard posted at the door.

"What do you mean, Synnen is inside with the king? Who is guarding him?" Finn hisses furiously at the pair of guards standing there. "Who else is in there?"

"His valet, sir, and his—"

"His valet! Well, that's a comfort!" Finn growls. "What were you thinking? Tell me exactly what Lord Synnen said for you to allow him inside."

The two guards look at each other and duck slightly in the face of Finn's wrath, and the one closest to me clears his throat and admits with a hint of regret, "He said, 'You will allow me to enter.' It made sense at the time, sir, to let him in."

"But now…" the other one looks slightly green as he realizes their mistake.

"Weak-minded fools," Finn barks, and raps on the door urgently. "Your Majesty!"

"Enter," says the king.

I slip back through the wall, careful to keep hidden beneath a side table. Across the room, a shift in the drapes catches my eye and I slink toward it while Synnen's attention is squarely on Finn.

"Ah, Finn, what is the matter?" the king asks, sounding slightly blank.

"Is it not obvious, Majesty?" Synnen interjects. "This guard is exhausted. He does not look fit enough to ride with the prince on the royal hunt."

"No indeed," the king agrees. "Take the morning, Finn, and rest before the feast. I shall send Glavin in your place."

"Your Majesty—" Finn starts, but he's promptly interrupted.

"Do as His Majesty bids," Synnen says darkly, "or he might issue a much less compassionate order."

"And where are your own guards, Sire?" Finn asks defiantly.

I reach the curtain and duck behind it to find two master Mages lurking there. One is in the colors of Solace; the other is of a guild I don't recognize. Both watch through the curtain in silence, as if it's not even there. Neither notice me. Their presence makes me feel a little better about the king's safety, but not much.

"His Majesty has no need of guards. I will, of course, protect him from any threats as we work together on the feast."

"Indeed," says the king. "Go, Finn."

The guard stands defiant until Synnen barks, "Your king commanded you to leave!"

"It will be quite a spectacle, all in honor of your most revered guild, Majesty," Synnen says with passion as Finn goes out and shuts the door behind him.

"Yes, yes," the king agrees. "And at the end, as you have so wisely convinced me, this old king shall relinquish his crown into your hands. It is a relief to know my kingdom will pass to one so capable."

"And finally, Sire, you'll go to your rest," Synnen says with a velvety tone that for a moment soothes me into thinking that everything he's saying makes perfect sense.

A few breaths later, I snap out of it.

With my heart racing, I back out of the wall and dash after Finn as he stalks down the polished corridors to the prince's annex, where a pair of guards allow him to enter Tirnon's chambers. Inside, the prince is being dressed in riding leathers by Erol and another man I haven't seen before.

"What word?" he asks as Finn crosses and bows to him.

"They're together in your father's chambers," Finn reports. "I've been dismissed from the hunt."

Tirnon thanks the dressers and sends them out. Once they're gone, he turns to Finn, his expression dark.

"I don't—"

Before he can say more, I slip to myself and step into Waking. Both men jump, startled. Finn's hand flies to his sword, but he stops when he realizes it's me.

"Sorry," I shrug apologetically.

"It really is unacceptable—" Finn growls.

"It's fine, Finn, considering," says the prince.

"I heard the king say he was going to give Synnen his crown at the feast," I tell them urgently. "I could go back in there right now. I could finish this before it gets any worse."

The prince shakes his head.

"Father is playing his role as he must. Remember, he's protected from Synnen's sway. It's all a ruse." The prince sighs and tugs a bracer onto his forearm with a scowl, and Finn helps him cinch the laces as the prince continues. "As much as I hate it, we must wait until tonight. If it were to happen now, his guild would scatter and strengthen. The Sorcerers allied with him would go unpunished. The only way to get them all together in one place is to make them believe they're being honored at the feast. And Synnen is so greedy and prideful, he'll never see it coming until it's too late for all of them. You must wait until the time is ripe, Elliot. As difficult as it is, we must be patient."

The way Finn looks at me, I can tell he objects to it all as much as I do.

"Have you slept?" the prince asks, deftly changing the subject. I swallow, mid-yawn.

"I'm almost always sleeping," I reply.

"Always sleeping, never resting, I imagine," the prince shakes his head. "Anod was telling me some of how it works for you. Go and prepare yourself for what you must do tonight, Elliot of the Grove. Know that your allies of Cerion will not fail, nor will you. But you must be at your best. Get some true rest. Take this day to collect yourself."

He crosses to the table at his bedside to take something out of a drawer, then presses it into my hand. I hold up the vial of purple liquid to the light, then sniff it.

"Lavender oil," the prince explains. "To calm and aid with sleep. It works some of the time… please, friend. Rest until the time comes."

I drop into a nearby chair as the prince and Finn discuss things in hushed tones. Across the city I speed, back to the chair at Mya's bedside where I curl up in fox form and pull myself through. Mya is still asleep in bed, but I can hear Silas downstairs chatting and laughing with the others.

With the prince's permission, I close my eyes and let myself rest for the first time in days. Choosing to go nowhere in Dreaming is usually a challenge, but I guess Mari and the prince were both right. I fall easily into a deep, dreamless sleep until I'm roused sometime later by Mya's hand stroking my fur.

"A fox would make us memorable, Mya. I'd prefer to go unnoticed."

"Please, Pa," Mya whispers hoarsely. Silence stretches between them, and I keep my eyes closed, listening as my heart races. They're talking about leaving Cerion. Leaving, and taking me with them.

"If it's that important to you," Silas agrees, sighing. "But he can't draw attention, and you must be responsible for him. Understand?"

"Oh, thank you!" Mya cries, sounding much younger and less self-assured than I've known her to be. "Thank you, Pa!"

"Yes, well, wake him up and we'll be on our way. We've lingered here long enough."

She blocks out the sun as I feel her move close to me, and her breath tickles my ear as she whispers, "Don't worry, I have a plan. I'm not leaving Cerion with him. I love you, Elliot."

My ear twitches as she strokes it, and it takes all my effort not to switch to my true form and gather her into my arms and kiss her, but the more I hear of her father, the less I trust him. The tingling at my ear and cheek seem to warn me with the same reservations.

"He'll find me when he wakes," Mya tells her father as they brush past me out the door. "He always does."

Once they're gone, I try to get back to sleep but fail. It's far too hot in this room with the summer sun blazing through the windows. The oppressive heat makes my skin itch beneath my fur. The salty sea air makes me thirsty. I slump from the chair onto the floor and stretch out under the bed, but it does little to cool me.

Annoyed, I switch to my true form and close the sun out with the shutters and flop onto the bed to sniff Tirnon's lavender oil, but that doesn't help much, either. I'm exhausted but too restless with thoughts of what happened last night and what I'm meant to do tonight.

What if I fail everyone and the crown goes to Synnen? What then? And what about Mya?

She loves me. That's what she said.

She needs her voice back. Maybe I can sneak it thanks to Elowyn's spell. Maybe I can snatch it away without Synnen suspecting me. I shift again and hop into the chair to curl up. The cobbles blur beneath me as I speed toward the palace on two feet to search.

I find Synnen alone on a parapet overlooking the city far below. It's a strange sight, because he isn't there at all. I can only see the green glow of the pearl bobbing at the same height where his neck should be. I think of the Sorcerer in the tower, visible to others, but not to me.

"I expected you'd be along," he calls to me with a cruelty that makes me wince. "This time, I am prepared."

He thrusts a hand out, and my feather sparks with warning too late. I'm flung backward through the sky, careening past Solace Hall, over the city gates, deep into the forest beyond the main road. I feel my fox self tumble toward me, the strands that hold me to myself taut and reeling in.

In the forest, I snap together on four feet. Nearby, a pack of dogs howl and bark. Horses' hooves thunder close. The prince's hunt. Overhead, the sky is black with storm clouds. My thoughts go blank. Instinct takes over.

Run faster. They chase.

Ears prickling.

Heart racing.

Hide.

Run.

Climb.

Arrows flying.

Jump.

Flee.

Still, they chase.

Barking.

Howling.

Thundering.

Rain.

Quickly, quickly.

Hooves churning earth.

Horse falling.

Man falling.

Run.

They fight. Swords clash. Magic flies.

Hide.

Up the tree, away from dogs. Away from arrows.

Arrows. I shift as the thought of weapons and fighting draws my true form forward. Back on two feet, it takes some time for me to catch my breath and sort out what just happened. I have never lost myself so fully into the fox before. Not even at the very beginning when I was first learning.

Something in Synnen's spell must have blocked me from myself. Even now, in this form, I feel like half of what I should be. The fox is pushed away, nearly nonexistent.

Far beneath the branches I cling to, the prince is under attack while his dogs clamber at the tree trunk, frantic for my scent. The dogs ignore the pair of red-clad Sorcerers who stalk closer, raising blackened hands to the sky. The storm broils above us, spilling its wrath with lightning bolts and hail the size of fists.

Sir Josten stands shoulder to shoulder with several of his guild mates, barricading the prince from the encroaching Knights in red.

"This is treason!" he bellows over the hiss of the hailstorm, and one of the Sorcerers gestures to a twisted oak towering over them. An earsplitting crack echoes across the forest, and the tree trunk snaps in half, careening toward the group of them.

One of the members of Solace dives for the prince, pulling him out of the way of the tree just before it lands with a thunderous crash.

Spells fly in the Sorcerers' direction, colliding into them, peeling away their wards. I draw my bow and fire my arrows before the first Sorcerer has a chance to recast her wards. My first one pierces her shoulder. My second is a killing shot straight through her heart.

Her partner lets loose a furious growl. While Solace and the Knights of Conquer clash together, swords flashing, the second Sorcerer looses a spell that splinters the branch beneath me, sending me plummeting to the ground. My panic shifts me again without thinking.

Fox.

Run.

No.

Prince.

Tirnon runs past me, scrambling to find cover as the Sorcerer's spells crackle over us. Lightning spears from the sky, striking a nearby tree, sizzling it to embers from the inside out.

"Run, Elliot!" he shouts as another bolt strikes the ground near our feet, throwing us both back.

I shifted again, and I didn't even realize it. Tirnon grabs my arm and pulls me up, and we slide together down into a ravine.

"Lower ground is never a good strategy," he says, panting. His right leg is singed, his trousers split open above his knee where a long, burnt gash seeps red.

"Lean on me," I say urgently, even though he's easily twice my weight. "We have to find cover before they reach us."

"I'm a fool," he growls, gritting his teeth against the pain as we creep along. "They mean to make it look like the storm was my end."

"Don't talk," I tell him, shaken by the thought of it. "Just move."

Above us on the ledge, the Sorcerer peers down. He calls out some taunt, some threat, but the tingling of my feather is so strong it makes my ears ring. He raises his hands, and the prince grabs me and we dive for cover behind a stone just in time to avoid another bolt.

"Ah," Tirnon winces, squeezing his thigh with both hands. "Go. You have no obligation to me. Run."

He's so concerned with his leg, he doesn't even notice the deep ribbons of slashes that bloom across his neck and chest, spilling his blood onto his riding leathers. I whirl to the side, looking for some escape for both of us, and nearly yelp in shock at sight of the white pebble path beside me.

"Elliot," Hana calls.

"Who was that?" asks the prince, wide-eyed.

Across the ravine, the Sorcerer raises his hands again. The black clouds churn, bending the trees, birthing a cyclone.

"Come on," I shout at the prince over the torrent of wind, tugging him with me toward the path. I have no idea if this will work, but it's our only choice. "Hurry!"

I prop him up as best I can as the pebbles creep closer. As soon as my feet touch them, the storm disappears. Washed in pink, everything goes silent.

43
PINK MIST

Surrounded by pink mist, Tirnon gapes at the sudden change in our environment. His eyes go wide as he moves away from me, staring at the pebbles under his feet and then his leg, which has stopped bleeding. The wounds along his chest and neck fade. He presses a hand to his thigh as the scarred, burnt gash heals to smooth, tanned skin once more.

"Elliot," he whispers, "where are we? What is this place?"

Home, I want to tell him, but the words won't come. It shouldn't have happened. He crossed the borders somehow. He should never be here. Soft tendrils of willow sway beyond the mist, the light from between them splashing yellowish-green rays across his curious face. Hidden somewhere within the fronds, Hana giggles.

On edge, Tirnon steps closer to me, his hand flying to his sword.

"What was that?" he whispers. "Did you hear it?"

"Hana, stop spying," I call, grinning. "Come out of there."

"Shh," comes her reply. "Don't say too much in front of him."

I turn in her direction, suddenly aching to see her smile, to feel the touch of her tendrils and look into her sparkling eyes. Silhouetted against the mist, a snaking vine unfurls, stretching toward me. I can't help but take a step toward it, even though I hear Tirnon's footsteps crunching on the pebbles away from me.

The mist swirls as Hana comes into view, her arms outstretched, her vines blossoming with cascades of fragrant purple blooms.

"Elliot!" she cries and runs to throw her arms around me joyfully. The purple-blossomed vines curl around my arms and legs, pulling me close, slithering into my hair.

"What took you so long?" she whispers, clinging like she's afraid I'll slip away. I graze my fingertips across the purple petals.

"These are new," I say, and the vine they sprout from grazes my cheek lovingly.

"So much has happened, for both us," she agrees, gazing at the blossom like a proud mother. "But don't change the subject!"

I tell her of everything that has happened since I left the Grove. It takes what feels like hours, but I don't mind. The feel of her vines holding me brings me so much comfort, so many memories of home, I could talk for a week and never mind.

"She loves you," she whispers, but there's no sadness in her tone. Like a true and loyal friend, she seems genuinely happy for me.

"She does," I say, beaming. I think of when Hana kissed me so long ago, back in the shade of the mossy awning. How wrong it felt.

I tell her about the puffs of clover on my feet—the slippers in Mouli's foyer—and she laughs.

"It was such an odd vision," she admits. "But now I understand."

"What?" I ask her. "What do you understand, Hana? None of it makes sense to me."

"You and I are linked, Elliot. Linked by heart and blood and deed and memory. Once this task is finished and you have followed the path set before you, I'll be the other end of the tether for you. Your anchor in the Grove," she says with reverence.

Her words make all the pieces of my life shimmer to a neat, orderly line that suddenly makes perfect sense. Through everything, Hana has been my dearest friend. More than Amma or Father, more than my brothers, she's a beacon of home. My love for her is my love for the Grove and all the good within it.

"My *ili'luvrie*," I murmur, stealing the elvish term. Hana nods.

"You already have the faith of the Prince of Cerion, its heir and its next king. Your bond is the bond we need in order to continue to thrive. You always spoke about how you felt like an outsider, how you felt as though you didn't have a place here. It's because you didn't. You belong out there, with them. With her. With him."

She gestures toward the cloud of mist, and it parts to reveal Tirnon standing at the edge of the pool. Aft'elu's figure hovers over him, their muscled arms outstretched, their wings glinting golden and sapphire in the sunlight, their skin dappled by the beams of light dancing through the canopy.

"You have been brought to this place as your father before you, and his before him," Aft'elu says, their voice like the whisper of wind through the leaves. "To witness the sacred beauty of the Grove, to gain an understanding of its power, to know, for all your life, what you have sworn to protect."

Tirnon bows his head as Aft'elu continues.

"The lives of men are as fleeting as the changing of the seasons. We know this, and we send with you our comfort and our allegiance. So long as a Plethore sits upon the throne, we shall never meddle in the affairs of men. We honor our treaties and expect the same from you."

"You have my word," the prince agrees with a bow. "As sure as my father's before me."

Aft'elu raises their chin, challenging that just slightly.

"More so," the prince says apologetically, and Aft'elu offers a haughty laugh.

"I should hope so," they say. "Go now, Tirnon Plethore, Heir of Cerion, to your home. Know that the Grove stands with you. Remember this moment, and our pledge."

Aft'elu opens their arms, and the mist slowly fades to reveal the unmistakable glory of the Ancients. The *Rianaves* tower over us, higher than the seaside cliffs, grander than the polished halls of the palace, more breathtaking than the gleaming dome of the Academy.

For what feels like half the afternoon, Tirnon gazes at the majesty of the ancient trees. I hear their voices thrum between them, whispering secrets meant only for his ears. When they're through, Tirnon steps forward into the pool of Lifesap, walking in a trance until the top of his head disappears beneath its mirror-like surface.

I run closer to peer into the sparkling pool. Its rippling surface shows the prince emerging in his rooms, all the way back in Cerion. He looks around for a moment, perplexed, then pulls open his door to see Finn waiting outside of it.

"Your Highness?" Finn asks, astonished by the prince's sudden appearance.

"Come in, Finn," says Tirnon. "Come in and tell me what I've missed while I was gone."

The surface of the pool shimmers and the vision fades. When I finally tear my gaze away, I find myself face-to-face with Amma and Father, and Kaini and Sulien. All of them embrace me. Amma weeps, Father murmurs how proud he is of me, Kaini clings to my arm, Sulien thumps me on the back. A few paces away, Hana waits, smiling.

"Face to face with a Sorcerer," Aft'elu's measured tone drifts to my ear. "Are you prepared, Courageous one?"

They sweep their hand across the pool and I see myself in fox-form, curled up on the chair beside Mya's bed. She bends to me and whispers, and her voice resonates through the pool, filling us all with a sense of excitement.

"Elliot," she whispers, "You can stop searching. I have my voice back. Don't put yourself in danger."

"Who's that beside her?" Hana asks curiously.

"Cort," I reply. "He was a pirate, I think, but not anymore."

The pink mist fades to reveal the Sanctum, where everyone has gathered for supper. Amma and Father guide me through to sit, and Hana kneels beside me in the grass. They recite the rites together, and for the first time I don't feel compelled to join in. The wisps bring our meals and sweep away to create rows at the front of the gathering like they did when they showed us Rubeus's secrets, except this time we watch what's happening at this very moment back in Cerion as guests arrive for the king's feast.

"This night," the wisps glow as the voices of the Ancients thunder through them, "will change the course of Cerion and our Grove for better or worse."

Hana's vines curl around my shoulders reassuringly. Amma pats my knee as I kneel. Kaini steals three honeyed rolls from my tray. Father beams a proud smile at me. Sulien grins, at first I think at me, but then I realize he's caught Hana's eye.

I turn to her and raise a brow, and her cheeks bloom pink as her vines stretch eagerly past me in Suli's direction.

"Watch," she whispers, and one young tendril tugs at my earlobe to bring my attention back to the wisps.

Through them, in Cerion, Synnen stands before the gathered guests. He boasts brazenly and cruelly of his accomplishments, obviously insulting and disrespecting the king. He sneers at Tirnon with disgust that the prince somehow managed to evade his plan to be dead in time for the feast.

"Everything is so red," Hana whispers, edging closer to me. "The color of poison, the color of blood."

Through the wisps, I watch Naelle and her father arrive at the feast, and I see the look of disbelief and joy in Tirnon's face as he rushes to greet her, offering her his arm.

"They made it," I whisper excitedly, and Hana's vines curl around my shoulders, hugging me.

Synnen sweeps Mya up to dance with her, murmuring into her hair. Furious, I jump forward, but Hana holds me back.

"Not yet," she whispers, Aft'elu's voice mingling with hers as my feather tingles. "Just wait."

"Enough dancing!" Synnen barks abruptly, and half the Grove

cowers at the rage in his voice. "It is time for entertainments, if it pleases His Majesty."

"Yes, yes," says the king. "Let us hear a song from our Master Troubadours, Master Tasiven Feathersoft and Lady Mya Songspinner."

Mya and Tasiven move to the center of the room and begin to sing the same anthem of Cerion that he taught her in the tunnels on the way to the arena. While they sing, I watch those around me as they tilt their heads to the side, listening with appreciation to the perfect harmony Mya and Tasiven create.

Midway through the song, Synnen's mouth goes slack. Several others in red around the room stare blankly ahead, mesmerized by Mya's voice. It's remarkable how she seems to have learned only to target certain people and leave others untouched by her influence.

"My countrymen, my allies," His Majesty's voice rings out over the song as he stands, his arms spread outward to address his people. "On this night, as I have mentioned, we come together to celebrate the strength of our people. But there is one group, one guild, which stands out amongst you all. The Knights of Conquer, all of whom are gathered here with us."

Hanna shouts, "Boo!" and many others here in the Grove follow her lead, hissing and shouting curses toward them.

"Under the guise of loyalty," the king continues, "they have swept through our kingdom sowing fear, destruction, and malcontent. Until now, we have had no real proof of this, nor have we been able to entice their leader, Lord Synnen, to return to us and provide an explanation that would ease our suspicions."

Mya and Tasiven continue to sing, and behind me the people of the Grove hum in harmony, their voices melding with the intent of the anthem, strengthening their hold on Synnen and his allies.

"And so, we are grateful they have chosen to honor us with their presence at this most honorable feast," the king continues, "to witness our proclamation that on this night, under suspicion of treason and charges of murder, conspiracy, coercion, and corruption, we proclaim the guild known as the Knights of Conquer dissolved, its leading Mages stripped, its foremost members banished to the Outlands."

We all cheer as the Mages of Cerion work through the crowded room, casting spells to put the mesmerized members of Knights of Conquer to sleep. Defiant and proud, Mya continues singing, holding the enemies captive with her voice. A Mage approaches the mesmerized Synnen and pulls his glove free and his collar, revealing the Mage Mark beneath.

A gasp echoes through the room and through the Grove, and Mya loses her focus for a moment, giving Synnen the opening he needs. He thrusts his hand forward and Mya screams and skids across the floor, smashing into a stone pillar.

I jump to my feet, spilling my supper across the moss, and sprint toward the wisps, screaming for him to stop as everyone in the feasting hall draws their swords, prepared to attack him.

"Stand down," Synnen commands, and most of the room press their hands to their ears painfully. It still has no effect on us in the Grove, except for the fury of being forced to watch and do nothing.

"Let me through!" I scream at the wisps, "I'm meant to stop him!"

"*Not just yet*," the *Rianaves* reply. "*Wait.*"

"You would defy me now," Synnen shouts in fury, "after all I have done to prove myself to this wretched kingdom? You are fools to turn your backs on the power within your grasp. All of you self-righteous Mages," he bellows, and I see Gaethon and others fall to the floor, screaming and writhing in agony.

"Everyone still loyal to a weak, dying king," he spits the last word, and His Majesty slides from his chair, sobbing in pain.

"Stop," Mya grasps at her own throat, struggling for air under the effects of his spell.

The Grove is silent aside from my ragged breath as I watch, waiting for my sign to charge.

"We are with you," Hana and Aft'elu say together, and behind me, everyone echoes their words. Even Father and Amma. Even the *Rianaves*.

"*We are with you. Go now.*"

I dive through the wisp wall, feeling my limbs shorten and prickle with fur. The power of the Grove charges through me as I cross the space like it's just two paces away and not the leagues I've come to know.

I crash into Synnen, aiming for the pearl at his throat, biting into it with all the power of the Grove behind me, crushing bone and tearing flesh.

The Sorcerer falls to his hands and knees, coughing and choking until he spits the large, glowing pearl onto the rushes in a pool of blood.

"No," he whispers as I snatch the prize between my teeth. I can feel the Grove behind me, watching me, though the wisps have faded between us. "No," Synnen begs as Cort, Tirnon, members of Solace, and all those loyal to the king approach him, swords raised.

"Elliot," Mya croaks from across the great hall, safe in Tasiven's arms.

"I've got you," Tasiven tells her gently. "Breathe, Mya."

Shaken by the taste of blood in my mouth and the power of her voice between my teeth, I duck beneath the tablecloth and gather my wits. With a little more effort than usual, I shift myself from fox to boy and spit the giant pearl into my hand, vigorously wiping the disgusting taste from my mouth and tongue.

"Mages," the king commands, "Strip him, here and now. Synnen Archomyn, in the presence of my court and by the power of the throne of Cerion, forfeiting all trials and formalities, I sentence you to stripping, and presently, to death."

There is no answer from Synnen except a sicking, gurgling gasp that tells me he may not even live through the stripping. Without wasting even a glance at the Sorcerer, I crawl beneath the rushes to where Mya is lying gasping in Tasiven's arms.

As soon as I reach them, the master Troubadour passes Mya into my arms and I press my lips to hers, drinking in her scent, trying my best to comfort her with my warmth. She clings to me, sliding her hands into my hair until I take one of them gently away and press the pearl into it, closing her fingers around it.

I smile through our kiss, reluctantly breaking it just long enough to whisper, "Found it."

The feather in my braid flutters excitedly, and along with the tingle of warmth that spreads across my cheek as I kiss Mya deeper, I could swear I hear the entire Grove in my ear, cheering my name.

Epilogue

The path of moss is soft and spongy beneath our bare feet as Mya and I walk arm-in-arm through a dense, vibrant forest that's a mix of Elespen's jungle and my Grove. Her voice blends in perfect pitch with the whisperings of the trees and the songs of hundreds of birds nestled in their branches. Though the trail is long and meandering, we don't rush. Our Dreaming is vast and intimate. We can spend as much or as little time as we'd like here. We could spend a lifetime, if we wanted to, only to wake in the morning after a night had passed.

Eventually, our trail opens to a meadow filled with Mya's favorite colors: blue cornflowers and poppies, yellow tulips, white daisies with centers like thousands of gold coins.

She stops singing and breathes in the scent of them, and I gather her closer and we kiss for ages until a soft rustle nearby draws our attention. At the edge of the meadow, the thick ferns part to reveal a path of white pebbles.

"They're coming," I whisper to Mya, who pales nervously.

I reach up and stroke the familiar dapple of freckles across her cheek, and her warm blush blooms beneath my fingertips.

"Don't be nervous," I say, smiling.

"What if they——?" she starts to ask, but I distract her with another kiss and she leans heavily against me, surrendering to it.

A giggle interrupts us, and Mya tries to jump away, but I keep my arms snug around her and kiss her cheek.

"Don't worry," I murmur. "They'll love you."

Together, we turn to see Hana standing at the edge of the meadow, her vines sparkling with dewdrops as they swirl excitedly behind her. She meets Mya's gaze and they study each other in silence for a long, curious stretch. Tucked close against me, I can feel Mya's heart thumping. Hana takes a step closer. Mya holds her breath.

Then, like she's greeting a long Forgotten friend, Hana grins, sprints across, and throws her arms and vines around the pair of us.

"Oh, Elliot!" she squeals excitedly, "I can't believe it worked. We're here, all of us, together! Mya, what a thrill to finally meet you!"

Her vines nudge me a step or two from Mya, who laughs beautifully as Hana hugs her again.

"I'm delighted to meet you, too, Hana," she says, her voice filled with relief and amusement.

A glimpse of red fur catches my eye at the end of the path. There,

Amma shifts from doe form to her true form. Tucked behind her in the ferns stand Father, Kaini, and Sulien.

"Good," Amma says with relief once she turns to check on the three of them. "No one got lost in their own dreams. Come, stay close to each other. Don't get distracted, Kaini."

"Yes, Amma," Kaini agrees, staring wide-eyed at Mya.

The group of them join us and greet me with hugs and kisses. Amma first, then Kaini, then Sulien, who thumps my shoulder before reaching to pull Hana close. Father takes me in a bear hug and beams at me with such pride that I feel like the sun itself couldn't outshine his joy.

"Everyone," I say after clearing the lump of emotion from my throat and stepping away to take Mya's hand, "meet Mya."

They greet her with a more reserved, more cautious warmth except for Kaini, who bombards her with questions I'm sure he'll forget the answers to once he wakes up. Mya answers graciously, and I'm about to tell Kaini to stop when something past him catches my eye.

The trees bend apart from one another at the opposite edge of the clearing, revealing a path of billowing, silver, cloud-like mist that carries the scent of scent of melted wax, flowers, and salt. Elf magic. With it comes another scent: earth, lavender, straw, and reeds.

"Mari!" I shout, and everyone goes silent and turns to see Mari emerge from the mist.

She and Amma lock eyes first, and Amma chokes back a sob and runs to her daughter, flinging her arms around her.

"Oh, my *Sheshi*," Amma whispers over and over as Mari buries her face in Amma's fringed shoulder. Behind them, Elowyn's lithe form swirls with the glow of sunlight on vapors. He meets Father's gaze and offers a respectful bow, and Father's brow furrows assessingly before he offers a subtle nod in return.

"Well!" Hana says cheerfully, "we're all here! Grandmother? Are you ready?"

Everything goes still at Hana's declaration, then the wisps come. Dozens of them in every color float from deep within the forest, hovering near each of us, blotting out the sky and the meadow and the trees.

Mya steps closer to me and clings to my arm, her eyes sparkling with awe and wispflame. The wisps converge at the center of the meadow and take the form of a woman, and Avela steps out of them.

Even Kaini goes silent as the Elder approaches us. Avela takes Hana's hand first, then mine. Mya starts to pull away, but I squeeze her hand tighter, refusing to let her go. For this, for everything, I need her beside me.

"Family," Avela begins without any ceremony or introduction, her voice strong and warm amid the soft jingling of chimes and bells. "Family across borders, across treaties, across realms. Elliot Eldinae, all you have been, all you are, and all you will become is centered around one thing. Family. Family is what you are born into," she gestures to Amma, Father, Kaini, and Sulien. "What you marry into," she gestures to Mari and Elowyn. "Family is who you choose," she smiles fondly at Hana, at Mya.

"There is a choice, always, my dear little fox," she says, taking my cheeks in her hands. "And there is no limit to the choice of family."

Her silvery gray eyes, framed with wrinkles and white lashes, dance just like Hana's. Avela smiles, and one hand strokes the vane of Aft'elu's feather. A tingle of magic shivers over me, and for the first time I realize they haven't come. They're not here.

Avela's eyes ask a question of consent, and when I nod, she pulls the feather free from my braid with nothing more than a gentle tug. A sense of utter loss floods through me, filling me with grief and loneliness.

"You are not alone," Avela says kindly, and Mya squeezes my hand, and Hana squeezes my other one, and when Amma and Father and Mari and the others place their hands on me, I feel their love flowing straight into my heart.

"Elliot, in the solace of the Dreaming, I offer you a choice. You may bind yourself to the Grove through Hana and work as its protector from beyond its borders, or you may wake in the Hamlet, never to return to Cerion."

Beside me, Mya holds her breath again. Hana stays impossibly still. I think of all I have accomplished since I left; the purpose I've found, the work I have left to do. I meet Amma and Father's gaze, and both of them offer a nod of understanding. For a fleeting moment, I wish I could bring them with me. I wish they could all see the wonders I've seen outside of our home. But I understand why there are protections in place. As difficult as it is to accept, after all that has happened, I understand why the Grove behaves as it does. As it must.

Though it's kind of the Ancients to offer me one last chance to remain, for me, it's barely a choice at all.

"Cerion," I say, turning to smile at my love. "I choose Cerion."

From her vest pocket, one of Hana's vines draws out a feather of silver hawk, its ends dyed the purple of mulberry juice. When she fixes it to the braid where the other one had been tied, I'm surprised not to feel filled up again with her presence instead of the other one.

The other one. Why can't I remember their name?

"With this token, let us be bonded through realms and across borders," Hana says, smiling. "It's done."

I slip my hand from hers and reach to stroke the feather.

"It's not what I expected," I admit, turning to Avela. "I feel...emptied out."

"What you feel is the loss of an omnipotent power, little fox. Hana's abilities cannot begin to match those of the Other."

"So, you can't speak through me, Hana? Make me say things?"

Hana's eyes go wide. "I couldn't. I wouldn't."

"You can't make me do things? Or do things through me?"

She looks at Avela and back to me again, "What an odd question. Even if I could do that, why would I ever?"

"It will not be the same as it was before, Elliot," Avela assures me. "Should we need you, Hana will call on you. When, or whether, you respond shall be your own choice."

The realization of what she's saying fills me with a sense of excitement and possibilities. This new promise begins to fill the emptiness left behind by the loss of...something. A mentor? A friend? A feather?

Avela is the first to leave once the ceremony is finished. The moment the wisps take her away, I barely remember she was here at all.

Mya and I spend the rest of the dream laughing and dancing and chatting and singing with my family until one by one they leave, whispering kind words in my ear, hugging Mya, filling me up with their affection and kindness.

Before Father leaves, he tells me he is proud of me and my choices.

Before Amma leaves, she tells me she'll see me again soon in Dreaming.

Before Elowyn leaves, he murmurs, "you are welcome in our home whenever your travels might take you to Ceras'lain."

Before Mari leaves, she pulls me close and whispers in my ear, "Brother, you're free."

Before Hana leaves, she leans in and conspires, "bring me some of those sweet rolls you keep talking about. Promise?"

Once we're alone, Mya falls into my arms with relief, her melodic laughter spilling into what was left of the emptiness, flooding it away.

"They were all so lovely," she says.

"I told you not to worry," I grin and press my lips to hers, and we kiss until she gasps and pulls away again. "I'm late. Mouli's trying to—"

She vanishes before she can finish, and as I wake in Solace Hall I can hear Mouli fussing at her from down the hallway.

"Master Feathersoft's squire is waiting, and you've not even had breakfast yet! Lazing about, sleeping all day! Ah!"

I can't make out Mya's answer, but her pleasant, soothing tone seems to placate Mouli some, and the two go on talking.

The hours-old scent of sweet spices and baking bread drift to my nose, and my stomach growls as I stretch my arms up over my head and blink awake. Gaethon sits at his desk beneath the window of our shared bedroom, making careful marks on the parchment spread before him. Acting on past experience, I wait for the motion of his quill to stop before I speak, to avoid annoying him.

"Did I miss breakfast?" I yawn once he reaches to dip into the inkwell.

"Indeed," he says. Meticulously, he sets down the quill and turns on his stool to face me. With an easy gesture he produces a plate of Mouli's warm sweet rolls and another plate piled high with eggs, sausages, and browned potatoes.

"I must say our arrangement is working out rather well," Gaethon murmurs, craning his neck to listen and make sure Mouli is still in Mya's room.

Cross-legged on the bed with a dish on each knee and my mouth full of sweet rolls, I nod in agreement.

"Though it is only a matter of time before she suspects I've been vanishing my meals," he smirks. "And woe to both of us when she does."

I raise one dish to him, offering up the eggs, but he shakes his head and returns to his parchment.

"I thought you might scout the East Wing wards today," he says, looking over his notes, "since His Highness will be out of the way. He'll be riding with Lady Naelle for a luncheon picnic."

Before I can swallow my mouthful to answer him, Mouli knocks softly. With lightning-quick reflexes, Gaethon flicks his hand out and my half-eaten breakfast vanishes. I force myself to swallow what I've been chewing to hide the evidence.

"Enter," says Gaethon, and Mouli pokes her head inside with slight trepidation.

"Oh, Elliot, you are awake," she says with relief, her eyes resting on me with an eager glint. In my short stay here at Solace hall, I've quickly become Mouli's favorite. "You missed breakfast. I'll fix you a plate before you two are off for the day. What would you like, Dear? I'm heating sweet rolls and frying some eggs up for Mya before she goes."

"Thanks, Mouli," I grin, patting my belly. "That sounds amazing. I'm starved."

Character Glossary

Aft'elu *(aft-EH-loo)* A mysterious figure from the fold.

Alayne *(ah-LANE)* A Sorceress of Cerion.

Alistar *(AL-iss-tar)* A Mage companion to Paewyn, traveling with Mya

Anod *(an-ODD)* A Mage of Solace guild.

Anten *(AN-ten)* An assassin of the Knights of Conquer

Avela *(ah-VAY-lah)* An Elder Seer of the Grove.

Celorin *(CELL-oh-rin)* An elf healer.

Ciri *(SEE-ree)* A female member of the Knights of Conquer.

Coren *(COH-ren)* An uncle of the Grove.

Cort Daborr *(CORT da-BOHR)* A reformed pirate, a friend of Mya's.

Crisanne Ethari *(KRISS-ann ee-THAH-ree)* Lisabella and Gaethon's mother. Wife of Josten. Healer of Solace guild.

Elliot Eldinae *(ELL-ee-ot ELL-din-ay)* A wood elf and dream scout of Sorlen Grove.

Elomae *(ELL-oh-may)* Mari and Elowyn's baby daughter.

Elowyn *(ELL-oh-win)* A high elf. Husband to Mari. Brother-in-law to Elliot.

Erol *(ER-ol)* A valet to prince Tirnon.

Evan *(EV-uhn)* An apprentice to Master Troubadour Tasiven Feathersoft.

Feren *(FEAR-ehn)* The oldest honored Elder of the Grove.

Filian *(FILL-ee-an)* A courtier of the Knights of Conquer.

Finn *(FINN)* Prince Tirnon's personal guard.

Gaethon Ethari *(GAY-thon ee-THAH-ree)* A Mage of Solace guild, brother to Lisabella, son of Josten and Crisanne.

Glavin *(GLAH-vin)* A member of the royal guard.

Gorhen *(GOR-ehn)* A Sorcerer of Cerion.

Grandymum *(GRAN-dee-mum)* A sturdy oak who cradles Amma's house.

Gwain Eldinae *(GWANE ELL-din-ay)* Elliot's father.

Hana *(HAH-nah)* A dryad, Elliot's best friend and neighbor on Grandymum.

Jevren *(JEV-ren)* A child of the Grove.

Josten Ethari *(JAH-stin ee-THAH-ree)* A warrior of Cerion. The guild leader of Solace. Husband of Crisanne, father to Lisabella and Gaethon.

Kaini Eldinae *(KAY-nee ELL-din-ay)* A healer of the Grove. Elliot's younger brother.

Keres *(CARE-ehs)* An adviser to King Victens, leaning allegiance toward the Knights of Conquer.

Kyli (KYE-lee) A child of the Grove.

Kyu *(KEE-oo)* Mari's sparrow who delivers letters to Elliot.

Lisabella Ethari *(liz-uh-BELL-uh ee-THAH-ree)* A squire of Solace guild, and a close friend of Prince Tirnon.

Loran *(LOH-ran)* A child of the Grove.

Lorelai Eldinae *(LORE-ell-eye ELL-din-ay)* Amma. Elliot, Kaini, and Sulien's mother. Married to Gwain. A deer dream scout.

Mari *(MAH-ree)* Elliot's sister.

Mouli *(MOO-lee)* Solace guild's cook and keeper of the hall.

Mya Songspinner *(MY-ah)* A bard with a magical voice, Elliot's love.

Naelle *(NAY-elle)* Daughter of the Earl of Kordelya, courting Prince Tirnon.

Nehkiti *(neh-KEE-tee)* The proprietress of the Pearl Peacock, an inn in Cerion.

Oakson *(OAK-son)* An uncle of the Grove, Hana's true uncle.

Paewyn *(PAY-win)* A mysterious woman traveling with Mya.

Rubeus *(ROO-bee-us)* A Sorcerer of Cerion, originally from Hywilkin.

Sare fox *(SAIR fox)* Elliot's fox friend who lives near Echo Pool.

Silas *(SI-luss)* Mya's father.

Sulien Eldinae *(SOO-lee-ehn ELL-din-ay)* Elliot's eldest brother. A warrior of the Grove.

Synnen Archomyn *(SIN-in ARK-oh-min)* The leader of the Knights of Conquer.

Tasiven Feathersoft *(TAS-iv-ehn)* A Master Troubadour of Cerion, who has taken Mya under his wing.

Tirnon Plethore *(TEAR-non)* Son of King Victens, prince of Cerion, the heir to the throne.

Valenor *(VAL-ehn-or)* A mysterious figure in the Dreaming.

Victens Plethore *(VIC-tens PLEH-thor)* His Majesty, the king of Cerion.

Waterfowl A dream scout of the Grove who can shift to a mallard.

Other Pronunciations:

Adalutu *(ah-dah-LOO-choo)* Warm greetings.

Av'alenia *(ah-vah-LEHN-ya)* Dearest one.

Celian vore estier'analla *(SEE-lee-an VOH-ray ES-teer ah-NAH-lah)* I am with you, always.

Rianave *(REE-ah-nav)* An Ancient tree of the Grove

Sifsivyan *(siff-SIV-yun)* Be at ease.

Acknowledgments

Book seven. Seven books! When I set out to write a story about Azi way back in 2014, I never imagined it was going to lead me to keep writing and writing! I never thought of myself as an author back then. Even now, it's a strange thing to think about.

Being an independent author is sometimes lonely work—especially during a pandemic! I started writing "Elliot" back around Christmas of 2019 and by autumn of 2020, I decided to completely scrap my 70k word manuscript to make a fresh start. It wasn't the story I wanted to tell. With the unending support of my friends and family, I started writing "Dream Scout."

To my *Av'alenia,* my dearest one, James…I could write a million words and it wouldn't ever be enough to thank you for your support, your love, your constant encouragement. Thank you for being beside me always, for reminding what really matters, for telling me again and again that my words are important, for always being there to check my tiny details. You are my partner and my favorite, and I love you so much!

Wesley, my *Sheshi* (I promise I won't start calling you that, really), I'm so proud of the independent, brilliant, helpful young man you've become. Thank you for understanding when I couldn't listen right this second. Thanks for not making me TOO crazy while we were all stuck inside together. Thanks for being an inspiration for Elliot. And thanks for being excited to read it! Love you, kid.

There's something to be said about a mom who will read every chapter as I write it, sometimes two or three rewrites of the same chapter, then read the entire book over again and tell me it's wonderful even when I know there are problems. I get my critiques from other places, but, Mama, you are the best for always seeing the best in me.

Rebekah…what can I say? Like Mom, you read chapter by chapter and send me all of your thoughts, and stir my imagination, and get just as excited as I am, and push me to write more in-depth. You help me to be a better writer in every way imaginable. You are my second set of eyes. You are a serious boost to my creativity and confidence, and honestly I don't know what I'd do without you. Thank you to the stars and back for being the best friend I could ever hope for!

So many others have helped me along the trail of this book, and in no particular order I'd like to say thank you from the bottom of my heart for your support, inspiration, encouragement, and helpful advice, especially Deb, Shabnam, Alana (@thorn_n_thistle_reads) and all my Bookstagram friends, Roxane, Dan, Penny, and The Porches writer's retreat in Norwood, VA.

About the Author

Missy Sheldrake is an epic daydreamer and a muse of positivity who weaves worlds full of character-driven, complex fantasy adventures.

In 2014, she dusted off an unfinished, Tassy Walden Award-winning manuscript from her college days, started writing her first novel, Call of Kythshire, and never looked back. In four short years, she completed the five-book Keepers of the Wellsprings series, an epic high-fantasy young adult adventure that was awarded the Golden Squirrel Independent Book Award in 2017 for Best Fantasy.

When she isn't writing, Missy can be found creating fantastical artworks in paint and clay, wandering hidden forest paths, and concocting plots for imaginary people who are beyond real to her. Find out what she's up to next at www.missysheldrake.com, on Instagram @m_sheldrake, on Twitter @missysheldrake, and on Facebook as Author/Illustrator Missy Sheldrake.

Also by Missy Sheldrake

THE KEEPERS OF THE WELLSPRINGS SERIES
Call of Kythshire
Call of Sunteri
Call of Brindelier
Call of Hywilkin
Call of Elespen

HIS MAJESTY'S ELITE
Songspinner

Find out more about these award-winning
young adult epic fantasy novels at:
www.missysheldrake.com